A SECRET TO DIE FOR

THE DCI COOK MURDER MYSTERY SERIES
BOOK 2

JACK CARTWRIGHT

CHESTNUT PRESS

ALSO BY JACK CARTWRIGHT

The DCI Cook Murder Mysteries

A Winter of Blood

A Secret to Die For

The Wild Fens Murder Mysteries

Secrets In Blood

One For Sorrow

In Cold Blood

Suffer In Silence

Dying To Tell

Never To Return

Lie Beside Me

Dance With Death

In Dead Water

One Deadly Night

Her Dying Mind

Into Death's Arms

No More Blood

FOREWORD

If Charles Dickens were alive today, what would he be writing?
   Would he still be the greatest? I think so...

The DCI Cook mysteries are inspired by both Dickens' stories, and the man himself, without whom the literary world simply wouldn't be the same.

Jack Cartwright

A SECRET TO DIE FOR

A DCI Cook Mystery

PROLOGUE
March 9, 1970

A dog barked somewhere far off, somewhere beyond the fields, and he pictured its nose against the ground, its head snapping from left to right as the pack replied one by one, picking up the hot trail the lead dog had locked onto.

His thick fingers, alien against her fair, young skin, grazed her cool cheek, then smoothed her hair the way she liked it. The way her mother often did.

The way she would never do again.

There was a stillness to the old barn. As if it had been forgotten by time, left to rot in the harsh winds that scoured the Lincolnshire Fens. Bright moonlight filtered through the spaces in the walls left by boards that the wind had long since torn off, and somewhere outside, something metal clanged softly in the breeze.

The dogs barked again, the lead dog on the trail, the pack somewhere behind it. But they were closer now.

Closing in.

He was on his feet in a heartbeat, which he knew because the thumping in his chest was loud enough for the dogs to hear, and he ran the few steps to the open barn door.

And there they were.

He couldn't see *them* of course – the men that held the leads. Those men from the village who were fit from toil and seething with rage. But the lights from their lanterns glowed and shook like fireflies dancing in the night.

Fireflies that were inching nearer.

But that was east. Towards the village. Towards the heart of that vile community where his fate would be decided by the bloodthirsty minds of the degenerate scum that called the place home. East was a known. East was where they would raise their shovels, forks, and even their guns. East was where he would eventually fall and curl into a ball. East was where he would lie staring at the moon one last time, and smile at the thought of peace as that bright, white circle in the sky grew smaller, and the incessant blows would fade to nothing.

West was darkness. West was the unknown. West was starting over, finding a new village of degenerate scum who pointed, stared, and turned their backs. West was leaving behind everything he had built. West was never seeing her again. Never feeling her touch. Never having somebody who cared at his side.

But west was hope.

It was almost impossible to discern the distance between those dancing flames and the old, weathered barn. The orange glows blurred after just a few moments of staring through his burning tears.

A few minutes, he thought. That's all he had. Enough time to say goodbye. Enough time to venture into the night and become a tiny, black dot in the distance.

He knelt by her side once more, no longer caring to wipe the tears from his eyes. She deserved his tears. She deserved every last one of them. But he held her hand. He had to touch her. If he could only wake her and tell her that everything would be okay, then he would.

He felt the connection. The parallels between them. Neither

of them had a chance to become. Neither of them had a chance to shine.

As if to exacerbate his thought, a single dog barked once, so close now that he heard the guttural snarls that followed, as if the beast was issuing a low and deadly threat in the wake of its vicious warning.

It was time.

He bent over her. She deserved that. A kiss on her cool forehead, and one more useless and gentle caress of her delicate skin.

And then he gathered his things. The shoes he had worn only once, the hat he would have worn so proudly, and the hellebore with its heather trim, which he tucked into her hand and closed her fingers around it.

"Sleep well, child," he told her, kissing her hand one last time. "God bless."

He stood and turned away, knowing that he would never see her again, and forced himself to refuse the lure of her sweet face. The lanterns were larger now. They were coming straight across the field from the east. Not in single file but spread out like a net. A viscous net that would tear the flesh from his bones.

And so, he ran west. He ran hard with only the moonlight to guide his feet and the growling dogs to coax him on. West was devastating loss. West was a blackness, vague and uncertain.

West was hope.

And so he ran there until he was nothing but a tiny, black dot in the distance.

CHAPTER ONE
March 28, 2024

A robin hopped onto the garden fence, its head twitching from left to right, up then down, and then it hopped again, this time to the ground, where it observed his new surroundings in much the same way, before tapping at the soil beneath the grass in search of breakfast.

Charles took a sip of his coffee and inadvertently spooked the little bird, and it flew off to the safety of the little maple halfway down Charles' garden.

The winter was a cruel time for keen gardeners. The hard work, effort, and time spent during the warmer months seemed to be wasted. A blanket of green was forming on the patio slabs, fallen leaves hunkered into the corners, and the joy of the outdoor space was replaced with a feeling of misery. It was like spending a full year working on a jigsaw puzzle and being just a few pieces from completing it when December came and pulled it apart, leaving just a few connected parts to entice the gardener back again.

His kitchen was no different. It seemed like every time he cleaned the place, put the dishes away, and wiped the worktop, he would return, only minutes later sometimes, to find that a bowl or a coffee cup had been placed there. He could almost understand if there were other items there, or if the dishwasher was full, but he made a point of leaving the door open so she could see it was empty.

That one bowl or coffee cup would then become magnetised, and if left unchecked, would attract all manner of items – post, hair clips, hair bands, moisturiser, hair brushes, and God knows what else she would remove from her pockets.

"Vanessa," he called up the stairs. "I need to pop out, love. Would you just clean the kitchen up before you go out?" He waited for an answer. "Vanessa? You there, sweetheart?"

He climbed the first few stairs and cocked his head, listening for signs of life. He heard the hiss of the shower and the dull hum of the extractor fan, and then he sighed in defeat.

"Give me strength," he said to himself, knowing that she could be just five minutes, in which case he would wait. Or she may have just started, giving him a potential thirty-minute wait, more if she decided to wash her hair.

He strode back to the kitchen, snatched the notepad from the shelf, and scribbled a note.

V, please clean the kitchen before you leave. Ta, Dad. X.

He left the note in plain view, where she couldn't fail to miss it, and then pulled on his coat, before removing his pen from his pocket and adding a line to the note.

P.S. Please wipe the shower down.

He kept his car keys in a little box that was fixed to the wall, the door of which was tiled with four tiles, each denoting a season's birds and flowers.

He'd been warned about keeping his keys in a box so close to the front door and had even tried to change his habits. But it was a nice box and it would be a shame not to use it. Besides, if he kept them on the kitchen worktop, there was a strong possibility of them disappearing forever.

There were some things, at least, that cheered him up, such as his new electric car which he had set to warm up while he drank his coffee.

He checked the address that DS Devon had sent through and entered it into the navigation app on the car's touchscreen. He then checked the distance and doubled it, giving him a sixty-six-mile journey there and back. The range suggested he had just ninety miles until the car's battery needed charging, which didn't leave him much wiggle room. But time was short and there would be a charger somewhere he could use. They were popping up everywhere now.

He eased the car from the driveway, still marvelling at how quiet EVs were. He was always reminded of his childhood when winter mornings in Glasgow would be an orchestra of starter motors and cold engines wheezing into life – old Allegros and Marinas, Cortinas and Fiestas. And if the ritual of coaxing the *old girl* – as his father used to refer to his car – into life was not bad enough, the first ten minutes of a journey would be just as horrific, with the heater on full, directed at the windscreen, and leaning forward with whatever item of clothing was at hand to clear a patch of fog to see through.

He felt smug. He *was* smug. They all laughed at him when he asked how to download an attachment from an email, or how to retrieve a file he had deleted from his laptop, and yet here he was driving state-of-the-art technology. The car had more technology than Apollo 11. It could do things that he never thought possible in a car. The steering wheel was heated, the little screen displayed the messages on his phone, automatic brakes prevented him from reversing into his house after a long shift, and the seats could even give him a massage on long journeys.

But not this long journey. Not with just thirty-four miles of power to spare. He lowered the temperature to conserve a little more, then turned the radio off. He didn't need it.

Within a few minutes, he was approaching Cherry Willingham. The roads were quiet and he settled into the drive, then cautiously, and against all principles, he initiated a call from his phone, checking his mirror to prevent being pulled by one of his white-hatted friends in the traffic department. They loved nothing more than to lecture him on how he should know better or how he should be setting an example.

"Guv?" Devon said when she answered the call. "You nearby?"

"Half an hour," he said. "What does it look like?"

"Well, do you remember that job we had down Monks Road? The bloke who had been lying in his own filth for days on end?"

"Aye, I do, how could I ever forget? Bloody hoarder, he was. You know, I spoke to Katy Southwell from CSI after that job. She reckons he had every copy of The Sun since April nineteen-eighty-five, all stacked up in his hallway, and every page three girl had been cut out and pasted onto his living room wall."

"And the cats, guv," she said. "Don't forget the cats."

"Oh God, don't remind me. I mean, that's just cruelty to animals, surely? What does one man need with twelve cats? And surely a litter tray or two wouldn't go amiss? The way people live, Devon. It just beggars belief."

"It does, guv. Takes all sorts, right?"

"You're not telling me we've got another hoarder, are you? Do I need to go back and change my clothes?"

"No, guv," she replied, and he heard her smile in her tone. "No, nothing like that. In fact, it's quite the opposite."

"Thank Christ."

"Elderly man found hanging in his study."

"Oh, for God's sake," he said and gave a sigh. "Medical examiner?"

"He's just arrived, guv. He should be done by the time you get here."

"Witnesses? Who found him?"

"The cleaner, guv. A lady from the village comes up and gives his house the once-over every week. She has a key."

"Aye right," he said. "You have a statement, I hope?"

"She's being looked after by local uniforms at the moment. I was going to wait for you," she said. "From what I can tell though, it sounds to me like she'd been there a while and was going to finish off in his study."

"So, the place has been wiped clean?"

"There's a strong chance, guv," she said. "CSI are setting up. As soon as you and the FME have seen the body, they'll shut the place down."

"What about family? Did he live alone?"

"Looks that way. I've asked Forsythe and Chalk to do some background checks when they've finished cutting him down from the chandelier."

"The chandelier? Who has a bloody chandelier in their study?"

"The type of man who also has a six-foot oil painting of himself hanging in the hallway?"

"What? What is this place?'

"You'll see," she said with a laugh. "You'll see."

CHAPTER TWO

March 9, 1970

Her dressing table was where Grace Lavender spent much of her mornings. But today was special. Today she would take extra care. She'd even bought a new lipstick and some cream, which an advertisement in a supplement had assured would restore her youth. She doubted it had magical powers, but she was happy with the result as she rolled her head in a clockwise movement to catch her reflection in the three mirrors from all angles.

And then she caught a little ray of sunshine in the doorway behind her and beamed.

"Morning, sweetheart," Grace said, carefully replacing the lid on her cream. Rosie was leaning against the doorframe, studying her every move. "Do you want to try it?"

The girl's face was a picture she would never forget. It was one of those mother-and-daughter moments. One of thousands. But this one was special.

Rosie ran to her side, using the dressing table to come to a stop, and Grace tugged the lid from the metal container.

"Just a little bit, now," she said, and gently touched her index finger to the soft, white cream.

"What does it do?"

Grace turned on her stool and, with her free hand, tugged Rosie gently into place.

"This," she began, "will restore your youth."

"But I'm already young."

"That's why you only need a little bit."

"But you're not old, are you?"

"No," she replied. "But it makes me feel good. A lady should always look her best. If you look your best, you'll feel fantastic, and if you feel fantastic, then nothing can stop you."

The comment seemed to intrigue Rosie, whose head cocked to one side.

"Why?"

Grace touched her index finger to each of Rosie's cheeks and then added a dab to her already smooth forehead, and the girl smiled at the sensation.

"Questions, questions," Grace replied, more to herself than to the girl. "Always the questions." In a circular motion, she worked the cream into Rosie's skin. Then, holding her by both shoulders, she appraised her work before turning her towards her reflection in the mirror, and Rosie gasped in wonder.

"Feel good?" Grace asked, and Rosie's grin stretched, revealing her wonderfully white teeth, perfectly straight, and marred only by a single chip in one of her incisors – her only flaw, and one she had earned by clashing with her sister over whose turn it had been to ride the bike they shared. "Now," Grace said, tapping her little backside, "help me into my dress, will you?"

She stood and walked over to the wardrobe, where hanging on a fat, wooden hanger, her dress hung ghoulishly like some headless bride, waiting at the far end of her long bedroom. At the other end of the room, Rosie ran to Grace's oversized bed and had to jump a little in order to perch on the edge of the mattress.

The dress was heavier than she remembered during the fitting. She held the hanger in her right hand and scooped the length in her left, then avoided stepping on the trailing, layered, lace skirt as she made her way over to the bed.

"Come on now. Shift," she said to Rosie, and the girl moved, leaving a space for Grace to lay the dress down on the bed. "What do you think? Do you like it?"

"It's pretty," Rosie replied. "Can I touch it?"

"Do you have clean hands?" Grace asked, knowing full well that she had bathed only the night before, and Rosie nodded emphatically. "Well, go on then." She held one of the sheer lace arms up, and Rosie ran a delicate little finger across the fabric.

"It's see-through," she said.

"Only the arms," Grace laughed. "Now, come on. Help me into it."

She unfastened the belt on her gown and let it slip from her shoulders onto her little stool. She took a moment to study herself in the mirror. The dress was for the villagers. It was the shiny wrapping which she hoped they would admire. But the new brassiere and silk slip she wore were for only one man, and she was sure he would appreciate the effort she had made.

Taking care not to catch the fabric, she removed the hanger and worked her arms into the garment, and then, with Rosie taking the weight of the material, she worked it over her head. Rosie was a natural. When the dress ruffled and failed to fall into place, she freed it with her deft, gentle fingers.

And they stood side by side before the full-length mirror in the corner of the room, and they beamed together.

"Mum?" Rosie said, and Grace cleared the emotion from her throat, finding her daughter's gaze in the reflection. "Do we have to call him Dad?"

It was a conversation she knew she would have to face but had never envisaged it at this moment when she was staring at her image one last time before she gave herself away.

"Where's your sister?" she asked, and Rosie shrugged. "Go and find her. I'll explain how it's going to be." Rosie stared up at her for a moment. "Go on," Grace said. "There's nothing to worry about. Hurry now."

The girl darted from the room, leaving Grace alone to savour the moment. She had longed for this moment, just as all girls do. It would have been nice for her mother to have seen her, to have tended her hair and helped with her shoes. But the girls were competent substitutes, and she was sure her mother and father would have been looking down with tears in their eyes. She took a few steps over to the mantle that bridged the fireplace and faced the individual images of her parents framed in gold on either side of the carriage clock.

"Come on, girls," she called out, seeing the late hour. "We've got to get you ready yet."

Nobody replied, but she could hear one of them thumping about on the floor above. She could almost trace their movements as they ran from room to room.

She made her way to the door and leaned into the corridor, peering down to the wide, spiralling stairs.

"Roșie? Polly?" she called, closing her eyes to tune into those thumping footsteps. She made her way to the stairs, held the old worn bannister, and peered up just as Rosie peered down from above.

"I can't find her, Mum," she said.

"Have you checked her room?"

"Of course."

"And yours?"

"*Mum*," she said as if Grace had questioned her intelligence.

"Go down and check the closet," Grace told her. "This is not the moment for a protest. She's had all month to state her position."

Rosie bounded down the stairs to the first floor, then ran past Grace onto the stairs leading down to the great hallway. Her bare feet padded across the wood, and Grace waited a few moments for the inevitable argument.

But Rosie appeared a few seconds later.

"It's empty," she said, craning her neck to peer up at her mother.

"Well, check the kitchens then, or the pantry. If she has her fingers in that cake, I shall be cross, tell her."

Again, Rosie disappeared. But the intrigue was all too much. The effects of the cream did little to mask her reddening face, and the calm morning she had enjoyed was giving way to a tempest beyond her control.

Her foot touched the parquet hallway floor just as Rosie reappeared.

"I can't find her anywhere." There was a panic in her voice fuelled by youth and immaturity, and one which Grace would need to curb. She marched into the parlour, finding the large room empty. Sunlight breached the spaces between the ill-fitting shutters, casting just enough light for Grace to be sure of its vacancy. She met Rosie in the hallway once more, this time her own anxiety building, sending tremors through her limbs.

And then she saw it. In the shadows on the hallway floor, a single shoe which she recognised at once. The girls had refused to be dressed identically for the day, to the finest detail. If Rosie was to wear pink then Polly would wear blue or yellow. If Polly was to wear lace-up shoes, then Rosie would wear slip-ons, no matter the discomfort.

She bent to collect the shoe then peered up at the ominous front door. As a single woman with two children, Grace had learned to take care. For years, she had fought the turned backs, the snide remarks, and even the foul spitting on the ground before her feet. For years, she had strived until she had risen to a position of respect, against all odds. But still, she had to take care. There was no man to keep them safe, so routine and good behaviour had been crucial. Routine that saw her shutters closed each night, her windows barred, and the giant, iron key in the great front door turned.

Slowly, she reached out, afraid to even look in Rosie's direction for fear of betraying her innermost dread. The brass handle was cool to the touch. The mechanism squeaked, reassuringly, as she turned the knob. And all things being well, she would feel the great slab of oak bump against its restraint.

But she didn't.

It opened with ease and then swung to its full extent, leaving Grace to stare out at the open gate and the extent of her property beyond. Leylandii lined the stone pavers, their tips lithe in the gentle breeze. The only unmoving object was Hugo Garfield, standing there in the lee of the open gate.

He said nothing, but it was the way he held his hat in his hands, and his slow way, purposeful not ponderous.

She stepped out to greet him and before she knew of her actions, she had descended the few steps, glancing left and right, silently praying that she would find Polly in a quiet corner reading in the morning sunshine. Praying that she would find her before he spoke. Because once he uttered those words, it would be too late.

But where once the two girls had frolicked, argued, and fought, where they had sat so many times upon a blanket, sharing a picnic with the dolls, now there was nothing. A void. A huge chasm that right there in that very moment, despite the reassurance from her intelligent mind, her heart was sure of. A mother knows. Grace knew.

The trembling that had been growing inside her finally overwhelmed her strength, and her legs finally gave. She dropped to her knees, stared up at the sky, and raised her hands to whatever the hell God could do such a thing, as Hugo came to stand before her. His face was a picture of sorrow, his eyes were two diamonds in the dawn, and his voice was the rumble of thunder overhead.

"I'm sorry, Grace," he said and put his strong hand on her shoulder.

And then she screamed her daughter's name.

CHAPTER THREE
March 28, 2024

"Well, I presume he didn't have fifteen thousand copies of The Sun stacked up in his hallway?" Charles said, as he climbed from the car and admired the old manor house.

"I'm not sure that he read The Sun, guv," Devon replied, and her familiar Sunderland accent raised a smile on his face. "More of a Times man if you ask me."

The driveway was long and straight for the most part but ended with a loop around a water fountain so that, should it be viewed from above, it would look like a giant lollipop. The house was as ostentatious as it was symmetrical, Georgian in style and design, with creeping ivy that should have been managed a long time ago.

"Any progress?" he asked.

"CSI are ready to go in," she told him, as they began walking towards the steps. "And the FME is waiting for you."

"And the cleaner?"

She pointed to a liveried police car that was parked to one side of the lollipop.

"They got her some coffee and she's ready to speak to us."

"Good job, Devon," he said, and then leaned in close to her, so he couldn't be overheard. "I told you that you'd make a good DS, didn't I?"

"Thanks, guv," she replied. "I feel a bit bad for Sergeant Hannaway, though."

"You know, the good thing about working for an institution as old as the force is that the procedures and processes have been honed over decades, more than a century, in some cases," he said. "But the bad thing about working for an institution as old as the force is that the procedures and processes have been honed over decades, too." She looked quizzically at him. "They don't like top-heavy departments, Devon. Two sergeants, two constables, and a chief inspector in one team? No chance. No, I had to make the call before they did. And trust me, if they'd have taken one of you, they'd have taken two or three. This way, it's me who gets to decide who stays. Besides, you sat the sergeant's exam. I can't take all the credit."

"Cheers, guv," she said.

"Aye, no bother," he said. "Now then, let's see about this body, shall we? Suicide is ruled out, I suppose?"

"I think we can be quite sure of that, guv," she said, and led him through the two huge, oak doors and into what once had likely been a powerful entrance hallway, before the wooden, panelled walls had faded, split, and bowed with damp. The parquet floor had seen better days too. It was clean, of course, no doubt thanks to the cleaner who was recovering from her discovery. But a floor like that needed more than cleaning once per week, in Charles' opinion. It needed love. The staircase had suffered a similar fate, bar the wrought-iron spindles that gleamed in the winter sun.

Two doors led from the hallway, one to the left and one to the right. They entered through the right-hand door into a library with a huge fireplace surrounded by three old sofas. The walls were adorned with hundreds of leather-bound books, at least one of which, Charles assumed, would be a volume of Burkes Landed

Gentry. Where there were no bookshelves, giant paintings hung in gilded frames, portraits and landscapes, pieces that at one time had meant something to somebody, but not anymore.

Further still was another door and Devon waited beside it.

"Well, if this is the library, then I can only assume that this is the study," he said, as he strolled over to her.

"Your knowledge of old buildings is spot on, guv," she said. "Does it remind you of your own house?"

He chuckled. It was good to see her in high spirits. All too often, she internalised her thoughts for fear of being reprimanded or made fun of. His influence was having an effect.

"My study," he told her, "is a spare bedroom on the second floor with a rug that doesn't lay flat, a blind that comes away in my hand whenever I try to use it, and an armchair that I've had since before I met my wife, back when I had hair and could go through the night without a visit to the bathroom." He peered into the room and shook his head. "And it almost certainly does not have a chandelier. In fact, I think it has a My Little Pony light shade from when the girls were wee bairns with pigtails."

"You don't know what lampshade you have, guv?" she asked, making a point of giving him room to pass her, which he did and stopped to stare up at the atrocity.

"I try not to look up," he mumbled and then turned to her. "In case I trip over the rug."

"Ah," she said, and he returned his attention to the deceased.

"Talk to me, Devon. Why isn't this a suicide?"

"How did he get there?" she asked. "There's no chair close enough. The desk is too far away, and aside from the obvious, guv—"

"His age?"

"He looks like he could barely climb the stairs, let alone climb onto a piece of furniture and tie a rope around the chandelier."

Charles studied the large hook from which the chandelier hung.

"Do you see that?" he said, pointing up at the old, iron fitting.

"The pulley, guv?"

"It's called a sheave block. Do you know what it does?"

"Lifts stuff, I suppose," she replied.

"No, the operator *lifts stuff*, Devon. The sheave block is a method of employing a mechanical advantage."

"A what, guv?"

"It makes the immovable moveable," he explained. "For every circuit that the rope passes through the two pulleys, the force required to lift the load is reduced exponentially." He pointed to the mechanism in the ceiling. "That particular sheave block has two pulleys, which means that instead of a force of seventy kilos being required to move a load of seventy kilos, you'd need only thirty-five. I mean, there's more to it than that. You'd need to factor in friction, the angle of the force, the give in the rope, and whatnot, but that's the general gist."

"Right," Devon said, sounding slightly unsure.

"What is he, do you think?" Charles continued. "Eight stone? Eight and a half, maybe?"

"What's that in new money? Fifty-five kilos? I'd say so."

"What do you think that chandelier weighs? Fifty pounds?"

"What's that?" she asked, doing the maths in her head. "Twenty-five-ish kilos? Yeah. Maybe a bit less."

"That's more than one hundred and fifty pounds hanging off that fixing. Eighty-odd kilos to you. Lucky the bloody thing didn't come tumbling down."

"Lucky, guv?" she said. "Or unlucky that it didn't?"

He grinned at her.

"Lucky for whoever inherits the old place," he replied and jabbed a thumb into the air. "Not many trades out there would know how to put that back up how it was, let me tell you."

She took the hint.

"Chalk and Forsythe have made some progress on the family. We'll go and see them when we've spoken to the cleaner."

He nodded his thanks and looked around the room. It could have been a set from a film or a period drama, with its large partner's desk, the leather chairs, and the tray to one side with its crystal decanter and a single accompanying glass.

Finally, and with more than a little reluctance, he studied the body in the open bag before him. The old man reminded him of his father. He'd been a broad-framed man in his younger days, barrel-chested, but not blessed in the height department. But as he had entered his winter years, that mass just seemed to fall off of him, like a tree discarding its leaves, along with its boughs and most of its bark. He was a shell of a man that, in the right wind, would have been blown from his feet.

"If you're still around when I go, Devon, do me a favour, will you?"

"Guv?" she said tentatively.

"Don't leave me lying about like this with people gawping at me. Get me in a bag, zip me up, and throw me into the ground. Just get it over with, will you?"

"I'll do my best, guv. But let's hope that's not for a long while yet."

He turned to leave the room and winked at her.

"Zip him up, Devon."

He left the room and waited in the library for her, taking a moment to peruse the spines of the books. Many were old ledgers, no doubt containing the financial management of the place when it had been an estate. It was one of hundreds of houses across the UK that had sold off its land. Few, like Gunby Hall, had passed the entire package to the National Trust to retain the heritage. But that took courage and devotion. Others, such as the house Charles found himself in, were kept for little more purpose than to retain some credibility. A sense of entitlement.

"Ready, guv?" Devon asked, and he realised that he hadn't even heard her come in.

"What would you have done, Devon? For a hundred years or more, your family owned and ran an estate like this. They may have even owned half the local village. The villagers would have looked up to them. Respected them and their lineage. They would have been grateful to have jobs, most anyway. Then the war came. Did you know this?"

"No, guv," she said.

"The war changed everything. Changed how we lived."

"Are we talking about the First or the Second World War?"

"Both," he said. "But the First mainly. We lost a lot of men, Devon. Places like this might have lost ten to twenty per cent of its young men. It affected farming in a big way, with no one to work the land. Add to that the need for men to help rebuild the cities and we found ourselves wanting. And then add to that the recession. Farms just couldn't pay their way. An estate like this might have had two, three, or four farms, each of the farmers renting the land. But if they couldn't make it work for them, they couldn't pay their way. And if they couldn't pay their way, the lord, or whoever he was, couldn't pay his own bills. Upkeep on a house like this? In the thousands, Devon." He shook his head at the sums in his head when he thought of maintaining the roof, the windows, the walls, the gutters, all of which were built and installed more than two hundred years ago. "What would you have done? Sold the land to developers? Many of them did. Many of them made good money, too. They took the money and made a new life somewhere. Or would you have stayed in this old place watching your bank balance, that same balance your forebears earned, dwindle away?"

"What are you getting at, guv?" she asked, to which he shook his head again sadly.

"Just getting a feel for who he was," Charles said.

"And?"

He fingered a copy of Romola by George Eliot, which Charles knew was a pen name. The true author was a lady named Mary

Ann Evans, whom, it is thought, used a male pen name to be taken seriously in a male-dominated world.

"It suggests that our man had an ego," Charles said, letting his hand fall to his side. He turned to her. "And people don't like egos. The ego is not the master in its own house."

"Freud?"

He nodded, surprised that she knew the quote.

"Of course, none of this means anything at all, Devon," he said. "But if I'm right, then this man had more than one enemy, and that doesn't bode well for us."

CHAPTER FOUR

March 9, 1970

It was the time of year when the dykes around the fields began filling with spring flowers. Water parsnips, fen violets, and fly orchids were among John Stow's favourites. Terry always said that they marked the turning of the weather. *When the wildflowers bloom, the sun will come soon*, he said every year, and it was a saying that John would be reminded of at the close of each winter.

But there was scant time to admire the budding daisies. Not when the dogs were out. Most of the men had been up all night and they had found something. But when he had asked what it was they had found, Terry had said to mind his business. Now they were hunting a man. A man whom the squire swore that he saw. A man who, as the squire had said, was undoubtedly guilty and should he be allowed to escape the area, then he would spread his poison throughout. He had said the words with a look of repugnance and had felt compelled to spit to rid his mouth of the taste.

And so it was. A dozen men or more and four dogs trudged through the fields. It was old man Mason's dog at the front. Terry had said that the squat spaniel had the keenest nose. The others, whose ropes were taut as a bowstring, were merely there to tear the flesh from the foul beast's bones.

They walked side by side, Terry and John, even though John's paces doubled in number to Terry's. Twice he had stumbled on the large, rock-like clumps of freshly ploughed, rich, dark soil. He wasn't the only youngster there. The squire had his boy and one or two others were walking beside their fathers.

It wasn't unusual for Terry to ask John to join him in the fields. But the occasion was altogether new. This was no pairing of stepfather and boy, no bonding over a task. It was a manhunt and the brooding silence of those sullen men with their boys spoke volumes.

"Now then," the squire announced, as he came to a stop at the head of a dyke, where four rough paths had been trodden. It was the point at which four farms met. The land was, of course, all the squire's but the tenancies belonged to the men, and even a man as arrogant as the squire wouldn't argue that he knew it as well as those who trod the earth day in and day out. The squire was a squat man, but for what he lacked in height and stature, his ample stomach proved to be a substitute. And if even that were questioned, his rumbling bark might be called upon to stand his ground.

He had deep-set eyes and a single eyebrow that John often likened to a caterpillar that wriggled as he spoke. It always seemed to him that the squire had a squint in his right eye, which caused that end of his one eyebrow to droop, making the caterpillar appear as if it were sniffing the air on the other side. Aside from that particular unfortunate adornment, the man's nose was pear-shaped, bulbous, and pitted like a strawberry, and with a colour not too dissimilar either. Terry had said once that he drank too much, but John had never understood how a few glasses of port each night could disfigure a man's face in such a way – unless, of course, he dunked his nose into the drink. But even then, he would have needed to drink his port from a tankard.

Even if his face had not been so unfortunate, among the group of men, he would have still been easy to identify. Whilst the other men, Terry included, wore the tarnished clothes of labourers and farm workers, the squire had elected to remain in fine tweed. His flat cap was not dissimilar to Terry's in style and colour, but Terry never wore a tie with his shirt. Not unless John's mum made him, at any rate.

"We'll split up here," the squire announced, once the men and boys had all gathered before him. He drilled his walking stick into the mud and made a show of leaning on it, then he pointed to an old barn at the edge of Terry's farm. "We found her in the old grain store," he continued. "Mason's hound caught the man's scent but lost it somewhere around here in the early hours. Shrimpy, you and your boy can go east in case he doubles back on us. Mr Fox and Mr Garrett, you can take your lads south. Which leaves Robert and I to take the westward path, and you, Mr Frobisher, to go north with *him*."

He made a disgusted show of identifying John but refused to make eye contact. His son, however, Bobby Garfield, made no attempt to hide his disdain. The scowl he offered John from his father's shadow was soon replaced by a serious look of agreement when the squire peered down at him.

"You'll each know your own farmland better than the rest of us," the squire continued. "So, let's make it quick. If the villain wasn't a vile coward, then he would have shown his face last night. As it is, we've got him trapped. He's out here somewhere, men, and the moment he shows his face, we'll have him. Now, I don't want any heroes. We've got dogs and they're rightly keen. Use them."

The group of men murmured their collective agreements and the squire tore his stick from the ground.

"Check the buildings, check the dykes, and above all, check your stables. If you see him, whistle," he said, then his squinty eye narrowed and the caterpillar raised its ugly head. "But mind the dogs have had their fill before you do, eh?" He stared at the men in turn, his smirk revealing a hint of yellow, tombstone teeth. "Now, get to it."

"I'm glad we're not with them," John said, working hard to keep up with his stepfather.

"Oh?" Terry said. Compared to the squire, his voice was light – almost singsong. Had John not witnessed the man single-handedly hitch the plough to their old draft horse or effortlessly heaving the harvests onto the cart, then he would have said that Terry was the lesser man. But the measure of a man was not in his voice, or even his money. It was in his heart.

"I don't like him," John said. "There's something about him. I don't trust him."

"Now, John, you remember what I told you about all that. Let he who is without sin cast the first stone. Are you without sin, John?"

"I think so."

"No. No, you're not. That's the point," Terry said. "See, when Jesus said that, he wasn't inviting the sinless to cast stones at the judged. He was proving a point."

"Nobody is without sin?"

"Nobody," Terry said.

"Even you?" John asked, and Terry came to a stop, briefly looking back to make sure they were out of sight of the squire.

"None of us are without sin, John," he said, shaking his head sadly. "We may strive to be, but the simple fact of the matter is that we can't be."

"But–"

"How many of those daisies have you plucked from the earth, John?" he said, and John shrugged. "How many lives have you ended or altered somehow?"

"None. I've never done—"

"You've never cut through a bird's nest to thin the windbreaks? You've never eaten a chicken or helped me string up a piglet?"

"Well, of course—"

"And are these not sins, John?"

"But those are animals."

"And which of the sins are most heinous?"

John thought for a moment. He knew the answer, but the way Terry was speaking, it sounded as if the answer was something altogether different.

"Thou shalt not kill?" he said, and Terry smiled.

"We're all God's creatures, John. The trick of life is to get through as well as you can. Be thankful for what we have. Be grateful when those with more help us and repay the debt when you can. All life is sin, John. Unless, of course, I should tell your ma not to feed you any chicken?"

"No, don't do that—"

"So let it be," Terry said. "Let the squire be the squire. Because just like us, he is doing what he needs to do to survive. He is the man his destiny calls for, and we are our own."

Terry spoke the words as if there were no other alternative but to follow the will of God. To play the hand he had been dealt. And it grated. It contradicted everything John had been taught – that if he worked hard and seized the day, then perhaps one day an opportunity might come his way. John gave the statement some more thought and he guessed that Terry had been watching him.

"Tell you what," he said, placing a hand on John's shoulder. He pointed towards the old slaughterhouse, a stone building close to the farm's privy and the granary. "Start down there and work your way along. I'll take a look in the stables. After that, we can check the dykes in the top field."

"On my own?"

"I'll not be far off," Terry reassured him, then delved into his pocket, retrieving a small, tin whistle. "If you see him, blow this."

John nodded and stared across the paddock at the line of old farm buildings. He knew them all, of course. But somehow, today they seemed different.

"Go on," Terry said. "The sooner we get this done, the sooner we can do some work. God knows the squire will still want his dues when the time comes."

As if to reiterate his remark, Terry turned and started towards the stables. He walked with an ease not only earned through familiarity of the land, but through knowledge of life. Wisdom. And John admired him for it.

"Terry?" he called out and then waited for Terry to stop, which he did. "Will they really hurt him?"

"I suppose," he replied.

"But what did he do to deserve it? Isn't it a sin?"

Terry smiled at him but said nothing at first. He often did that when he did not know what to say. "There's more than one way to interpret the words of the Lord," he replied. "Now go." He turned and started off again. "I'll see to it that you get a slice of bread with your lunch."

The slaughterhouse doors were large enough for two men to manoeuvre livestock inside, yet the room was too small for the beast to run amok. From the central beam in the eaves, a chain hung, and on its end was a great hook in the shape of an S. The floor was bare stone and would be covered in straw when the building was in use. The eaves were the only real place to hide, and they were void of life, save for a pigeon which he could hear but not locate.

The privy was even easier to check. The door was open, and unless whoever it was they were looking for was willing to take refuge in a cesspit, then John was certain he wasn't in there.

The granary, however, was a different story.

It was a wooden structure with a cat slide roof, set back from the slaughterhouse and privy for reasons which made perfect sense in the height of summer when the blowflies spawned.

But the door shouldn't have been locked. It had been open. He had seen it. He was sure. Terry had been in there before they had left to meet the squire and the men, and the chain was so awkward that it usually stayed closed until John did his evening round.

Slowly, he walked across to the building, finding a broken slat to peer through. Of all the buildings, the granary was the worst, especially during the harvest when the earwigs came in their millions to feed on the grain.

The chain was heavy and pinched John's fingers when he tried to tug it free from the clasp. At its end was the large padlock, which swung and cracked against the wood.

If anybody was inside, they were sure to have heard him. Perhaps it was for the best. Perhaps they could hide in a sack or the loft and John could escape none the wiser.

The door swung open of its own accord and came to rest in the position in which John was familiar with seeing it.

The morning hadn't been a bright one. Not yet anyway. The sun was low to the east far behind him. But in contrast to the gloomy granary, the sky was blinding.

But such are the wonders of life, with all its little foibles, that contrast became even more evident when John stepped inside and looked up into the loft, where two bright and glassy eyes were suspended in the shadows above.

CHAPTER FIVE
March 28, 2024

"Can I ask you something, guv?" Devon asked as they left the house.

Charles nodded to Katy Southwell, the young woman who led the CSI team. "All yours, Miss Southwell," he said. "Try not to make a mess, eh?"

"I'll do my best, Charles," came the reply as she pulled her mask into place.

"Why have we landed this one?" Devon asked. "It's in the middle of nowhere. Surely there are other teams more local than us?"

"Funny you should ask," he said. "And you're right, of course. There's a team out near Horncastle led by a DI Larson if I'm not mistaken. This is their patch, by rights. Plus, there's the team in the Fens, led by…what's her name now? The posh one who thinks the world owes her a favour?"

"DCI Bloom, guv?" she said.

"That's her. Piece of work, she is, let me tell you," he said. "And there's another team out near Boston that handles much of the coastal work. But you know what happens when politicians lose their marbles, don't you?"

"No, guv?"

"Criminals lose their scruples, Devon. The British people are feeling the pressure. Tempers are frayed, believe me. Did you know that, as a national average, we're solving ten per cent of all reported crimes? Ten per cent. We've got bobbies jacking it in after three years on the job, senior officers taking early retirement because they simply can't do their jobs with all the woke agendas forced onto them, and to top it off, we've got a bloody general election coming up. Nobody dares talk about our need for more resources, because all it will do is add fuel to the political fire. I tell you, Devon, in all my years, never have I seen it as bad as this."

"So, we have to travel thirty miles across country to deal with something that a local team is too busy to? That's just inefficient, guv."

"Ah, sounds to me like you're ready for your DI exam. You summed it up perfectly," he told her, as they neared the liveried car where a female uniformed officer was chatting to the cleaner.

"Thank you, Constable," Charles said. "Mind if we have a wee word with her? You might want to grab yourself a cup of tea or something."

"Be my guest, guv," she said, and then politely left them to it.

"How are we doing now?" he asked, and dropped into a crouch, then immediately wondered if he would be able to get back up without assistance.

"This is Joanne Childs, guv," Devon said.

"Morning, Joanne. Bit of a rough morning for you, eh?"

"You could say that," she said, and he placed her with certainty as a local woman from those four words alone. "I never expected it, see?"

"Of course you didn't. Nobody expects to see that. But the important thing is that you called us. You did the right thing."

She smiled at the comment but it did little to ease her manner.

"Did you know him well? Been cleaning for him long?"

"Hugo?" she said. "Yes, I've been cleaning for him for years now." She looked behind Charles and into the sky above as if in thought. "Thirty years, give or take."

"Thirty years?"

"That's right," she said. "My mum used to clean for him too. And my old nan. She was the housekeeper back in the day, you know?"

"Well, well," Charles said, "I expect I could learn more from you and your old nan than I could from that library in there."

"I dare say you could," she replied, and she pulled a tissue from her sleeve to dab at her nose. "Sorry."

He waved the apology off.

"You said his name was Hugo. Is that right?"

She nodded.

"Hugo Garfield," she said, then added, "although, we used to call him the squire, see?"

"The squire?"

"S'right. Same as his dad, and him before."

"Forgive me, Joanne, but it's not a title you hear often these days."

"No, it's not. But he was the squire back in the day, and I suppose it stuck."

"Do you know how old he was?"

"I do," she said. "Ninety-eight."

"Ninety-eight? Wow. That's some good going. I'll be lucky if I even get close."

"Won't we all," she said. "I only know that because I went to his seventieth, see? He invited us all. Well, I say he did. It was his daughter-in-law who did it all. But I remembered the date because it was the same day as my thirtieth."

"Oh, so it was a joint birthday?" he said, to which she laughed.

"Oh no. No, I doubt he even knew it was my birthday. He didn't let on if he did."

"That would mean he was born in nineteen-twenty-six."

"S'right," she said. "The things he must have seen, eh?"

"That's right," he agreed. "Nineteen-twenty-six. That's around the time places like this began to lose their dominance, am I right?"

"Suppose, yeah," she said. "My old nan used to talk about the old days. There used to be an army of them back then. Hall boys, butlers, cooks, you name it, they had it. Course, they all started dropping off after the war. Didn't need them no more, did they?"

"Or they couldn't pay them," Charles offered.

"Same thing," she said. "Course, my old nan kept her job and few others, but most of them went."

"That must have upset quite a few people."

"I expect it did, yeah. But what were they supposed to do, keep them on and fall into debt? No, the times were changing, weren't they?"

"I expect they sold the land off, did they?"

"Sell the land? No. Well, not until later anyway. No, he kept it. Lose the land and then what? He would have been nothing more than a sad, old man in a house he couldn't afford to keep. No, he kept it alright. Up until the last minute."

"Hence why he was able to continue to use the title of squire, even when his counterparts had all given in?"

"Something like that. No, I remember when he sold it all. It was in the eighties. I hadn't long started. My mum was getting on, see? Needed someone to take over, and, well, what with us being so close to them for all these years, he trusted us, didn't he? And do you know, even when it had all been sold off and all he had left was the house and the grounds, he kept me on." She nodded at Charles and pointed a finger his way. "That's loyalty, that is."

"He sounds like a fine man, Joanne," Charles said. "But even fine men cross paths with others from time to time."

"How do you mean?"

"Ah, I was just wondering if you know of any arguments or fallings out he might have had recently."

"Fallings out?" she said. "There's nobody to fall out with. The old beggar hadn't left the house for a decade, and there ain't nobody comes to visit, not that I've seen."

"How very lonely," he said. "You must have been some comfort to him, then."

"Well, course. I done his dinner for him when I could. I mean, half the doors haven't been opened for years. It's not like I was run off my feet, was I?"

"Well, when you put it like that, I'd say he was lucky to have you." He smiled at her. In the short time they had spoken, she seemed to have chirped up. Talking did that, he thought. It was good for the soul. "You said he had a daughter-in-law," Charles said. "Which suggests that he has a son, or had, at least. Is he still alive?"

"S'right. Bobby his name is. Bobby Garfield. He's a lawyer I think. Last I heard he was up in the city. One of them big firms in Lincoln."

"I wonder if you have his details, Joanne?" he said. "I'm afraid I'm going to have to reach out to be the bearer of bad news."

"I don't. No reason for me to have them, is there? He probably don't even know who I am, does Bobby," she said, and then looked up at the house. "But I know where to find them if that helps?"

CHAPTER SIX
March 9, 1970

The fields were as alien to John as the granary and the rest of the buildings had been on that strange spring day. It was like he knew none of them. The grass, the fields, the old, wooden structures. All of them existed, but only in his dreams, and now he saw them for what they were in the pale, evening light.

The farmhouse they called home stood over the outbuildings, still a few hundred metres from where he and Terry walked side by side.

"Do you think one of the others found him?" he asked, taking a few steps to keep up with Terry's one.

"We'd have heard the whistles," Terry replied. "Or the dogs, at least. No, he's gone." He sighed heavily.

"Do you think they'll ever find him?"

"I don't know. I hope so. God has his ways, John. Everything happens for a reason. You'd do well to remember that."

"But where will he go? Won't people be looking for him everywhere? Aren't the police looking for him?"

"The police? Out here?" Terry shook his head gravely. "No, the squire wouldn't give them the time of day. Damn near useless anyway. What are they going to do that we haven't? We've searched every inch of the fields and outbuildings. The other tenants have all done the same. No, he's somebody else's problem now, John. But mark my words, the good Lord will bide his time. A sin is a sin, after all."

Terry's final statement was sobering enough to command a pause in the exchange and for John's keen eyes to find a red-tailed kite hanging in the air above the stables and the granary.

"Can I know what he did?" John asked as innocently as he could.

"It's probably best that you don't," Terry told him. "Not from me at any rate."

"But he was a bad man, wasn't he?"

"He was a sinner, John," Terry replied, a little shorter than before. "Now then, let's leave it there, shall we? We don't want to upset your mum. Speaking of your mum, you're not to mention any of this. You understand? If she knew we'd been out all day, she'd be spitting feathers."

"But how will he get away?" John pressed. "Where will he go?"

"What is all this?" Terry said, offering a sideways and curious look down at him. "Something you want to tell me, John?"

"I'm just curious, that's all. I mean, the squire looked right foul, didn't he? He must have done something awful. Isn't he a God-fearing man, Terry?"

"The world is a big place, John. We can't all think alike."

"But you said once that God made us all in his image," John said. "How can he make bad people then?"

"God works in mysterious ways. Who are we to judge his decisions, John?"

"I still don't get it," John replied. "Where's he going to go and how is he going to get there? Nobody from Baumber would help him, would they? And it's a long road into the city. He can't walk all that way."

"Men like that find a way," Terry said with a shrug. "Maybe he'll find a kind soul driving a lorry from Skegness. Somebody passing through, you know? A fisherman, other farmers. You've seen how busy the roads are these days."

"You mean he could hitch a lift?" John asked. "Why would somebody help a man like that?"

"Maybe he has some money on his person. You'd be surprised what people will do for a few coins."

"But he doesn't have money. He doesn't have anything," John said, and Terry's long paces came to an abrupt stop.

"John? Is there something you want to tell me?"

"What? No! The squire said so, didn't he?"

"Not that I remember–"

"He did. Or somebody did. Maybe it was one of the other farmers?"

Terry eyed him with obvious suspicion.

"Maybe," he said, his tone low and gruff. He inhaled and then outstretched his arm to touch John's shoulder. "Come on. Let's not give your ma reason to give you a hiding."

Large puddles had dominated the farmyard for longer than John cared to remember, leaving a few narrow paths of loose, dry stones for them to navigate. And while Terry led, John took a moment to study the old granary, thinking that he just might see the glint of a bright, red, glistening eye staring through a gap in the boards.

"Come on, John," Terry said, watching him from the rear door, and John kicked into gear, trudging through the edge of a puddle thoughtlessly. "You sure you're all right?" Terry said, grabbing hold of John's shoulder to stop him.

"Course," he replied, then pushed through into the house.

"Boots," a voice called out, shrill and bad-tempered.

Behind him, Terry kicked off his muddy footwear and gave them a bang over the threshold before slotting them onto the two wall hooks to keep them off the damp floor. He grinned at John. He was good like that. Although technically he was John's stepfather, it was often the case that the two of them relied on each other. They were on the same side, as it were, against his mother's wrath. They had both seen the gentle side of her, and they knew deep down that she only wanted the best for their household, but it was her execution of those dreams that proved to counteract their purpose. They created a void between them all, a chasm which only served to drive Terry closer to John, which seemed to further infuriate her and fuel that burning bitterness.

He edged past John and pushed through into the kitchen, unleashing the warm aroma of freshly cooked pastry.

John took a moment to bang the loose mud from his boots and then hung them below Terry's. Once he had asked his mother why they couldn't dry the boots in the kitchen near the oven, but he may as well have asked to keep them in the pantry. The look she had given him was one of absolute outrage, and the pitch of her voice, which seemed to rise in line with her mood, had reached scandalous heights.

Inside the kitchen, he hung his coat beside Terry's and then dropped his hat onto the kitchen table beside his seat.

"You can get that off there," his mother snapped, as she dumped rather than placed a jug of fresh water down to accompany dinner. "Hang it up, won't you?"

John pushed himself from his chair and hung his hat beside Terry's.

"And wash your hands," she told him. "I haven't spent the day slaving in here for you two to soil it."

Beside the sink, Terry handed him a sliver of soap, and John began to work up a good froth.

"What have we got?" John asked, hoping to encourage some of his mother's more moderate tones before they sat down to eat.

"Shit and sugar," she replied. "You'll get what you're given."

"Pie?" he asked. "It smells good."

"Well, smell it all you like, but you won't be having any. That's for the church." The sting of disappointment was a series of talons embedding themselves into John's gut. "You've got liver casserole and you'll like it. If you think I've time to stand in here making you a pie, you've got another thing coming."

"Casserole it is," John said, which wasn't so bad. At least it would be warm.

"You can fill the fire basket, too," she called out from inside the pantry.

"Now?" He stepped over to the pantry door and leaned inside, hoping for a glimpse of kindness. "I've just washed my hands."

She looked him up and down, then softened.

"No, love, it can wait until after dinner. But mind you do it before bed." He eyed the pie on the shelf, beneath a checkered tea towel. "Do you want some?" she asked, and he felt his face light up. "Well, then you'll have to come and help out tomorrow. Maybe you can help me with the teas?" She ushered him out of the little pantry, then followed, closing the door behind her. "Now sit."

* * *

For as long as he could remember, the clock on the wall in the kitchen had woken John in the early hours, kept him awake at night, and on those bitterly cold mornings when all he wanted to do was curl into a ball beneath his blanket, it had been the source of dread. But tonight, it played an altogether different role.

It had taken every ounce of John's willpower to stay awake. Yet, as was the way, he had slipped into sleep several times. The first time he heard it, he had counted the chimes, both dreading the prospect of hearing the eleventh and twelfth and longing to hear them in equal measure. Yet there had been only ten. And in the hour that followed, his mind had put forward arguments causing him to doubt the first chime he had heard. He had been asleep after all. Perhaps he had started counting on the second or the third, in which case, the next hour the clock would announce would be either twelve o'clock or one o'clock.

It was the type of mental battle that proved all too much for John's young mind, and no sooner had he been certain that the next chimes would mark midnight hour, he succumbed to the argument, lulled to sleep by the toing and froing.

But when the clock tolled once more, he sat up in a start, wide awake, certain it was the first of twelve that had woken him.

And it was. The second chime sang out, which meant that there could be only ten more. And by the time the song of that dreadful twelfth chime had faded, John was dressed.

There was no question of his mother or Terry being awake. They would have retired when the fire had died down. John knew the drill. Terry would have put a log on the coals, large enough to carry through the night, smouldering and smoking, ready to be stoked in the morning.

But that left only two doubts in John's mind. The first was that he inadvertently woke either of them. But he had planned for that. He knew the boards that creaked and he knew the sounds of the house. If they found him downstairs, he would tell them he thought it was morning and feign being sleepy.

The second of the doubts was far more worrying – Terry's evening rounds, during which he would lock the tool store, the barns, and the granary. And given the heightened state the villagers were enjoying, he might have even rechecked the buildings.

He might have found him.

But the only way to find out was to go through with his plan.

And so he did.

His bedroom door opened onto the landing, and as his eyes adjusted to the gloom, the shapes of the handrail and the staircase took form, shades of blacks and greys in the bitter gloom.

The embers in the kitchen fireplace glowed, and although the air was warmer in there, the floor was icy cold through his woollen socks. He found the keys hanging on the hook near the back door and carefully scooped them off then tucked them into his pocket.

The pantry was dark but he knew the layout well enough that he could grope around for one of Terry's beer bottles, which he slid into his jumper. Then there was the pie. He had given the burglary some thought. He could have taken a slice of pie, wrapped it in a towel, and carried it out. Hell, he could have taken half of it. But that would leave little doubt as to the culprit, and the idea of suffering his mother's wrath for the weeks that followed was just unbearable. No, it was better to take it all and then stage a robbery.

He could see his mother's face in his mind's eye, the disappointment and the rage. But it was too late now, and if he got to that stage, he would just have to lie his heart out to avoid the lashes of the willow.

He didn't bother tying his bootlaces. They were cold, and to walk quietly across the courtyard, he had to lift his feet high so the heels didn't drag in the mud. Unlocking the padlock quietly with one hand proved to be a challenge, and it took far longer than he had anticipated. Twice he thought he had heard a noise from inside the house, but he saw no lamplights.

He slipped into the darkness inside, pulled the door closed behind him, and then stared into the black, searching for those two glowing eyes.

"Are you here?" he whispered and then listened. What if Terry had found him and taken him to the squire? What if all this had been for nothing? What would happen to him?

But to the last question, the answer was already there in his mind.

He would hang. Terry had said so. He had said that a jury would spit at him for what he had done and that they wouldn't even have to leave the room to come to a decision.

"I've got something for you. A pie," he said. "And some beer. You must be hungry." He waited a few moments longer. Something moved in the corner of the room, where the shadows were so dark that John could have put his hand down there and felt nothing. A bottomless pit. A window into some other world, maybe?

"I can help you escape," he whispered. "I know a way out—"

A large, strong hand closed around his mouth and a sharp point dug into his neck.

"Are you alone?" the voice said, and John nodded. The man's hand tasted of sweat and the earth, salty and stale. He held up the pie, although it was barely discernible in the darkness. "You tell anyone?"

John shook his head as much as the man's grip allowed.

"You promise me, boy? I'll do it. I'll stick this in your neck if you lie to me."

He relaxed his grip enough for John to speak.

"I promise," he said. "I never said nothing to no one."

The point was removed from John's neck, and he turned to face the man who, in the gloom, was nothing more than an outline in the finger of moonlight that groped through a gap in the old, wooden walls.

John held the pie put to him.

"I got this for you," he said, placing it into the man's hands and then reaching into his jumper. "And this."

"For me?"

"It's all I could get. But it'll help you on your way."

The man pulled back the towel and then broke a piece of pastry from the crust. Then without uttering a word, he scooped a large hand into the pie and stuffed it into his mouth. Two mouthfuls he ate like that, long enough to deem John not a threat, and then he fell back to lean against one of those old, wooden uprights. He pulled the cork from the beer and glugged a large mouthful, the way Terry often did in the summer when Ma would bring lunch into the fields.

Then he stilled. His moonlit eyes washed over John as if he was trying to understand him.

"What's your name, boy?" he said.

"My name?"

"You do have a name, don't you?"

"It's John. John Stow."

"And you live here, John Stow, do you?"

John pointed in the direction of the farmhouse.

"That's our house."

"This your old man's farm, is it?"

"My old man?"

"Your dad?"

"No," John told him. "No, my dad died. The farm is Terry's."

"Terry? Now who might Terry be?"

"He married my mum. We came to live here with him after Dad died."

The man considered those words, and although it was too dark to discern his expression, John felt every touch of his stare, as if his two big hands had reached out and were tracing his features.

"Sit," he said eventually, and John dropped to the cold ground, folding his legs beneath him as he did in school assembly. "He must be a good man, this Terry. A kind man?"

"He is," John told him. "He's nice."

"And your ma? She good too, is she?"

"Good? She's a Christian. She don't do no wrong."

"You a Christian, are you, John Stow?" he grumbled, taking another handful of pie. "God-fearing, are you?"

"I don't know," John said. "I suppose."

"You believe?"

"In God? I suppose so. I mean, he ain't never spoken to me. But Ma says he won't. Not until I'm old enough, and only then if I done good."

"And have you?" the man asked. "Done good, that is?" He took a mouthful of beer, swished it around his mouth and then set it down with a clink.

"I think so. I ain't never done nothing bad if that's what you mean."

"No," he said. "No, I suppose you ain't. Not yet anyway."

John waited for him to chew his next mouthful before asking what he had been meaning to ask. "Did you do it?" he said. "To the girl? They said you did bad things to her."

"You think I did, do you?"

"I don't know," John replied. "No?"

"And tell me, John Stow, if I did those things, would you be out here helping me?"

"Suppose not."

"So, I'll ask you again. Think I did those things, do you? Think I'm a bad man, do you?"

"No," John said. "No, I don't."

He tipped the dish to his mouth and tapped it until every last crumb had gone, and then set it down beside the beer.

"You said you know a way out."

"I do," John told him. "Terry said that you could get a ride on a lorry. There's loads that come from the coast."

"And where might they be heading?"

"I don't know. Lincoln, I suppose."

"And why might some lorry driver decide to give a man like me a ride?"

"You'd have to pay him," John said. "Terry reckons they'll do almost anything for a few extra quid."

"A few extra quid? And what makes you think I've a few extra quid on my person?"

"I don't know," John said, seeing the flaw in his plan. "I could find some maybe. It won't be much, but I know Ma keeps a jar in the kitchen."

The man said nothing, but his head turned to face the door,

and that finger of moonlight spilt across his shiny head like a pool of water in a dark forest.

"Shall I go and see?" John asked.

"No," he grumbled. "No, you've done enough, John Stow." He climbed to his feet and stretched. From where John was sitting on the ground, the man seemed like one of those giant poplar trees that lined the south field. He reached down and yanked John to his feet with almost no effort at all. "Which way's this road, then?"

"That way," John said, pointing in the darkness.

"I can't see," the man said. "Show me."

For a terrifying moment, John thought the man was asking for John to go with him. He couldn't do that. He couldn't leave Ma and Terry. They would know that he'd helped him. Everyone would know.

He reached out and took hold of the man's giant hand. It was larger even than Terry's, yet softer. Terry's had hard callouses where his fingers met his hands, but this man's hands were soft. Strong but soft.

John raised the man's arm. It was a dead weight, and he had to stand beneath it to rest it on his shoulder. Then he fumbled with the man's fingers, extending his index finger so that it pointed in the right direction. "That way," he said. "Just keep walking. Keep to the edge of the field until you can't go no further. There's a dyke you'll have to jump. After that, you'll be on the squire's land. There's hedges there. Follow them to the road."

"How far?"

"A mile," John told him, knowing the route well. "It's the main road from the coast. You won't have to wait long."

"You know what I'll do if what you told me is a lie?" he said. "You know I'll come back and find you, John Stow?"

"It's not a lie," John said. "It's the truth. Honest, it is."

"All right," the man grumbled, then dropped to a crouch.

"Now then. Just answer me this. Why would a boy like you help a man like me, after all what they said about me?"

John gave the question some thought. The man's face was close enough to smell the pie and the beer on his breath.

"I just wanted to help you," John said. "I felt sorry for you."

"Felt sorry for me, did you?"

"They said you done those things. They said you'll hang for it."

"And do you think I should hang, John Stow? Think I should go to the gallows, do you?"

"No," he said. "Not unless you actually did it, and I don't think you did."

"What makes you so sure?"

John shrugged.

"Because if you killed that little girl, then I suppose you could have killed me," he said. "And I ain't dead yet."

CHAPTER SEVEN
March 28, 2024

"Hugo Garfield," Forsythe said, and the detective constable then slapped his notebook down onto the bonnet of Charles' car. "Local squire back in the day."

Forsythe was of average height and lean with it. His hair was a nondescript side parting and his face bore no stand-out features. Charles likened him to some of the boys at his school, those individuals who were neither the bully nor the bullied, the slowest nor the fastest, neither the smartest nor otherwise. His ex-wife might have called the man boring, in fact. But there was something to be said about such men, and something to be envied.

"That's right," Charles said, and he collected the notebook from the bonnet and held it out with a smile. "Ninety-eight years old. One son, namely Bobby Garfield. Anything to add to that?"

"His wife died back in two thousand and ten, guv," he replied. "Since then, he's become something of a hermit."

"A hermit is somebody who chooses not to interact with the world. Was our man alone by choice or through ill health?"

"We've requested his medical records, guv," Chalk said. "Along with his financial records. We're just waiting for access."

"Good. Before we run away with ourselves, I want to see what resources we have to hand," Charles said. "The high street isn't too far away. In the absence of any ANPR cameras, I think we're going to be reliant on shop cameras. With any luck, one of them might have an outward-facing camera."

"Guv," he replied, in acknowledgement.

"I saw a post office, too. That's our best bet," Charles said then turned to Forsythe. "Let's see what we have in the way of eyewitnesses. I'm no pathologist, but he hadn't been there long in my opinion. A day at the most. Talk to the locals, see if they saw anybody suspicious, or if they saw anybody coming up the drive. Places like this draw attention. You never know, we might get lucky."

"Yes, guv," Forsythe said. "I'll try the pub too. You know how people talk."

"Do that," Charles said, then turned to face Devon. "In the meantime, you and I need to pay a little visit to the son, Bobby Garfield. Nothing like being the bearer of bad news to end the week well."

"It's not all bad news, guv," she said and nodded at the house. "I suppose he'll inherit."

"If you're inferring that he might have had something to do with his father's death, Devon, might I suggest we hold that thought until we've spoken to him? I'm all for theorising, but let's not let it get in the way of good police work, eh?"

"Got it, guv," she replied. "Just wanted to get some ideas going, that's all."

"The last thing I want to do, Devon, is stifle your creativity, but that man in there, this Hugo Garfield was at one time, a powerful man. His son, Bobby Garfield, is a lawyer in Lincoln," he said. "I think we might need to tread lightly."

"Well, there's always the cleaner, guv," she replied and then glanced at the gardens. "Seems strange that an old man like Hugo Garfield would have his house cleaned every week despite him not using most of the rooms, and yet he couldn't have paid a gardener to come. And who cooked the rest of his meals?"

"He was still able-bodied," Charles said. "I didn't see a wheelchair or a stick. He might have been two years from hitting the bullseye, but as far as I can tell, he was still quite capable."

"If he really had lived a reclusive life, then surely he would have done away with them all?"

Charles stared at her then at the gardens. She was right, of course.

"By which you mean that perhaps he wasn't as reclusive as the cleaner suggested," he said. "Very good." He turned to Chalk and Forsythe. "We'll meet back in Lincoln this afternoon. Call if you need anything."

"Guv," Chalk said, leaving them to it.

Charles checked his watch. It was barely eleven o'clock, but there was one more person he needed to see, which would pass the time before he could badger Southwell for some hints.

"Find the medical examiner, will you?" he said to Devon. "Ask him to meet me around the back."

"Have you had an idea, guv?" she said, following his gaze to the side of the house.

"No," he replied. "But houses like this often had tremendous topiaries. It would be a shame to leave without seeing it." He winked at her and left her standing there by his car. "With any luck, there will be a walled kitchen garden," he called back over his shoulder, then muttered to himself. "Now that would be a treat."

Where there had once been lawns, wildflowers grew, their seeds having blown in from the fields so that now they were meadows that stretched far into the beds, blurring the once sharp delineation between the two. Trees thrived that should have been tamed, an orchard of apples and pears that had long since outgrown their welcome.

But to the rear of the house, the damage was even more

evident. He held a rose between his fingers and bent to smell it. There was little wood on the stems, and the tallest of them stood only three feet from the tended soil. But the rose between his fingers was just one flower of a hundred or more. They ran in two lines on either side of a footpath that led from the rear doors to the far end of the grounds, mirroring the drive to the front of the house, but instead of leading to the road, the path led to distant hornbeams and beeches, which once upon a time might well have been hewn into delicate balls or shapes with sharp lines, but now appeared forlorn and dishevelled.

He turned in a circle, noting that from no conceivable angle could the rose garden be seen from the road.

"You summoned me, Squire," a voice said, and Charles smiled to himself as two figures came into his peripheral – one short and rotund, the other tall and lean.

"Oh, I'm not one for summoning, Doctor Saint," Charles replied. "I just thought that we could discuss your findings away from the circus. A little more peaceful, don't you think?"

His jacket sleeves finished short of his wrists, and there was enough of the old-school type in him that he wore a tie, yet with his oversized ears, nose, and hands, it gave him the look of a man dressed as a schoolboy, reminding Charles of a film he had seen once, where a boy wishes to become a grownup and thanks to the magic of an old, creepy arcade machine, his wish is granted.

"I'm tempted to take a cutting," Saint said and nodded at the roses.

"Me too, and I don't think the owner would mind, do you?" Charles replied, then offered a look as if to test his morals. "You know what I'm going to ask, don't you?"

"I do," Saint said, and he too bent to smell the roses. "The same questions that you all ask. You want to know how and when the victim died."

"And I suppose you'll give me the same answer?"

"I can give you an idea, based on my findings–"

"But we'll have to wait for the pathologist to provide something for us to go on?"

"More than fifteen hours judging by the progression of livor mortis."

"Blood pooling?" he asked, and the doctor nodded.

"But rigor mortis is still quite evident, so less than twenty-four."

Charles checked his watch. "Sometime between eleven a.m. and five p.m. then. We can work with that."

"But?" Saint said, seeming to enjoy debating what was typically a cold and brutal topic to discuss. "What you really want to know is the cause of death."

"Am I that transparent?"

"The rope," he said flatly. "I'm quite certain that Doctor Bell will agree, but it's her call, as you know. Haemorrhaging in the eyes, discolouration of the lips," he said. "And a look of utter terror on his face." The comment caught Charles' attention. "You don't get that from a lab. One of the perks of seeing them in situ."

"A perk?" Charles replied.

"An insight, then," he said. "The question is, how did he do it?"

"No," Charles said. "No, the question is who did it." He turned to stare at the roses and the wild gardens beyond. "One of the questions, anyway."

"And what's the other?"

"Who pruned these roses?" Charles said, and he smiled up at the big man. "Thank you, Peter. I suppose now we are armed with enough information to pay a visit to the victim's son."

"I don't envy you that," Saint said.

"Oh, you get used to it," Charles told him. "You could call it a perk of the job." Saint grinned freely, and as he walked away, Charles nodded down at the roses. "I won't tell if you don't."

CHAPTER EIGHT

March 10, 1970

"John!" His ma's voice seemed to fill the house like air in a balloon, threatening to pop the windows from the frames. He opened his eyes to the morning, although how much sleep he had managed was anybody's guess. He had watched from his window, hoping to see a glimpse of the large man making his escape, and he had felt a sense of pride. He had done a good thing, and for that, he was now called upon to bear the brunt of his mother's anger. "John Stow. Get your backside down here right now."

She stood with her hands on her hips, her apron fastened tightly around her waist and her hair pulled into a tight bun the size of a fist.

"What's wrong?" he asked, and found Terry sitting at the table with a bowl of porridge, but he refused to make eye contact.

"You know damn well what's wrong," she said. "Where is it?"

"What? Where's what, Ma?"

"The pie I made for the church," she said. "Where is it?"

"I haven't—"

"Don't you dare lie to me, boy."

"I'm not lying," he protested. "Honest. I didn't eat it."

"Well, who did? The bally fairies?"

"I don't know," he said.

"Came down in the night, did you?" she said.

"No–"

"Thought you'd help yourself–"

"I didn't Ma, honest. Check my bedroom."

"Oh, I will."

"Smell my breath," he said. "If I'd eaten it, wouldn't you be able to smell it?"

She cocked her head to one side, licked her lips, and then with one of her long, bony fingers, beckoned him. He came to stand before her, feeling his knees trembling, and then looked up. She pulled his mouth apart and cautiously peered inside. Finally, she sniffed at his breath.

"See?" he said.

"Get away from me," she said and shoved him towards the table. "Your breakfast is cold. You slept in."

"Did I?"

"Had to get the fire going myself, didn't I?" she said. "And you didn't get the wood. First job for you."

John took his seat opposite Terry but failed to catch his eye. The porridge was as his ma had described, cold, which he would just have to suffer. To ask for it to be heated on the stove would be akin to stepping onto the gallows that man had spoken of. He managed the bowl in eight large spoonfuls, gagging as the lumpy cereal coated his throat. Terry didn't utter a word, unlike Ma, who rambled to herself about how she would have to make another pie, and the cost of it all, not to mention how she wouldn't have time to make them lunch.

Terry sipped at his coffee, seeming to mull something over in silence.

"Are we going out in the fields today, Terry?" John asked.

"No, boy," he replied. "You'll be home today."

"But I want to go out with you–"

"I said you'll be home today, damn it," Terry said, in a rare display of frustration, silencing John. But the outburst had clearly enraged Terry. He shoved himself from his chair and strode over to the sink, where he peered through the window to calm down.

"Ma—" John began.

"Have you finished your porridge?"

He looked down at his bowl.

"Yes, I—"

"So go and get the firewood before the embers die out," she told him. "I don't want to spend half my morning building a fire. I've already enough to do, what with making another pie. And no doubt your school clothes need scrubbing. They weren't in the basket when I looked."

"I don't know," he said. "I put them in my cupboard like you told me to do."

"Not on a Friday, John," she said, tapping his head. "I told you to put them in the basket at the end of the week so I can wash them. We might not have much, John, but we do have pride. You hear me?"

"Yes, Ma."

"So, fetch them down. They'll have to stand in front of the fire for the day if I've any hope of drying them."

He turned towards the staircase.

"Now where are you going?" she asked.

"To get my school stuff," he said.

"Fire," she told him, infuriated. "I told you to get the wood in before the embers die out. When you're done, you can get your school gear. Listen, boy. Listen to me, will you? Or I'll clean your ears out in the river, I will."

"Sorry," he said and traipsed across the flagstone floor to the old, wooden porch where he and Terry kept their boots. A keen eye might have spotted that where the mud on Terry's boots had dried and hardened, the mud on John's boots was still wet. He made a show of reaching for the keys on the hook then noisily worked the lock. "Ma?"

She said nothing and slammed the pantry door closed before shuffling across the kitchen to her husband.

"And you can stop your moping as well. Time you were out there, ain't it?" she said.

"Ma?" John said, and again he was ignored.

"Bally fields ain't going to plough themselves, are they? I suppose we're ready for the lambs, are we?"

"Ma!" John said, and she glared at him indignantly.

"How dare you?" she said. "Ain't you got no ears? Can't you hear I'm talking to Terry? And where's the wood? Bally fire'll be out and it won't be me who makes it up again."

"But, Ma, the door," he said, and stepped out of the way so she could see. "It weren't locked."

"You what?"

"The door wasn't locked. I just went to unlock it but the key wouldn't turn. It was already open."

She turned to her husband.

"You didn't lock the door?"

"Course I did," he replied. "I always lock it. You saw me go out there, woman."

"And look," John continued. "There's mud on the floor. It weren't me."

"Well, it weren't me neither," Terry said.

"You made us take our boots off in the porch, Ma," John said. "Couldn't have been us, could it?"

She stared at the careful trail of mud that John had made not six hours before and it led her bitter gaze to the pantry door.

"Well, I'll be damned," she muttered to herself. "Someone's been in here."

"Don't be daft, woman," Terry told her.

"Well, tell me then," she said. "You was it?"

"You know it weren't me. You saw me take my boots off when I did the rounds last night. You were sweeping the hearth, remember?"

"Oh, I remember all right."

"And I ain't been up long enough," John added, then he widened his eyes as if he had been struck by a revelation. "You don't think it was him, do you?"

"Who?" she said.

"The man. The one we were looking for."

"Oh, get out of it. What would he want in here?"

"He could have been hiding," John said, then ran to the door again, and peered out into the cold morning. "Look," he said, pointing emphatically across the courtyard. "The granary door's open. He was here, Ma. He was bloody here."

The use of the word bloody earned him a clip across his ear, and he rubbed at the side of his head while his mother took a look for herself, stepping out of the way for Terry to have a look, and in a heartbeat, he was tying his bootlaces.

John said nothing but instead chose to read the silent looks his mother and Terry exchanged.

"You just stay inside," his mother said, pointing at John as if somehow the entire thing had been his fault. She watched as her husband strode across the courtyard to the granary, grabbing a shovel from where it stood beside a pile of manure. John sidled up to his ma and peered through the window as Terry eased the heavy granary door open. He glanced back at them and then stepped inside.

"It was him, weren't it?" John said.

"Be quiet, John."

"It was, I know it. It had to have been him."

"I said be quiet," she said, her eyes not leaving the granary door until a few moments later, when Terry reappeared shaking his head, and then held something up for them to see. It was the pie dish and the red and white tea towel.

"See, Ma?" John said. "It was him who took it. Not me."

The remark earned him a left ear to match his still red and swollen right.

"You got the firewood yet, have you?"

"No, you said to stay—"

"Get the bally firewood, boy. That's the third time I've told you this morning. There won't be a fourth. Mark my words."

Rubbing his ear and wincing at the whining tinnitus, he ambled over to the porch for his boots, moving aside for Terry to come back inside. The boots were cold and damp, and the laces encrusted with mud. But the loud ding of the pie dish being slammed onto the kitchen drainer suggested that all was not over for John.

"Check the granary, did you?" Terry said.

"Eh?"

"Don't eh me, boy. I told you to check the granary and the stables."

"I did," John said.

"With your eyes shut?"

"No, course not, Terry—"

"Well, how did you miss him, then?"

"I don't know. It was dark. Maybe he was hiding."

"We know he was hiding, damn it. That's why we were looking for him. What did you expect to find, him sitting inside the granary with his feet up and a bally newspaper on his lap?"

"No, I—"

"Well then," Terry said, as he slid the empty beer bottle across the worktop. "Next time I ask you to do something, boy, see that you do, will you? Half the county out looking for him and here he was under our noses."

"Should we tell the squire?" John asked, and Terry leaned on the sink, his eyes closed and his head hanging low, much like the previous day. "Do you think they could still catch him?"

"No," Terry said, the anger abating from his voice. "No, he'll be long gone by now. Likely made his way to the road."

"But they still might get him."

"And have the squire and God knows who else round here?"

Terry said. "What do you think they'll make of me, eh? Too dumb even to find a man on his own property? Maybe they'll think it was me who hid him here? How about that then? No. Old Terry Frobisher can't be trusted, he can't. Let them all down, that's what they'll say. I'll be outcast. Won't even give me the time of day." He shook his head. "No, they needn't know about it. Far as they're concerned he's gone, and good riddance, too." He straightened and ran his tongue across his lips as he often did, then turned to face John. "Get your boots on," he said. "You can help me outside."

The idea of being outside with Terry brought a light into John's dark mood. A light which, if luck was on his side, might just wash away his mother's temper.

"I'll just get the wood in," he said excitedly.

"And John," Terry said, eyeballing him from across the room. "You do what I say to the letter, you hear me? I ask you to do owt and you see it's done. You hear?"

"Yes, Terry," he replied. "I'm sorry if it was my fault."

"S'all right," Terry said, including John's ma in the stare he embedded into the room, drawing a line beneath the entire episode. "Now get to it. We've work to do. And if anybody speaks of it, what do you tell 'em?"

"Nothing. I'll never speak of it again," John said, shaking his head. "Not as long as I live."

CHAPTER NINE
March 28, 2024

Range anxiety was a relatively new but all too real phenomenon. Had the readings on the dashboard been correct, then Charles would have had thirty-four miles left in his car. But when he parked on the first floor of the multi-storey car park, there were only twenty-one miles left.

Still, a little anxiety and careful driving were worth it when he thought of the one hundred pounds he used to pay to fill his old car with petrol. Twenty-one miles was easily enough to get him home, where he could charge it overnight for just twelve pounds.

Devon pulled into a space nearby and flashed her lights to let him know she was there. Walking through the town centre on her own was another form of anxiety altogether. He hadn't said anything to her about it, but her recent weight loss efforts were evident. He supposed it was one of those things that people like him would never understand. Not truly anyway. He could empathise. It seemed like stick-thin women and girls were plastered on the covers of every magazine, and on advertising posters, and, of course, they walked the streets in their hundreds. She had explained it once, how she felt, and what triggered her anxiety, and very often it was down to her police work, which involved studying – discreetly – individuals. Watching a man in a shop, for example, as he leered at stereotypically perfect women, and then glanced only fleetingly in her direction.

It was a feeling of being invisible, despite being the largest person in the room, she had said.

But she looked good. She was pretty, he thought. There was no doubt about that. And he had tried to tell her that he had never exactly been an oil painting in his younger years, yet he had managed to snag a beauty, with whom he'd had children. His married life that followed wasn't really a shining example, but the point was that he had fallen in love, and so would she, one day.

She waited at the front of his car while he climbed out and pulled his jacket on.

"Apologies for the separate journeys, Devon. We'll drop one of the cars off at the station when we're done here," he told her. "We've got a briefing anyway and with any luck, we'll have some kind of action plan."

"I was mulling it over while I drove, guv," she said, as they started towards the stairs. "I think it's worth having the will checked out."

"And as much as I adore your enthusiasm, Devon, I'd like to just tick some boxes before we begin pointing the finger."

"I know, but–"

"Let's inform the next of kin, arrange the viewing, and by that time we should have reason to point our fingers."

"Guv," she said, a little disheartened, "I was just going to say that if the son is a lawyer, then perhaps he has access to the will. Perhaps he even wrote it?"

They descended the stairs, making way for a young woman with a pushchair and two toddlers heading in the opposite direction. The toddlers were running amok, sprinting back and forth on the landing.

"Can I help you there, love?" he asked.

"Oh, would you?" she said, and he bent to pick the front of the pushchair up. "Bleeding lifts are out of service again."

"I'm not sure if I'd get in them even if they were in service," he replied with a pleasant smile. "Which floor?"

"Fourth," she said, and a small part of Charles regretted his generosity. "Packed to the rafters, it was when I got here." She had a southern accent, somewhere close to the east or south of London.

"I'll see you at the bottom," Devon called, and she grinned at the situation he had found himself in.

"Typical, ain't it?" the woman continued. "Bloody dozens of spaces down here now."

"Ah, I need the exercise," he said, allowing the toddlers to go on ahead of him. "You stay close now. Don't go running off."

"They won't," the mother said. "They're good kids, really."

"Yours?"

"They are," she said, her pride stifling her embarrassment.

He studied her while they managed the pushchair, noting that she couldn't have been much older than Vanessa. She caught his scrutinising eye and blushed.

"Sorry, I didn't mean anything. I just wondered if you were looking after a nephew or–"

"No, they're mine," she said. "My husband wanted to get it over and done with. Well, we both did really. Except, people tell you about the tantrums and the nappies, and whatnot, but it's the little things they don't tell you, ain't it?"

"Like carrying a pushchair and shopping bags up to the fourth floor of a car park?"

"Yeah, like that. The day-to-day stuff, you know?"

They reached the fourth floor and he straightened his back, trying not to make a fuss.

"Well, there you go."

"Oh, you're a love. Is that your daughter down there?"

He opened his mouth to explain, then thought better of it. Not everybody warmed to police officers.

"Yes," he said after a pause. "Yes, we're just out doing a bit of shopping."

She eyed his much smaller frame and then his facial features.

"She seemed nice," she said. "Must be lovely when they're that age. My old man passed away a few years ago. He would have loved to have taken me and the kids shopping."

"I'm sorry," he said, which she dismissed with a wave of her hand like it was something she did every time she spoke of her father. He was going to ask how he had died but felt the question intrusive, and he hesitated.

"Anyway, I mustn't hold you up."

"I can help you to your car," he said.

"Honestly, there's no need. The kids can help from here. It's just those stairs, you know?"

"I do," he replied and held the door for her. "Well, it was lovely to meet you."

"Yeah, thanks," she said, corralling the toddlers to keep them close in the car park. "I really appreciate your help."

He descended the stairs and found Devon tucked into a corner, leaning against the wall and scrolling through her phone.

"Shall we?" he said, and she shoved off the wall.

"Chalk sent an email. Looks like Robert Garfield is the next of kin," she said. "No siblings."

"Well, that simplifies things, doesn't it?" he said, sensing that she was pursuing the inheritance motive. "Where are we heading?"

"Guildhall Street," she said. "Do you know, I can't remember the last time I came into town?"

"Yeah, I'm not much of a shopper," he replied, and he waved a hand over his attire. "As you can see."

"No comment, guv," she said. "But, I'll say this, if ever Vanessa suggests you both go shopping, I'd take her up on the offer if I were you."

"What are you saying?"

"Oh, nothing," she said, clearly fibbing. "But a few more shirts wouldn't go amiss."

"A few more shirts?"

"I hope you don't mind me saying, guv, but people in the station don't look at the calendar to work out what day it is."

"This is my Thursday shirt."

"I get it," she said. "It's orderly. It's organised, and in our line of work, it helps to make home life as easy as possible. I just wonder what people would do if you were to shake it up a little?"

"Shake it up?"

"Yeah, you know? Maybe a new cardigan or something."

He nodded and recognised how her roundabout approach had turned into a direct hit.

"Aye, maybe," he said. "Maybe the station would fall apart. How would people even know what day it was? The last thing I want to do, Devon, is to mess with the Gregorian calendar."

An elderly man was sitting on a flattened cardboard box in a shop doorway, with an old hat by his feet. He had keen, bright eyes, and sat upright, as if his situation had yet to break his pride. Charles dropped a pound coin into the hat as he passed.

"Get yourself a cup of tea, man," he said, without breaking stride.

"Much obliged, sir," came the reply.

"You don't give them money, do you?" Devon said.

"Aye, I do. That might be me one day."

She peered back over her shoulder and lowered her voice.

"You probably just bought him a fix."

"A what?"

"Drugs, guv. He'll be high as a kite by dinnertime."

"You really think so?" Charles said, glancing back at the man who had to have been at least as old as he was.

"I know so, guv. I don't give them a thing."

"That's not very charitable, Devon."

"Charity begins at home, guv. Didn't anybody tell you that?"

"I must have missed that lesson," he replied, as they stopped outside the address, which was little more than a doorway between two banks. He reached up and pushed the buzzer, then waited for somebody to answer. But the door opened instead and a man started when he saw them.

"Hello," he said. "Can I help?"

He was around Charles' age, somewhere in his sixties. But the difference in dress was night and day. His grey, three-piece suit was immaculate, his knitted tie was presented in a double Windsor, and his black Oxfords had recently been polished. He wore no wedding ring, but instead, a small, gold signet occupied his right pinkie.

"Good afternoon," Charles said. "We're looking for Robert Garfield."

"Bobby?" the man said. "I'm afraid you're out of luck. He's on annual leave. Have you made an appointment?"

"No, no," Charles said, and then reluctantly presented his warrant card. "I'm DCI Cook. I just need to have a word with him regarding a personal matter."

"Oh dear," the man said. "Well, if you pop upstairs and ask for a Mrs Hyke, she'll give you his address."

"Freely?" Charles said, and the man was intuitive enough to understand the question.

"It'll be fine," he said.

"And you are?" Charles asked. "In case Mrs Hyke is reluctant to provide his details."

"I'm the managing partner," he replied and extended his hand for him to shake. "John Stow."

CHAPTER TEN
March 11, 1970

"The divine right of kings," Mr Matheson announced from the top of the class, scrawling the words as he wrote them and then underlining them with an angry swipe of the chalk. He turned to face the class. "Was King Charles the First correct when he assumed such a right?"

Being relatively new to the class, John had been seated near the front at the desk that was closest to the door, a position that, though favourable for a fast escape, came equipped with a bitterly cold draught that seemed to soar through the old school house in search of bare and fresh shins in which to sink its teeth.

"You, boy," Matheson said, pointing at John. "Stow."

Slowly, John eased his chair back and rose from his seat. But words failed him.

"What's the matter with you? You have a tongue, don't you?"

"Y-yes, sir."

"Well, then?" he said. "Was King Charles correct in his position?"

"I don't know, sir," John said, much to the amusement of the class, who all silenced at Matheson's glare.

"You don't know?" John shook his head and stared at the

scratched names on the desk. Someone named Freddy had, once upon a time, loved Rose, so much so that he had carved it into the wood for eternity. "Well, would you care to hazard a guess?" Matheson stepped across the room in three easy strides and stopped before him. "Did being a king grant King Charles immunity from his fellow man? Or can a king only be judged by God?"

"I suppose that all depends, sir," John told him.

"Explain yourself," was Matheson's reply.

"Well, who made him king, sir?" John said. "Did God do it?"

"You know well enough that God did not make him king, Stow," Matheson said, and he launched into a booming recital that John had heard before. "Kingdoms are won and lost through battle and bloodshed. They are passed down through generations, and in the case of King Charles the First, they are both bequeathed and borne of blood. Yes, he inherited his title, but he had to fight for it, and it was a fight that he lost with dire results."

John nodded his understanding.

"I think a man is a man, sir. I think that sometimes a man can think he's better than the rest of us and maybe he is. Maybe because the king was rich, he could do as he pleased. But even if that were true, God wouldn't allow it. In God's eyes, we're all equal. The Bible tells us that."

"It does indeed," Matheson said thoughtfully.

"So, if all men are equal, then how can God have given one man the right to do as he pleases? Even if God had made him king, and he hadn't inherited the kingdom, or won it in a battle, how could God then grant him rights that no other man has? If he did, then the Bible would be wrong."

Matheson stared into John's eyes with what John could only describe as curiosity.

"Did your previous school teacher teach you that?" he asked.

"No, sir. It's just what I think. We're either equal or we're not."

"And are we equal?" Matheson asked, and John felt all eyes in the room bearing down on him.

"I think we are, sir. Deep down, I think we are. It's just that some people have more money than others. Some people have to work harder."

"And where does God fit into this curious ideology, Stow?" Matheson asked. "Does he not judge any of us? Is that the concept to which you are alluding?"

"No, sir. I think he does judge us. But not on what we've got, or on who we are, or if we're a farmer or a lord. I think he judges us on whether we're good or bad. That's why we sit together in church. Because we're all the same."

"Sit down," Matheson grumbled then turned to the room and filled his chest. "You will, in your own time, read chapters twelve to fifteen. You will then write for me, in your own words, an essay on the divine right of kings. How would the public react to a monarch making such claims today?" He glanced at the clock on the wall behind him and then at the blackboard. "I want you all to copy down what's on the board, and then you may go," he said.

John scribbled down the notes that Matheson had made on the board, and not wanting to be the first to leave, let a few others go before him, slipping into the bustling crowd for safety.

But no sooner had he stepped from the doorway onto the small playing field, than a voice sang out into the afternoon air.

"Oy, Stow?" The voice was light, a boy's voice, and it was familiar. He turned to find Bobby Garfield at the top of the steps with his two cronies, both of whom looked as if they needed a good bath. Garfield pointed in John's direction, and as if they were on one of Matheson's battlefields from days gone by, he issued a command to his followers. "Get him!"

It was becoming a regular occurrence, one that John hoped they would soon grow bored of. His school shoes were stiff and flat, making his footfalls hard and clumsy. He leapt from the lane into the trees and ploughed through brush and broken sticks, fallen in winter and yet to fade into the earth. A few seconds later, they followed, the undergrowth giving way as if three wild horses had burst through.

Clutching his schoolbag, John flew out of the trees into the open fields. They weren't Terry's fields, but he hoped that the tenant was nearby and would see them off. He would take a scolding from a tenant farmer over another beating from Bobby Garfield and his mates any day of the week. But the field was empty. Deep furrows made running even harder, and despite them closing in on him, he strived to avoid trampling the seeds, knowing full well how Terry would feel should his own crops be trampled.

He ran towards the dyke on the far side of the field, beyond which was the main road. If he could make it there, then Bobby might grow tired of the charade and choose to head home to his father's manor. After all, he was the squire's boy, and John had to run through his land to reach Terry's.

He was just a few steps from the dyke, preparing to launch himself across the wide ditch when the first foot caught his ankle, and he stumbled forward. It seemed like barely a second had passed when another hard shoe caught his backside, and the momentum carried him forward, sending him down the bank and into the freezing water at the foot of the dyke.

The three of them stood there at the top, looking down at him, pointing and laughing like they had never seen such a sight.

"Stinky Stow," Garfield said. "Maybe you should wash your clothes while you're down there. Then you won't stink like an old fireplace."

"Bugger off, Garfield," John said, shoving himself to a seated position and wiping the muck from his face.

"You what?" Garfield said, and the laughter had gone. He turned to his mates. "Get him out of there."

"I ain't going down there," one of them said. "My mum'll bloody murder me if I get covered in mud."

"I said get him out of there," Garfield told him, and if ever John had doubted Garfield's father's identity, he didn't any longer.

The two boys scrambled down the dyke, and as much as John resisted, they overpowered him with ease and dragged him to the top, to his feet, holding him upright in front of Bobby Garfield.

"Do him, Bobby," the one to his right said. Ian Mason was his name. John remembered Terry talking to his father at the market one day.

"Yeah," the other said – Harry Pepper, who as far as John knew lived in the village, and his parents ran the pharmacy. "Show him what we do with outsiders round here."

"Shall I?" Garfield said.

"Hit him," Mason added. "You're not gonna let him get away with it, are you?"

And that was all the encouragement that Garfield needed. He reached back, closed his fist, and slammed it into John's nose. The two boys let him go and he rolled back into the dyke, face down this time. He choked and pushed himself to his knees, and then stared up at them. The punch had been nothing. His nose wasn't even bleeding, and given the chance with any of them on their own, John was sure he would come out on top.

But Garfield wasn't done. He collected John's bag from the mud and unfastened the buckles.

"No," John said. "All right, I'm sorry. I shouldn't have told you to bugger off. I'm sorry."

His words went unheeded, and staring him in the eye, Garfield upturned the bag, letting the contents spill into the mud, where a few sheets of paper caught the spring breeze that carried them across the fields.

"Don't cross me, Stow," he said. "I own you. Just remember that."

CHAPTER ELEVEN
March 28, 2024

The house was within walking distance from Guildhall Street, an impressive five or six-bedroomed semi located on Beaumont Fee. Aside from the size, the red-brick building looked no different to the nearby houses – sash windows, large entranceways, and multiple chimneys, which signified multiple fireplaces, which further signified the house had originally been designed for wealthy Victorian residents. It wasn't quite suitable for the upper echelons of society but was for no less than the middle class.

"Bit of a step down from the manor house," Devon remarked.

"Maybe in size and stature," he replied. "But a house like this in this part of town probably cost similar to the old manor house out in the middle of nowhere. Maybe not quite so much, but close enough to be out of the range of an ageing police officer."

"I don't know, guv," she said. "I can see you rattling around in a place like this in your retirement."

"Well, you'd be wrong on two fronts," he told her. "First of all, unless I want to live out my days in poverty, retirement is a long way off. Secondly, if ever I rattle around, just put me out of my misery, will you?"

"I couldn't do that," she said. "Just think, you could have different pyjamas for the days of the week."

"Aye, that'll keep me happy while I stare out of the window all day with nothing to do but the crossword. No, Devon, while there's breath in my body, I'll be working. You mark my words."

Charles imagined the original door would have been accompanied by an actual bell, or at least a pull, which would be connected by wire to a bell somewhere inside. He was almost disappointed to find a modern camera doorbell.

The door was opened by a woman whom Charles deemed to be in her late thirties. Her hair had been pulled up and fixed to the top of her head with an oversized clip, and Charles immediately wondered if she too left them lying around on the kitchen work surface. She had large, brown eyes that were as soft and caring as a mother's touch.

"Good morning, ma'am," Charles said. "We're looking for Robert Garfield. Do we have the right house?"

She nodded but gave nothing else away.

"You do," she said. "Is he expecting you?"

"I doubt it," Charles replied, and he held up his warrant card, letting the little wallet fall open. "We just need a few words."

"Police? Is this about one of his cases?"

"No, ma'am, I'm afraid not."

"Well, what should I tell him?"

"You could tell him that Chief Inspector Cook would like a few minutes of his time," he said. "Sorry, may I ask who you are?"

"Me? I'm Dot."

"Dot? Would that be short for Dorothy?"

"It would, yes," she said and then took a deep breath. "You'd better come inside. I'll see if he's available."

She held the door open for them and then left them in the hallway while she disappeared into a back room. The floor was made up of black-and-white, checkered tiles, and the walls were a faint, floral-patterned wallpaper, holding a mirror, an old-fashioned barometer, and an old Vienna wall clock with its swinging pendulum marking the passage of time with each sweeping traverse of its walnut frame.

"Think you could manage the stairs in a few years' time, guv?"

"Less of your cheek, Devon," he said. "I can still manage stairs, all right. I might need a wee bathroom break in the middle of the night, but I'm not past it yet. Besides, I always fancied a little bungalow when my time comes. Somewhere quiet. Out in the Wolds or on the coast, maybe. Somewhere with a wee garden and a decent view."

"That's a bit cliche for you, guv, isn't it? I always thought you would go against the grain."

"Going against the grain, Devon, is a luxury saved only for the inconvenience of others," he told her. "But when it comes to my own convenience, I think the old folk have it right. Get rid of the stairs, make all the surfaces and floors wipe-down, ditch the bath and the shower for a wet room, and fill the kitchen cupboards with microwave meals. Then all anyone will need to do is pop in every six months or so to see if I'm dead yet."

"Crikey," Devon said, surprised at his bluntness. "Not that you've thought about it much."

"He can give you a few minutes," Dot said from the doorway, and she held the door for them to indicate they should go through.

"I think of little else," he said quietly to Devon, then smiled at Dot. "Through here?"

"The door at the end of the corridor," she said.

It wasn't so much a corridor as a small hallway, gloomy and without purpose, except to provide a path to areas of more importance. It was a lot like France, Charles thought, gloomy with its only real purpose to provide a route to Italy.

The door at the end of the so-called corridor was open and Charles gave it a light knock as he entered.

"Mr Garfield?" he said, and a portly man in his sixties stood from behind a large desk. He held out his hand for Charles to shake, which was more of a formality than a sign of him being genuinely pleased to see them. "I'm Chief Inspector Cook and this is Sergeant Devon. I wondered if we might take a few moments of your time."

"I invited you in, didn't I?" he said.

He wore a green, tweed jacket over a Tattersall shirt, opened at the neck. The room had, at some point, been converted into a study, but given the low light and claustrophobic air, Charles felt its original purpose might have been the butler's pantry or some other servantage function.

The two side walls had been filled with old bookcases, not dissimilar from those at the Manor House, while the wall behind the desk seemed purely to accommodate a small fireplace.

"May we?" Charles said, indicating the two guest chairs, which, if he wasn't mistaken, were the same as the old farmhouse breakfast chairs in his own house.

"Of course," Garfield said.

"I'll get to the point, Mr Garfield–"

"It would be appreciated."

"There's no easy way of saying this. It's your father," he said. "I'm afraid he was found dead at his home this morning."

If Garfield felt any emotion at all, then he kept it in check. He swallowed once and gave a small cough to clear his throat, and then blinked his blue eyes a few times to conceal his truest thoughts.

"Dead? My dad?"

"Hugo Garfield is your father, is he not?"

"He is. Of course he is, but–"

"I'm sorry, it's never easy to deliver news like this, but given the circumstances..."

Garfield sat back in the plush, leather seat, and stared at the bookshelf to his right where, in front of a series of books titled Harvey on Industrial Relations and Employment Law sat a photo of whom Charles presumed was Hugo Garfield many years younger.

"Are you okay, Mr Garfield?" he said. "Do you need a minute? I appreciate this can be difficult news to hear."

"I'm fine," he said sharply. "He was ninety-eight years old. I shouldn't be surprised."

"Oh? How so?"

"Because he was ninety-eight, Inspector. I've been preparing for this day for twenty years or more. Never thought it would happen, though."

"Was he ill at all, Mr Garfield?"

"Bobby," he said. "Call me Bobby, please. My clients call me Mr Garfield, and unless you're planning on paying me—"

"Okay then. Was he in poor health, Bobby?" Charles said, to which Garfield simply shook his head.

"Nothing that any ninety-eight-year-old man out there hasn't been through at some stage or other," he replied. "What was it, anyway? Did he have a fall? My wife has been telling him for years he needs to get out of that house."

It was difficult to respond to such a question. There had indeed been a fall of some description or a drop at least. But delivering news of a recent death required a gentle approach.

"Did he have cause to be upset, Bobby? Was he experiencing difficulties, perhaps?"

Garfield stared between them, curiously, his face reddening.

"Just say what it is you have to say, Inspector," he said, and following a brief glance at Devon, who sat politely with an indifferent expression, Charles said what he had to say.

"Your father was found in his study by a Mrs Childs."

"Joanne," he said. "She cleans for him, or should I say, she cleans up after him."

"He was hanging from the chandelier, Bobby," Charles said, and Garfield gave his first look of shock. He stared at Charles as if searching for a telltale sign that he might be lying. But Charles remained straight-faced, offering enough empathy in his eyes to soften the blow.

"Hanging?"

"I'm sorry, Bobby," he said again. "I imagine this is extremely difficult for you, but being his next of kin–"

"How?" Garfield asked, cutting him off. "How on earth did he manage to do that? The man could barely tie his shoes let alone climb a ladder."

"Well, that's just it, Bobby. There was no sign of a ladder."

"A chair, then," he said, his tone more malicious than grateful. "This is hardly the time for being pedantic, Inspector."

"I'm afraid there was no chair either," Charles told him. "Not within reach, anyway, and certainly none tall enough for him to... make the necessary preparations, shall we say?"

"What are you saying?"

"I'm afraid that your father may have had assistance," Charles told him and then spoke frankly for the avoidance of doubt. "And whether that assistance was through kindness or otherwise, this is likely going to escalate into a murder investigation, Mr Garfield."

CHAPTER TWELVE
March 15, 1970

The four days that followed the dyke incident were each punctuated by similar escapades involving a long run through various landscapes, culminating in some kind of physical attack from either Garfield, his two friends, or in the case of Friday's episode, all three of them. The final attack had been all too much for John to conceal, and the excuses he had given to his mother about the state of his clothing, and the various bruises that were appearing, were wearing thin.

"Now then," Terry said when he saw John ambling along the side of the field that sat between their farmhouse and the squire's property. He did his best to conceal the limp from his deadened leg, but his swollen lip and bloodied nose were out of his control. Terry jumped down from the Massey Ferguson, tugged his gloves off, and then waited for John to arrive. "Been in the wars, have you?"

"Ah, it's okay," John told him. "We were just playing, that's all."

"Oh, aye? What were you playing?"

"Football," John told him as if there could have been any other answer.

"Right, and you were the ball, were you?"

"Very funny," John told him as he hobbled past.

"Course, I could always drop you back at the house on the tractor." John stopped on his good leg and eyed the length of the field. It was doable but would easily take him half an hour or so. "Or you could walk back, and then have to tell your mum why your clothes are ruined again, and why you're limping, and of course, why your face looks like a cow's backside."

Despite the unrelenting urge to cry his eyes out, John managed to keep his emotions at bay.

"You won't tell her, will you?"

"Not unless you lie to me," Terry replied. He leaned against the tractor as if the day was mid-summer and the sun was beating down. He wore his shirt sleeves rolled up with only a thin vest and a light scarf beneath. It was the first week for a long time that the ground wasn't too wet to get the crops in, and almost every farmer in every direction was making the most of the mild weather. "What happened, John?"

"It's nothing," John said, immediately realising the lie.

"Okay then," Terry said, pulling his gloves on slowly. "We'll talk about it tonight over dinner."

"Sorry. Okay, I'm just having some trouble, that's all. It's nothing, though. I can handle it."

"You being bullied, John?" Terry asked, to which John shrugged. "Anyone I know?"

"Nobody that matters," John said, and again Terry started back towards the little step to climb back onto his tractor. "Okay, it's Bobby Garfield. He's had it in for me since we moved here."

"Bobby Garfield?" Terry said, almost as if he disbelieved it. "That useless sack of spuds? He couldn't fight his way out of a wet paper bag. He might be able to buy his way out–"

"And his two mates," John added, to which Terry nodded his understanding.

"I see. One of them's old Pop Mason's boy, isn't it?" Terry asked. "I've seen them about. Who's the other?"

"Harry Pepper."

"Keith and Jill's boy? My my..." Terry said. "Well, Bobby Garfield hasn't fallen far from the apple tree, has he?"

"What does that mean?"

"It means his dad knows how to surround himself with people with less up here and more down there," Terry said, pointing first to his temple and then to his biceps. "Looks like young Bobby Garfield is following in his dad's footsteps."

"Yeah, well, he'll get what's coming to him. They all will," John said.

"Not while you're living under my roof, they won't," Terry said. "I don't want you going anywhere near Bobby Garfield."

"But, Terry–"

"No buts about it, John," Terry said. "And if you want my advice, you'll stay well away from them. All of them."

"I have to see them every day."

"Just walk away."

"But they chase me."

"And what do you do when they chase you?" Terry asked.

"What?"

"What do you do when they chase you?"

"I bloody run, don't I?"

"Hey now," Terry said, wagging his finger. "Don't let me hear you say that word again. You know what your ma would say."

"Sorry," John said. "But what am I supposed to do?"

"Stand your ground," Terry told him as if the answer was as simple as slicing bread. "What would you do if you were in with the chickens and one came at you?"

John shrugged again. "Run?"

"No, you stand your ground, John. You go at them," Terry explained. "You don't have to hit them or kick them. But you have to show them you're not afraid. Same with horses. Keep your distance but don't let them get the upper hand. Do that, and you'll be on the ground 'fore you know it."

John pictured the scene. He could see himself descending the school steps into the little playground, and then hearing Bobby Garfield bellow from the top of the steps behind him.

'Get him!'

But instead of running, he imagined what it would be like to just stand there. To face them head-on or maybe even walk at them, meeting them halfway. He wondered how they would react. They certainly wouldn't hit him in eyesight of the school window, where old Matheson might see them from the classroom window.

"Thanks, Terry," he said, and to his surprise. his mother's new husband came and put his arm around him, leading him back to the tractor. "You won't say anything, will you? To Ma, I mean."

"No," Terry said. "No, tell you what, we'll tell her you stopped to help me on the way home and slipped down into the dyke or something."

"I fell down the dyke on Monday."

"Well, then we'll say something else. One of the springs popped off the cultivator."

John glanced at the back of the tractor.

"You haven't got the cultivator."

"I know that and you know that," Terry said. "But your ma doesn't. Don't worry, boy. I'll take the blame."

"Really? You'd do that for me?"

"Oh, aye," Terry said. "Listen, you and me need to stick together more. Your ma is a strong woman. One of the reasons I love her, as I do. I can take it and she'll not be as mad at me as she would be at you."

He helped John up onto the tractor, where he carefully dropped onto the little wheel arch. Terry pulled himself up and the seat springs accommodated his weight with a few gentle squeaks.

"Terry?" John called, as he fired up the great engine and the exhaust bellowed black smoke for a few seconds before the old

Massey idled. He turned to look at John, eyebrows raised. "What would you do if you walked into a field with a bull in it?"

"Is the bull charging at you?" Terry said as if it somehow made a difference.

John nodded. "Full pelt."

"Ah, under those circumstances, Johnny boy," Terry replied, dropping the tractor into gear and staring at John long enough for him to see that twinkle in his eye, "I would run like hell."

CHAPTER THIRTEEN
March 28, 2024

"Was that your wife or..." Charles began, and he jabbed a thumb at the study door.

"My daughter," he replied, far too consumed by the news to pick up on what could have been perceived as an insult. "Dorothy."

"Would you like us to fetch her?"

"No," he said. "No, I'll tell her in a bit. She should hear it from me."

"Honestly, it's no trouble."

"I said I'll do it," he snapped, then turned his face away. "Sorry. This is somewhat of a surprise."

"Excuse me for the intrusion, Bobby, but is your wife around? It's often good to have somebody with you at times like this."

"No, she's away, I'm afraid. She has enough on her plate without all this. It can wait until she gets back."

"Anywhere nice?"

"Just away," he replied, then read into Charles' expression. "Her mother's. She's poorly, and like my father, quite elderly. None of us is getting any younger, are we?"

"Bobby, I'm obliged to run through the procedure with you.

Quite often in these circumstances, having knowledge of the protocols that we must follow helps people in your position."

"I'm a lawyer," he replied. "I am fully aware of your procedures, believe me."

"They can be quite intrusive," Charles said.

"Yes, I know, and I'm also keenly aware that they can be quite time-wasting," he countered.

"Well, let's not waste any time then," Charles replied. "We will, of course, need you to identify your father at some point in the next day or so."

"I expected that," he replied, and he dragged an A4 diary across his desk, flipping it open to the marked page.

"Before then, the pathologist will need to carry out some investigative work. I'll confirm a time and date with you when we know more."

"Investigative work?" He set his pen down in the fold. "Are you suggesting that my father will have to endure being prodded and poked and God knows what?"

"I'm sure that the pathologist will employ suitable finesse," Charles said. "And as for your father enduring any discomfort–"

"So why the need to cut him open? Why can't they just show him a bit of respect? He was the squire, you know? People looked up to him."

"I understand that the processes might seem unnecessary. However, we must ascertain the cause of death, and we must ascertain if he had help in any way."

"Help? Who would've helped him?"

"Well, that's precisely the type of information that you might be able to help us with, Bobby. Look, we're on your side here. Your father is dead and that is quite possibly – no almost certainly – the most devastating news a man can hear. But if a crime has been committed, then we simply must get to the bottom of it. Is that clear, Bobby?"

He nodded submissively.

"Do you want us to come back? We've quite a few questions to ask, but if you'd like some time to come to terms with it all?"

"No. No, now is as good a time as any," he said. "No point in reopening the wounds."

"Quite right," Charles said and then glanced across at Devon. "Some tea, maybe?"

"I don't want tea," Garfield said, then pulled his poor manners into check. "But of course, if you want it."

"I'll see to it, guv," Devon said, and Garfield looked up from his desk.

"You'll find Dot out the back somewhere. She'll be working, but she'll show you where the things are."

"Thank you," Devon said, catching Charles' eye as she left.

Charles waited for Devon to leave the room and then made a point of making himself comfortable.

"When I lost my dad, it hit me pretty hard," he said. "We weren't close. Never had been, in fact. But knowing that he was no longer there, that was a difficult transition for me."

"Thank you," Garfield said. "For sharing that, I mean. We were close, my father and I. Not so close that we hugged or anything like that. He wasn't an emotional man. But I feel like he knew he had me. He groomed me, in fact. Up until I was in my mid-teens, I was being groomed to run the family show."

"The estate, you mean?" Charles said, and Garfield nodded.

"Estates like ours, at that time at least, were delicate affairs. The balance was knife-edge. We had tenant farmers, we had investments, and staff, of course. All of that had to be managed. Succession was key. But I think my father knew it wouldn't last. It couldn't last. The world was a changing place back then, more so than it is now."

"So, you became a lawyer?"

"Kicking and screaming, yes," he said. "But it made sense. If the estate survived, then I would be competent enough to succeed him. If it failed, as many did, then I wouldn't be destitute.

My father was not a loving man, Inspector, but I am grateful for his foresight. If I'd had my way, then I'd probably be sitting in a big, cold, and damp house burning books to keep warm."

"I'm sure he knew what he was doing," Charles told him, then shifted the conversation. "I wonder if you know of anybody who might have had something against him?"

Garfield laughed.

"How long do you have?" he said. "My father was the squire and his father before him. The locals didn't exactly bow and scrape willingly. They kept him at arm's length." He pointed a finger at Charles and peered down the length of his arm as if it were a rifle. "He could have ruined any one of them in a heartbeat." He clicked his fingers for effect. "And they knew it."

"But that was back in the day, was it not? I was thinking of anybody whose nose might have been put out of joint more recently."

He stared across at the old photo once more.

"Not that I can think of," he said.

"In which case, I must ask if there could be anybody who would have been willing to help him. Somebody close maybe, who might have known about some ailment, or illness? Or close enough for him to ask?"

"Help him kill himself? Not a chance," Garfield said. "I mean, there's always Joanne, but she doesn't seem the type."

"You'd be surprised at how often types go against the grain, Bobby. Anybody else?"

He shook his head.

"You have to understand, Inspector. My father was a very private man. He kept himself to himself. I used to speak to him once a week. I'd visit once per month to make sure he was all right. Other than that, he had nobody. Not really."

"And when did you last visit?" Charles asked.

"Are you asking for my alibi, Inspector?"

"No, I'm merely asking when you last visited him. I was going to follow up with something along the lines of, how did he seem? But now that you mention it, we might as well get it out of the way."

Garfield sighed and leaned back in his chair, eyeing Charles with suspicion.

"I was here. I haven't left the house for days."

"You've taken annual leave, I believe?" Charles said. "Any reason? Are you planning on going away? Meeting your wife, perhaps?"

"No. I'll be staying here," he replied and gestured at the stack of ledgers on the desk. "My father's accounts, if you must know."

"He still writes them out by hand?"

"Always did," Garfield replied, then tapped the stack of old books. "All the way back to my old grandfather's days. My wife and I have been going through them for the past couple of weeks to see where the money went."

"How fascinating. I'm sure there are some memories in there."

"Not happy ones, I'm afraid," he replied. "And as for fascinating, we'll have to wait and see, won't we?"

He smiled up at Charles from behind his desk, conveying the end of their little chat.

"I will need to access your father's last will and testament, Bobby. His financial records, too. Digital if possible. As much as I'd love to sift through the years to see what life was like one hundred years ago, I doubt I'll have the time. I hope that won't be perceived as intrusive."

"Not at all. I can tell you all there is to know if you like," he said. "Everything goes to me, and there is absolutely nothing to be had. The sad truth is that my father died penniless, Inspector."

"You have the house, at least."

"Oh yes," Garfield said. "Just what I need. An old relic from the past that costs more to maintain than the land is worth."

"Will you keep it?" Charles asked. "I can't imagine a family like yours, Mr Garfield, selling a place with so much family history. You must be quite torn."

"Torn? Not really. You see, my family, like so many others, has survived because we are survivors, Inspector. The Massingberds sold most of their estate at one stage. A few generations later, they handed the house and grounds over to the National Trust before moving on. They survived. Which is exactly what I intend to do – survive. It won't be easy, and you're right, to sell the old place will be heartbreaking. But survival is not a matter for the faint of heart, is it?"

Charles conveyed his empathy with a friendly smile.

"I'll be in touch about the identification," he said, placing one of his contact cards on Garfield's desk. Garfield studied the card, then looked up at him. "For the will. You said you would send it."

"I'll look forward to hearing from you," Garfield replied, and he retrieved a business card of his own from a pile in his top righthand drawer, which he then slid across the desk. "I'd like to say goodbye to the old boy." He straightened in his seat and prepared to get back to work. "I'd also like to draw a line under this whole affair."

CHAPTER FOURTEEN
March 16, 1970

A variety of shops lined Alford's High Street, and on Saturdays, a steady stream of cars passed through, at least one per minute – Ford Cortinas and Vauxhall Vivas, Austin Healeys and Morris Minors, and of course one or two foreign imports, such as the Volkswagen Beetle.

John watched them cruise by in awe. Families headed to the coast, couples made their way to Horncastle and Lincoln, and locals went about their daily business. It was a time when the motor car had made its mark, yet some, Terry included, still favoured the pony and trap. Other farmers had invested in trucks, large, open-backed vehicles to transport their wares, that seemed far too large for the narrow roads. It seemed to John that every month that he and Terry came to the market, more and more cars were on the roads, grumbling through the old market town, coughing and spluttering, and often leaving a trail of grey smoke in their wake.

The market square was off the main road, situated in a paved triangle space filled with livestock pens, stalls, and men of all shapes and sizes – red-faced, roly-poly men, tall and lean men, stout men, broad men, small men, and servicemen who still carried their battle scars. He saw men with missing legs or missing arms, blind men, men whose faces had been melted away, and men who bore no physical scars but seemed to stop and stare, their faces white with fear and polished with sweat.

The variety of women was equally as impressive. Some walked with their arms linked through their husband's. Some walked alone and with purpose. One lady, a rather rotund creature with bosoms as large as John's head, most of which was on show, yelled from the corner of the street about the amazing quality of the fish that her husband was selling in his shop further along the High Street.

It was the voices, John thought, that was the most interesting – the large lady's whine that cut through the heavy, baritone and the thundering men's voices as they announced to all and sundry the prices of vegetables, butter, and cuts of meat.

"Stay close now, John," Terry told him, as he led them through the melee. "I don't want to be hanging about here all day. You hear me?"

"Yes, Terry," John replied, having to shout to be heard above a man who was barely larger than he was in height and frame, yet whose voice seemed to come from the earth beneath his feet.

"Over here," Terry said and dragged John through a gap to stand beside a stall filled with hessian sacks.

Pleased to have found a spot from which he could safely observe the chaos, John waited while Terry negotiated the price of a brown sack that stood as high as John's waist and resembled, in part, he thought, the fish seller's buxom wife.

A man with a scar that ran from his eye to his mouth pushed an old, wooden cart, stomping through a pile of fresh horse droppings undeterred. John admired his arrogance, as the crowd seemed to part to let him through, then close around him like a fish through water.

Two dogs scoured the old, cobbled stones for scraps dropped by careless shoppers, never straying too far from the butcher's stall where strings of Lincolnshire sausages hung beside cuts of mutton. It was too early for the lambs, even John knew that. In a few months, the racks would be filled with fat legs and chops.

"Snap to it, John," Terry said, as he crouched to heave the great sack onto his shoulder. He walked lopsided under its weight, edging past crowds, between nattering men, and on one occasion, he bellowed for a few children, who were younger than John, to simply, "Move out the bally way before you get trampled!"

John hurried behind Terry, not wanting to lose him in the crowd. Occasionally something would catch his eye, such as a shop window in which a family of mannequins displayed the modern family. The man wore a sharp suit and flat cap, the woman wore a knee-length, floral dress, and the boy's outfit wasn't too dissimilar to its father's, but in place of the jacket, he wore a waistcoat. He stopped to admire the make-believe family, picturing how he, his mother, and Terry might look wearing it all and then deemed the notion ridiculous. Terry would destroy the suit in a heartbeat, Ma wouldn't be able to do her chores wearing such a short dress, and his own outfit would remain in his little cupboard for fear of being tarnished, most likely until it was far too small. And of course, he would no doubt be scolded for growing too fast.

He dragged himself away from the display and found himself trapped in an endless cage of backs, bums, and legs. He jumped into the air in the hope of spying Terry or perhaps the large sack, but he saw nothing. The crowd urged him on, nudging him this way and that, and in his panic, he stumbled into one of those little treasures that the pack horses enjoyed leaving behind. His knee was wet with it and the palms of his hands were soiled, leaving him with little option but to wipe them on the sides of his already sullied trousers.

"Get out the way," a voice called, as a heavy boot landed beside him.

"What do you think you're doing down there?" another said.

He earned himself a kick from one man for irritation alone, and at one point, he even had to snatch his hand away before his fingers were trampled.

He climbed to his feet amidst a few fast-moving knees and spied the shop fronts to one side, where he found relative sanctuary in a doorway.

"Now then," a voice said with familiar authority. "If it isn't young Master Frobisher."

The squire wore one of his tweed suits, similar to that of the man in the window. Beneath the heavy jacket, he wore a waistcoat with the gold chain of a pocket watch hanging freely. A silk scarf had been tied around his neck, and his shoes had been polished to a shine.

Behind him, his entourage came to a standstill. Two men, each carrying a sack on either shoulder stopped and waited, the strain of their loads evident in their expressions. And behind them, Bobby Garfield stepped into view, perusing the wares in the windows with casual indifference.

"I'm a Stow, sir," John told him. "Ma's a Frobisher, but not me."

"You live on Frobisher's Farm," the squire said. "You're a Frobisher in my book, and I doubt that you're here alone. Where's your father?"

"He's dead, sir," John told him, which earned him a glare.

"Don't be smart with me, boy. I don't care for impertinence." Bobby came to stand beside him, mimicking his father's posture, with his fingers tucked into the corners of his waistcoat pockets. He watched John as a kestrel eyes a field mouse.

"I'm here," a voice said, and a red-faced Terry stepped out of the melee and came to stand beside John. "Is everything as it should be, Squire?"

The squire's watchful eye lingered on John for a moment, then turned on Terry, who was having to adjust the sack on his shoulders.

He glanced back at the two men to whom he had no doubt paid a pittance to carry his vegetables, and then back at John.

"I think so," he said eventually. "In fact, I'm rather glad to have seen you, Frobisher. The question of rent is up. It's that time of year, I'm afraid. Well, if accuracy is something you seek, then it's actually been and gone. You've started this year's crops already."

"I have, Squire," Terry said. "Soon as the fields were dry enough. Same as the other tenants."

"Yes, well, you see, the other tenants are all paid up. It's their land for another year. You, however–"

"I'll get it you," Terry said. "Give me a week. That's all I need."

Terry's ability to stand his ground was, in John's opinion, admirable. Even with the great weight on his shoulder, he managed to remain resolute yet respectful, and John recalled Matheson's feeble attempt at singling him out.

All men are equal in God's eyes.

"And then, of course, there is the topic of last week's manhunt," the squire continued, changing tack. "You know there's a rumour that he escaped onto the main road."

"Is there?" Terry said, and the squire's eyes narrowed a little.

"Which of course means that he must have passed across my land from your plot."

"I wouldn't know," Terry said. "Less, of course, he came from old Pop Mason's field, through mine, and then yours."

"I suppose that could have been possible had Pop Mason not assured me that his outbuildings and dykes were thoroughly searched."

"As were mine, Squire."

"I see," he said, and stepped closer to John, taking his sweet time as if he was prolonging the conversation and therefore Terry's discomfort. "End of the week, Frobisher," he said. "You've a family to feed now. Wouldn't want to see you all begging in the streets now, would we?"

He tipped his hat and Terry followed suit as he made his way, clicking his fingers for the two men with sacks to follow. Bobby brushed past John as he passed, and then peered over his shoulder to glare at him.

"Are you okay, Terry?" John asked.

"Me? Oh aye, I'm okay," he replied.

"Do we owe him money?"

"Listen," Terry began, taking a moment to reassure John despite his weighty burden. "Men like you and me will always owe men like Hugo Garfield. It's a fact of life."

"But all men are equal. That's what the Bible says."

"Ah, all men are equal in heart and body. But position, now that's a different story."

"But we won't be homeless, will we?"

"Listen, John," Terry said. "If I paid the squire what I have to when he asked, he'll no doubt invent some new debt. But if I hang on to it, if I wait until he comes to me, asking for the money, who has the power then?"

"I don't know."

"Not him," Terry told him. "When a man with the kind of money he's got comes knocking at your door for rent, it tells you who needs it most. Let them come to you, John. Meet them on your terms. You'll do well to remember that."

"Right," John said, not quite understanding.

"Now then, let's get out of here," Terry said, seeking a gap in the stream of passing bodies. "If we're not back by lunchtime, your ma will have us both hung out to dry."

CHAPTER FIFTEEN
March 28, 2024

The incident room was a lively place, too lively for Charles' liking. He preferred space and silence in which he could think and empathise, put pieces of the jigsaw together, and truly work himself into the minds of the individuals.

But telephones rang, people chatted or called out, and printers, those loathsome beasts of burden, lazily spewed sheet after sheet from their mouths, which often went unread. They were just slipped into a file somewhere. It was, like most police work, a box-ticking exercise. An investigation could not be opened without a crime number. It could not then be handed to Charles and his team without reasonable confidence a crime had been committed. And he could not even begin to question individuals to the degree he would have preferred without the body first being identified. The process was designed to remove the risk of the force investigating the death of somebody who was still alive, and thus, to prevent a senior spokesperson from having to stand in front of a circus of journalists and news reporters, cap in hand.

If only the same consideration would be given to the individuals who actually performed the work, they might find that their ninety-per-cent failure rate would improve.

But the world had gone too far. It had become too sensitive. The decision-makers had been shamed into giving every single minority group a voice, which in the case of racism and gender equality was absolutely fine. Perfect, in fact. But these days, even prisoners had rights. Even when the whole country knew that a particular individual committed a crime on a particular date, at a particular time, unless all shreds of doubt were wiped out, they would walk. They would be free to enact their crimes again and again.

It was thankless and did little to make the streets safer, in Charles' opinion.

He would have wagered that at least ninety per cent of the chatter and phone calls were not investigative enquiries to find a culprit. Nine times out of ten, the officers knew who had committed the crime within twenty-four hours of the crime being reported. No, the calls and chatter were discussions on how they could provide the CPS with a case that ran very little risk of not producing a conviction.

"Guv?" Devon said, dragging him from his thoughts.

"Sorry, yes?"

"We're ready when you are," she said politely. He was seated in his chair beside the whiteboard, which itself sat on a wobbly easel, so that every time he made a mark, the whole thing threatened to collapse.

Chalk and Forsythe were sitting beside her at the little table they had commandeered as their own, and one which Charles defended vehemently. All too often, he had returned from a crime scene or his enquiries and discovered a rogue team in their spot. One of them had even rubbed his investigation from the whiteboard and replaced it with their own scribbled notes.

"Hugo Garfield, ninety-eight," he said, and then with one hand holding the board steady, he wrote the name at its centre and then added the word, *Prelim*.

"Prelim, guv?" Chalk said.

"Preliminary. It means we haven't got the go-ahead to make enquiries yet. But we can make plans so that if and when such a time arrives, we aren't starting from scratch." He added a name and then spoke it aloud. "Robert Garfield. Son. Late sixties." He drew a line to connect the two names, and then on the other side of the victim's name, he added another. "Joanne Childs. Cleaner." He added one more word beneath the victim's name. "Hanged."

On the far side of the board, he began a list, narrating the key elements of the investigation as he wrote them.

"Autopsy, identification, CSI, financial statements, LWT..."

"Guv?"

"Last will and testament'" he said, without turning from the board. "Eyewitnesses and CCTV." He recapped the pen and turned in his seat. "Robert Garfield is married. Do we know the name of his wife yet?"

Chalk scrawled through her notes and findings quickly.

"Rose, guv," she said, and Charles wrote it on the board, connecting her to her husband, and in the format used by family trees, he added the name of their daughter. "Dorothy Garfield."

"Not bad for six hours," Devon said, and Charles studied her, looking to see if the comment was genuine or just plain flippant.

"Before we start, does anybody have any plans for the weekend?" he asked, ignoring Devon's comment.

"The wife wants to take the kids out," Forsythe said.

"And if I were to ask you to work?" Charles said. "Don't feel obliged. I don't want to be the thorn in anybody's relationships."

"I can probably get out of it," he said.

"Good, thank you. I'll give you as much notice as I can. I think, at this stage, everything depends on the pathologist," he said, looking over at Devon. "And that will be our first port of call tomorrow morning. In the meantime, we can only go with what the FME told us and our guts. Chalk, Forsythe, what did you learn today?"

They exchanged glances, and being a man of manners, Forsythe nodded for Chalk to go first.

"I've managed to find a security camera in the post office, guv, just like you said. They're sending me the footage as soon as they can."

"That's good. Give them until tomorrow morning and then call them. Tell them you need it sooner."

"I'll try, guv," she said. "But I don't think Mr Garfield was particularly well-liked."

"What makes you say that?"

"Because the lady behind the counter told me as much, guv. I'd tell you exactly what she said, but it's not the type of language you enjoy."

"Well, there's food for thought," Charles said. "Forsythe?"

"Same, guv," he said. "I knocked on a few doors and got nothing. The pub was interesting, though. Element of old photos of the house up on the walls, but nobody really wanted to say much."

"The landlord?"

"Yeah, he seemed like a nice bloke. He gave me this." Forsythe said and slid a slip of paper towards him. Charles reached out and examined the slip, and then rolled his eyes, before removing the cap from the pen and starting a new list in the top left-hand corner, titled *Motives*. Again, he narrated as he wrote. "Debt."

"I hardly think a sixty-quid bar tab warrants a murder, guv," Devon said.

"If he owes money to the pub, Devon, then the chances are that he owes money elsewhere. Where are we with financial statements?"

"Tomorrow morning, guv. The magistrate signed the request off this afternoon."

"Good. So, we have the CCTV, financial records, and the pathology report coming tomorrow," he said. "Now let's talk motives." He tapped Joanne Child's name with the pen. "Anybody?"

"She seemed pretty normal to me, guv," Devon said, and Charles left a silence for one of the other two to speak.

But nobody did.

"I agree," he said finally. "She did seem quite normal. But let's get our ducks in a row, shall we? Forsythe, follow up with the emergency services, will you? I want the recording of her call."

"What for, guv?" Chalk asked.

"Because that is, currently at least, the only true evidence we have. Her voice, reporting the death of her employer, presumably from the room in which he was hanging. And seeing as the information is from an internal source, we do not, at this stage, need a crime number to make the request."

"Got it," Forsythe said, and he made a note in his notepad.

"While you're at it, why don't you focus on her and her family? She said they had worked for the Garfields for years. See if there's any information available on them."

"Righto," he replied, and Charles turned his attention to Chalk.

"Assets. See if he had any other properties, Chalk, will you?" he asked her, then addressed the team as a whole. "And then we have the will, of which Robert Garfield assures me that he is the sole beneficiary."

"That's quite the motive, guv," Devon said. "I had a look on Rightmove earlier. The old manor house will probably go for somewhere north of two million quid."

He nodded slowly, then gauged the expressions of the others, who, from a glance at least, seemed to be falling in with Devon's line of attack.

"Two million pounds, eh?" he said. "That's quite a sum of money. Enough to murder your father for?"

"For me, no," she said. "But people have done similar for less."

"They have," he agreed. "Tell me, the house in Beaumont Fee. How much would you say that was worth?"

She shrugged and looked to others for assistance.

"Beaumont Fee?" Forsythe said, inhaling a deep breath. "How many bedrooms?"

"Five or six."

He pulled a face that suggested he was mulling it over, then came up with a sum.

"I'm going with low seven figures."

"One million?" Charles asked, to which he nodded.

"In the region of," he said.

"Have you missed your vocation, Forsythe?" Charles asked. "Is there a budding estate agent lurking inside of you?"

"No, guv," he replied. "The wife and I enjoy a bit of house porn."

"House porn?" Chalk said.

"Yeah. You know. We browse houses that we'd like to live in. We imagine what it must be like to live there. "Kelly always goes for the ones with a large master suite, dressing room, and en-suite. My go-to places have a decent bit of land, an outbuilding or two, and maybe a decent office space."

"Oh, I do that," Chalk added.

"The question is," Charles said. "If Bobby Garfield's house is worth a million pounds, does he really need his father's money?"

"Depends if it's mortgaged or not," Devon said. "And of course, how much he has in the bank."

"Which we won't know until we can access his financial records," Charles said, bringing the briefing to an end. "And we can't do that until we can officially begin the investigation. So, I suggest that we leave it there. Wrap up any paperwork you have outstanding and get a good rest tonight. Tomorrow is going to be busy and I don't want any distractions. Got it?"

"Got it," Devon said.

"Right," he said, checking his watch. "Let's park it. I'll see you all in the morning."

"You off early, guv?" Devon asked.

"Early?" he said with a laugh. "No, I thought I'd take the time to look at the property market."

"House porn, guv?" Forsythe asked.

"If that's what you want to call it," he replied with a smirk. "I call it research myself. But what you do with your spare time, Forsythe, is entirely down to you." He stopped at the door and thought about what he wanted to say. "I want you all to think about something," he began. "Not all motives for murder are clear. It's not always money, or revenge, or hatred that drives a person to do such a thing. Sometimes a person can think they're doing the right thing when, in fact, they're not. Not in the eyes of the law, at any rate. Just think about that, will you?"

CHAPTER SIXTEEN
March 18, 1970

Matheson was bull-like in more ways than one. When he addressed the class as a whole, his eyes often appeared dead, as if he was looking through, rather than at, an individual. His shoulders were broad, which John presumed was more a result of pies than hard graft. The top of his legs resembled tree trunks, and the straining jacket, with its worn elbow patches, was crumpled at the collar, like great folds of skin.

"Now then," he called to gain their attention. "Times tables. One of the most important skills of life, maths is. Master the intricacies of mathematics and the English language, and who knows, some of you might just stand a chance."

It was Karen Gutteridge who raised a hand first, stopping Matheson mid-speech, and he raised his eyebrows in anticipation.

"Why, sir?" she began.

"Why what? Be clear, girl."

"Why are numbers important?" she said. "I mean, my mum's a cleaner. I'll probably work with her. She don't need her numbers. I don't think she even knows them."

"I see," Matheson said, and then peered at them all, perhaps searching for similar opinions among the sea of bored faces. "Can any of you explain to Miss Gutteridge why the ability to add, subtract, multiply, and divide numbers might serve you well later in life, regardless of your chosen occupation?"

Nobody said a word.

"Or perhaps some of you might be keen to understand why calculating an area might one day come in useful?"

Again, nobody dared to raise a hand.

"You, boy," he said, and even without looking, John knew that he was the target of Matheson's fat finger. "You seemed to be full of ideas last week. Perhaps you can explain?"

John stood and his chair squealed across the floor.

"Explain why numbers are important, sir?"

"Yes, come along. If I wanted a recital, I would have bought a parrot."

"Well, you need to count, don't you?" John suggested. "I mean, everyone needs to count, don't they?"

"I don't know, do they?"

"My ma does. She has to count when she bakes. I've seen her, sir."

"Ah, baking. Give me an example of how your dear old ma might implement mathematics whilst baking if you will."

John gave it some thought and glanced around the room, spying Garfield, who ran his index finger across his neck slyly.

"Come along, boy."

"Half fat to flour, sir," he said, then explained. "Pastry, I think. I remember she told me once, that she uses half the amount of fat as she does flour."

"Very good," Matheson said. "Anything else? Area? Why might you dear old mother benefit from understanding how to calculate an area?"

"I don't know, sir," John said. "But my stepdad does, I suppose. He's a farmer. He's always measuring the fields for seeds and whatnot."

"And whatnot?"

"Sorry, sir. He just does it. I don't know how. But he said once that he needed to buy the right amount of seed for the field. Too much and it would go to waste. Too little and he wouldn't have enough. He does that by area, I suppose."

"I imagine that he does," Matheson said, then gestured for John to sit before turning to the back of the room. "You. Stand." John turned in his seat and saw Garfield slowly rising from his seat. "Give me an example of why somebody who cleans for a living might be required to understand basic mathematics." Garfield's face reddened, and he stared down at his desk, saying nothing. "You do understand basic mathematics, don't you?"

"Yes, sir."

"Four eights," Matheson said.

"Sir?"

"Four eights. Come on, you should know this."

Garfield employed the use of his fingers while Matheson tapped his foot loudly.

"Thirty-four, sir," Garfield said eventually.

"Wrong," Matheson told him, then glanced across John. "Stow?"

"Thirty-two, sir."

"Good," he said, returning to Garfield. "Seven nines."

Garfield squeezed his eyes closed as he tried to work the sum in his head.

"Fifty-four, sir?" he said doubtfully.

"Stow?"

"Sixty-three, sir."

Matheson stared at Garfield, who, as John had, found solace in his desk.

"Do you have your times table scratched onto your desk, Garfield?"

"No, sir."

"Then why are you staring at it?"

Garfield raised his head and looked fearfully into the man's eyes, who strode over to him.

"Why might somebody who cleans for a living be required to employ mathematics in order to get by in life?"

"Don't know, sir. Maybe they need to work out how much money they owe?"

The comment earned a brief snigger from Mason and Pepper and a lengthy glare from Matheson.

"And what is it that you plan on doing, when and if you ever leave this school house, Garfield?"

Garfield shrugged. "Go home and have my tea, sir?"

"An occupation, damn it, boy. What is it you intend to do when you become an adult if you ever get there, that is?"

Again, Garfield shrugged. "I suppose I'll work with my dad."

"Ah," Matheson said, knowingly. "As the local squire?"

"Yes, sir."

"You are therefore here not to learn but to pass the days until such a time exists in which your father hands you his land?"

"Sir?"

"You will inherit your father's fortune, Garfield. I cannot dumb it down any further, I'm afraid."

"Yes, sir. That's always been the plan."

"And you think that will be enough to carry you through life, do you?"

"It worked for him, sir."

"Do not be petulant with me, Garfield. I have neither the patience nor the stomach for it."

"Sorry, sir. But it's true. It was always his plan. He doesn't want me to be a cleaner, or a farmer, or anything like that."

"Rather short-sighted, don't you think?" Matheson said. "I mean, do you honestly think that in twenty years' time, or even in ten years, that men like your father will even exist?"

"Sir?"

"Who cleans your home?" Matheson asked, to which Garfield gave another shrug.

"We've got a housemaid, sir."

"Who cooks your dinners?"

"The cook, sir."

"And what of your father's affairs? I presume he pays tax, and I presume he pays a significant amount of it."

"He has a man of business, sir. I think he does all that."

"The gardens?" Matheson said. "I've seen your home. The gardens are beautiful. Not the work of a man who employs a housemaid and a cook, I imagine."

"We've a gardener, sir."

"I see," Matheson continued, and then began to stroll around the room as if he was walking the roses in Garfield's garden. "Sixty years ago," he began, "at the turn of the century, men like your father would have employed half the village. Your grandfather did, I presume?"

"He did, sir. Yes."

"Butlers?"

"Yes, sir."

"Footmen?"

"Two, I think."

"Maids?"

"Too many to count, sir."

"And not just gardeners but gardeners' assistants, too. Not only cooks, but cooks' assistants. Hall boys, drivers, pot washers, and maybe even a valet."

"That's right, sir. He did."

"And now?" Matheson said. "You have a cook, a housemaid, and a gardener. Anybody else?"

"No, sir."

"No butler?" Matheson said, sounding surprised.

"No, sir. He died and Father didn't replace him."

"No footmen, no assistants, no hall boys?"

"No, sir."

"And in twenty years' time, how many staff do you think your household will employ?"

"Don't know, sir."

"None is the answer," Matheson told him, staring him in the eye as if to punctuate the point he was making. "The world is changing. Families like yours are coming to an end, dear boy. However, that sizeable garden of yours will still need tending. Your house will still need cleaning. And the pies that you eat for your tea, Robert Garfield, will still need cooking. Now who on earth is going to do that?"

Garfield shrugged again.

"I suggest you start paying attention. For a boy of your age not to know your times tables is a disgrace. Take a leaf out of Stow's book, why don't you?" John felt his face blush and Garfield's eyes bore into the back of his head. "I want to see a marked improvement from you, Garfield." He glanced up at the clock on the wall. "That goes for all of you. When the day comes for you to finally leave this institution, you mark my words, you will be on your own. If you choose to rely on family fortunes, or if you choose to follow in your parents' footsteps, then you're setting yourself up for a potential disaster. A life of ruin. Not all of you, but some." He stared directly at John but spoke to the room. "There is a world of opportunity out there. The world is changing, and perhaps for the first time, all men are equal. Seize those opportunities with both hands is my advice. Understood?"

"Yes, sir," the room chorused, save for John, who was transfixed.

"Good. Now get out. Go home to your teas and think about what I have told you. Think about your futures."

The edge of the playing field was just yards away. Five or six steps. Three, if he were to run. But Bobby Garfield's shrill voice sang out and John stopped in his tracks.

"Stow!"

Garfield stood at the top of the steps, flanked by Mason and Pepper, and John eyed the distance between them, wondering if Garfield could even calculate the distance in yards, let alone convert the figure into a fraction of a mile.

Two hundred yards, he thought. Just under an eighth of a mile.

It was a good head start. Enough even to outrun them if he ditched his bag along the way. He eyed the lane, which seemed endless, and then turned back to face Garfield as he descended the steps.

"Get him," he called. But this time, there was no joy in the command. Not like it usually was. This time there was a genuine malice to his tone.

Mason and Pepper both ran while Garfield walked at a brisk pace. His shoulders were down, his head leaned forward, and to adopt Terry's analogy, he was a raging bull.

John faced them head-on and Mason and Pepper slowed a little.

He let his satchel slip from his shoulder and he tossed it to the ground behind him, at which Mason and Pepper slowed further.

Garfield continued on, however, surpassing his friends, until they walked in arrow formation, spearheaded by Bobby Garfield.

"Well?" he said when he drew close enough. "Run."

But John stood his ground. His heart thumped like the pistons in Terry's old Massey and his palms became clammy.

And then he took a step towards them. Garfield slowed a little but not much.

"I told you to run, Stow."

"Bugger off, Garfield," John told him, doing his best to force some depth into his quivering voice. "I'm not running anymore."

"You'll do what I tell you," Garfield said, and he marched right up to John, opening his mouth to bark some crude insult. But John's fist put a halt to the words and knocked Garfield back a few steps. Mason and Pepper stared at each other as if wondering what to do. But there was no time to stand and watch. No time to let him recover. So, John hit him again, and again, and again, until Garfield fell to the ground, cowering.

"Well, don't just stand there," he shouted at his friends. "Get him."

John stared at each of them, daring them to come at him. He held his fist to his side, poised to strike.

"Bugger that," Mason said.

"Yeah," Pepper agreed. "I'm not getting involved."

"I told you to get him."

"Why don't you stand up and fight your own battle, Garfield?" John said, surprising himself at his own words.

Both Mason and Pepper took a few steps to one side then rejoined behind John, making a hasty retreat to the lane.

"I'll see you tomorrow, Bobby," one of them called out, leaving a tearful Bobby Garfield on the ground, dabbing at his bloodied nose with his shirt sleeve.

"You bloodied my nose," he said, holding his head back. "I'm going to tell my dad about this."

"You tell him," John said, and he held a hand out for Garfield to hold onto. He pulled the boy who, since John and his mother had moved to the area, had made his life a misery to his feet. With one hand holding his nose, Garfield snatched up his bag and pushed past John in a last-ditch attempt to assert control. "This ends now," John said and held out his hand for the squire's son to shake. "Truce."

Garfield stopped and studied the peace offering – and sneered.

"The only thing that ends, Stow," he said, "is your peasant family. You're finished. You hear me? Done for."

CHAPTER SEVENTEEN

March 28, 2024

The note he had written was still on the kitchen worktop, only now it was obscured by a used cereal bowl with Crunchy Nut Cornflakes welded onto its side. The rest of the worktop was unchanged. If anything, there were even more hair accessories scattered across it, plus the addition of another coffee cup. He dropped his bag onto one of the chairs that he had recognised in Bobby Garfield's study and then plonked down into another.

It was defeat. That's what it was. The energy he usually found to blitz the kitchen and recover some semblance of order had gone. The fight was in its early stages. It was in his mind. He could suck in a deep breath and get to work. It would take just ten minutes. But there was no lesson there. He would be creating a rod for his own back. Or, as the front ranks of his mind put it, he would be holding up the rod that his ex-wife had created.

It was a simple task. Clean the kitchen. But the complexities surrounding it were a minefield of personalities, tempers, and emotions. It had been less than a year since Vanessa had reached out to him and those early days had felt glorious. For the first time, he had seen a chance to make up for lost years, during which he could only dream of hearing her voice.

But in the pursuit of a clean kitchen, he could drive her away. He was, as his father might have once said, bent over an electric fence with a raging bull on either side.

He slipped his jacket off and hung it over the back of the chair before unbuttoning his shirt sleeves and rolling his cuffs to his elbows. The dishwasher was still as he had left it – empty. Filling it took moments. He was tempted to time himself so he could state the time it took him to do so.

He picked up the note, which came with its own temptations. Perhaps he could stick it to the fridge with a magnet for her to see. But that felt somewhat passive-aggressive, and instead, he crushed it and binned it, alongside the remains of last night's dinners.

He sprayed the surface with the lemony kitchen cleaner, and then set to work scrubbing, and after a final buff, he could almost see his miserable face in it.

It was as he was rinsing the cloth and hanging it up that he heard the front door close. It was typical, he thought. It was as if she had been watching, waiting for him to finish before coming in.

"You all right, love?" he called.

But there was no reply.

He opened the kitchen door and peered out into the hallway, but found it empty.

Then, as if in answer to his question, he heard the radio come on from inside her room upstairs.

Slowly, he trod upstairs and came to a stop outside her door. He held his hand up to knock but thought better of it. She'd only just got home. Who knew what kind of a day she'd had? The last thing she needed was for him to start going at her about the state of the kitchen when she'd been dealing with the public all day.

So, he waited. He walked off to his own room, where he undressed, folded his clothes, and then slipped into something a little more comfortable – a pair of Nike tracksuit bottoms she had bought him. He always felt a little silly wearing them, a little too old for the style. But they were comfortable, far more so than anything else he owned. He pulled a plain white t-shirt on and then slipped his feet into his slippers. He could see why the kids dressed in such a way, but would never dream of leaving the house like it.

Downstairs, he re-entered the kitchen and opened the freezer. He was about to remove a ready meal – beef in a rich mushroom sauce. But he closed the drawer and opened the fridge. Courgettes, aubergine, and chicken breasts all stared back at him. There were peppers too. He could do something with that.

He sliced the vegetables and laid them out on a tray before giving them a fine coat of olive oil and a sprinkling of sea salt. Setting them to one side, he began working on the chicken breasts and decided on an old tried and tested spice rub of turmeric, cloves, cayenne, ground coriander, and a touch of ground cinnamon to sweeten them. He coated the chicken on another tray, and then placed them both into the oven, before slicing the peppers, which he then fried with garlic.

A good twenty minutes had passed since Vanessa had arrived home, and he hoped the smell of home cooking, especially with the spices, might lure her downstairs. He found a microwave rice sachet, which according to the packet was infused with Moroccan spices. So, he shoved it into the microwave, slammed the door, and set the timer.

"Smells good," Vanessa said from behind him.

"I thought we could eat together," he said, making a show of checking the oven before he turned to see her. Her eyes were puffy and red, and her smile was forced. She sat down in the chair with his jacket on and scrolled through her phone.

"You all right, love?" he asked.

"Yeah, I'm fine," she told him, then set her phone down on the table. "Actually, that's a lie. I'm not fine."

Dinner would be another twenty-odd minutes, so he collected

a bottle of red from the rack on the side, along with two glasses, and took the seat beside her.

She waited for him to fill one of the glasses before she held up her hand.

"Actually, not for me Dad, thanks."

"Oh, things must be bad," he said, hoping to raise a smile. But it didn't. "You can talk to me. You know that, aye?"

"I know," she said. "It's just that, well, sometimes it's hard. Sometimes the words fail me. Sometimes things happen that you just can't help with, you know? I have to be a grown-up, don't I?" She laughed at the comment, but the humour didn't last. Then, just as he'd seen hundreds of people in his career do, as they sat opposite him in an interview room, she sucked in a deep breath and began her confession. "I'm thinking of moving out, Dad."

And there it was. The words weren't so much a jab to the stomach that winded him, but more of a knife wound, a stab to the heart that took his breath away.

"All right," he said and then lured her gaze from his fumbling fingers. "Is it me?"

Immediately, she sat back in her chair and sighed.

"See, I knew it. I knew you'd make it about you."

"All right, so it isn't about me—"

"This is a mistake," she said and made to leave the table. But he reached out and held her wrist. "What are you doing, Dad?"

"Talk to me, love. All right, so it isn't me, then what is it? Do you need some space? Is it a chap? Have you met somebody? Because if you have, you know that's great. I just want you to be happy, Vanessa. That's all."

"Yeah, well," she said, "I don't think that's going to be possible. Not in this lifetime, anyway."

She pulled her hand free and shoved her chair back.

"Vanessa, come on," he said, as she made her way to the door. "What is it you want from me? Money?"

She stopped but didn't turn, and even though he couldn't see her face, he knew what expression she would be wearing. Her eyes would be closed, her mouth downturned, and those little crinkles in her cheeks would be pronounced as she stifled her tears, just as they did when she was a young girl.

"No, Dad," she said. "I just wish I could turn back time. I wish somebody would understand me. I wish I could understand me." She peered over her shoulder shyly. "Right now, I don't even like me, let alone understand me."

"Well, I like you," he said.

"Yeah, right. The daughter you thought you'd never see again? The daughter who doesn't wash up after herself or clean the shower?" she said. "I saw the note, Dad. I'm just a disappointment."

"You're not a disappointment. Not to me you're not. Just tell me what's brought all of this on. If I know what's bothering you, then... I don't know, maybe I can help you? If you want your own space, then that's fine. It's understandable, in fact. I couldn't have lived with my parents at your age."

"You were in the force at my age, Dad," she said. "What do I do? Work in a bloody shoe shop?"

"Aye, you work in a shoe shop. And bloody lucky they are to have you. We all have to start somewhere."

"I've got a degree, Dad. I should be out there making a difference."

"You do make a difference," he said, then softened, realising his tone was becoming harsher. "I'll bet that some woman went home today with an armful of wee kids and was grateful that you took the time to fit shoes on their feet. Am I right?"

She shrugged. "Probably."

"And although you didn't realise it at the time, Vanessa, you made that woman's life just that little bit easier. She probably didn't even realise it at the time, either. But you did. It's not about money or positions of power. Yeah sure, you have a degree, and when the time comes for you to use it, it'll be there. But right now, you need to focus on you. You need to understand your value. You need to believe in that value, love. Look at me. I'm an old has-been. People at work know today is a Thursday because of the shirt I put on this morning. They probably laugh at me behind my back because I'm useless with computers," he said. "But do you know what? Every now and then, I make a difference. Some grieving mother or wife or husband is grateful that I put everything I've got into an investigation and brought somebody to justice, and that's no more or less important than helping a mother at her wit's end get through her day."

"What are you saying, Dad? That I should wear clothes according to the day of the week?"

He laughed.

"It simplifies doing the laundry," he said. "Listen, I don't know what the point is. In fact, forget about the woman with the kids. Forget about the degree and using it one day. You make a bloody difference to me, love. You brighten my day. This time last year, I could only have even dreamed of having a conversation with you, let alone having you back home. There's nothing you could do, Vanessa, that would make me love you any less. Nothing."

"I'm not so sure about that," she said, and then looked back at him. "I'm pregnant, Dad. And I have no idea who the father is."

CHAPTER EIGHTEEN
March 18, 1970

He was mildly surprised not to find Terry's tractor in the top field. There was still plenty of daylight, and even with John's limited knowledge, he could see that only half of it had been sown. He could even see where the tractor's wheel marks had veered off course and had returned to the farmhouse.

It was one of those late afternoons in springtime when a blue sky belied the chill wind that swept across the land from the Fens and was then channelled by the undulating Wolds. The ground wasn't as boggy as it had been, the temperature milder than previous days, and rows of daffodils marked the edge of the fields in their thousands.

John ran along the edge of the dyke, keen to see Terry and to tell him about his episode with Garfield. He imagined the pride in Terry's eyes and he foresaw some kind of warning about not telling his mother. The warning was inevitable. But what John really hoped for was perhaps a squeeze of his shoulders, and maybe even a demonstration of how he had hit him.

From afar, the farmhouse and all of its outbuildings appeared lonely, dwarfed by the rolling hills yet dominant in its surroundings.

A soft glint of sunlight caught John's eye as he ran – something black and shiny beside the house. He ran further, his senses translating the possibilities more so than his intelligence.

It was a car, he saw as he drew nearer, a sleek, black car parked near the back door. Nobody ever used the front door. In fact, John couldn't even remember the last time it was opened.

But he knew the car. He had seen one once before.

The day they buried his father.

He ran to it and peered through the window. It was a Jaguar. A mark two, he thought. Elegant woods lined the dashboard and door trims. The seats were leather and stuffed so thick they ought to have burst. The chrome trimmings shone even more so than the huge, glass windows.

"In here, John," a voice said, and he found Terry at the back door, his expression tired and grim.

Terry held the door for him and John burst into the kitchen.

"Ma?" he said in a sudden panic. "Ma, are you okay?"

"We're through here," she called, and just hearing her voice was like music.

He stepped through into the parlour, a room he had only been allowed into twice before. It was the best room. The furniture was nicer and even polished. A rug protected the floor and the walls were clean. It was a room that Terry and his ma saved for best. For when the vicar came or Terry's sister, who lived somewhere out on the Yorkshire coast. But it was a room saved for guests of a particular calibre, as was evident by the stranger in the room. He sipped tea from Ma's best china. He wore a suit even smarter than the one John had seen in the shop window, and his shoes appeared to have been polished by the same man who had cleaned the Jaguar.

"I thought you were dead," John said to Ma.

"Don't talk nonsense," she told him, then addressed the man. "You'll have to ignore him. He's got a wild imagination."

"They tend to have at that age, do they not?" the man said.

His voice was light, like a boy's, and he made such an effort to pronounce his *t*s that it seemed to impede his ability to speak at a reasonable speed.

"I saw the car," John explained. "It's a Jaguar. Like the one when Dad died. The one that took us to the church."

"I can assure you, my boy," the man began, "that nobody has died. Nobody here, in any case." He set his tea down and stood to appraise John, turning him around as if he were the boy mannequin in that window in Alford. He squeezed John's upper arms and shoulders and then examined his fingernails. "You've been fighting," he said.

"No, sir," John replied, to which the man offered a knowing glare.

"Your knuckle is swollen and cut. A boy's tooth, I shouldn't wonder." He held John's stare as if he could read his mind. "Well?"

"You been fighting, John, have you?" Terry said.

"Better bally well not have been," his mother added, then addressed the man. "He knows better not to fight."

"Perhaps you fell?" the man offered the waited for John to respond.

"Yes, sir. On the lane."

"I see. Well, you shall have to learn how to stay on your two feet if you are to succeed, my boy."

"Succeed, sir?"

"In life," he said, retaking his seat on one of the floral-patterned sofas. "Mr Matheson tells me you are a bright young boy."

"Mr Matheson?"

"Your school teacher?"

"Yes, sir."

"And are you?"

John shrugged.

"I suppose so," he said.

"Stand up straight," the man said, and John did as he was told. "Chest out. Legs straight. Shoulders back."

It took a moment for John to work through the list, and when he thought he had done as the man had requested, he felt he was standing to attention like the service men did each year down at Alford.

"Your stepfather here agrees with Mr Matheson," the man added and then looked to Terry who leaned against the doorway with his arms folded. "Mr Frobisher?"

"He is that, all right," Terry concurred. "Not afraid of hard work, that's for sure."

It was nice to hear Terry verbalise the things John had always thought that he thought. But still, there lingered a terrible secret that it seemed as if nobody in the room save for the stranger was privy to.

"What exactly is it you want him for?" John's ma asked. "He ain't done no wrong, not really, and they ain't calling the lads up no more. So, I'm told anyways."

"Rest assured, Mrs Frobisher, your son is in no trouble at all. And as for being called up, word in parliament is that such duties are a thing of the past."

"So, begging my pardon, sir, but what's this about?" she asked, to which he smiled, and from his pristine, leather bag, he removed a small file, from which he withdrew a small collection of papers, each headed with the words *Swain and Swain LLP*.

He handed them each a pile, including John, and then politely sipped from his teacup.

The words were a fuzzy blur that seemed impenetrable to John. He hadn't even reached the third line before he had to start over.

"Education?" Ma said, and the man smiled at them each, in turn, finally resting on John.

"My dear boy," he began, "it is with great pleasure that I am here. Your aptitude and moral standing have served you well."

"Sorry, sir?" John said.

"You are to be privately educated," the man explained, and his hard eyes bore into John as a nail being driven into a beam. "In fact, from this moment on, I should consider your life well and truly changed."

CHAPTER NINETEEN
March 29, 2024

As a rule, Charles avoided Vanessa's bedroom. That was her space. She wasn't a child, she was an adult, and adults needed a space to call their own. But today was different. Today was a day for reparation, and like all moments of hardship, it would be made easier with a nice cup of tea.

"You okay, love?" he said.

"I'm fine, Dad."

"Can I come in?" he asked, which was followed by a short pause and the closing of a drawer.

"Yeah, sure," she said, and he pushed open the door. She was sitting up in bed with her laptop on her knees. "That for me?"

"I thought you could do with one," he said, and he set the mug down on the bedside table before perching on the edge of the mattress. "How are you feeling?"

She laughed scornfully.

"Like I'm at the crossroads of my life, Dad, and the path I've been trying to find is now closed."

"Roadworks?"

"Something like that."

"So, take a detour. Follow the diversion," he said. "There's more than one way to get to where you're going." He gestured at the laptop. "What are you up to?"

"Oh, nothing much," she said, looking away.

Even if he hadn't spent his career dealing with habitual liars, he could have spotted her deception. She used to do the same thing when she was young. Her eyes would dart from left to right and she would scratch her head as a distraction.

He leaned forward and peered at the screen.

"Dad?"

"Houses?" he said. "You're looking at houses?"

"Flats, actually. It's not like I could afford a house, is it?"

"Is this what they call house porn?"

"Sorry?"

"House porn," he said. "One of the guys at work was telling me about it. He and his wife–"

"I know what house porn is, Dad," she said. "I just wasn't ready to hear that word coming from your mouth."

"Ah, come on."

"Besides house porn, as you put it, is when you look at houses out of your budget. Your dream house. All the flats I can find are neither within my budget nor my dream house. I'd be lucky to get a one-bed flat over a chip shop."

"Decent chippy?" he asked, and she shook her head, clearly not in the mood for humour.

He reached for the laptop.

"May I?" he asked and she let it go and reached for her tea.

"This one looks nice," he said. "Decent sized bedroom, nice kitchen."

"Eight hundred pounds a month," she added. "And then there's council tax, leccy, shopping, nappies. The bloody list goes on."

"All right, so we'll set our sights a little lower," he told her, scrolling through the page of properties. "There's a two bed here. Five hundred quid a month. Christ, that's a bargain."

"Yeah, and my child can grow up with a drug habit and have a criminal record before he or she turns eighteen. Have you seen where it is, Dad?"

"Ah, right," he agreed. "Yeah, I'd steer clear of there."

"Let's face it. I've messed up."

"Ah, poppycock," he told her, and he set the laptop down beside her, but his thumb caught a button and the web browser minimised, revealing the screen behind. "What's that?"

She closed the laptop hurriedly and spilt her tea in the process.

"Nothing, Dad. Look, thanks for the tea, but can I—"

"Vanessa?" he said, and he opened the laptop's lid to read the web page. He stared up at her but she refused to look him in the eye. "Abortion?"

"I'm just considering my options—"

"That is not an option."

"It is an option, Dad," she said firmly. "It's my body. I get to choose."

"Aye, and you're my daughter. I get to tell you what I think."

"I don't have to listen."

"No, you don't. But I'll say it anyway. You're looking at this whole thing like it's a mistake. I don't know why, but you seem to think you're going to pay for this mistake every day for the rest of your life. But you're not. You're really not."

"Oh right, yeah, I suppose I should just forget about the first twenty-five years of their life and focus on when they can go out and bring in some cash."

"Listen, when your mum and me had you, I could barely feed us, let alone buy all the stuff you needed. Your mum had to wash your nappies out in the sink. You were weaned on boiled bloody carrots and mashed potatoes. And any toys you had were from the car boot sale."

"Even the rocking horse?"

"The rocking horse?" he said, remembering it fondly. "No, I

made that myself. We had a wee house on Monks Road and somebody had tossed out an old wardrobe and some other bits."

"You made it?"

"Aye, I did. I mean, it wasn't brilliant, but it kept you happy."

"I loved that thing."

"Aye, I know. And it was hard. I wanted to give you what you wanted, but the fact is that we didn't have the means. Like you right now. You want to give your baby everything it needs, but you won't be able to. You don't hold it against me, do you?"

"No," she said.

"And your baby won't either. You might want to give them everything you need, but what they really need is love. Nothing more. Maybe a cardboard box every now and then. Kids love a cardboard box. But love, you can do. I know you can. You're full of it, sweetheart. Same as your mum."

She shook her head, unable to conceal the smile that was bursting from inside her.

"You really think so?"

"I know so," he told her. "Find some places."

"I can't—"

"Find some places," he said again. "We'll go and see them together, all right? You're not alone in this, love." He rubbed her head the way she had always hated, but she didn't pull away. He strode over to the door and looked back at her. "Just make sure wherever you find is somewhere close. I don't want to be traipsing halfway across the county to do my grandpa duties."

There was barely a single space left in the hospital car park, but after completing three full loops, Charles finally found one, which, because of the neighbouring car being parked at an obscure angle, was difficult to get into. And then, of course, came the tricky business of opening his door far enough to climb out without damaging either car. To get into the space, he'd had to mirror the neighbouring car's angle, leaving just an inch or two between his rear bumper and that of the adjacent car, which was parked correctly.

Human nature was a funny business, he thought. How easy it would be to berate the offending driver, pinning all kinds of behaviours on whoever it was, such as selfish, arrogant, pig-headed, or just plain rubbish at driving. But he rose above it. Perhaps they had been having a bad morning. Perhaps their daughter had confessed to bearing the child of an unknown man with no means to provide for them.

He strode across the car park, noting the clear skies. The morning was fine and fresh, the type of morning that invoked smiles on faces, unless, of course, you were working a murder enquiry, about to witness a dead body being opened up, or in his case, both.

"Guv," Devon called. He had seen her on the far side of the car park but avoided stopping to watch her run to close the gap. She wouldn't have appreciated him seeing her run.

"Morning, Devon," he said, without breaking stride, and he noted how out of breath she was when she caught up with him. "How was your evening?"

"Ah, you know?" she replied but said nothing more to elaborate on the statement.

"Aye, dinner, tv, and bed?"

"Actually, no. I had a Zumba class."

"Zumba?"

"It's a fitness thing. Kind of like a cross between keep fit and dance lessons."

"Dance lessons? Sounds like hell. I'm guessing it wasn't a waltz?"

"No, more Latin than that."

"Latin, crikey. You're not going in for that Strictly thing, are you?"

"Considering I can't bear to look at myself in the mirror, guv, I very much doubt that seeing me wobble all over the TV is going to help my self-esteem, is it?"

"Ah, well, as long as you're happy. I've seen a shift in your demeanour, you know? Ever since you started this whole weight loss thing. I mean, it's none of my business. I think you're a great detective however you look and feel. But if Zimba—"

"Zumba, guv."

"Aye, right. If it makes you feel good, then you go for it."

"Cheers, guv. I like it," she replied. "And for once, I wasn't the biggest girl in the room. It was worth the fifteen quid for that alone."

"Aye, right," he said, not wanting to press the topic of her weight any further. "So, you're all fired up then, are you?"

"I don't know about being fired up, guv," she replied. "My backside is killing me. What about you? Dinner, tv, and bed?"

"Aye, something like that," he told her. "Caught up with Vanessa, made us both dinner, then I left her to it."

There was very little else he could say about his evening. He couldn't tell her that, despite cooking his daughter a meal, he had ended up throwing the lot in the bin. And he couldn't exactly talk about Vanessa's news. It wasn't his secret to tell.

They were deep into the hospital's maze of corridors, with neither of them particularly looking forward to the task ahead when Devon spoke again.

"Guv?"

"Aye?"

"Do you really think there's something in what you said last night? You know, about the whole assisted suicide thing?"

"Aye, I do. I mean, there's easier ways. An overdose is how it's usually done. But that's the thing about people, isn't it? You never really know what's going on inside their heads. Sometimes you can have an idea of what they're thinking," he said, reaching up to push the buzzer, then stepping back. "And in other cases, it's like they're a whole different species."

The door opened to reveal the forensic pathologist, a woman with whom Charles was familiar but had never quite clicked.

"Ah, thought it was you, I did," she said, and he was reminded of her thick Welsh accent. "Come for the show, have you?"

"Good morning, Doctor Bell," he said, waving Devon through the doors before him. "To be honest, this is one show I'd like to be late for. One I could get the gist of through a report, perhaps?"

"No such luck," she replied. "It's started already, but you're just in time for act two. You know where the PPE is, don't you?"

"In the cupboards," he said, and he watched as she studied Devon opening doors and retrieving their gowns and masks. "We'll just be a moment. Don't wait for us."

She let the heavy doors swing into place with a swish and a cold draught ran through the room like a lost soul searching for an escape.

"I swear they do that for effect," he said, as Devon handed him his gown.

They gowned up and donned their masks, and then with a quick nod to make sure she was ready, he led them through the heavy doors.

Doctor Bell, or Pip, as she preferred to be called, was standing at the nearest of the half a dozen or so stainless-steel benches with a small trolley beside her containing her instruments, various tools, and dishes.

"Now then," she said, which Charles recognised as a very local greeting, despite being from Wales, him being Scottish, and Devon being from the Durham coast. "Don't get too many this far gone, if I'm honest."

"I thought he was only up there for a day?" Charles said.

"I wasn't referring to how long he was hanging for, Inspector."

"Ah, well. That seems to have set the tone," he said. "Do we have anything yet?"

"Oh right, here we go again. Another one in a rush, are you? I thought you were different, I did. But just like all the rest, you are. I had Chief Inspector Bloom in here the other day. Woke me up, she did. Got me out of bed and then wanted a report by lunchtime. And do you know what I told her?"

"I'm not giving you the hurry up, Doctor," Charles said, refusing to engage.

"I told her she could stand there and watch me and see it all first-hand. It'll save her reading the report, I said."

"And did she?" he asked.

"Well, no," she said. "And seeing as you had to ask, I can only assume you haven't met her."

"I've heard of her and her mannerisms," Charles said. "Let's just say her reputation precedes her."

"Right, well let's just say that she didn't get her report by lunchtime," Pip said, proudly. "That'll teach her to give me the hurry up."

"Nobody wants you to hurry up, Pip," he said. "Your work is far too important to be rushed. I would appreciate it if we could ascertain a few things as a priority, but after that, I'll stay as long as you need me to."

"Right," she said suspiciously. "Time of death?"

"What we really need is to understand if the old man was murdered, Pip."

"I see."

"We can't open a murder investigation without a murder having taken place, can we?"

"I suppose not," she said.

"He was found hanging by a rope from a chandelier. CSI have the rope and are examining it as we speak. But if there is something you can tell us that might give us a shortcut—"

"Then you can open your case?"

"Then we can begin our enquiries, Doctor," he corrected her. "Which might give us a head start on bringing a murderer to justice." He leaned on the bench, being careful not to touch the pale corpse. "Now I would say that was a good cause, wouldn't you? Tell us what you've found so far, and Sergeant Devon here can be excused. There's no need for us both to be here."

"I can stay, guv," Devon said.

"There's really no need. I have a meeting after this anyway. I'll see you back at the station," he said and then turned to the pathologist, who seemed to digest the information, and then adjust her expression to hide her true thoughts.

"Well, as it happens, there was something," she said, and she pulled back the sheet to reveal the old man in his natural state, folding it at his waist.

"Bruises?" Charles said, spying the blueish-black mark across the man's arms. She raised her eyebrows but said nothing. Instead, she exposed his feet and held one up for them to see. "Grazes."

"He was dragged," Devon said, peering at the heavy scuffs on the men's heels. "Did they occur—"

"Post-mortem? No. These occurred while he was still alive, Sergeant. The bruises too."

"So, he could have been dragged across the room by his arms, tied up, and hung?" Charles said.

"There's every chance," she told him. "He didn't die of a broken neck."

"What are you saying, that somebody could have hauled him up from the ground?"

"That's exactly what I'm saying," she said. "Saw him in situ, did you?"

"I did, aye."

"And I'm guessing a man of your maturity, Inspector, is aware of the difference between a long and short drop?"

"There was nothing for him to climb onto," he said. "No chair, no ladder. Nothing."

She nodded slowly and thoughtfully, and then pulled one of

his hands into view, reaching up to adjust the huge, round LED that hung from an arm above the bench.

"See this, do you?"

Charles put his glasses on to see what she was referring to. The man's hands were scratched and some of his fingernails were broken.

"He struggled. He was awake at the time?"

"As conscious as you are right now," she said, and then gently returned his hand to his side. "I've been through the FME's report, and at this stage, I can see nothing that indicates anything different, although I can narrow the window down a little. This man died from asphyxiation sometime between the hours of eleven and two on Wednesday afternoon. His digestive system allows me to hone it in a little, but that's all I can give you until the lab provides a report. They may find traces of Benzodiazepines or something similar, which may have been used to sedate him or at least stop him from escaping, but I can't see any physical evidence of that."

"It all helps, Pip," he said, to which she seemed indifferent.

"So, without further ado, we shall swab his body and gather all the data for the lab. We might be lucky and find something else, but I'm not hopeful." She stared down at the man on the bench for a while and then returned her vacant gaze to Charles. "Even with no further evidence, I think it's safe to say that you have grounds for your murder investigation, Inspector. Even if it isn't conclusive."

CHAPTER TWENTY
March 19, 1970

The Grange was a formidable house, encased in ivy through which at least a dozen windows stared out at the Lincolnshire countryside. The lawns were long but shaped, suggesting they had been tended not long before, but they were in dire need of some attention.

A pair of huge front doors loomed from beneath a great, stone archway, and there were so many chimneys that John wondered how many fireplaces were inside and who cleaned them.

Surrounding the property was a wrought fence, allowing passersby to glimpse its majesty, but not come too close.

"Well, John," Terry said, as he eased old Barney to a halt. The faithful Percheron slowed and then stopped with a swish of his bushy tail. "This is you."

"It is," he replied automatically.

"Sure you want to do this, are you?" Terry said. "It's not too late, you know?"

"It's my chance," he replied. "I know it."

"Your chance at what?"

"My chance at life," John told him. "At making something of myself."

"You've got the farm. It'll be yours one day," Terry said. "You'll be master."

John stared at the house. He could have sworn something moved behind one of the upper windows.

"John?" Terry said softly.

"Do you think I'm doing the right thing, Terry?" John asked.

"Well, if it were me, I would have tossed him on his ear," he replied. "Who does he think he is, coming to our house and messing with your head like that?"

"It's private education. I could be someone."

"You are someone, John. You're my boy. All right, I know you're not *my* boy, but you might as well be. Think of your ma."

"I do," he replied.

"Well, what's she going to do with you gone?" Terry asked. "What are we supposed to do when I'm too old to get out in the fields?"

"I don't know," John said, and he looked up at the house once more. "All I know is that if I don't take this opportunity, then I might never get another."

"Opportunity," Terry scoffed. "It's just an education, John. Bits of paper, that's all. They won't do anything for you. You won't learn anything. Piece of paper don't teach you how to run a house, does it? Won't pay the bills, will it?" It was the first time John had seen him close to tears. Perhaps it was because of those tears that he looked away. "Anyway, who's paying for all of this? That's what I want to know."

"It was Mr Fisher's client," John said.

"I know, but who? Could be anyone for all we know."

"The contract just said that he wished to remain anonymous."

"Contract," Terry scoffed again. "I ask you. Who makes a contract with a young boy and pays for him to have an education? Whoever it is, isn't right in the head, John. Mark my words. No good'll come of this."

"I've got to do it," John said. "And if it all goes wrong, then I'll come back and work on the farm."

"Will you now?" Terry said. "We'll have to see about that."

"I'm not deserting you or Ma," he explained. "I'll still be home every night. I'll still work at the weekends. The only difference is that I'll be going somewhere else to be schooled. Here," he said and looked up at the house with its huge dormers protruding from the roofs like bared incisors. It was like staring into the devil's mouth. "I am grateful, you know?"

"Are you?" Terry muttered. "Well, you do a fine job of hiding it."

"I am," he said. "I'm grateful for everything you do. Ma too. But I can't be a burden forever. I have to find my own way at some point. And that time is now. It's a start, and if it doesn't work out, I'll find another way."

"Will you now? Sounds like playground talk, if you ask me."

"Well, it's not," John told him. "When my dad died, we had nothing. Nothing but Ma's pride and an empty cupboard. She spent nearly every last penny we had on his funeral so the village wouldn't know we were poor."

"I know well enough how poor you were before I met your ma, John."

"Well, don't you see? I don't want that. When the day comes for me to say goodbye to Ma, I want the best for her. And we won't just have one car, we'll have three. And she won't be buried in a pine box, it'll be a proper casket. And before that, she won't have to scrimp and scrape to feed you and me. She'll have what she wants." He could see how his choice of words might have stung, but there was no malice or contempt meant, and he refused to take them back. "I mean to make you proud, Terry. Both of you."

Terry cleared his throat and wiped his face with his handkerchief, then shuffled in his seat.

"Well, go on then," he said quietly. "You all right getting home?"

"It's not too far. I can cut across the hill," John said.

"Right then," Terry said and gave Barney a gentle tap with the whip. He performed a tight circle and on his return refused to look in John's direction. "Make us proud then, John," he called out and waved his hat once as the trap picked up speed. "It'll change nowt. You mark my words."

———

Never before had John stood before two such imposing doors. They were at least ten feet tall, and together, they must have spanned twelve feet. If somebody had told him that they had been hewn by the gods from giant oaks in a magical forest, he might have believed them. As if to make them appear even larger, they stood atop a set of stone steps made round by decades and decades of footfall.

But there was no sound of feet right then. There was no sound at all, save for Terry's final words echoing around John's mind.

John took a deep breath and then wiped his clammy hands on his trousers before reaching up for the brass lion's head that stared out at the gates as if defending the doorway from the horrors of the outside world.

Brass met brass, loud and arrogant, and the door opened under its own weight, allowing John a glimpse of the inside. The hallway was wooden and larger than their kitchen, and a huge staircase rose up like a snake. He expected somebody to come, but nobody did. He shied from peering inside for fear of a reprimand. But as the minutes passed, his curiosity outgrew his manners.

Gently, he pushed the door open further and stepped inside, only to be greeted by a familiar smell. It was the smell of Tuesdays when his mother tore through the house cleaning everything in sight. She would rip the rugs up and beat them in the courtyard, and that was the smell.

Dust.

It lay over everything, the once polished banisters, the old bench that stood to one side, and even the floor bore foot marks, where somebody not so long ago had trod.

"Hello?" he called out. "Mrs Lavender?"

A door opened somewhere upstairs and the breeze coughed up a great swathe of dust.

"Hello? Is anyone there?"

A shadow moved. He was sure it did. Somewhere on the upstairs landing. He moved to the stairs, which weren't steep and narrow like they were at home, but so wide and shallow it seemed to take two of them to match the height of a single one of the farm's. Progress was slow and the journey a dizzying spiral, and all the while he climbed, his eyes barely left the shadow on the landing. He was nearing the top when footsteps rang out. Light feet, running, and a door closed the moment he stepped onto the landing corridor. It was one of two corridors, placed on either side of the magnificent staircase. The floor was solid wood, similar in tone to that of the parlours, but having seen far more use. The planks seemed to go on forever, past doorways and beneath rugs until they joined at the end window. There were five doors off that single corridor and John tried the handle of the first. It was locked.

"Is anyone here?" he called out, as he tried the second door, which surprisingly swung open.

"You must be John Stow," a voice said, feminine yet cracked with age.

The room was vast with a fireplace as large as the stable doors, and the curtains of all four of the windows had been drawn. At one end was a bed, a huge four poster like the ones John had read about. There was a dressing table, mirrors, armchairs, and tables, but more than anything, there were shadows. Shadows so deep that only the strongest of lights might touch them.

It was from one of the shadows that the voice had come. He saw her, the outline of her anyway. She sat in a chair close to the bed and set a book down on the table beside her.

"I am, ma'am."

"Well, the first thing you must learn, my dear boy," she said, "is to knock before you enter a room." She rose to her feet and stepped out of the shadows, the deep lines in her face seeming to draw the darkness with her. Her eyes ran over him like tiny, black insects, scrutinising, studying, tearing him apart to reveal what lay beneath. "The task is bigger than I thought, I see," she said and then clicked her fingers at a lone carver chair in the centre of the room. "Sit, and we shall begin."

CHAPTER TWENTY-ONE
March 29, 2024

Guildhall Street on a Friday morning was sparsely populated compared to the High Street not two hundred yards away.

Charles took his time, savouring the relative peace and quiet, while he mulled the investigation over. There was little doubt in his mind now that Hugo Garfield had been murdered, just as there was little doubt that Hugo had been dragged across the floor, the rope wrapped around his neck and then hauled up using the sheave blocks designed to maintain the chandelier.

The question wasn't so much who, but why? Compassion or hatred? The two were vastly different and would require severely different approaches.

"Morning, sir," somebody said, and he saw the man he helped the previous day sitting in a doorway.

"Morning," Charles said then tapped his pockets for some change.

"There's no charge for saying hello," the man said. "We don't always want money, you know. Sometimes good manners are enough."

Charles heard the comment and couldn't help but smile.

"Well, if good manners is your currency, then consider yourself a rich man," he told him. "Have a good day."

"You too," the man replied, and Charles felt his eyes track him along the road.

He found the Swain and Swain doorway and pushed the buzzer. Moments later, a young woman responded, her voice sounding tinny through the tiny speaker.

"Swain and Swain," she said, and the little nuances of her tone inferred that he should introduce himself.

"Ah, good morning," he began. "I was wondering if I might speak to John Stow?"

"I'll just see if he's available. Do you have an appointment?"

"Actually, no, I don't," he replied. "I was just passing, you see?"

"I'm afraid you'll need to make an appointment."

"I just need a minute of his time," Charles told her. "I spoke to him yesterday. He'll recognise me."

A small silence ensued, during which he imagined her conferring with the lady in charge. Mrs Hyke had been her name. She was the lady who had provided Robert Garfield's home address.

"Can I take your name, please?" she said over the intercom.

"Of course. It's Charles Cook," he said. "That's *Detective Chief Inspector* Charles Cook."

Another silence, and he was tempted to count to ten when the little electromagnet clicked open and he heard her voice over the accompanying buzzer.

"Would you like to come up, Inspector?"

He made his way up the stairs. The interior was typical of an old building in the city. It was old enough to be listed, either grade one or two, but not so esteemed for the interiors to be overly protected. The stairwell appeared to be the original, but the walls had been painted. Perhaps a few holes and dents had been filled, but not much more. The real joy of the space began when he reached the door at the top and entered the Swain and Swain offices. The room was as long as the terrace of shops, occupying the full first floor. Partition walls had been built to create a line of offices along the window wall, which did little in the way of natural daylight for those occupying the central space, but provided those lucky enough to have earned a private office a wonderful view of the street below and the Guildhall with its ornate arches.

The girl he had spoken to stood from her seat and smiled politely.

"Would you like to follow me?" she asked and then walked away before he could respond. Instead, he trailed after her, nodding a good morning to Mrs Hyke, who observed him from over her large glasses as the eyes of a lioness might track its prey. "Just in here," the girl said, opening a door for him. "If you'd care to wait, he'll just be a moment. Can I get you a coffee or a tea?"

"Coffee," he said. "White no sugar. Thank you."

She closed the door behind her and he mooched over to the window. It was prime office space in a nice part of the city. A short walk from most places. It was one of the reasons he enjoyed Lincoln. The city was old. It had history, but it wasn't sprawling like London. You didn't need to take a cab to get to the other side. The worst-case scenario was that you had to endure Steep Hill. But even that wasn't so bad. In fact, he found it harder to walk down the hill than up it.

"Terribly sorry about that," a voice said from behind him, and he turned to find John Stow closing the door behind him. He held out a hand to shake, and then swept it across the room, proffering one of the eight leather seats all neatly placed around a large meeting table. "Please," he said. "How can I help you?"

"It's me who should be apologising," Charles said, accepting his offer and selecting the seat with a fine view of the old Guildhall. "I feel guilty for taking your time if I'm honest."

"Is he okay?" Stow asked. "I presume this concerns Mr Garfield?"

"It does, it does," Charles replied. "And yes, he's fine. Given the circumstances, you know?"

"No, sorry. I'm not following."

"Ah, yes. Well, there's no reason for me to withhold information any longer, is there? I'm afraid Mr Garfield Senior was discovered dead in his home on Thursday morning."

"Hugo?"

"Aye, you know him?"

"I know of him," Stow said. "Through Bobby, of course."

"Ah, yes. Robert, you mean?"

"I think now that his father is dead, there's nobody left who uses his real name," Stow told him. "How did he take it?"

"Ah, you never can tell, can you? I mean, he put on a brave face, and he said himself that he'd been expecting it for years. But the truth is, Mr Stow—"

"John, please."

"Aye, well. The truth is, John, that none of us know how we'll react when the time comes, do we? Knocked me for six when my old man passed, and I always thought I'd handle it well."

"Bobby is a strong chap," Stow said. "He'll need some time to arrange the affairs, of course."

"Ah yes. The affairs. That's when the real secrets come out, eh?"

"Secrets?" Stow said.

"Aye. You know? Debts here and there. A strange box found in the attic."

"You found a box?"

"No, I just meant that—"

"I see," Stow said. "Well, I'll have my secretary send some flowers to his house, and maybe I can look at organising some compassionate leave for him."

"There's something else, John," Charles said, and he double-checked the door was closed. "Between you, me, and the gatepost, I'm afraid the question of Mr Garfield's death has raised a few questions. I don't wish to speak out of turn, but we're treating the death as suspicious."

"He was murdered?"

"Like I said, it's confidential," Charles said. "I don't want people's imaginations to run away. But there are a few questions that, quite frankly, are baffling me. And given the man's age and his wealth–"

"His wealth?"

"Aye," Charles said. "I mean, that's no two-up-two-down out there, is it? He must have been a very wealthy man in his day."

"I suppose that all depends on your definition of wealthy, doesn't it?" Stow said, cryptically. "I was always under the impression that the money had long gone, and that was why Bobby became a lawyer. But then, what do I know?"

"Well, be that as it may, his father wasn't claiming benefits, was he? If I'm honest, John, the whole affair is spiralling. I wonder if you might be able to shine a light on a few things."

"Shine a light, Inspector?"

"Look, the last thing I want to do is trouble Robert with all of this. I know what it's like to lose your dad. He's been very helpful so far. He sent me a copy of the will. Haven't had a chance to look at it yet, but I'm loathe to go back to him armed with a barrage of questions. I'd sooner let him grieve. Do you know what I'm saying, Mr Stow?"

He studied Charles for a moment and then cleared his throat.

"I think so," he said. "In the absence of my colleague, and to spare him from turmoil, you would like me to provide you some kind of character?"

"Not a character, as such," Charles explained. "You said you knew him. His father, I mean."

"No, I said I knew of him, but only through his son."

"Was that recently?"

Stow sucked on his lip and then released it with a puckering sound.

"We knew each other as children," he said. "His father was the local squire."

"And your father?"

"My father was dead," Stow said. "My mother remarried. A farmer. We lived just outside the village."

"Hagworthingham? Is that right?"

"Correct," Stow said. "But I'm afraid I knew very little of Bobby Garfield or his father, even as a boy. We lived worlds apart, you see. Him the son of a rich squire and me a lowly farmer's boy."

"I do see," Charles said. "But if you don't mind me saying, you seem to have done very well for yourself."

"Thank you, yes. I've achieved, and I'm proud of that."

"And I hope you don't mind me saying, but there can't be too many farmer's boys who speak as well as you do. I'd have put you down as an Eton lad?"

He shuffled in his seat and cleared his throat again, clearly embarrassed by Charles' observations.

"Sorry, I didn't mean to embarrass you," Charles said. "I was just a little surprised at your story, that's all."

"I was fortunate," he explained. "And please don't apologise. I was lucky enough to have received a private education, without which who knows where I would be today?"

"Well, there you have it," Charles replied, and he slapped his hand on the table. "A real rags to riches tale. Farmers boy to managing partner of Swain and Swain, and all because of your education."

"Like I said, I was extremely lucky," Stow said thoughtfully. "My education changed my life."

CHAPTER TWENTY-TWO

March 19, 1970

The chair was hard and cold, and seemed to have been placed directly in a slice of light that the curtains failed to contain, and in which tiny particles of dust seemed to enjoy an endless dance.

She had been pretty in her day, John thought. It wasn't a subjective opinion but a fact, evidenced by her high cheekbones, large eyes, and lips that invited him to stare.

Beneath the silk dressing gown, her slender body moved with grace – feline and purposeful. Yet for all her natural beauty, grief defined her dominant features. The lines that he had heard his mother refer to as crow's feet seemed to have been carved with a chisel. Rows of them, all culminating in a single mass that was swallowed by dark rings that encircled those wonderful eyes.

Her hair was a tangled mass of curls that had, at one time, been pulled into a tight bun. Since then, strands had broken free on either side of her face, and they swayed gently when she stepped out of the shadows to stand before him.

"You know my name," she said. It hadn't been a question, yet John felt obliged to say something if nothing more than to break his stare.

"Mrs Lavender," he said.

"And you know who I am," she said, again, not a question.

"Only that you're going to help me."

"Help you?"

"Teach me," he said. "Mr Fisher said, that you–"

"Mr Fisher knows nothing," she told him flatly. "I could summon Fisher now, and for a kiss and a coin, he would do whatever I ask. I could tell him to strip naked and run through the village, and he would do so."

"Why would he do that?" John asked.

"Because I would tell him to," she replied.

"But surely not. Surely there are things that he wouldn't do?"

She stepped over to John, close enough for him to inhale the smell of perfume and cigarette smoke that would come to be synonymous with her presence.

"And here lies your first lesson," she said, and she dropped to a crouch before him, laying her hands flat on his thighs, seeming to enjoy his discomfort. "Not all men are equal, John Stow." She watched him and he did his best not to be distracted by her touch. But her fingers probed as if she was gauging the muscles in his legs. "Men want what men want, and the only remedy is for their desires to be satiated."

"Satiated?"

She stood faster than she had crouched, and her robe swirled as she turned to walk away. She peered at him through her dressing table mirror.

"When you woke this morning, did you eat breakfast?" she asked.

"Yes, thank you," he said. "I've eaten."

"It wasn't an invitation to dine with me. It was a question."

Her mood perplexed him. Her choice of words intrigued him, and the way she moved was alluring.

"I did," he said. "I had porridge."

"And you were hungry before you ate, were you not?"

"Ravenous," he said.

"And when you had eaten?" She turned back to him, head cocked. "Were you still hungry?"

"No, ma'am," he replied, and then he understood. "My hunger was satiated."

She smiled.

"Now take that feeling of hunger and apply it to all of man's needs."

"Like thirst, you mean?"

"That is one example," she said. "But I want you to think bigger. Think of a man you know. What does he have?"

"Love," John replied, thinking immediately of Terry. But his response wasn't received as he intended. She turned away again, choosing to examine her face in the mirror.

"Bigger still," she said.

"Money?"

"Ah," she said, snapping back to face him. "Now we're getting somewhere."

"Money? Men want money?"

"Some," she replied. "What does wealth bring?"

The sliver of light that breached the curtain's defences, faded as some distant cloud passed across the sky, and a chill climbed John's spine like tiny, bony fingers. The only wealthy man he knew of was the squire, who seemed to breed clouds of gloom over those around him.

"Power," John said.

"Good," she replied. "Power and wealth. When a man has those things, his hunger is satiated. He can then seek to satiate some other need."

"Some other need? Surely if a man has enough money, then he can buy whatever else he needs."

"Sometimes," she told him. "Now picture Mr Fisher. Picture him a wealthy man."

"I thought he was wealthy. He had a nice car. A Jaguar."

"Fisher is not wealthy, John. Fisher is a paid man. He told you himself, did he not, that he is working on his client's behalf?"

"He did."

"And so why would a wealthy man work for somebody else? Why would a wealthy man not be in a position to do as he pleases? You do not suppose that he enjoyed coming to see you, or me, do you? Surely you cannot believe that a wealthy man would choose to spend his time satiating the needs of another?"

"I suppose not," John said.

"So, Mr Fisher is not a wealthy man. Not in its true definition, anyway. And so, revisiting my earlier remark, should I summon him and make a request for a kiss and coin he would, of course, accommodate my needs."

"Just one coin?"

She smiled.

"Hungry men have a price," she said. "A wealthy man might laugh in my face at such a request in return for any number of coins." She crossed her legs, allowing just enough bare flesh to be revealed, and her eyes followed his all the way up to her knowing grin. "But a kiss?"

"A kiss?" he said, blushing at the sight that seemed to pull his eyes from hers.

"The second of man's needs," she told him. "Sex."

"Sex?"

"Companionship. Intimacy."

"Love?" he suggested, to which she laughed, and slowly slid a cigarette from the packet on her dressing table. She used a lighter to light it, inhaled deeply, and then blew a cloud of smoke across the room that seemed to wake the sliver of sun and the dancing dust worked itself into a frenzy.

He inhaled the second-hand smoke and let the cloud dissipate.

"Lust," she began, "is far more appropriate." From the table-top, she reached for a little brass bell, which she rang twice before setting it down, silencing the delicate tone.

Barely a moment passed before the door through which he had entered opened inwards, and the meaning of that word became evident.

CHAPTER TWENTY-THREE

March 29, 2024

"I hope you're all well rested," Charles said, as he entered the incident room and found Devon, Forsythe, and Chalk seated at their little table. He slipped his jacket from his shoulders and tossed it onto his chair. "Because today is the day we make things happen."

"Somebody had his porridge this morning," Forsythe said.

"They did," Charles replied. "Some of us have also spent the last two hours watching a ninety-eight-year-old man being cut open, prodded, and dissected. So, if it's okay with you, I'd like to make sure that little episode wasn't for nothing."

"Bad one, was it?" Chalk asked Devon, while Charles looked for his marker pen.

"It wasn't how I like to start my day," she replied. "Let's put it that way."

"Autopsy," Charles said, to regain their attention, and he tapped on the list he had made the previous day. "Identification, CSI, financial statements, LWT, eyewitnesses, and CCTV." He removed the pen lid and wrote beside the first item. "Bruises, grazes, asphyxiation."

"He was beaten up and then hung?" Forsythe asked, which was a reasonable assumption albeit wrong.

"Bruising on his arms and grazes on his feet, suggesting that he was forcibly dragged from somewhere," Charles said. "Cause of death was asphyxiation. Hugo Garfield did not die from a broken neck. This was not a long drop. Which means that it was not a quick death. Marks on his fingertips suggest he struggled somehow—"

"And the scratches, guv?" Devon added.

"No, the scratches weren't part of this. The scratches were from the garden. More specifically, from pruning his roses, which suggests that he was not as feeble as we might have originally thought. The rest of the garden might have been left to ruin, but his roses were well-tended. He was an able-bodied man. Not lithe by any means, but able. We should bear that in mind."

"So how did he end up hanging from the chandelier?" Chalk asked.

"Well, that's for us to work out. The chandelier in question hangs from an iron hook which in turn is connected to a pulley system," he said, not wanting to go into the details of mechanical advantage. "This is important. It's a hook, and back in the day when chandeliers were not only prized by their owners but were cleaned by somebody else, they were hung from hooks and lowered to make them easier to remove for cleaning." He snapped the pen lid back on to stop it from drying out while he spoke. "Now, that ceiling was what, twelve feet high?"

"Give or take," Forsythe said, nodding.

"The average man is what, six foot and one-hundred-and-eighty pounds?" Charles said. "Plenty enough weight to hoist the old man into the air. Not easy, by any means, the pulley system wouldn't have been designed to hoist that kind of weight, but it's extremely plausible, don't you think?"

"I suppose anybody heavier than Hugo Garfield could have managed it," Chalk added. "In theory, anyway."

"I agree," he said. "The point is, that none of this is conclusive, the bruises could be unrelated. Elderly people bruise very easily. The grazes on his feet could have been from any number of incidents. The same could be said for the marks on his fingertips. But when you put all that together, alongside the fact that he was found hanging with no obvious means of getting himself up there, then we have a strong case to open a murder investigation."

"I thought it was open," Forsythe said. "Are you telling me that all we have done so far is prove that he could have been murdered?"

"I am," Charles told him. "If you speak to some of the top brass they might explain that it is a system designed to increase efficiencies, maintain public trust, and protect valuable resources. I call it red tape, myself."

"So, we could have a murder," Devon added. "In fact, in light of what we now know, it's highly likely that we do. However, it is also possible that whoever did this did so out of compassion. It's down to us to prove that a murder took place."

"So, somebody dragged him into his study and strung him up out of compassion?" Forsythe said. "They need to work on their bedside manner, if you ask me."

"As I said, the bruises, cuts, and grazes could be unrelated. Not only do we need to understand who did this and why, but we also need to develop the actual sequence of events. If you put this in front of a jury as it stands, you'd be laughed out of the courtroom. Which brings me to the next point on our list." He tapped the board again. "CSI. Has anyone seen the report?"

"Came through this morning, guv," Chalk said, and she slid a stack of stapled sheets across the desk. He left them there and raised his eyebrows expectantly.

"Summary?"

"The place has been wiped clean, guv. Doorknobs, floors, walls, bannisters, the lot. Everything aside from the study."

"Which we know from her account that Joanne Childs left until last," Devon said. "Coincidence, or just bad luck?"

"What do we know about her?" Charles asked.

"Not much," Forsythe replied. "Her husband works in a local agricultural supplier as a forklift operator. Two kids, both in their late teens. Mortgage, but nothing outrageous." He shook his head. "Nothing in the public domain about her and nothing to suggest that she had anything to hold against Hugo Garfield. If anything, she's going to be out of pocket."

"Is she a full-time cleaner?" Devon asked.

"She is," Forsythe replied. "She works for one of these agencies that pop up. Cleans various houses in the area."

"Have another look at her. See what you can find," Charles said. "If nothing more than to rule her out of the picture."

"The magistrate will want to know why she's a suspect, guv," he replied.

"Well, she found the body and wiped the place clean, didn't she?" Charles replied. "I'm sure you can make something of that." He turned back to Chalk. "Anything else in the CSI report?"

"As it happens, yes," she replied. "Something we all missed. There were two dirty glasses in the kitchen."

"Crystal?" he asked, and she checked her laptop.

"Yes, guv. How did you know?"

"Because very rarely do you buy a set of three crystal tumblers," he explained, much to her confusion. "Did he have a visitor that morning, or the evening before?"

"It's possible," she replied. "I don't know about anybody else, but when I do my housework, I leave my kitchen until last. If he did have a visitor, then maybe they shared a drink and he took the glasses out to the kitchen for Joanne Childs to clean the next day?"

"I agree," Charles said. "There's nothing more infuriating than cleaning the kitchen and then finding a plate or a glass in another room. Had the kitchen been cleaned?"

"Not to the same standard as the rest of the place, guv."

"Which might suggest she was also going to finish in the kitchen when she'd cleaned the study. Can somebody reach out to her? Ask her about the glasses? Don't go heavy on her. We're just trying to build a picture here, and until we know more, we going to need her help."

"I'll do it," Forsythe said, scribbling a line in his notepad.

"Good, thanks," Charles replied. "Identification will take place this afternoon. Devon, can I task you with lining up our friend Bobby Garfield?"

"Guv," she said, making a note of the request.

"Financial statements," he said, then took a deep breath. "Chalk, what do we have?"

"It's a minefield, guv," she said. "He wasn't your average man with a current account, a savings account, and a credit card. The man has accounts all over the place, most of which have been bled dry over the years, presumably to keep the place running."

"Well, let's start with the basics," he said. "Any large sums in or out recently?"

"No one-off payments," she replied. "I mean, there are large sums. Council tax on that place is enough to make your nose bleed, for a start."

"I'm sure it is," he agreed.

"The payments to the cleaner are there, but as you can imagine, they're minimal. Then there's the bills, which considering the size of the place, are fairly low."

"It's oil-heated," Charles said. "And by all accounts, he didn't use half the rooms, so we can assume he only lit the few rooms he did use."

"There are no significant transactions, guv," she said. "But if you were to total up his net worth, minus the house and any shares he may have had, and not taking into consideration any debts he may have, then you're looking at somewhere in the region of one-point-two million pounds."

The team digested the figure in silence and their various expressions amused Charles. Devon shook her head at such a sum, while Forsythe seemed to be less than impressed.

"Enough to kill for, Forsythe?"

"Depends, guv," he replied. "He's married, so any property worth more than a million is subject to inheritance tax. Which is what?"

"Forty per cent," Charles replied.

"Which leaves what, seven hundred grand?" He said, pulling a face. "If what you said about his son being the sole beneficiary is true, then does he really need seven hundred grand?"

"Plus the other assets," Devon added.

"Right, but still. It sounds to me like he's already wealthy," Charles said. "I'd rather have my dad around for a bit longer if I'm honest. You said the house is around the two million mark. Add to that the one-point-two the old man had in cash and you've got three-point-one. He's going to pay around a million in tax on that, which gives him a total inheritance of somewhere in the region of two-point-one million."

"Assuming he's factored in the tax and the debt," Devon said. "He was going through his father's accounts, was he not?"

"He's a lawyer, isn't he? He'll know the rules like the back of his hand."

"I agree," Charles said. "But then we don't know the ins and outs of their relationship, do we? Plus, as you quite rightly said, he will know the laws like the back of his hand, but he'll also know the loopholes. He'll know how to work the money to avoid paying tax."

"Like a trust, you mean?" Chalk said, and Charles jabbed his pen at her, as Devon began scrolling on her laptop.

"Exactly like a trust. A trust is the most tax-efficient means of passing on your assets. If I created a trust and made my daughter the sole beneficiary, and then willed my assets to the trust, then not only would she not pay tax, but should she marry and divorce, then her husband would have no claim on those assets. You hear of this thing all the time."

"Not in my circles you don't, guv," Forsythe said. "Most of my friends can barely go on holiday this year."

"I think it's safe to say that the Garfields move in far different circles to you or I, Forsythe," Charles told him and then turned to Devon. "Which leaves us with just one question. Who stands to benefit from Hugo Garfield's death?"

She finished scrolling and then turned her laptop to face them all. The screen displayed a scanned document, signed by Hugo Garfield and witnessed by a man named Jeremy Fisher.

"Everything goes to a trust, guv," she said. "The cash, the house, the contents, the lot."

He snapped the lid back onto the pen and nodded his thanks.

"It looks like we need to find Mr Fisher, whoever he is," Charles said. "If Robert Garfield is the sole trustee, then I think we have an avenue to exploit."

"There's just one thing, guv," she said, closing her laptop. She leaned back in her chair and let her head fall back in thought, and then snapped it upright. "Let's just say for argument's sake that Robert Garfield did all this. Yeah, sure, he's the sole trustee, he gets the lot, and he couldn't wait for the old man to die to get his hands on the family treasure."

"Aye," Charles said, wondering if she was going to suggest what he had been thinking. "It's a bit brutal, isn't it? I mean, dragging a man across a floor and then stringing him up while he was still alive? That's not exactly compassionate, is it?"

"It's not," Charles agreed. "That is, if that *is* what happened, which we don't know for certain yet."

"But even if he wasn't dragged, guv, he was still strung up by a rope," she said. "That's not the work of a man who is out to make a few quid. That's the work the work of somebody filled with hatred."

"Somebody who wanted to see him suffer, you mean?" Charles said.

"Yeah," she said. "The motive is not financial. It just doesn't fit. It's bigger than that. It's…"

"Revenge," Charles said, finishing the sentence for her. "CSI found two glasses in the kitchen. Somebody had been there, and if that somebody passed by the *post office*, Chalk," he said, emphasising the name of the place, and letting her fill in the blanks.

"Then we'd have them on CCTV," she said. "I've had a look through it, guv, but you're talking about two-hundred-odd cars in the timeframe you specified. If we had something specific, then we might be able to single one out."

"What does Robert Garfield drive?" Charles said, clicking his fingers three times and then pointing at Devon.

She made a show of recalling the cars on the drive, squinting, and biting down on her lower lip.

"Black Audi," she said. "Plus, there was a Volkswagen Golf on the drive, which I presumed belongs to his daughter, Dorothy."

"Colour?" Chalk said.

"Deep red," Devon replied.

"Leave it with me," Chalk replied, and she got to work analysing the video file.

"The pathologist has messaged us," Forsythe said. "Looks like she's prepared the body."

Charles checked his watch.

"Shall we get hold of Bobby Garfield?" Devon asked.

"No," he said. "Forsythe, Chalk, can I ask the pair of you to deal with that?"

"Shouldn't be a problem, guv," Chalk said.

"Call him to make the arrangements. You won't need to go in with him. Just be there to receive the verdict."

"What about us?" Devon asked.

"There is another person on my mind," Charles said. "Somebody we haven't spoken much about."

"The wife?" Devon said, to which he nodded and underlined her name on the board.

"Rose Garfield. She's currently away visiting her mother," he said. "Now there's somebody I'd like to talk to."

"Want me to find the mother's address, guv?"

"Yes," he said, thoughtfully. "Yes, let's go for a little drive."

CHAPTER TWENTY-FOUR

March 19, 1970

The doorway framed her as if she had been crafted from oils, and the artist, adept with his brushes, had captured perfection. She was a masterpiece. The very epitome of beauty.

And he knew in that very first second of the hunger she spoke. A new hunger. A hunger that, until now, had never even stirred, in places that had never before been woken.

Her dress appeared to have been painted onto her lithe form, it hugged her so, a mask of black satin that shone like skin in the hot summer sun. Her shoulders were bare and her figure was celebrated from her young, tight bosom to her smooth and slender ankles. Long, white gloves reached beyond her elbows, over which a delicate bracelet of gold swayed with the weight of its many topaz fruits.

Her mass of thick, blonde ringlets had been draped across one shoulder, pulled back to reveal two more topaz fruits that hung from her ears, glistening in the gloom like stars in the night sky.

"Come in, Rose," Mrs Lavender commanded rather than asked. And Rose entered. Thin heel straps embraced her ankles like snakes and her exposed toes seemed as if they had never seen bare earth or soil. "This is John Stow," Mrs Lavender said. "Won't you say hello?"

Rose came to stand before him, her expression that of the mannequin's – numb and indifferent.

"Stand, John," Mrs Lavender said. "When a lady enters the room, you must stand."

And so, John stood, more than acutely aware that his clothes were a far cry from hers. He had worn his Sunday best for want of anything else to wear. But still, he might as well have been in rags.

She held out a gloved hand, which he took gladly but felt only a polite and gentle squeeze before she pulled away.

"It's a pleasure to meet you, Master Stow."

Her voice was syrup, sweet and smooth, and he wanted more. It was as if somebody had filled his mouth with marbles and his mind with fog.

"John?" Mrs Lavender said. "Won't you greet Rose?"

"How do you do?" he said.

"Come now," Mrs Lavender said. "That is no way to greet a lady."

"Sorry," he said, finding himself breathless.

"And don't apologise. What are you sorry for?"

"I don't know," he said. "I don't know what to say."

"Well, tell me how you feel. Tell her how she makes you feel?"

The idea of revealing how she had made him stir seemed laughable, how his heart was beating faster than a steam train, and how his hands were wet with sweat at the very sight of her.

"Well, John?" Mrs Lavender said. "Are you pleased to have met her?"

"I am," he told her.

"Well, as lovely as it is, I am most certainly not the one to be told, am I now?"

She stared at him and then nodded at the girl before him.

"It's delightful to meet you," John said to Rose, and that

porcelain face of hers broke into a fleeting smile, before returning to its more natural and indifferent state.

From her seat at her dressing table, Mrs Lavender appraised the pair of them, as if she were eyeing two statuettes, picturing how they might compliment her mantle.

"Do you want her?" she said.

"Sorry?" John replied.

"What are you sorry for?"

"I-I just–"

"Do you want her?"

"Do I want her?" he said, doing his best not to apologise again. "Do I want her for what, ma'am?"

"For your own? To keep. To have. To admire," she said, and she rose from her seat to move closer. "To touch." He found himself blushing again and unable to look either of them in the eye. "To hold," she continued. "To feel. To be felt by." She stopped, apparently amused at his embarrassment. "To love?"

"Not to love," he said, to which she cocked her head.

"How so?"

"Love is something you feel," he explained, just as his mother had when she had told him about Terry. "Love is something that grows. It's shared."

"Very good," she replied.

"So, what would you do with Rose?" she asked.

"I don't know."

"Do you want to touch her?"

He hesitated, but felt her disdain.

"Yes."

"Do you want her to touch you? Hold your hand, maybe?"

"Yes," he replied.

"Why?"

He gave it some thought and dared to look at Rose who apparently found the corner of the room far more interesting.

"Because she's beautiful."

"Just beautiful? A rock is beautiful to some. A tree, a flower, a river. Even a painting. Do you want to hold one of those things, John?"

"She's the most beautiful thing I've ever seen," he said, and Rose looked at him. She had the same large eyes as Mrs Lavender, the same skin, the same hair, and the same figure, and in some way, they shared the compliment.

"What would you do to have her?" Mrs Lavender asked.

"Ask?" John suggested.

"Ask?" she replied, and then sighed. "A kiss. What would you do for a kiss from my sweet Rose?"

And then he understood.

"Anything," he said without hesitation. "I'd run through the village naked if need be."

"And if all the money in the world was at your fingertips?" she pressed.

"I would run through the village naked," he said again, and as that first lesson reached its climax, he looked into Mrs Lavender's eyes, seeing something similar to pride. "And then I would be truly wealthy."

CHAPTER TWENTY-FIVE
March 29, 2024

The Grange was like a scaled-down version of the Manor House in which Hugo Garfield had been found. Clearly, some efforts had been made to maintain the front, but it was minimal. By road, the house was a few miles from Hagworthingham, but Charles imagined a walk through the hills would be shorter and far more pleasant.

A wrought-iron fence surrounded the property, which was less of a deterrent for trespassers and more of a trellis for the various climbing plants that had claimed a section for their own, masking the inside from the out. But once inside, the fence and the foliage were impenetrable walls. Like the Manor House, The Grange was of Georgian design, albeit slightly older than its larger counterpart.

A white BMW was parked at the foot of the steps, which led up to a pair of old doors. The number plate suggested the car was a 2023 model, new and expensive.

They climbed the few steps and used the old, brass knocker to gain the occupant's attention. The heavy brass sent a dull thud through the old oak and beyond.

"This is more my style," he said to Devon. "Much more manageable, don't you think?"

"Manageable? Can you imagine doing the hoovering in a place like this? It would be like painting that bridge. What is it, the Forth Bridge? The one that takes a year to paint and then they have to start again?"

"I think you'll find that's an exaggerated myth, Devon," he told her. "And anyway, I'll bet this place leaks energy like a sieve. No double glazing, and I'll bet the walls aren't insulated. It would be like living in a wind tunnel in the winter months."

They heard footsteps beyond the door and it opened to reveal perhaps the most beautiful woman Charles had ever seen. Despite her age – he guessed her to be in her sixties – it was as if she had been carved from ivory or shaped from porcelain. She had an ageless quality usually reserved for Hollywood stars.

"Hello?" she said when she caught Charles staring. "Can I help you?"

"Sorry," he said, shaking his head, and he saw Devon's wry grin in his peripheral. "We're looking for Rose Garfield." He fumbled for his warrant card and held it up for her to see. "Sorry," he said again.

She wore a tight skirt of respectable length, a blouse that accentuated her fine figure, and her dyed blonde hair hung in ringlets on her shoulders, still full like a young girl's.

She leaned forward to read his ID and then pulled a questioning face.

"Is something wrong?" she asked.

"I'm afraid so," he said. "Do you mind if we come inside? We won't take too much of your time."

"Am I in trouble?" she asked.

"Oh, no. nothing like that," he said, reluctant to give too much away until they were inside.

She stepped to one side and allowed them to enter.

"This is a lovely place," he said, looking around the old hallway, which appeared to be in a state of disrepair and without the caring touch of a cleaner such as Joanne Childs. A large staircase dominated the space, leading up to two further floors. Beams of light cut through the dust that seemed to hang in the air above them.

"It used to be," she replied, closing the door behind them, with a boom that seemed to reverberate around the room. "I'm afraid it's become too much for my mother."

He waited for her to invite them through to a lounge or somewhere more comfortable. But she seemed intent on remaining in the hallway, occasionally glancing up the stairs.

"How can I help?" she said.

"Well, it's a rather delicate matter, actually," he began. "It's about your father-in-law. Hugo Garfield."

"What about him? Has he had a fall? Or has he finally pushed the boundaries of his tax assessment?"

"Neither, actually," Charles said. "I'm afraid he was found dead yesterday morning."

She gasped and her expression stiffened. She stepped over to one of two occasional chairs to the side of the large space, holding her hand to her mouth.

"That's terrible. Does my husband know?"

"He does, Mrs Garfield. I'm sorry to be the bearer of bad news."

"But he hasn't said anything. He would have messaged me."

"In his defence, he did say that he would tell you when you got back. He said you had enough on your plate."

"But he'll need me. He shouldn't be alone."

"Your daughter is with him," Devon said. "Dot?"

"Right," she said, and then shook her head, still processing the news. "But how? Who found him? How did it happen? Was it painless?"

"It was the cleaner who found him."

"Joanne? Oh dear. She must be devastated. I must go and see her—"

"And as for the manner of his passing, I'm afraid it wasn't as peaceful as you might have hoped," Charles said. "Your father-in-law was found hanged in his study, Mrs Garfield. I'd love to tell you that he didn't feel a thing, but—"

"Hanged? Why would he hang himself?" she said. "And how?"

"We're still establishing the facts, so the last thing I would want is to cast aspersions."

"I know he was in trouble," she said. "Financially, I mean. Bobby and I have been going through his accounts to see where all the money went, but I didn't realise it was this bad."

"I'm not sure you're quite following," Charles said. "You see, should his death be considered a suicide, then it's unlikely that either myself or my colleague, Sergeant Devon here, would have come to see you."

She unravelled his gentle articulation of the facts and then stared up at them.

"But if it wasn't suicide, then…"

"Then we would need to establish who was there at the time," Charles finished for her.

"Murder? Are you saying he was murdered?"

"I'm saying that in the short space of time we've had to gather information, we can assume with reasonable confidence that Hugo didn't take his own life, nor did he die of natural causes."

"Good Lord," she said. "This is awful. What did Bobby have to say? Is he okay? I should call him—"

"I would appreciate it if we could finish our discussion first, Mrs Garfield," he explained. "You see, being the wife of a lawyer, I imagine you're fairly familiar with the processes we must undertake."

"My husband may be a lawyer, Inspector, but I'm afraid I tend to tune out when he and his cronies talk shop."

"Well, then I'll explain, shall I?" Charles began, and he took a few slow steps around the room, enjoying the sound of his heels on the parquet floor. "When something like this happens, there are a few things that need to take place to allow us to investigate effectively. First of all, the body needs to be identified, which your husband and two of our colleagues are taking care of as we speak."

"I should be with him," she said.

"I think he'll be fine," Charles said. "It might be best to let him say goodbye in his own way." He took another few steps. "Once we have officially confirmed that the body is that of Hugo Garfield, then we need to ascertain the whereabouts of his closest friends and family."

"You're accusing me?" she asked, immediately defensive.

"Not really," he said. "You should think of it more as us laying the groundwork to find whoever is responsible and bringing them to justice. Let me explain." He shoved his hands into his pockets to signify that he offered no real threat, and then took a few slow steps away from Devon. "When we find the person," he said. "And find them we will, the case may go to trial, during which time their defence lawyer will seek any possible areas of doubt that his or her client killed Hugo Garfield." He held her gaze, hoping to convey how serious the matter was. "If, for example, we failed to ascertain the whereabouts of your father-in-law's closest family, that defence team is going to raise that as a red flag for the jury. How can the jury possibly find his or her client guilty when the prosecution, i.e. the state, i.e. the police force, haven't even questioned the immediate friends or family when more than eighty per cent of homicides are carried out by individuals who were close to the victim? Do you see what I'm saying, Mrs Garfield? This isn't an accusation. This is me hoping to convey to you that I plan on doing everything in my power to bring justice to your father-in-law. He was a ninety-eight-year-old man. I believe that he deserved to die on his own terms and that whoever took that privilege away from him, Mrs Garfield, deserves to receive the full penalty of the law."

She nodded once and crossed her legs.

"Quite the speech," she mused.

"You're aware of the facts now," he said. "This isn't an accusation. This is how our justice system works." He took a few steps towards her and then stopped. "So? Where were you, Mrs Garfield, between the hours of eleven a.m. and two p.m. on Wednesday?"

"She was here," a new voice said, with a similar velvety tone to Mrs Garfield's but with somewhat harsher intonations. He looked to the landing above them and saw the elderly lady peering down at them. Her hair had yet to be brushed and she wore an old nightgown that stopped at her bare ankles. "She was here with me."

"And you must be—"

"Rose's mother," she replied. "Is it true? Is it true what I heard about dear Hugo?"

"I'm afraid it is," Charles said.

"Then I shall pray for him," the old lady said, and turned her haunting stare onto her daughter. "Rose, dear, help me to dress, will you?" She turned to shuffle away and called out. "Find me something black to wear. Today is a sad day. A very sad day indeed."

The old lady disappeared into a corridor and Mrs Garfield stood to open the door for Charles and Devon.

"Mrs Garfield," Charles said, stopping in the doorway. "When we spoke to Joanne Childs about her employment, she mentioned that you organised it on his behalf, is that right?"

"It is," she said. "She's a good woman. The family have worked there for years, and as I understand it, they need the money."

"And you're not aware of any reason why she, or anybody else for that matter, might have held a grudge against your father-in-law?"

"I'm not really the one to ask, Inspector," Mrs Garfield replied. "I don't really know her."

"You just said that she was a good woman," he said. "Or were you simply being polite?"

She held the door tightly and stared into his eyes.

"She worked tirelessly at that house for decades and my father-in-law was not an easy man to like. He wasn't one who gave thanks freely. He believed in the old ways," she told him. "In my book, that makes her a saint, and if you knew him, then you would probably agree."

CHAPTER TWENTY-SIX
March 22, 1970

His first week of private education had been nothing short of eye-opening. His time, it seemed to him, was to be split between academia and experience, the former to arm him with sufficient knowledge and expertise in which to gain a position whereby the latter could be employed to great effect.

Rose was elusive and occupied some other part of the great house during those academic sessions. But as receptive as he had been to Mrs Lavender's tactile approach to his learning, his mind rarely ventured beyond that china-doll skin. There seemed to be no schedule. The agenda of the day was set by Mrs Lavender's mood. She had a way of explaining mathematics that he could only describe as enlightening. Language, both Latin and English, rolled off her tongue with such elegance that mimicking her became second nature, and he imagined himself speaking to Rose in this new tongue, not as the grubby, little farm boy from a distant village, but as an equal.

When academics were finished, Rose would be called in. It was the highlight of his day. He had learned how to stand and sit, never before knowing that such practices could be deemed right or wrong. He had learned how to smile, where to look and where not, and even how to enter a room.

Twice she had pulled him back from his daydreams, and on the third, she snapped the book closed, and that dancing dust rose at the disturbance as she proceeded to return to the shadows beside her bed.

"That's enough for today," she told him, and he checked the clock on the mantle.

"It's early," he said.

"I said that's enough. Now I need to rest."

It was enough of a hint that he felt little obligation to stay. At the door, he stopped and looked back, finding her form in the shadows.

"Ma'am," he said, to which she grunted. "Thank you. For what you're doing, I mean. I'm grateful."

She said nothing and moments passed like sand slipping through an hourglass.

And then he heard it. The soft rattle of sleep.

He closed the door quietly and walked slowly along the corridor, wondering what he should do. The walk home would take nigh on an hour, leaving time still to help Terry in the fields. But time had never been a commodity for him. Like money, there had never been enough of it. Yet he found himself holding a gold coin. An afternoon to himself with nowhere to be.

Neither Rose nor her mother had ever spoken of the house, where to go, where not to go. In fact, he hadn't seen Mrs Lavender outside of her room. Not once.

The corridor was one of two and now the second beckoned him. He wondered if Rose was down there somewhere. He wondered what her bedroom was like, imagining that his own paled in significance. He imagined she slept on a great, soft bed, with white sheets and plump pillows. He imagined she bathed in a large tub, leisurely lathering her skin, polishing it to perfection.

He imagined how she might laugh if ever she saw his own

iron-framed bed, with its lumpy mattress and its lonely, old pillow. How she might baulk at the idea of sleeping in such a confined space, with no fireplace to call his own and with the moisture from his breath running down the window panes.

He took the stairs slowly, leaving behind any ideas of wandering the halls. The large front door opened with a creak and the bright spring daylight filled the hallway, like flames seeking pockets of air to feed on.

But the sunlit wooden floor was perhaps the smallest distraction. Rose was sitting on the steps, gazing out at the gardens before her, as if she wondered what life was like on the other side.

"Is it nap time?" she asked, and then finally looked up at him. "She tires easily recently."

"She said that we'd done enough for today."

"Then you should go home," she told him, returning her vacant stare for the world outside to enjoy.

"I should," he agreed but remained where he was. She was different somehow. In the lessons she had looked like royalty, but now, sitting on the steps wearing a simple frock, she looked normal. Like she could have been any of the girls he had known, albeit with far more beautiful skin and eyes to die for. "You don't like me, do you?"

She rolled her eyes and sighed, but said nothing.

"It's okay," he told her. "You don't have to like me."

"Well, thank heavens for that," she replied. She plucked a crocus from a planter within reach and admired it in delicate hands.

"Perhaps you will when you get to know me," he said, and although her head remained still, her eyes rolled up to meet his. Her fingers, however, plucked blindly at the flower petals, and she dropped each one to the ground.

"Perhaps," she said and then discarded the tortured plant before adjusting the way she sat, moving into a position from where she could observe him more freely. "Sit."

"You want me to sit with you?"

"No, I want you to sit," she said, then pointed to the far end of the steps. "Not with *me*. Over there."

John descended two steps, then dropped down, adjusting himself, as she had, to a position from where he could study her.

"What are you doing here?" she asked, to which he shrugged.

"I don't know. Learning, I suppose."

"But what are you learning? What can my mother teach you that the world out there cannot?" She cast her hand across the sky. "Why aren't you at school with other children like you?"

"Like me?"

"Like you," she said, unabashed. "Poor children."

The comment was sharp and caught him beneath the ribcage.

"You ask a lot of questions, don't you?"

"Isn't it my right?" she said. "You come to my house, you tire my mother, and you leer at me like a salivating dog. Yet not once have you told me of you."

"I haven't had the chance," he said. "Not with Mrs Lavender, your ma, I mean."

"So now is your chance. Tell me about you. Tell me all about John Stow."

It wasn't a question fuelled by intrigue. It was a demand, and from how John heard those words, they were fuelled by nothing short of indignance.

"My dad died," he began, and her face softened briefly before she caught herself and corrected her expression.

"Oh?" was all she said.

"It was just Ma and me for a while. We had to sell Dad's farm. Ma rented a place. A little cottage out near Boston. She got work as a cleaner in some big house and that's when she met Terry."

"Terry?"

"Her new husband."

"Ah, your stepfather. Does he beat you? You hear such awful tales of children being beaten by their stepfathers—"

"No, no," he said stopping her from venturing down a wrong path. "No, he's not like that. He's a good man."

"Better than your father, then?" she suggested, an idea that he had never considered until that moment.

"No. He's different. But not better. He means well. He's a God-fearing man."

"And are you a God-fearing boy, John Stow?"

"I don't know," he replied, after a time. "I suppose I am a bit. But there are things I just don't understand. I can't make them out."

"Perhaps, I can help," she said. She moved again, tucking her legs up to her chest, and wrapping her arms around her dress to preserve her modesty. "What don't you understand?"

The cool manner in which she had first greeted him was now gone and she seemed genuinely interested in hearing what he had to say.

"All right then," he said, mirroring her posture minus the dress. "If God is so great, then why did my dad die?"

"Perhaps he wasn't as good as you say he was?" she suggested, an answer he had never once considered.

"But he was."

"If you say so."

"He was," he said. "He was a good man. He didn't have much, but he was a good man."

"So, what could be the alternative?" she pressed. "If your father was, as you say, a good man who deserved to live, then why did God let him die?"

"I don't know," John said. "The same way I don't know how bad people are allowed to live."

"Perhaps there is no God," she said, and she smiled sadly. "Perhaps there was a God, but he grew tired of us and moved on. Too many bad people."

"Is that what you think?" he asked. "That God has moved on?"

"Maybe," she said thoughtfully. "Maybe this is hell and all the good people are destined to die?"

"But I'm good," he replied. "I'm alive, aren't I?"

"Are you? Do you really believe that you are a good person?" she asked, and she pushed herself to her feet, straightening her dress as she did. "Have you never sinned, John Stow?"

"All I know is that my father was a good man and he died."

"My father also died. My sister too," Rose replied as she stepped past him and pushed open the door. She looked back over her shoulder at him. "So where does that leave you and I?"

CHAPTER TWENTY-SEVEN

March 29, 2024

It was common for the team to carry out group calls from their vehicles. Charles idled the car from The Grange, still marvelling at the lack of road noise. The call was so clear that he could whisper and be heard.

"Guv?" a voice said when the call was answered.

"Chalk, are you with Forsythe?"

"I am, guv. We're just on our way back to the station."

"How did it go?"

She hesitated as if searching for the words, and then spoke freely.

"Odd, guv," she said.

"Are you referring to the pathologist, or something else?"

"Well, her too," Chalk said. "But I meant him. He's a cold man, isn't he? He barely showed any emotion at all."

"Was it a positive ID?"

"It was, guv, yes. Although it felt more like a transaction than a formal identification."

"Well, it takes all sorts, Chalk. It takes all sorts."

"How about you two? How did you get on?"

"I'm pleased to say that Rose Garfield displayed more emotion than her husband," Charles said. "She was with her mother, who I might add must be as old as Hugo Garfield was, or thereabouts."

"Must be something in the water up there," Forsythe said.

"Aye," Charles replied. "Or the air. Listen, I want to look into Joanne Childs. Forsythe, have you managed to call her about the glasses yet?"

"Yes, guv," Forsythe said, speaking up to be heard over the road noise from his car. "It's as we thought. She usually cleaned the kitchen last thing. She did see the glasses but was waiting until the rest of the house was done. She said she usually leaves by the back door, as that's what key she has. Saves dirtying her floors or something."

"The back door?" Charles said. "The one that leads out to the rose garden?"

"I'm not sure," he replied. "I didn't go out the back."

"What else do we know about her, aside from what you mentioned in the office?"

"Not much, guv. She's a cleaner, she votes, she claims child benefit."

"Any previous we should know about?"

"Not really, although she did make a complaint about Bobby Garfield back in nineteen seventy-one."

"What type of complaint?" Charles asked. "Did they leave their breakfast things for her to tidy up?"

"No, guv," he said, his tone serious. "I dug the report out of the archives. It hasn't even been digitalised yet. She claimed that Bobby Garfield sexually assaulted her while she was working at the house."

"What?"

"That's what it says. She claimed that while her mother was working, they were playing in one of the bedrooms. He pinned her down and groped her."

"So, what happened? Was he arrested?"

"No, nothing like that. There's a subsequent statement from

her claiming that she had made the whole thing up. They were just kids playing."

"So NFA, then?" Charles said. "No further action?"

"None at all. She would have been thirteen or fourteen at the time. She was made to apologise to the boy, and that was the end of it."

"Right," Charles said. "I wonder why she would make such a claim?"

"Money, guv? Maybe she was looking to earn a few quid?"

"Extortion at thirteen?"

"They were poor, guv," Forsythe said.

"Hold on, let's not pin a guilty badge on her just because she's female," Devon added, and Charles stared at her. "What?"

"What does being female have to do with anything?" he asked.

"It just does," she said. "I'm just saying that he could have groped her, that's all. Not every young, poor girl who makes a claim about a rich boy is lying about it. Maybe there's something to the claim."

"Nineteen-seventy-one," Charles said. "How old would Bobby have been?"

"Fifteen or sixteen," Devon said after a moment of doing mental calculation.

"I don't see how it ties in," Charles said. "I mean, the families have known each other for more than a century. They had servants for God's sake. I'll wager that if something happened between Bobby and Joanne Childs, it was not the only occurrence, and I'd also wager that both parties were consenting. I've had daughters. They can be as curious as boys at that age, and what they lack in strength, they make up for up here." He tapped his temple at Devon and she shook her head in disgust. "And before you say it, that is not a sexist comment, and nor am I a misogynist, as you well know."

"Well, as you said, guv," Devon replied sharply, "it doesn't tie into Hugo Garfield, does it? So, I can guess it's a moot point."

"I guess it is," he said and then returned to Chalk and Forsythe. "Listen, you two. Carry on doing some digging when you get back. I want to pay a visit to our friend Joanne while we're up here. We'll call you when we're done."

"Righto, guv," Chalk replied, and the call ended.

Charles glanced across at Devon who stared out of her window.

"Devon?"

"Guv?" she said.

"I'm not going to argue about this," he said.

"Well, that's fine by me."

"We can't know what happened. That's all I'm saying. And even if we did know what happened, it was fifty years ago, and it was Bobby Garfield who she accused."

She inhaled a deep breath, filled her chest, and then let it out.

"I know," she said. "I just get riled up when we talk about that kind of thing."

"And that's understandable," he said. "But like I said, you know me. I am in no way sexist. There's some truly awful men out there."

"And there are awful women, too," she conceded. "And yes, I get it. There are women who cry rape or assault or whatever unnecessarily."

"And do you accept that two young teenagers, from different classes, in the same house, might have just let their curiosity go too far?"

"I do, guv," she said.

"We're talking about the nineteen-seventies, Devon," he told her, remembering the era with mixed emotions. "The world was a very different place to what it is now." He pulled the car to a stop, and checked the address was correct. Then finally, he looked back over to her. "Look, let's just ask her about it. Let's ask her what happened," he said. "And if I'm wrong, then I'll gladly accept it."

"Can't say fairer than that, guv," she replied.

"But we have to bear the time in mind. We can't liken it to the societal norms of today," he said. "We have to remember what it was like back then. The divide between the rich and poor in these parts was huge." He stared through the window at the little cottage. "It was another world, Devon."

CHAPTER TWENTY-EIGHT
August 5, 1973

For more than three years, John had walked the hills to The Grange, twice per day, in every weather that God, should he exist, could throw at him.

And yet, in all that time, progress seemed only to grace his education, be that academic or otherwise. The rest of his world seemed to stand still.

The summer days were long, and although he still harboured an unhealthy infatuation with Rose Lavender, her perpetual rejections and icy glares had sent it scurrying to that secret place inside him that she, he remembered with great clarity, had stirred for the first time.

Not only was John well-mannered, articulate, and a proficient dancer, capable of holding his own at any debutante's soiree, but Latin had become second nature, his knowledge of the English classics spanned the length of Mrs Lavender's library, and he was more than capable of composing a letter, a contract, or even a will.

Yet still, the little bedroom in the old farmhouse was where he slept each night.

There had, of course, been an element of guilt at first. His education had proven to be so demanding that he once again found himself short of time. The gold coin he had once held had been spent, and he was reminded daily of his lack of wealth, which as a result, created friction.

His mother prepared meals but he often dined alone. Terry walked the fields but often without John. A barrier had formed, or as his ma had once said, he had climbed a wall from which he could never climb down.

He stood when his mother entered the room and all she did was scoff. He greeted them each morning, as Mrs Lavender had shown him, and they simply laughed at his choice of words. He had tried several times during those three long years to create a separation, to walk across the hills each morning, and with each step, he would become somebody new, only to discard the facade on the return journey. For a time, the dual personalities had worked. He had managed to slip back into the old John Stow convincingly enough that they had chatted for a while, him and his ma.

But each time she spoke, and he heard himself correct her, a part of the old John died.

"You stopping by for tea?" she would ask, and he would ask her if that was a question or a statement.

"Suppose you'll be too busy with books to help with the harvest eh, John?" Terry had once said, and every abused syllable had stung him.

But it was more than that.

The way they stood annoyed him. Ma slouched and Terry insisted on keeping his hands in his pockets during Church services. The way they held their knife and fork, the way they chewed, their improper greetings, the way the cutlery was tossed onto the table instead of being placed in the correct places, the way Terry belched when he drank beer, the way he passed wind after a meal, and the way they dressed – heaven forbid. Did they have no sense of style or common decency?

"I'm off, Ma," he said to her. He wore his newest suit and she her oldest pinny. But she didn't look up from the old sink. If anything, she scrubbed the skillet harder than before. "I'll be back tonight."

"Righto," she replied, which was something, at least. "I'll beat the red carpet and lay it out ready for when your highness returns."

"I shouldn't think that will be necessary, Ma," he said, and she shook her head at his words. "What is it? What's happened?"

"What's what?" she replied, sounding bored already.

"Why are you treating me like this?"

"I'm treating you no different than I did three years ago, John. At least back then you had the good grace to help us out from time to time."

"I still help."

"Yeah," she said. "A few hours at the weekend don't butter no parsnips, John. Perhaps if you found the time to put your airs and graces to one side—"

"I'm still the same person," he told her, and for the first time, she set the skillet down and stared at him.

"I wonder," she said.

"You wonder what?"

"Where my little boy went," she replied. "You know, there was a time when it was all you could think of to get out there with Terry. To take over the farm and become the master." She turned back to the sink and snatched up the skillet in a strong hand. "Now look at you. You dress like one of her ladyship's dolls, and you speak, well, I don't know what it's like. But it ain't how I taught you. That I do know."

"I'm bettering myself, Ma. Can't you see that?"

"Bettering yourself? Is that what you call it?"

"I can make something of myself, Ma. I stand a real chance. Mrs Lavender thinks I could do well if I get a chance. Think of it, Ma. If I got a job in a local business, I might earn good money.

Enough to buy a car or even a house. Think of that. You wouldn't have to work so hard. Neither would Terry."

"Oh, right. And who'd pay the rent on this place and see it clean?"

"I would," he said. "It's what I want to do. I want to look after you. I want us to be comfortable. Don't you see that? You can't go on working forever."

"Hey, I'm thirty years old, not ninety."

"I know, but, Ma, you've been working since when? Since you were fifteen?"

"S'right," she said, proudly, as she laid the skillet onto the drainer. "You weren't even a week old when I pulled my pinny back on. As for your father, God rest his soul, he never even stopped."

"Just like Terry," John said.

"Aye, just like Terry."

"He's what? Thirty-one? Thirty-two?"

"He is," she said, grabbing another pan and dunking it into the steaming water.

"He's going to be working until he's dead, Ma. He'll work himself into an early grave," he said. "Just like Pa did."

The pan hit the drainer with a bang.

"Now, you listen here. You might have an education that none of us deserve, but don't you dare talk like that. You've no right. You hear me? No right."

"It's true, though," he told her. "I'm fifteen, Ma. I could be working in another year. Mrs Lavender said that I'll need to sit some exams, but she thinks I'll pass. She said I can do a degree while I work. Think about it. By the time I'm twenty, I could be earning good money. Enough to take care of us all."

"Oh aye, and I could marry a prince if I could only find a frock to fit."

"I'm serious, Ma. And look, I know you think that I've changed–"

"You have—"

"And I know you think that I have no claim to greatness. But the world is changing, and the way I see it, I have two options. More than most, I grant you that. I can go out there and work with Terry. And when he dies an early death, which he will, I can take over. And when I die an early death, you can be alone, poor, and hungry."

She listened but said nothing, continuing to work while he spoke.

"Or?" was all she said.

"Or I can seize the opportunity, Ma. I can make a go of it," he told her, and she dabbed at her eye with the cloth. "I want children and I don't want them to be poor like us. And what money I earn can help them, so their children can go on to do even greater things. This isn't just for me. It's for us all. I can set us and future generations up for life. And that is what I mean to do."

"You want to be rich, you mean?" she said. "Well, money don't buy you happiness. You remember that when you're all alone in your ivory tower."

"Not rich, Ma," he said, and he pulled at her arm, dragging her from the sink, and then waited for her to look him in the eye. They were the same height now. It had been so long since he had stood beside her that he hadn't noticed how much he had grown. "Wealthy."

"Rich. Wealthy. Same thing, int it?"

"No, Ma," he said with a smile. "It's not the same thing at all."

CHAPTER TWENTY-NINE
March 29, 2024

The front door of the cottage opened onto the High Street, as did the other houses in the old, stone terrace. It wasn't hard to picture the old building and the surrounding village fifty, or even a hundred, years before. Newer houses had been built since, of course, but many of the old places had survived. It was the type of village that Charles imagined where the locals would claim the village just wasn't the same as it had once been.

They did that, he thought. And even he had been guilty of it in the past. Claiming their own memories as the best times and that anything since was simply an affront to originality, forgetting, of course, that the places had existed before anyone, and that at some point, those original stone buildings had been new. Perhaps somebody back then had claimed the place had been better before they had been built?

"You okay, guv?" Devon said.

"Me?" he said, snapping out of his little daydream. "Yes, yes. I'm fine." He knocked on the door and stepped back, peering up at the old, cast-iron gutters and the window recesses. "Beautiful, isn't it?"

"And cold," she said. "And probably damp, too."

"More of a brick-built, new-build type of woman, are you?"

"I'm not fussed about the architecture," she replied. "I just like to be warm and dry." She pointed down to the bottom of the old, wooden front door. "You could get immigrants through that gap, guv."

"What?" he hissed. "You can't say that!"

"Can't I?" she replied. "Why not?"

"Well, it's racist or something, isn't it?"

"I didn't mention a particular race? I was just talking about poor individuals from war-torn countries who need somewhere to sleep."

"Well, I don't doubt that somebody might take offence," he told her. "You know what people are like. So keep those thoughts to yourself, will you? The last thing we need is a complaint."

"You're right," she said. "Besides, they wouldn't be given an old place like this. They'd be given something newer and nicer."

"A brick-built new-build, you mean?"

"Warm and dry, guv. I can't say I blame them, can you?"

The door opened, thankfully bringing the conversation to an end, and Joanne Child's expression sagged when she recognised them.

"Good afternoon, Mrs Child," Charles said. "You remember us, I hope?"

"I do," she replied, then stepped back for them to enter, checking the footpath outside to make sure nobody had seen them before closing the door. "I wondered if you'd be back."

"Oh, you know how it is, Joanne," he said. "Investigations like this are rarely straightforward. We do try to limit the number of times we need to speak to people, but sometimes we aren't always in full possession of the facts. Questions arise, as I'm sure you understand."

"Are you staying long enough for tea?" she asked. "I've just made a pot."

"Tea would be lovely," he said, and she led them through to a kitchen barely big enough to swing a hamster, let alone a cat. The floor was terracotta-tiled and the rough, textured walls appeared to be the original plaster.

"There's not much space, I'm afraid. We always wanted to break through into the lounge but it's so expensive."

"I quite like it," Charles said. "Not everything has to be shiny and new, does it?"

"Spoke to your man earlier," she said, as she placed the teapot onto the kitchen table and then beckoned for them to sit. "He asked about those glasses."

"Ah yes," Charles said. "We just wanted to understand why they were left there."

"Well, like I said to him, I always clean the kitchen last, see? That way, I can slip out the back door without going over my nice, clean floors." She smiled pleasantly and laid out three cups. "Shall I be mum?"

"Please do," Charles told her, then watched as she poured the teas and then settled into the seat at the end of the table. He added his own milk, then passed the jug to Devon. "We were in the area, and I thought I'd stop by to go over the statement you made."

"To catch me out, you mean?" she asked, to which he smiled.

"Listen, when you see something like you did, sometimes it's easy to forget things. Little things. But it's often those seemingly insignificant things that make a difference."

"Right," she said, then wrapped her hands around the cup. "I let myself in the back door as I always do. Put the kettle on, you know?"

"And were the glasses there then?" he asked. "Or did you move them from elsewhere?"

"No, they were there. It's not unusual to find dirty plates and whatnot. But like I said—"

"You usually leave those until last?"

"That's right," she said. "Anyways, I filled the kettle up, put it on to boil, hung my coat up, and fetched my apron from the pantry."

"That's your routine, is it? You don't go to see him first or anything?"

"No, I don't bother him," she said. "I like to make a dent in the cleaning before he knows I'm there, or I'll end up spending all morning making him lunch."

"I see," Charles said.

"No, I get myself set up. Run the water for the mop, that sort of thing, and then have a nice cup of tea before I get started."

"In the kitchen?"

"That's right. I like to keep out of his way."

"And did he ever join you in the kitchen?"

"Him? Join me in the kitchen? He'd need bleeding Theseus' string to find his way out again. No, he never went in there."

"So, who put the glasses in the kitchen?" Charles asked, to which she shrugged.

"Whoever was with him, I expect."

"I see," Charles said. "Sorry, go on."

"Well, when I'd had me tea, I got started. Upstairs don't take long. It's only his bedroom and the little bathroom he uses. Downstairs, now that's where the work is. Bleeding dust in that place, I tell you. I don't know where it comes from."

"Time," Charles said. "It's just time leaving its mark. So we don't forget, you know?"

"All I know is it's a pain. Anyways, I'd pretty much done. All I had to do was his study and the kitchen. Course, everything else is done by then, so if he asks me for some lunch, it's not really a problem, you know?"

"I see," Charles said.

"Anyways, so I knocked and went in, as I normally do. And there he was. Hanging from the chandelier like a bleeding Christmas decoration, he was."

"And that's where I need some help, Joanne," he said. "Was it ever part of your role to clean the chandeliers? I mean, they must have needed cleaning at some point. Especially if, as you say, the place was so dusty."

"Clean them? Course we did."

"We?"

"Sorry, back in the day. Me and Mum used to do it together. It would take us an afternoon just to do one of them."

"But you never do this alone?"

"God no," she said. "No, told him straight, I did. Said I haven't got it in me to get them down, clean every little bit of glass, and then pull it back up. It would take me a week now just to do one. And there's four of them in that house."

"But you could, if you were asked to," he asked, and again she shrugged.

"I'd have to remember how Mum used to do it. There's a rope in the corner over by the light switch. Wouldn't dare touch it now, course. The whole bleeding lot would probably come down."

"I think you'd be surprised at how strong they are," he said. "I certainly was. Tell me, while you're cleaning, you must use some strong chemicals in that old house."

"I do, yeah. Bleach mainly, plus some wood soap and whatnot."

"So, you wear gloves while you're doing this? To protect your hands, I mean?"

"I do. Mum never used to and her hands were like a rhino's backside by the end. Always told her, I did. Mum, I said, one day you'll be sorry for not wearing gloves–"

"Sorry, Joanne," he cut in before she ventured onto another tangent. "The pathologist and the medical examiner both agree that Mr Garfield died at between eleven a.m. and two p.m. on Wednesday. I wonder, and this is purely for our records, you understand, if you could tell us where you were at that time?"

"Me?"

"Yes, you," he said, and she puffed her cheeks out.

"Wednesday, you say?"

"That's right. Between the hours of eleven and two."

"I had lunch in the George and Dragon," she said. "Do that from time to time, I do."

"Alone?"

"That's right. Just saves me making it. I make it myself and I'd have the same old thing. Ham sandwich. Nice to get out and have someone cook you a meal from time to time, ain't it?"

"And the bar staff could vouch for you, could they?"

"I suppose," she said.

"The landlord?"

"No, he weren't about. It was a young girl. I'm buggered if I can remember her name, though."

"That's fine," Charles told her. "I'm sure they'll remember you."

"Well, I don't know about that. Lunchtime in the George and Dragon? You ought to get down there. Honestly, best pub food for miles, it is."

"Maybe we'll stop for some food when we ask them about your wee lunch break," Charles said, spying Devon's note-taking from the corner of his eye. "Listen, there is one more thing I wanted to say. I hope you don't mind."

The carefree expression she had worn slipped like wax slipping from a candle. She swallowed hard, and then wrapped her hands around her tea again.

"Go on," she said.

"Only that I'd appreciate it if you didn't travel, Joanne," he said, rising from his seat, much to Devon's obvious chagrin. "There's a chance I may need to talk to you again before this is over."

CHAPTER THIRTY
August 5, 1973

A strange mood had fallen onto The Grange, even more so than John had grown accustomed to. Although it had been years since he had knocked on the door, he had never been able to bring himself to enter without announcing his arrival, which he did with more than a little trepidation.

He wasn't quite sure what it was but something was different about the house, something which was made clear the moment he knocked and entered Mrs Lavender's bedroom.

Occupying the centre of the room, where an old carver chair had once been placed for him to sit, was a table and chairs. A clean, white tablecloth had been draped across the table, along with a brass candelabra, two sets of cutlery, wine glasses, and napkins. Even the chair backs were covered in linen, and for once, the ceiling light had been turned on, casting a warm glow across the setting.

"Sit," Mrs Lavender said, from her seat in the shadows, and so he did as he was told, selecting the seat furthest from the door with his back to the windows. "You are, for all intents and purposes, required to entertain. To dine." Mrs Lavender continued. "You will, to the highest standard, behave in a manner befitting a young man of your education."

"But who—"

"And such a man does not stoop so low as to ask irrelevant questions," she said. "Your task is to entertain, and entertain you will." She re-entered her world of make-believe and her voice softened to suit. "You are surrounded by the finest in the land. The Duke of Sussex and his wife are dining beside the windows, Lord Grimsby is enjoying supper with some of his old army cronies. You know how they enjoy a bottle of port and a cheese board. And you, John Stow, must behave accordingly."

The set-up was surreal. Her description of the diners around him was no more vivid than his dreams yet she somehow brought them to life. Lord Grimsby and his pals guffawed, the Duke of Sussex and his wife enjoyed a fine meal, with the head waiter standing in attendance at all times. But there was something missing, and he was close to opening his mouth and voicing his opinion when her words rang true.

He pushed himself from his seat and strode over to the end of the room.

"I didn't say you could leave," she said to which John said nothing. "I asked you to return to your seat," she said, her voice a little sharper.

On a broad desk inlaid with green baize was a record player. On the floor beside it were three brass glacettes, each containing a dark green wine bottle and ice.

"I assume you can hear me but are choosing not to answer me," she said. "There is nothing more ill-bred than ignorance, John Stow."

But John continued with his task, selecting a jazz LP from the broad selection.

"What are you doing, John?" she asked, and again he remained silent, until at least he had carefully lowered the arm, placed the needle, and heard those first piano chords dance.

"You described a fine restaurant, ma'am," he said. "The Savoy, perhaps? In fact, I could picture the scene so well, I could even hear Lord Grimsby and his chums laughing." Light brushes on symbols joined the teasing piano, and the beginnings of a jazz rhythm began to form. "I've been asked to entertain a beautiful young lady, and entertain I shall," he said. "I know of no young lady who prefers silence over a fine band."

"But jazz?" she said.

"Had a real waiter been in attendance, I might have requested something a little more suitable, ma'am."

"You could have asked for something classical."

"A man befitting the presence of Lord Grimsby and the Duke of Sussex does not stoop so low as to ask irrelevant questions, ma'am," he said, returning to his seat. "He has all the answers that he needs."

She said nothing. He couldn't even see her face, so dark were the shadows in which she seemed to thrive. He slid the paper menu from the tablecloth and examined its contents. She had done a fine job. The meal was a set menu, a starter, main course, and pudding, each of which was paired with a wine of which he knew nothing.

The first of the jazz numbers was just coming to an end when he heard a gentle knock on the door. He stood, as he had been taught, and Rose entered without invitation, coming to a stop beside the chair. He was reminded of that very first meeting with her when he had likened her to an oil painting. and today was no different. Her dress was not dissimilar, figure-hugging and elegant. The jewels that were set in her bracelet, necklace, and earrings were red instead of blue, and her hair had been cut short, collar length, and it framed her magnificent cheekbones.

He took the shawl from her shoulders and set it to one side while he helped her sit. He took his own seat, remembering all he had been taught.

"You look lovely," he told her.

"I'm thirsty," she replied.

"Some water?" he said, to which she shook her head.

"Something stronger."

Her tongue darted across her red lips and the reality of his shortfalls made itself clear.

"I could fetch some wine," he said, which seemed to please her. He looked to the shadow, finding only darkness, and then found solace in the menu.

"What will you do, John?" Mrs Lavender asked.

"Ordinarily, I would discreetly catch the attention of a waiter."

"Pity. They all seem to be busy," she said.

"So, I'll fetch it myself," he told her, then excused himself to Rose and made his way over to the glacettes. He selected the bottle that the menu had suggested to accompany the entrée – grapefruit with a maraschino cherry, paired with a rosé.

He returned to the table with the entire glacette, half-filled Rose's glass, and then took his own seat, from where he admired the way she held her glass, the way her lips pursed, and the way her eyes never wavered from his.

"Won't you join me?" she asked.

"Join you?" he said, and she raised her glass. "Wine? No, I don't... I mean, I've never..."

"You cannot let a lady drink alone, John," Mrs Lavender called out, reminding him that they were not alone.

Tentatively, he filled his glass, and Rose held hers up in a toast. He joined her of course and then sipped.

"To education," he said.

"To education," she replied.

It wasn't his first alcoholic drink, being allowed a sherry with Christmas dinner. One time, he had stolen a mouthful of John's beer, and then sought a place to spit it out without being seen.

But the wine seemed to evaporate in his mouth. The tiny bubbles massaged his gullet and slipped down in a heartbeat.

"What are we eating?" she asked, and he scooped the menu from the tablecloth.

"The starter is a grapefruit," he told her. "Then there's a steak tartare and a selection of cheeses."

She sank the contents of her glass and placed it down on the table, her fingers caressing the stem. Catching her eye, he reached for the bottle, filled the glass, and then slipped it back into the glacette.

But her roving eye wandered to his glass.

"Please don't let me drink alone," she said, and he took another sip. "More," she urged, and after a deep breath, he took a mouthful so large that bubbles seemed to spill from his nostrils, and he forced the drink down before entering into a huge coughing fit.

She just sat there, a wry smile growing across her face, and an empty glass in her hand.

"Shouldn't we eat?" he said.

"I'm not hungry," she replied, and she rolled the glass around on its base.

He recovered sufficiently enough to pour her a fresh glass and used the napkin to tidy himself up.

"Drink," she told him. "It'll make you feel better."

"I'm not sure if–"

"Drink," she said again quietly, leaving little room for argument.

And so, he drank, and it did feel better. And when he had finished his glass, Rose refilled it.

"How do you feel?" she asked, as he took another mouthful.

"All right," he said.

"Just all right?" she asked.

"No. Good," he said. "Really good. This is nice."

"The wine?"

"No," he said. "You. Being here. Doing this with you."

The comment seemed to amuse her. The corners of her

mouth flexed briefly before she set her glass down and leaned back in her chair.

"I'd like to dance," she said flatly.

"Dance? What here? Now?"

"I thought a man befitting such an audience had all the answers he needed?" Mrs Lavender said from her corner.

He eyed Rose and she stared at him expectantly.

"Then, we'll dance," he told her, rising from his feet, and the wine hit him with full effect. He staggered to the side and held onto the table to steady himself, but the tablecloth slipped under his grip and he fell, taking with him the contents of the table.

He lay there for a while, dazed. The spilt wine had soaked his suit jacket, and when he tried to climb to his feet, he felt the sharp, broken glass piece his hand. It didn't hurt, which surprised him, and he lay back to stare at that wonderful ceiling and that wonderful light with all its wonderful, twinkling glass pieces.

He awoke in a dream. It must have been a dream. The bed was larger even than the one Ma and Terry slept in. The room was vast, bigger than their kitchen, and the floor was covered in a beautiful, cream carpet with a faint, floral pattern. The wall coverings were also floral but bold in colour, contrasting the delicate carpet. Bright, green flower stems with a repeating pattern of vivid violets seemed, at first, to sway in the breeze. Among them, nestled into the foliage, tits and finches frolicked, some of them calling to the others, some with their beady eyes fixed on some distant grub or worm. But there was no breeze, and the birds didn't call, and the vivid image that had been alive not moments before stilled.

He lay back, letting the huge, soft pillows swallow his head. He wished he could savour the moment, prolong the dream somehow. But he knew that the moment he climbed from the bed, he would wake, and the memories of the place would fade.

The blankets were soft and warm and they smelled of the outside, and through the window in front of the bed, only the tops of trees and a glorious, blue sky could be seen.

The sun was low in the sky and birds sang. Real birds, this time, of that he was sure.

A tassled rope hung beside the bed and he knew immediately its purpose. If he pulled it, perhaps a butler would come, or a maid. He had seen them before in another life. His old life. His real life. But for now, he would enjoy the dream. Perhaps he was a lord, or a squire, like in the old days. Maybe, if he stood and peered through the window, he might see gardeners tending his beds. There might be an army of servants working downstairs, cooks, assistant cooks, a housekeeper with maids, hall boys, underbutlers, footmen, all of whom waited for his next command.

He sat up in bed, resting his head against the soft, quilted headboard. Briefly, he thought of his own bed, his real bed in real life – an old, iron frame that was chipped and scratched and squeaked when he moved. But he couldn't think of that now. He couldn't risk letting this dream slip away.

It was as he sat up that he realised something. Something truly odd. The fresh air licked at his bare chest. He lifted the blankets and the sheets, and...

"Oh God," he said aloud, searching the room for his clothes. But he found no sign of them, his new suit, the one Mrs Lavender had paid for, and the shirt and the shoes.

It was okay, he told himself. Maybe they would come to dress him. A valet, perhaps, who would lay the day's clothes out for him, and then he could go down to breakfast. He wondered what delights would be in store for him – bacon, maybe, and sausages, black pudding and tomatoes, fresh bread and cold butter.

Not porridge. Anything but the lumpy porridge that he was used to.

"How are you feeling?" a voice said.

But it wasn't a man's voice and they hadn't used a suffix, such as m'lord, or sir. In fact, the tone had hardly been subservient at all. It had been rich, smooth, and creamy, and...

"Rose?" he said, as she pushed the door closed behind her.

Aware of his nakedness, he pulled the blankets to his chest. She placed a glass of water on the bedside table and then perched on the edge of the bed.

"You gave us quite a fright."

"A fright?"

"You fell," she told him, and the image of that white tablecloth slipping from the table, dragging with it the glasses, the candelabra, and the cutlery came to mind.

A pang of utter regret followed and snuffed his dream as his father used to snuff his cigarettes.

"The wine," he said, narrating his memory as it revealed itself. "How long—"

"Most of the day," she said, knowing what he was going to ask.

"And my clothes?"

"I've laundered them. I'll find you something fresh while they dry, don't worry."

She had changed from that decadent dress she had been wearing into her plain frock. As glamorous as those pretty dresses made her look, he preferred her in the frocks. Perhaps because she wasn't so out of reach.

"But who undressed me?"

"I did," she replied as if the question had been daft. "You couldn't do it on your own, could you? You could barely walk."

He found himself tongue-tied at the prospect of her seeing him unclothed.

"I'm sorry if I ruined the dinner party."

"What does a man not do?" she asked, and he realised immediately.

"Apologise?" he said, and she nodded. "And your ma? Is she upset?"

"Upset? No."

"But she's disappointed?" he asked, and she nodded slightly.

"It's nothing that a little more practice won't overcome."

"Practice? You mean, we have to do this again?"

"Of course," she replied. "Mother says we have to do this again and again until you are ready. She said that she cannot let a student of hers into the big, wide world in such a state of unpreparedness."

"It was the wine," he said. "I was doing well. I'm sure of it. I did everything right."

"You didn't finish the evening," she told him. "We didn't even eat."

She reached forward and touched his bare skin, letting her delicate finger trace the outline of his shoulder.

"You're strong," she said. "It'll come. In time." Her fingers tugged at the blankets, and he released them from his grip, allowing her to explore his chest. She tugged at those fine hairs that had been growing there these past few years, like a field of crops, secretly inching their way from the soil until one day they were ready for harvest as if they had appeared overnight. "This is not the body of a man destined to sit at a desk."

He said nothing.

"Do you want to sit at a desk?" she asked, and her fingers ventured beneath the covers, following the crop to his stomach. He held his breath as she circled his belly button, tantalising.

Awakening.

The stirring he had felt that time. It was real now. Unrestrained, and...

She held him.

"I think you are destined for great things, John Stow," she said.

"Am I?" he said, aware of how feeble he sounded.

She removed her hand and studied his curious gaze as she

unbuttoned her frock, slowly. One by one, the buttons popped open, and inch by inch, her soft, creamy, white flesh was revealed. She took his hand and nuzzled his fist until it opened like a spring flower, before sliding it into the opening in her dress, closing his fingers around her, and squeezing them tight.

He groaned a little at the touch, at the shock, and at the taboo, and then writhed as once more she took him in her hand.

"Oh yes," she said. "I think you are destined for great things indeed."

CHAPTER THIRTY-ONE
March 29, 2024

It was late by the time they were back on the road. They rode in silence, which would have usually suited Charles as he could have enjoyed the Wolds whilst mulling over the investigation and his daughter's predicament.

But the silence had a cold edge to it. Something unsaid but tangible nonetheless.

"Ready when you are," he said, and she glanced his way briefly, before staring back out of the window. "Suit yourself."

"You know you can be a right pig, sometimes, guv?"

"Aye, I know that," he said.

"You always think you know better, don't you?"

"One of my flaws, of which I have many."

"Just because you're older and you have more experience."

"I know," he said. "I'm afraid it's one of those traits you always tell yourself you'll never adopt, but it just kind of happens. You get old and suddenly you think you know better."

"Can you stop being so…"

"So what?"

"Accommodating," she said. "So bloody agreeable."

"Ah, I see."

"If you didn't want to ask her about the nineteen-seventy-one complaint, then why did you tell me we would talk about it?"

"Well, I had planned to—"

"You just skipped over it, guv. Right when I thought you were going to ask her, you just told her not to leave the country."

"And you would have asked would you?"

"Bloody right, I would have."

"You would have let her know that we knew about the complaint from all those years ago so that when we go back to her, she can have an explanation ready for us?"

"Eh?"

"Well, would you?"

"I'm not following?"

"You don't think we're done with her, do you?"

"I don't know," she replied. "I just assumed that we left because there was nothing left to say."

"Ah right, and the first thing you do is give me the cold shoulder based on an assumption, Devon? An assumption?"

"Well you did say that we'd talk to her about—"

"Aye, and we will. But not yet. Maybe if she hadn't have lied, then I would have broached the topic. But as it stands, we have her alibi to check out."

"The pub?"

"Aye, get Forsythe on the blower, will you?"

She fumbled with her phone and then set the call to loudspeaker.

"Sergeant Devon," Forsythe said when he answered the call, "how's it going with the old man?"

"It's going very well thanks, Forsythe," Charles called out and then waited for the silence, which would then be followed by a lame excuse.

"Oh sorry, guv," he said. "I didn't think—"

"No, you didn't," Charles told him. "Listen, I need you to talk to your landlord at the George and Dragon. Joanne Childs has said she was in there alone during the time the murder took place. Can you just corroborate that, young man?"

"No problem, guv," he replied. "And listen, I didn't mean–"

"I know exactly what you meant, Forsythe. Lucky for you I'm not easily offended, eh?"

"Thanks, guv."

"How long?"

"Two minutes?" Forsythe said.

"Make it one," Charles said, then nodded for Devon to end the call.

"Listen, guv, I'm sorry. I shouldn't have jumped to conclusions," Devon said. "I should have known you would have a plan."

"There's nothing wrong with jumping to conclusions. Instinct is fine, Devon. We have that for a reason. But where I'm concerned, you should know me by now. I'm not out to further my career. I'm not out to get anybody. I just want to live a quiet life, surrounded by good people, until one day I can curl up and die, knowing that the people I love, and that includes you, Devon, are happy and safe. That's all I want."

"Thanks, guv," she said shyly, and her phone began to vibrate in her hand.

"Better get that."

"Guv?" Forsythe said.

"That was quick. What, do you have a hotline?"

"You said to hurry, so I did," Forsythe explained. "Turns out he was working the bar on Wednesday. Said something about his staff being on holiday."

Charles and Devon exchanged glances and he hoped that she was thinking what he was.

"Don't tell me, he doesn't remember seeing Joanne Childs?"

"Hasn't seen her for two weeks," Forsythe said.

"Oh, so she does actually go in there, then. It wasn't an outright lie?"

"Apparently, guv," Forsythe said. "Last time he saw her, she was with some woman. A businesswoman or something. Hasn't seen her since. He said he'd talk to his other bar staff in case they've seen her at any point."

"No need," Charles said. "Listen, are you with Constable Chalk?"

"I am, guv. She's sitting right here."

"Get us on loudspeaker, will you?" Charles asked, and the background noise suddenly shifted. "You both there?"

"We are," Chalk said, her voice loud and clear.

"Good, build me a file on Joanne Childs, will you? I want her phone records, financial records, medical records, whatever you can get."

"Do you think she's up to something, guv?"

"She's telling lies, Chalk. That's never a good sign," he told her. "From where I'm sitting, Joanne Childs had access to the house, found the body, wiped the place clean, and even knows how to lower the chandeliers. Now we learn that not only did she make a complaint against the family all those years ago, but she lied to us about her alibi. I've given her the benefit of the doubt until now, but I'm afraid my generosity has run thin."

"When are we bringing her in, guv?" Chalk asked, and Devon peered across at him, expecting him to turn the car around.

"It's late now. If we bring her in, we'll have twenty-four hours. I'm not wasting precious time while we build a case. Devon and I will pay her a visit first thing in the morning. If she still chooses to lie, then I'll bring her in."

"Got it, guv," Chalk said.

"Good," Charles said. "Get me anything you can on her. Anything at all. It's time she told us where she really was on Wednesday, and what really happened in that bedroom back in the seventies."

CHAPTER THIRTY-TWO
August 5, 1973

If he had thought that simply waking in the room had been a dream, then to witness Rose writhing above him, lost in a whole another world, as bare as the day she had been born, must have been something far beyond the imaginary world of sleep.

They were connected yet free. The passion was shared yet each of them occupied some other land, some other place, coming together at those times when he held her, only to be shoved away in her pursuit of a sensation that only she could find and only he could provide.

Her body was soft yet firm. Her skin was perfect yet adorned by freckles that did little to taint the perfection. Her hair, loose now, hung in great curls from her shoulders, beneath which her breasts danced and teased. He gripped her thighs for fear of her falling, such was the ferocity of her bucking, like a wild horse, tethered to a hitching post.

She was an ocean, powerfully untamed. Her waves rose to great heights, her body tightened and stretched, and her face, that beautiful face, was pained to the point of pleasure, before dipping into one of those great, stormy troughs, and the cycle began over.

Sweat formed on her brow, on her chest, and on her

arms, and she leaned on him, pinning him to the bed as the storm began another surge. Each surge was greater than before and he saw her as fluid as the water, frothing and tempestuous, dominating the tides yet riding the free winds toward ecstasy. He felt her harden inside and buck at his touch. She leaned into him, wrapping her arms around him as the last of those great waves rose to unseen heights. Her body pressed against his, and he writhed, groping and touching, and savouring the overwhelming feeling that surged through his body.

And with a cry, she rode that crest, seeming to hover over him in a state of absoluteness. Until at last, the wave was swallowed by the ocean, and crashed down, taking with it every ounce of his energy.

He couldn't recall how long they had stayed like that. The moment would live in perpetuity inside his mind. Her face was buried in the crook of his neck, and he felt the tension she had stirred dissipate. It was as if he had lived his full fifteen years with a weight hanging from his naval, which now had been untied. Now it had been freed.

She rolled off into a crumpled heap beside him, and as much as he wanted to roll over, to smooth the hair from her face, to caress her milk-white arms, and to trace the outlines of those wonderful breasts, he couldn't. It was as if he was still pinned beneath her weight. Bound there to be used at her will for eternity. To live in that dream world for the remainder of his days. That cool breeze glanced over his body, finding those parts of him that still glistened with sweat and their fluids combined.

But all dreams must come to an end eventually.

"Your education is over," a voice said, new yet familiar, and he sat up in a hurry to find Mrs Lavender standing not six feet from the bed. "You will leave and never return to this house, John Stow."

He reached for the blankets but Rose had tugged them from

the bed, tossing them to the floor, so he covered himself with his hands.

"Over?" he said. "But I haven't done my exams."

"I cannot teach you now," she said, and he turned to Rose. She lay exhausted, a wry smile on her pretty face as if she had known all along the outcome.

"But I didn't mean to..." he began. "It wasn't my fault."

"You were lured by temptation," she said. "You are not the first man to have been so, and you will not be the last. That I do know. But I cannot have you here, not anymore. Now leave."

"But my clothes," he said.

"Do not belong to you," she replied before he could finish.

"But I can't—"

"You recall the first day of your education?" she asked. "By which I am not referring to your first day in the village schoolhouse. I mean your first day here. You do recall it?"

"I do," he said softly.

"And do you recall your response when I asked to what lengths you would go to just for a kiss from my sweet Rose?"

He laughed nervously, remembering the day as clear as the skin on Rose's slender shoulders.

"Yes," he said.

"Then go," she told him. "Go and find your way home. It'll be dark soon."

"But I can't. Not like this. What if somebody sees me?"

"Then you should be quick about it, John Stow," she said.

He climbed from the bed, his legs trembling from his time with Rose, his first time, and the fear that Mrs Lavender commanded. He peered back at Rose, who lay on her side, resting her head on one hand, unabashed by her nudity.

"You could have been a great man, John Stow. You had an opportunity like no other. But let me ask you this," Mrs Lavender said, and he stopped in the doorway to look at her one last time. "Was she worth losing your education for?"

He stared at Rose, with her curls barely covering her chest and her arm laid across her body like a sleeping snake atop a rock smoothed by the ocean.

"Yes," he said to Mrs Lavender, though kept his eyes firmly on Rose's. "There's not a thing I wouldn't do for your daughter, ma'am. Not a single thing."

CHAPTER THIRTY-THREE

March 30, 2024

"Are we going in, guv?" Devon asked.

They were parked a few doors down from Joanne Childs' cottage and Charles was going over the facts in his mind.

"Not just yet," he replied, offering little else to ease ambition.

His phone rang through the car speakers and the little screen displayed green and red buttons. He hit the green button.

"Forsythe?" he said.

"Guv," Forsythe replied. "We've been through it all. The warrant came through last night and we've been through her phone bills, bank statements, anything we could get our hands on."

"And?" Charles said.

"Nothing, guv. Nothing concrete anyway. We're still matching up the phone numbers she's called recently, but it's just family."

"What about two weeks ago when the landlord said he saw her in the pub?"

"Checked that. Nothing."

"No secret text messages?"

"Nothing. Not a thing."

"What about her bank statement?" Devon asked. "Anything at all?"

"No luck there either," Chalk said. "She's doing the part-time work and claiming benefits."

"But she pays bills, I imagine."

"She does, guv," she said, and he heard her lift the sheet of paper and slap it down as if she had flipped it over. "But there's nothing untoward in here. She hasn't paid anything out and hasn't received anything but what she earns."

"Any card payments to the pub for last Wednesday?"

"Not for last Wednesday. But there is one for two weeks ago," she replied.

"Well, that's something, at least. Medical history?"

"Couldn't get it, guv. Not in time, anyway."

"Fair enough," he said, knowing that such information was extremely difficult to get with far more certainty than they had. "So what do we have?"

"Everything but a motive, guv," Chalk said. "We can place her there to find the body, she's lied about her whereabouts, and she had the means."

"Unless there's more to the nineteen seventy-one thing," Devon said.

"I'm not sure," Forsythe said. "I mean, she's worked there ever since. If somebody assaulted me, I wouldn't go back once, let alone every week for decades."

"She was a kid when it happened," Devon said. "We don't know the ins and outs."

"Well she's had fifty years to have done something about it," Forsythe said. "It's hardly still relevant, is it? And besides, the claim was against Bobby Garfield. Why would she off the old man fifty years later?"

"He's right," Charles said. "We'd never get that to stick without a confession of some sort."

"You're hopeful, aren't you?" Chalk said as movement caught Charles' eye.

"I am indeed," he said. "Stay close to your phones."

He hit the red button on the screen and climbed from the car, catching Joanne Childs as she was locking her front door.

"Mrs Childs," he called out, and her expression melted once more. "I wonder if we could get a moment of your time."

"Again?" she said. "I'm running late–"

"We'll drop you off when we're done," Charles said, leaving her very little room to manoeuvre. Devon climbed out of the car and opened the rear door for her, inviting her to take a seat with a sweep of her arm.

Reluctantly, Joanne climbed in and closed the door behind her.

"Sorry about this," Charles said, and with a few taps of his screen, he located the climate controls. "Warm enough?"

"Plenty, thanks," she replied. "But I am in a hurry, so could we do this while we drive?"

"Oh, I'm not sure if that's wise," he said with a little laugh. "I'm not sure if I could explain how I came to be questioning a suspect in a murder investigation whilst driving and fit it all in that little box you get on the insurance form."

"A suspect?" she said, and her eyes widened. "What? What do you mean a suspect?"

"Oh, it's just a label," he said, brushing the comment off.

"It's a label I'd rather not have, thank you very much."

"Well, perhaps we can address that then," he replied, and he turned in his seat to face her. "I've spoken to you twice now and my colleague has spoken to you twice. That's four opportunities that you've had to tell me about an incident that happened way back in nineteen seventy-one."

She closed her eyes and let her head fall forward into her hands.

"It's time to talk," Devon told her.

"She's right," Charles added. "This is your fifth opportunity. There won't be another. In fact, unless you start being honest with us, I'll drive us right back to Lincoln and we can have this conversation in a more formal environment, namely an interview room with a solicitor present."

She sat up and rubbed at her forehead then dabbed an eye with her cuff.

"Come on, Joanne. You're not going to make me drive all that way just to have a wee chat, are you? Just tell us what happened."

"It's not that easy," she blurted out. "Don't you get it? I've had to live with it my entire life. Have you any idea of what that's like? Have you any idea what it's like to see him and speak to him, knowing what he did? I can still feel his hands on me, you know?"

Charles glanced at Devon, who turned in her seat to face Joanne, and he nodded for her to take over. Sometimes, regardless of the individual, a woman's voice was needed. Sometimes, Charles thought, he was ashamed to be a man.

"Joanne," Devon said, finding a tissue in her bag and handing it to Joanne. "Joanne, who are you referring to here? Was it Hugo? Is that who touched you?"

"No," she spat, as she took the tissue. "It was Bobby. Bobby bloody Garfield. Untouchable Bobby. It was him."

"So Hugo wasn't involved?"

"Oh, he was involved," she said. "He was egging him on. He was telling him to do it. To be a man." She let her hands fall into her lap, defeated, and stared out of the window.

"Joanne, can you tell us what happened, please? It might help us here. It might help us understand who Hugo really was."

"Oh, I can tell who he really was. He was a bloody narcissist. It was all power to him. Power and money. That's all he knows. Or knew, anyway."

"It happened in one of the bedrooms. Is that right, Joanne?" Devon asked, to which she nodded, and then took a deep breath.

"I was helping my mum. Well, she had me there on the

pretence of helping, but I think it was just a way of avoiding having to pay for childcare. She used to take me with her, give me a duster and send me on my way while she did the real cleaning. Anyways, I was in one of the bedrooms when Hugo walked in. I was always told that if someone came into the room I was in, I should make myself scarce. So I did. I tried, anyway."

"He stopped you from leaving?"

"He did, yeah. Not physically. He just said I could stay and carry on," Joanne said. "Then he called Bobby in. I was a couple of years younger than Bobby. I can see him now, in all his fineries, while I was in my rags. That's what he called them, see? Hugo. He made Bobby stand there while he gave a lesson on class and hierarchy. He explained to Bobby how we were different. How I would always be a dirty little scrubber girl, and how he would always give the orders. How he would always be in charge, and that servants were there to serve. Anyways, he told Bobby to show me that he was in charge."

"He did what?"

"Told him to show me who was boss," she replied. "So Bobby did. He stepped up to me, his face was right here, it was," she said, holding the palm of her inches from her nose. "Told me to get on my hands and knees, he did. Like a dog or a horse."

"And you did?"

"What was I supposed to do? I couldn't tell them to bugger off, could I? Mum'd get the sack, wouldn't she? Then what? I'd be dragged home and bleeding flogged."

"So you got on your hands and knees?" Devon asked, to which she nodded.

"He rode me. Kept slapping my backside and I had to crawl around the room with his fat arse on my back."

"Do you mind me asking what Hugo was doing while this was happening?" Charles asked.

"Oh, he was just standing there by the door at first. I s'pose he left at some point, because when Bobby finally got off and rolled me onto my back, he weren't there no longer." She quietened and the bitterness faded from her voice. "That's when Bobby knelt on me. Pinned me down, like. On my shoulders, see."

"I see," Devon said, and Joanne sighed.

"Anyway, you can imagine what happened next. He was a boy going through puberty. He was curious, and then all of a sudden he had this power. So he used it."

"He raped you?" Devon said.

"No, no. nothing like that. I doubt he even knew what to do," she said. "He just felt me. All over, like. Hard he was. Rough, if you know what I mean? Not nice at all. Squeezing me, and prodding me, and making me…" She stopped and closed her eyes. "He made me touch him, he did. His…thing, you know?"

Devon glanced across at Charles, but her expression was unreadable.

"Anyway, it didn't go on for long. When it was over, he just stood up, buttoned his trousers, and told me to clean the place up."

A silence hung in the air and Charles faced forward, out of shame more than any other reason.

"Did you tell your mother?" Devon asked.

"God no. Not at first, anyway. No, I didn't know what to do, so I just kept quiet. I told a girl at school what had happened, and she must have told her mum, see? Next thing you know, the local policeman came to the school. Took me into a room, he did, and made me tell him what happened. Next thing I know, my mum was involved, and she was raging."

"At Bobby?"

"No, at me. Called me a little slut and all sorts."

"She did what?"

"Yeah," she said, nodding at the sheer indecency of it all. "Said I provoked him and that if she lost her position there, she'd have to send me away. So I had to tell the policeman I'd made it up. That we were playing, and that he hadn't done anything."

"Joanne, that's awful," Devon said. "Truly awful."

"Yeah well. True what he said, though isn't it? Men like that will always be the ones in control."

"But if you don't mind me asking," Charles said. "Why did you go to work there? You were just a kid when this happened. But you went back as an adult and you worked there for decades."

"I know," she said. "And I don't really have an answer for it, except that after a while, if you're told that something is your fault for long enough, you kind of begin to believe it." She stared at him in the rear-view mirror. "Believe it long enough and the truth just kind of fades away, don't it?"

It was a sad story to have heard but one that Charles knew would resonate with hundreds or even thousands of people who had endured similar circumstances.

"This puts me in a very difficult position, Joanne. As harrowing as your story is, the fact remains that we're here to investigate a murder, not a sexual assault claim that took place fifty years ago."

"Guv?" Devon said.

"I'm sorry, but it's true, and I'm sure the circumstances will be taken into consideration. In fact, I'll make sure they are. But, Joanne, can I ask you to see this from my perspective for a moment? I have a dead body in a house to which you are a key holder. That's what we call opportunity. He was hanging from a pulley system that you know how to operate. We call that having means. And now we have this."

"Motive?" she said, nodding. "Why do you think I kept quiet about it? Was hoping you wouldn't bring it up, if I'm honest."

"Add to that the fact that you cleaned the house from top to bottom, and then you lied about being in the pub on Wednesday, Joanne—"

"I was—"

"We've spoken to the landlord," Charles said. "I have no choice but to arrest you on suspicion of murder."

"Arrest me?"

"Aye, the evidence is damning, Joanne. If you weren't at the house, then where were you?"

"It doesn't matter where I was. You should be talking to Bobby bloody Garfield. He's the one who saw him last."

"And you saw Bobby, did you?"

"No, I didn't see him. But there were two glasses from the squire's study in the kitchen. Nobody else goes in there."

Charles looked across at Devon who acknowledged the point with a nod.

"The thing is, Joanne, whether Bobby was there or not doesn't matter right now. Right now, I want to know where *you* were. It's important, love. If you can't tell me where you were, then I'm going to have no alternative but to arrest you."

She said nothing, and again she closed her eyes and controlled her breathing.

But it was a small vibration that disturbed the moment, and she pulled her phone from her handbag. She stared at the screen for a moment and then handed it to Charles.

"You want to know where I was," she said. "Talk to her. She'll tell you."

CHAPTER THIRTY-FOUR
August 5, 1973

The world could be a cruel and heartless place. If it wasn't bad enough that humans could be capable of such wickedness, fate and destiny were equally as brutal.

It was as if the skies had seen his naked form standing atop the steps of The Grange and had at that moment decided to punish him. The blue sky he had seen not an hour before through the bedroom window seemed to slip from view, and in its vacuous wake, great brooding storm clouds came together. The breeze he had felt lick at his sweat, their sweat, had grown since, and the elms that lined the grounds swayed as if in warning of the gale to come.

He was grateful for The Grange's location. The old manor house, once majestic and rich was lonely and secluded, and the lane that it graced was devoid of traffic. He ran at first until the stones had torn the soles of his feet, and then he limped towards the break in the hedge, where he could make use of the soft grass beneath his feet.

Twice he had to drop into the dyke at the side of the road, pressing himself flat against the bank while a Ford passed and then a farm truck trundled by.

When he reached that break in the hedge, where two fields met and the dykes interlinked to drain the land of water, he stopped for a moment to inspect his feet. He considered his route home and where the chances of passing others might be. The Wolds were, of course, notorious for hikers and dog walkers, but the hour was late, and he was hopeful not to come by any.

The grass was soft underfoot in comparison to the lane and he made good progress. The army of heavy clouds that had started to form when he left The Grange, had begun to release their soldiers. Small droplets at first formed a sheen across his body. But now he was deep into the hills with a view of the farm and the distant village, those droplets grew large and heavy and stung his skin, and the wind that before had merely swayed the treetops now surged across the land like a swarm of locusts devouring the landscape. Branches of trees that had died now cracked and fell. Debris from the not-so-distant winter was carted across the open fields, and it seemed that the blood beneath John's skin had retreated, leaving him pale, shivering with cold, and questioning his tenacity to finish the journey.

But the answer to that question became abundantly clear when he rounded a corner and found three bodies sheltering beneath an oak.

"Stow?" the first voice said. "No. It can't be."

John stopped in his tracks, covering his modesty with his hands.

"It is," another said. "It's bloody well John Stow."

They emerged from their shelter, quite unable to contain their laughter. Mason was crying at what he saw and Pepper was so intrigued that he seemed to study John's body with fascination.

And Bobby Garfield simply strode towards him, his eyes never leaving John's.

"Well, well, well," he said. "Out for a stroll, Stow, are we?"

"Bugger off, Garfield," he said, as they circled him like hyenas.

With the flat of his hand, Mason slapped at John's buttock,

and he grimaced at the sting that followed. He shivered and he was unable to wipe the rain from his eyes for fear of revealing himself.

"You owe me," Garfield said.

"I owe you nothing," he replied, hearing the fear in his own voice.

"Oh, I think you do," Garfield told him. "For that time you hit me. You never even apologised. And it's a timely meeting, too. I'm off tomorrow."

"Off where?" John said and winced at the next slap that gave him a matching pair of burning buttocks.

"I'm on my way," Garfield told him. "I'm out of here. Father wants me to have a career. He wants me to take over the estate, of course, but said I needed some experience."

"How wonderful," John said. "For us, anyway."

Garfield eyed him curiously.

"What are you even doing?" he asked him. "What, are you sick in the head or something? Is this how you get your kicks?"

"What? No."

"My dad told me about people like you. Exposing yourself to young boys like us," Garfield said. "What do you say, boys? Think he's one of them perverts?"

"Yeah, he has to be," Pepper said. "He was probably just waiting for some poor girl to come along so he can show them his tallywacker."

"I think you're right," Garfield said. "Where have you been then, Stow? Where are your clothes?"

"At home," he said.

"So you just happen to be out here without your clothes?"

"Look, I told you to bugger off and I meant it."

"You're a pervert," he said.

"Here, I'll bet it was him who did that young girl a few years ago. One of the Lavender girls. You remember?"

Garfield's eyes widened at the idea and his face twisted in repulsion.

"Polly Lavender," he said. "I remember her. It was that bloke who took the blame though, wasn't it? Jimmy Sutherland. My dad still talks about him and how he got away. He told me once what he'd do if he ever found him."

"Is that right?" John said. "And what was that?"

Garfield stepped closer so his face was just inches from John's.

"He would set the dogs on him. Have them tear him apart. He said he'd make sure they tore his balls off before he lost consciousness. You know? So he could really feel the pain where it mattered."

"Sounds charming," John said. "I didn't realise your dad had such an imagination."

"Oh, he does," Garfield replied. "But not nearly as good as mine." He lashed out and his fist connected with John's nose, forcing him to stagger back into the embrace of Mason, who held him upright and then shoved him forward. John put his hands out to prevent himself from colliding with Garfield, who grabbed his opportunity and took hold of John's most intimate of parts.

John froze and Garfield stared at him. In the three years since they had last spoken, he had filled out. But unlike John, whose body had matured and hardened through work on the farm, Garfield's, it seemed, had filled out through good eating and scant exercise.

But his hands were strong and held John tightly.

"What do you think, boys? Should I just tear them off?"

"Yeah, rip them off. Feed them to the dogs," Mason said. "At least he wouldn't be able to hurt anybody else."

"Yeah, I reckon old Mrs Lavender, as mad as she is, would be pleased," Pepper said. "Here, maybe we could post them through her letterbox?"

"No," John said. "Just leave me alone, will you?"

The cold had begun to take its toll on John's body now and he shook uncontrollably, to the point that he feared Garfield might actually do some damage simply by holding onto him as he did.

"How do feel about being dogs, boys?" Garfield said, to which John sensed their pleasure, and his two counterparts began to bark and howl like wolves. "I'll give you a ten-second head start."

"Excuse me?"

"Ten," Garfield said, and his grip on John relaxed. "Nine..."

John shoved him out of the way and took to his feet. There was an easy mile before him but the ground was soft underfoot. He heard them behind him, cackling, laughing, barking, and howling, and they closed in with ease, grabbing at his buttocks, and his arms, and eventually tripping him over so that he stumbled and fell to the ground.

There was barely even time to recover when the blows began to rain down on him. Kicks and punches landed like rain on his head, his arms, his torso, his legs, and, of course, those parts of him that Rose had awakened. He curled into a ball, as tightly as he could, but a kick to his back caused him to stretch out in pain, leaving him wide open for the final blow, which came in the form of Garfield's right boot landing directly between John's legs.

―――

How long he lay there, John didn't know. His body had even numbed to the cold and no longer shivered and trembled. His fingers were swollen but not broken, his arms ached from the beatings and the parts of him that Rose had devoured had swelled to twice their normal size.

The irony taste of blood sat at the back of his throat and one of his eyes was almost impossible to open. He crawled at first, no longer caring if he was discovered by a hiker. Slowly and tentatively, he made his way down the hill towards the sprawling farm that he called home. The darkness had fallen while he had slumbered and only his familiarity with the path and the light in the kitchen window guided him.

It was an hour or more before he was on Terry's land, where he felt safe for the first time that afternoon, and another half an hour passed while he climbed to his feet and slowly picked his way along the dyke to the courtyard, where the stony ground formed an impassible barrier. He dropped to his knees, doing everything he could to restrain the tears that burned in his eyes. He wanted to call out, but what would he say? He wanted to be held and to be nurtured in a soft, warm bed. Not the big bed he had shared with Rose, but his bed. The little, iron-framed single bed with the lumpy pillow. That was all he wanted. He found a spot beside the granary that was out of the wind and tucked his knees to his chest. He could sleep there and maybe he wouldn't wake. Maybe he would slip away as his father had. Maybe he wouldn't ever have to explain his predicament to a single soul.

Maybe Rose would hear of the episode and be haunted by her conscience or guilt?

The back door opened and light spilled from the doorway onto the courtyard. Voices filled the night, one of them familiar and one of them recognisable, but he couldn't quite place it.

And then he watched from the shadows, just as Mrs Lavender often had, as two men walked the side of the house.

"You'll be sure to tell him," the first man said without stopping.

"Oh aye," Terry replied. "That I will. He'll be glad to hear it, I'm sure. Though how his mother feels about it is a different story."

"She'll come around," the man said, as a car door opened and the interior light of a gleaming Jaguar lit the front of the house. "She'll have to if she wants him to make something of himself."

The car door closed and the big engine fired up. Headlights lit the lane and then retreated, leaving only Terry's heavy boot steps on the gravel.

"Terry," John called out from his place of sanctuary.

"John? That you?" He followed the sound of John's voice and found him with ease. But the look on his face was one of absolute horror. "What the devil have you done, boy?"

"I need help."

"I'll say you do."

"Is Ma awake?"

"She is," Terry said. "We're going up soon. She's been waiting all evening for you. You've caused one hell of a stir, John. I won't lie."

"I can explain," he said. "I just need help getting inside."

Terry mulled it over and glanced back at the house before removing his jacket and wrapping it around John's shoulders.

"Wait here. You hear me? Wait. I'll be out when I can."

He stood and John felt the warmth that the jacket offered and groaned in delight. Terry's heavy boots disappeared into the house and the door slammed, leaving John alone again, thinking of every conceivable reason he could give for his position and realising how wildly they would be perceived.

The moon had passed by at least a few degrees by the time Terry returned, making a show of doing his rounds.

"You go on up, Mary," he called out. "I'll be right there."

John hadn't heard the response, but when Terry came to him and dropped to a crouch, he presumed he had heard his mother acknowledge his call.

"Now then," he said, and with one arm beneath John's arms and the other under his legs, he raised him from the ground as easy as if he was plucking the third-born lamb from a birthing pen. He set John down in one of the kitchen chairs and set about filling a bowl with water.

"Had your ma scared out of her wits, you did, John."

"I didn't mean to," John replied. "It was never my intention to cause her upset."

At the sink, Terry turned and gave him that look he saved for when John phrased his sentences as he had been taught by Mrs Lavender.

He took the bowl from the sink, and placed it on the kitchen table, then proceeded to plunge an old cloth into the water and dabbed at John's wounds.

"Where does it hurt most?" he asked, to which John covered himself with the jacket and raised his foot.

"They're terribly sore," he said, and Terry apprised them before cleaning the filth from the hundreds of tiny cuts.

"Anything else?"

"Bruises, I think," John said, and he saw Terry glance down at his genitals and then look away respectfully.

"If the swelling don't go down, you'll have to see a doctor. If it hurts to pass water, then say something."

"What about Ma?" John said. "What do I say to her?"

"Can't you tell her the truth?" John shied from answering and Terry caught his cowering expression. He screwed the cloth into a ball and dropped it into the water. "What happened, John?"

"I can't say," he replied.

"Well, if you want my help, then you'll say something. You go missing for half a day, the bally solicitor tells us that Mrs Lavender no longer feels she can give you an education, and now you turn up, naked as the day you were born and covered in bruises." He glanced at the doorway and then lowered his voice to a hiss. "If you want my help, John, then I need to know."

John studied his face for signs of sincerity, then saw it and sighed.

"It was Rose..." he began, then heard his cowardly words and stopped himself. "Rose and I, we did things. Things we ought not to have done."

"All right," Terry said. "Suppose she kicked you out, did she?"

"Mrs Lavender?"

"Well, I doubt it was her daughter, John."

"Yes, she did," John said. "She caught us and threw me out

with no clothes. She said they didn't belong to me so I was to walk home naked."

"Bit harsh," Terry grumbled.

"No. Not really," John said, and he swelled with pride at the courage he had found. "I did something wrong. I should have fought the temptation."

"Aye, you should have. But we are all human, John. You're a man now. A red-blooded man." He looked John up and down. "What about all of this?"

"The bruises, you mean?" John said, buying time to construct an explanation, but he found only the truth. "I met Bobby Garfield and his mates on the way home."

"They did this?"

"They said I was probably a pervert."

"What?"

"And that's why I was out on the hills with no clothes on."

"Why didn't you tell them the truth, for God's sake?"

"What, and have them tell the village that Rose isn't virtuous? She would never forgive me. Her life would be ruined. She'd have to move away."

Terry listened in apparent awe.

"You let them think you were a pervert to save Mrs Lavender's daughter from ruin?" he said, to which John simply nodded. "Well, John, you surprise me. Whatever the old girl taught you, it's done you well, son."

John looked away in shame.

"Terry?" he said, as his stepfather reached for his other foot to begin dabbing at the wounds. "They said something about Polly Lavender." Terry stopped his dabbing and turned his face away. "Was that who that man had hurt? Jimmy Sutherland? The man we were looking for that time?"

"None of our business is what it is, John," Terry said, resuming his cleanup operation with renewed vigour.

"They said that it was probably me who did it and not Jimmy Sutherland."

"You what?"

"They said the squire should set the dogs on me. Have them tear my..." He gestured at his groin. "They won't do that, will they?"

Once more, Terry tossed the cloth into the bowl of water and he stood to pace over to the shelf near the back door, from where he retrieved an envelope and then glanced back at John as if he was unsure of something. It clearly pained Terry to deliver whatever news the envelope held, but he did so anyway. He pulled a seat from beneath the table and sat down opposite John.

"She must have called him the moment you left," he began. "Mr Fisher, I mean. Came straight away, he did. Told us to give you this."

Terry held out the envelope for John to take, and he saw it had been opened.

"What does it say?" John asked.

"You can read, can't you? Better than we can too, no doubt."

John slid the letter from the envelope and then pulled the lamp closer. The first paragraph explained that due to unacceptable behaviour, John's education with Mrs Lavender was to cease with immediate effect.

He made it to the second line of the second paragraph when he looked up at Terry.

"I'm to go to Lincoln?" he said, to which Terry nodded.

"He said you can finish your exams there in your new position," Terry told him. "As an apprentice lawyer."

"An apprentice lawyer?" John said, staring at the letter dumbfounded. "Me?"

"Your ma wasn't going to tell you," Terry said. "Don't want you to go."

"And you?" John asked. "What do you think?"

"I think she's right to want you close," Terry explained. "But in light of today, I think perhaps you should go, John."

"I'm to run away?" John said.

"It's for the best," Terry told him. "I think the further you are from Bobby Garfield, the better, don't you?"

CHAPTER THIRTY-FIVE
March 30, 2024

They watched as Joanne Childs hurried back to her house, opened the front door, and went inside. She glanced back at them briefly before wiping her eyes and slamming the door.

"Call the team, will you, Devon?" Charles said and then rubbed his head to rid the images of Joanne's story from his mind.

"Chalk, it's me," Devon said. "You're on loudspeaker. Is Forsythe with you?"

"He is, yeah," she replied, and then she set her phone to loudspeaker so they could talk as a foursome.

"Have we got her?" Forsythe asked. "Should I book her a room downstairs?"

"No," Charles said and then sighed. "We let her go."

"What? Why?"

"Because it wasn't her," Charles said. "And that's typically what we do when somebody cannot be guilty of a crime."

"But I thought we were sure. We had it all lined up."

"We did," he replied. "But she couldn't have been in two places at once. It transpires that Joanne Childs lied to us about her whereabouts because she was working."

"So what? Why didn't she just tell us?"

"She's claiming benefits," Chalk said.

"Bingo," Charles told her, and he heard Forsythe slap his hands on the desk. "Her boss called while she was sitting in the back of my car."

"And I suppose she corroborated the story?"

"She can provide CCTV of her as well."

"Brilliant," Chalk said.

"Not for her," Devon said. "She was calling to see why Joanne wasn't at work, and subsequently, to fire her."

"She lost her job? Well, that'll teach her for signing on and working, won't it?"

"Whilst I sympathise with your beliefs in the welfare system, Chalk," Charles said, "we're not investigating fraudulent benefits claims. We're investigating a murder, and Joanne Childs losing her job has just cost us a valuable witness."

"Sorry, guv?"

"Play the long game, Chalk. She's just lost a large part of her income. Do you think she'd be happy to give evidence now? Because I don't. In fact, I doubt if she'd give us the time of day if we asked. Do you see what I'm saying?"

"I do, guv," she replied. "So what now?"

"Bobby Garfield," Charles said. "Joanne seems to think he had been there at some point. She said that only he ever went into the study with his dad and that's why there were two glasses."

"Two glasses that she conveniently didn't clean?" Chalk said. "Sounds like a set-up to me."

"Be that as it may," Charles said. "Forsythe, how did we get on with the CCTV? Do we have a black Audi?"

"We've got black cars, guv, but I'd need a specialist to confirm the make and model."

"Well, line it up, then," Charles told him. "Is there anything that could be an Audi?"

"Yes, there is, but not on the Wednesday. It passed through the previous day around four p.m. Black saloon car, four doors, single occupant. The image is too blurry for details. No return trip, not on that route, anyway."

"Well, let's run with it," Charles said. "Believe me, after what Joanne Childs just told us about him, we can be pretty sure that he'll have something else to hide. Men like that don't change. They just get smarter."

"I'll get it confirmed, guv," Forsythe said. "Are we focusing on him now?"

"I'd say he's all we have. Press CSI for some kind of data on the glasses, will you? Fingerprints, DNA, or preferably both. We'll come at this from two directions – the car and the glass. Maybe that will convince him to explain why he lied to us."

"Will do, guv," he replied. "Are you both coming back now?"

"Not just yet. While we're out here, I might take a wee look around at the house. I want to get a feel for Hugo Garfield and his many enemies. I think that his secrets died with him," Charles said. "The question is, which one of them pertains to his murder?"

―――

The manor house was empty but not quite quiet. It was as if the old place was alive somehow; its workings, its structure, and history all created a sense of life, of being.

"If walls could speak, eh?" he said to Devon in the hallway. "They must have seen a thing or two."

"I wonder if they'd prefer to forget them though, guv. Can you imagine being a servant back in the day? In a place like this, I mean? Downstairs you've got people who could barely afford to live all serving a family who by all accounts thrived on the blood and sweat of others."

"Ah, it wasn't all that bad," Charles told her. "Not in every house, I mean. I mean, sure this wasn't the only place like that. But don't be disheartened, Devon. Not every man who employed others was like Hugo or Bobby Garfield. There were some good people, too. Good employers. And the people were grateful not just for the jobs, but for the roofs over their heads."

"I think I'd find it hard to bow and scrape, guv," she said.

"Oh, we all bow and scrape at some point in our lives. We all report to somebody, don't we? Our wives, husbands, children, bosses…"

"God?"

"Sometimes," he said. "In a sense, anyway. He gets the final word, doesn't he? He's the one that sees everything we do."

"Do you believe that?"

"Me? I'm not sure. I think there's something in it. Maybe not God in the image that we're taught. But there's something we don't yet know. Our morals, maybe? Or our peers? We don't like to be judged, Devon. Nobody does. And we don't like the unknown. Can you honestly, hand on heart, tell me that you've never wondered what will happen when your time comes? Have you never wondered if you'll come to stand at the pearly gates to be judged? Or have you never done anything that you thought would send you to hell?"

"I'm pretty sure I'm not going to hell, guv. I'm a police officer, after all."

"I know plenty who are," he replied.

"Well, not me," she said. "But yeah, I have wondered. I think, to me anyway, God is more about the people I know. My nan for instance. I often wonder if she's looking down on me. I wonder if she sees everything I do."

"Everything? Could be embarrassing."

"She was a good woman," Devon replied with a smile. "She would know when to give me some privacy."

"Very decent of her," Charles said. "And would she object to you rifling through a dead man's possessions?"

She glanced across at him, and he held out a pair of blue latex gloves he had produced from his pocket.

"Where do you want to start?" she asked, taking the gloves.

"If you were a man like Hugo Garfield, where would you keep your secrets?"

"Not his sock drawer, guv. Anything but his underwear."

"I think he might have had a wee bit more class than that," Charles said with a laugh. "But we may as well start in his bedroom. Myself, I'm keen to see what the old place is like."

The staircase was broad enough for five or six people to walk side by side and each step was so shallow that vertical progress seemed slow as if the architect was intent on the ascender having time to enjoy the ornate ceiling mouldings or the hand-carved spindles.

The stairs split to the left and right, where a large landing gave access to various hallways and the gallery, from where the old squire, or even the butler, might have peered down to the lobby.

Most of the rooms were just that – rooms. A few of the beds had been made but most had been stripped, and in those rooms, dust had settled on the furniture. It was only the rooms in which the beds had been made ready for guests, which had been recently dusted and polished. A basket of wood had been provided beside each fireplace and old family portraits hung in various positions of prominence.

"I wonder if this was Bobby's room," Devon said, and she stared at the patterned carpet as if imagining Joanne Childs' story.

"Well, if it was, then he certainly made his escape," Charles said, as he closed a bedside drawer and opened another. "Empty."

Devon opened a free-standing wardrobe that was large enough for Charles to fit most of his possessions into, let alone just his clothes.

"Same here," she said, and so they moved to another room. "This looks more like it," she said from an open door. Charles joined her and found a four-poster bed that had been made, and a chair, on which a pair of royal blue pyjamas had been hung. A dressing gown hung from a hook on the back of the door and an old paperback book was on the bedside table. Charles opened one of the drawers.

"Here we go," he said. "Hugo's medication, I presume. This was his room, all right." He tugged the gloves tight and smiled at her. "Let's see if he was hiding anything."

They were meticulous, neat, and, despite the claims that police searches were often hostile and disrespectful, they took care to replace any items that were removed from drawers and cupboards.

But there was little to be found and Charles was reminded of the day he had been through his father's bedroom. It was not long after the funeral had taken place, and he had expected to spend hours reminiscing about little nuggets of history that he might come across.

But those nuggets were few and far between. The fact remained that, like Hugo Garfield, his bedroom had indeed just been a bedroom.

"I think we're done here," Charles said.

"Thank God for that," Devon said, stuffing the old man's socks back into a drawer. "Where next?"

Charles held the door for her and let her pass before him.

"The one room that only two people visited," he said. "Unless of course, all that was a lie."

The study was as they had left it, minus the body bag, the rope, and the smell of death.

Charles made a beeline for the leather chair behind the desk and took the weight off his feet for a moment.

"What are you doing, guv?" Devon asked.

"It's been a long day," he told her.

"It's ten past eleven," she said, and he grinned.

"I just wondered what it must be like to sit behind a desk like this, commanding your estate. The room is bigger than my lounge for God's sake."

"You don't have a My Little Pony light shade in there, too, do you?"

He laughed aloud. "No, the wife wouldn't have allowed that."

"Your wife?" she said. "You've been divorced for more than a decade, guv."

"Aye, I know. I was there, remember?"

"And you haven't changed the lights?"

"What for?"

"I mean, you must have decorated."

"Why? There's paint on the walls. That's the good thing about paint, Devon. It tends to stick to whatever you put it on."

"I know, but surely you would have updated it in ten years? I do mine every couple of years. I paint the walls, get new cushions and curtains if I fancy it."

"Every couple of years? Christ, Devon. What do you do with the old stuff?"

"Get rid of it," she said. "Give it to someone. Sell it online or something."

"And then you go and buy new stuff from a shop?"

"Yeah. It's nice to have a refresh."

"Do you think this place has ever been refreshed?"

"Never, guv," she said. "Not since King George went mad, I'd say, judging by the state of the place. I mean, who has wood-panelled walls these days? And as for the rug. Columbus could have brought that home from Persia."

"I don't think he ever visited Persia," Charles said. "Not that I know of anyway. He was too busy discovering the Americas."

"Well, one of them old explorers must have brought it back. Look at it. It's older than the house." While she rattled on about how old the rug was and how the room needed a good refresh, Charles thumbed through a stack of papers on the bookshelf nearest the desk. "I can't even imagine having to dust this place," she said, pulling a book from one of the cases and blowing onto it to create a cloud. She set it down on the desk and pulled more out. "Look at this."

"It's hard not to," he said, waving the dust away from him.

She created an eclectic stack of books, flipping through each one to see if any loose pages fell out. There were old books on landownership, farming, and even landscaping, plus newer books on plant species, genetics, and biology.

"I'll bet he didn't even read these," she said, as she flipped through the pages of the book on genetics. A single piece of paper fell out and dropped lazily to the desk. They exchanged glances and she picked it up. "It's a photo," she said, turning it over for him to see. The image was of the rear garden, where a younger Rose Garfield was crouched beside her daughter, with Hugo in the background, tending his roses.

"So he did have a heart at least," Charles said, and she continued to peruse the books. But something caught Charles' eye. A piece of headed paper. "This might be something," he said, thinking aloud, and he turned the sheet over for her to see.

"What does it say?" she replied, stooping to examine the printed letter. She reached for the light switch, then stooped again. "That doesn't make sense."

But Charles had followed her hand when she reached for the switch and now something else had caught his eye.

"What is it?"

"I don't know," he told her and then stood to examine a half-moon-shaped dent in the wall. He fingered the space and felt the chalky dust on his fingertips.

"Did CSI empty the bins?" he asked.

"I believe so, guv," she said. "Although, unsurprisingly, they haven't been through them yet."

"Ask them to prioritise it," he told her, as he collected the remaining crystal glass from the tray on the table and held it up to the dent in the wall. He looked at Devon. "It's a perfect match."

"I don't get what that means," she said.

"Neither do I. It's just something that Bobby said to me when we went to see him." He cast his eye over the paperwork and the books. "Get onto Chalk, will you? Have her arrange for this lot to be collected."

"What, all of it?" she said, horrified at the amount of work that would take.

"Yes, all of it," he said. "Every last scrap. I don't know what I'm looking for, but I know it's in here somewhere."

CHAPTER THIRTY-SIX
August 6, 1973

The bruises on his legs and arms were angry and purple, and the tiny lacerations on the soles of his feet felt like he had slept with them in a red ants' nest – and boy had they feasted.

He could live with the pain and discomfort. But the deformities would take some explaining – the swollen lip, the bruising around his eye, which he was sure would only get worse as the days passed, and, of course, his genitals, which thankfully resembled their previous state, although the area was tender to the touch, and urinating had been a somewhat delicate affair.

He stood at the door and wondered if and when he would next look back into his old room, with the old, iron-framed bed, his little cupboard, and the few possessions he could call his own. It was with a heavy heart that he closed the door behind him and ventured down the stairs, familiar with every creak and groan as a blind pianist might finger the ivories.

He took a deep breath to endure those tiny ant bites and entered the kitchen, setting his bag down beside the door. His mother didn't move a muscle. She just sat there at the kitchen table with her back to him and her head in her hands.

"It won't be forever, Ma," he explained, to which she gave no reply. "I'll be back."

"No, you won't," she said, her voice thick with tears, and he went to her, placing his hand on her shoulder. She reached up and held it, still averting her eyes. But it felt good. It was perhaps the first sign of emotion he had seen from her since the day they buried his father. "You'll make new friends. You won't be back."

"Of course I will," he said, taking the seat beside her, and again she turned away and blew her nose into a handkerchief. "I'll send money, Ma."

"I don't want your money–"

"But I'll send it anyway," he told her. "And if it goes well, then I'll send plenty." He pulled at her arm so that he might see into her eyes. "I meant it when I told you, Ma. I mean to make a go of it."

"I just don't see why you have to," she mumbled. "You've a perfectly good life here on the farm. There's nothing there that we can't give you."

"There's plenty, ma," he said. "And besides, how long is it since a Stow ventured into the great unknown, bound for glory?"

Despite his emphasis, she still found no humour in his words.

"Let him be, Mary," Terry said, from the back door. He kicked the mud from his boots and then stepped inside. On any other day, he would have removed them entirely for fear of a scolding, but this was no ordinary day. "He must go and find his way. We can't stop him."

"Well, you've changed your tune and I don't know why," she said. "You were dead against it all when Mr Fisher was here."

Terry stared at John from across the room.

"Aye, well, had time to think, haven't I?" he replied.

"Oh, done some thinking, have you? Suppose you'll be telling me next that you've been at John's bally books."

"I wondered what I would have done had I been given an opportunity the way he has," Terry said. "And I'll tell you this for nowt. If that boy goes and fails, then he tried. He'll have a home here as long as I'm alive. But if he don't go, Mary, if he stays here, then the three of us will always wonder. We'll wonder what might have been. We'll wonder who he could have been, and if, when the last lump of wood goes on the fire, he could have done better. And he could. You know that, Mary. You know he can do well. He's a mind on him, see?" He tapped at his temple with a fat index finger. "And if he don't use it to his advantage, then what really have we done for him but hold him back?"

John gave his mother's hand a squeeze. He was right, and despite the choice of words, the sentiment was powerfully articulated.

"Now then," Terry said. "I'll be in the truck when you're ready, John. Don't be long now. We've a long road ahead."

He collected John's bag and gave him a nod of support before leaving through the back door.

"He's right, Ma," John said, and she shoved herself from her seat and strode over to the dresser in which Terry had stored the envelope. She opened a drawer and removed the old biscuit tin. "No, Ma–"

"I won't hear another word on it," she said, removing a little, brown envelope which she clutched to her breast for a moment before turning to face him, steeling her jaw and holding her head high. "This was your father's. He wanted you to have it."

"What is it?" John asked.

"It's money. Not a lot, but it'll be enough to see you through if you're mindful."

"Ma, I don't need–"

"I want you to have it. Your pa wanted you to have it," she said. "And he isn't around to argue with now, is he?"

She handed him the little, brown envelope and he slid it into his pocket.

"I will be back, Ma," he told her. "I promise you that I'll be back."

She smiled and held both his hands in her own.

"That's the thing, John," she said. "I don't want you to come back. Not on my account. You want to do this then do it you will. You give it everything you've got and don't be steered by anyone. You hear me, John? You do the right thing. I know you know right from wrong. I know you're a good lad. Just be mindful. The city ain't like round here. Folk'll eat you up in a heartbeat if you give them half a chance, and they'll think nothing of spitting you out in the river."

"Mr Fisher's letter said I'll have somewhere to stay."

"I know, and I'll write when I can. But just mind you keep to yourself, John. The world out there can be cruel and I won't be there to help."

"I know, Ma," he said.

She reached up and touched his swollen lip.

"Should I ask how that happened? Or who did it?"

He shook his head.

"Somebody who doesn't matter anymore," he told her. "Somebody who will amount to nothing."

She nodded.

"Unlike you?"

"Unlike me," he agreed and then leaned to hug his mother for the first time for as long as he could remember. "Bye, Mum. I'll look forward to your letters."

"Bye, love," she said, then pulled away and dabbed at her eye. "Go on, then. Or Terry'll leave without you."

He stopped at the back door, turned back for one last look at the old kitchen, and then smiled at his ma, before slipping away to find his fortune.

The truck was noisy on the outside and cold on the inside, and black smoke bellowed from the exhaust.

"I bet old Barney's glad you bought this," John said as he climbed into the cab. "He'd have hated taking me all the way to Lincoln."

"He wouldn't have made it," Terry said, as he released the long handbrake and set the old truck in motion. "You got everything?"

"Everything? I have nothing to my name," John said with a smile. "So whatever I have when I return is a gain, is it not?"

"That's one way of looking at it," Terry replied. Watching Terry drive the truck was still odd to John. In the trap, with old Barney pulling them along, he used to sit back and enjoy the views. But the truck seemed to scare him. His eyes barely left the road.

They rode in silence for a while until the old, second-hand truck nosed towards the village and seemed to creep past the squire's big house for fear of waking the Garfields. The driveway was long and lined with miniature evergreens, each one neatly clipped into a tall, conical spike. The lawns had been cut fastidiously and the edges could have been drawn on, they were so sharp. Even the trees that had been planted with care and precision seemed not to dare drop a single leaf – two maples and a little copse of silver birches. Daffodils and crocuses dared to raise their heads only in those spaces near the trees, providing some much-needed colour against the formidable backdrop of red brick and stone.

John watched the house and searched its windows for fear of Bobby seeing him and making subsequent inquiries as to his whereabouts. It should be a clean start.

He lowered the window as far as it would go and then leaned out for one last look.

"I'll be back, Bobby," he whispered aloud but to himself, letting the wind carry his voice towards its target. And then he thought of her. Rose. And he spoke to them both. "One day, I'll be back. You'll see."

CHAPTER THIRTY-SEVEN
March 30, 2024

"Vanessa?" Charles said when he pushed through from the custody suite into the long corridor towards the main entrance. She turned and her mouth opened, but no words followed. "What are you doing here? Everything all right, love?"

"Hi," she replied. "Yeah, yeah. I just popped in to see you, that's all. They said you were out, so I'll just catch you later on."

"No, it's fine. I can spare a moment or two," he said.

"No, honestly. It's fine. It can wait."

"Devon, go and prep the others, will you?" he said. "I'll be up in a wee while."

"Dad, it's fine," Vanessa said, as Devon pushed through into the stairwell.

"Nonsense," he told her and peered into a vacant interview room. "You didn't come all the way down here just to walk home again, did you?"

She relented and then slipped past him into the room, taking the seat that was typically occupied by a suspect.

"Do I need to read you your rights?" he asked, hoping to raise a smile, but he failed.

"Come on then," he said. "Talk to me. Do you need money, love? I can help if you need it—"

"It's not money, Dad," she replied then realised her tone. "Sorry. Thanks, Dad. But it's not money."

"You worried about the bairn? Is that it?"

"I've found somewhere," she said. "A place. It's nothing huge, but it's nice and clean, and it's safe."

"That's great," he said. "Whereabouts?"

"It's in Branston," she told him.

"Branston? That's hardly walking distance—"

"I know, but it's safe, and they're buses into town. There's a co-op and everything I need."

"And the rent?"

She inhaled long and hard and then fumbled with her fingers.

"It's more than I was looking for, but it's a house, Dad. Two beds with a little garden. There's even a park we could walk to. I want to go and see it. I know you'd approve. It's a new-build. Nobody has ever lived in it."

"New-build?" he said. "Warm and dry?"

"Warmer than your house," she said.

"Aye, well," he said, then thought about it. "You came all the way down here just to tell me that?"

"Yeah," she said. "I thought you'd be happy for me, that's all."

"But you haven't seen it yet?"

"Well, no. But I've seen the pictures online. I want to go and see it. This will get snapped up, Dad."

"I see," he said. "Do you have a deposit?"

"Just," she replied.

"And the rent?"

"The first year would be hard, but when the baby gets into nursery, which by the way is in the village, then I could do more hours."

"Right," he said. "Right, fine."

"Sorry?"

"It's fine," he said. "We'll make it work. Whatever it is that you need, we'll make it work."

"Are you serious?"

"Aye, I'm serious. What do you think your old man is, some kind of monster?" He pushed his chair back and opened the door. "Set a viewing up."

"For tonight?" she said, and her eyes filled with hope, something he'd never been able to argue with.

"Aye, tonight. Just text me, will you?" He smiled and held the door for her, and then walked her to the exit into the public waiting room. "It's going to be okay, Vanessa. Whatever it takes, all right?"

"I know," she said, and then she reached up and kissed him on the cheek before heading out of the building.

"Do all your suspects kiss you when they leave?" Mansfield said, a duty sergeant who was as reliable as the rain. "No wonder you made chief inspector."

He held a fresh cup of tea and was no doubt coming down from a break.

"My daughter," Charles told him.

"Blimey?" Mansfield said, and then looked Charles up and down. "Take after her mum, does she?"

"In many ways she does," Charles admitted, letting the door swing closed. He walked past Mansfield and through the next door into the stairwell. "But not in every way, thank God."

"Bobby Garfield," Charles announced as he entered the room. He clapped his hands together a few times, more to liven himself up than anybody else. He flipped the board around to use the other side and then snatched up the marker pen. "What do we have on him?"

"Positive ID on the car, guv," Forsythe announced. "We managed to enhance the number plate. It's his car."

"Opportunity," Charles said, scrawling the words *CAR POS ID* onto the board. "Time?"

"Four-twelve, guv," he replied, so Charles made a note of the time. "What we don't have, unless I'm mistaken, is his exit. If he drove from Lincoln and back again, then he should have been caught on that camera."

"I'll check later dates," Forsythe told him.

"Could have been at his mother-in-law's house, guv," Chalk said. "It's only a few miles away."

"You're right, he could have," Charles agreed. "In which case, why didn't Rose Garfield or his mother-in-law say so when we visited?" He looked at each of them in turn, but nobody had an answer. "I spoke to Rose Garfield about her husband. She said she wanted to call him. She had every opportunity to say something." He shook his head and tapped Bobby's name on the board. "No, he was up to something, and my guess is that whatever it was, his wife doesn't know either." Forsythe nodded his agreement and made a note in his pad while Chalk contemplated what the reason could be. "The glass," Charles said, keen to move the conversation along. "Has Katy Southwell come back to us yet?"

"She has," Devon said. "There's an email in your inbox. One glass had Hugo Garfield's DNA on and the other was a partial match, which suggests it was his son. He has no other children, so nobody else would have his DNA."

"Bingo," Charles said to himself, but aloud. "So we know he was there. What we don't know is *why* he was there and *when* he left. I think it's reasonable to assume that he both knows how to work the chandelier hoists and is strong enough to use them, so that gives us a means," he said, scrawling the narrative onto the board as he wrote. He finished with a single final word. "Motive," he said. "The hard part."

"I still say it could be financial," Devon added.

"I thought he was broke," Chalk said.

"Ah, that's where I could have been wrong," Charles admitted. "We found a letter in Hugo Garfield's study this afternoon. It looks like he was in negotiations with the National Trust about handing the place over to them."

"What, for free?"

"There's no mention of a sum at this point. All we know is that they were discussing it."

"Why the National Trust?" Chalk asked, to which Charles clicked the lid back onto the pen and set it down before perching on the edge of a desk.

"How do you think the National Trust come to be running big estates? Think about it? They didn't own them way back when the estates were thriving, but they do now. If you were a landlord, Chalk, and times had moved on so much that your way of life was dwindling, what would you do? Your estate would be haemorrhaging cash, you can't pay your staff, and the house your family has called home, for hundreds of years in some cases, is about to go under the hammer? What would you do?"

"Give it to the National Trust to preserve?"

"Exactly," he said. "The Massingberds did it when any chance of an heir fell by the wayside. Others have done the same thing when they simply cannot make ends meet. Would you want to be the one who, after generations have passed through, lets the candle go out?"

"This way, Hugo would have walked away with enough to live on for the rest of his life," said Chalk.

"They may have even rented it back to him," Charles said. "That happened, you know? Some of the house would be opened to the public while he could have lived in another part. It's big enough, let's face it."

"So, are we saying that Bobby's motive could have been that he didn't want to let the house go?" Chalk said. "He killed his father before the house was lost?"

"At this stage," Charles replied, "I can't make head nor tail of it. It's a big house worth somewhere in the millions, so you'd think he'd be keen to get his hands on it."

"Unless he just wants us to think he's not interested," Devon said.

"Or he could have organised the whole National Trust thing himself," Forsythe said.

"Why the hell would he do that?"

"Isn't it obvious?" he said. "His dad has a relatively small amount in the bank. Now, he could spend that money fixing the lead work on the roof, leaving Bobby Garfield with no inheritance, or Bobby could arrange for the house to go to the National Trust, leaving them without the headache and Bobby with a small inheritance but an inheritance nonetheless."

"I still say this isn't financial," Devon added. "I see what you're all saying, but it doesn't sit right with me. Whoever murdered Hugo Garfield watched him writhe in agony. I just can't see Bobby Garfield doing that to his dad to get an inheritance that, by all accounts, he doesn't need."

"Unless Bobby had a reason to hate his father," Charles said, thoughtfully, then snatched up his jacket. "Chalk, Forsythe, carry on digging, will you? Get me Bobby Garfield's financials. Let's see if he needs the money."

"Where are you going?" Devon asked.

"We are going to see Bobby Garfield," Charles said. "His father died because of something he did, was going to do, or something he knew."

"A secret?" Devon said, suggesting the Joanne Childs incident.

"Possibly," Charles told her. "Whatever it was, it was bad enough to die for."

CHAPTER THIRTY-EIGHT

August 6, 1973

Lincoln City was a marvel to behold. The buildings on the edge of the city seemed to grow closer together as they neared. Large houses with acres of land gave way to smaller houses with barely enough room for a vegetable patch. And they mirrored each other so that John wondered how on earth the occupants knew which house to be theirs.

A huge, brick building dominated one side of the road with walls so high that surely no sunlight could reach inside.

"What's that?" he asked, and Terry followed his gaze.

"Prison," Terry told him flatly, then pointed to a sprawling collection of buildings opposite. "And that's the hospital. And I don't want to hear about you going to either one of them places. You hear me?"

"I do," John said, in awe of the sheer size of the institutions. Ahead of them, jutting from the rooftops was a huge, stone tower, ornate even from a distance. "And that?"

"That?" Terry said as if he should have known the answer. "That's the cathedral. Have you really never been to the city?"

"Never," John said. "It's huge."

"Tallest building in the world," Terry said, with an element of pride in his tone. "For a good while, anyways."

"I suppose Ma wouldn't mind if I were to go there?"

"I don't think she'd mind one jot, John," Terry said, with a smile. "Now listen, there's places here that you've no place being. You hear me? You're here for one reason and one reason alone."

"I know, Terry. It's okay."

"No, you're not listening. I mean it," he said, his expression grave. "Think of it like this. You want to do well here. You've got this place you need to be and it's at the far end of a long road. So far that you can't see it. But you know it's there. You've seen it in your dreams."

John listened intently to Terry's rudimentary explanation and could only wonder at how a man whose hands were stained with the earth and who displayed so little emotion could find such depth in the matter at hand.

"I have," John told him.

"But there's other paths, see? And people. Bad people at every junction. Now, they want you to take their path and they'll do almost anything to steer you away, you get me?"

"I do," John said.

"But you have to stay firm, John. You have to keep your mind fixed on where you want to be. There'll be times when you have to stand up to them and I want you to do just that. Don't be afraid of them. Don't be afraid of using this," he said, tapping his temple with his finger. "You're smart, John. You've a good head and that's your power, see? That's what you've got that the others don't, you hear?"

"I understand," John replied.

"Do you, though?"

"I do," he said. "Honestly, I do."

"Every day, when you wake up, wherever that might be, I want you to picture it. I want you to picture why you're there. Focus,

John. Do that, and there'll be a statue with your name on it before you know it."

"I doubt that."

"I don't," Terry said, as he pulled the truck into a siding and came to a stop. "And your ma don't either. All right? Believe in yourself, John. You're not like the others."

Outside, there seemed to be people everywhere. It was like an oversized version of Alford Market. Some walked with purpose, others for something to do. Some carried huge bags, while others seemed to sit on wooden benches, whiling away the time. And the cars. There were dozens and dozens of them. Trucks, too.

"You're on your own from here," Terry said.

"You're not coming with me?"

Terry shook his head.

"No, city ain't no place for me. We don't get on much," he replied. "You've the letter, I suppose?"

"I have," John said, pulling the folded paper from his pocket.

"Right then," Terry replied, and he pointed through the windscreen. "See that chap over there? The one with the big hat?"

"The policeman?"

"S'right. Ask him where to go. In fact, whenever you find yourself off the right path, ask a policeman. They'll steer you right. Mark my words, they will."

John smiled at him.

"Thanks, Terry," he said. "For everything, I mean."

"Don't thank me," he said. "Place won't be the same without you, but you'll always be a part of it. You know that, right?"

"I do," he said.

"And you'll always be welcome. If this don't work out, or if you lose your way, then you make your way home, you hear? We'll not think ill of you."

"I will," John told him.

"Go on then," Terry said, and he extended his arm towards

John. He took it and they shook hands. "You're a man now, John. This is it for you. This is your chance. I know it."

"I do too," John said, and he gathered the handles of his bag and peered through the windscreen. "I just know it is."

CHAPTER THIRTY-NINE
March 30, 2024

It was Rose Garfield who answered the door. She wore a pair of dark jeans and a loose t-shirt that exposed a slender shoulder and bra strap. It wasn't, in Charles' opinion, a look that many women in their sixties adopted, let alone pulled off. But pulled it off she had. She held the door open and stood with one bare foot placed atop the other.

"Devon?" she said. "Am I right?"

"Close," Charles told her. "It's Chief Inspector Cook. My colleague here is Sergeant Devon." He held out a hand to present Devon.

"Apologies," she said. "How can I help?"

"It's your husband we've come to see, actually," he told her. "Would it be possible to come in?"

"I'm afraid he's rather busy—"

"It's important that we speak to him," Charles said, recognising the attempt to put them off. "We could, of course, pursue a more formal route. But none of us wants that."

"I see. Very well," she said, reluctantly stepping to one side. "He's in his study. I'll go and fetch him."

"Oh, no need," Charles said. "We can speak in there. In fact, I think it's best if we do. Alone, if possible."

She studied them both for a moment and then relented with a sweep of her arm.

"You know the way, I presume?"

"I do."

They had barely reached the door from the hallway when she called out to them.

"Go easy on him," she said, and they stopped to look at her. "He's under enormous pressure right now. Add any more weight to his shoulders and I'm afraid he'll break."

"I'll bear that in mind," Charles said and then left her standing there.

They found Bobby Garfield sitting at his desk with his head in his hands. At first, Charles thought he might be upset, but when Garfield raised his head, there was little but frustration in his eyes.

"What do you want?" he asked.

"Just a wee word," Charles said, then took a seat without being asked. Devon took the spare chair and for what seemed like thirty seconds or more, they all simply stared at one another.

"Well?" Garfield said. "I've done what you asked me to. I've answered all your questions—"

"Not quite," Charles told him. "There are just a few more things we need to know."

Garfield closed the ledger on his desk and slid it to one side with a heavy sigh.

"Right," he said. "Go on then." He checked his watch. "You've got ten minutes."

"Ah now, see, I was hoping for a wee bit more than minutes, Mr Garfield. In fact, this might be easier down at the station."

"Out of the question," Garfield said flatly. "I've got all this to get through, I've got the funeral to arrange, and I'm supposed to be meeting a surveyor at the house."

"A surveyor?"

"Yes, a surveyor. Is there a problem?"

"Well, no. It just surprised me, that's all. So often I deal with individuals who can barely cope with the loss, let alone the deceased's assets."

"Well, there's no point in waiting, is there?" Garfield said, and he placed his hand on the ledger. "That house is costing several hundred pounds per day and that's without even heating it or boiling the kettle."

"I see," Charles said, thinking back to what Forsythe had mentioned. He nodded and let his gaze linger for a moment.

"The clock is ticking, Inspector."

"Oh yes," he replied. "Yes, sorry. It's just that when I usually have these conversations with people, Mr Garfield, just a day or two after the death of a loved one, not only are they not making plans to sell assets or going through financial details, but they usually have some questions for me."

"Such as?" Garfield said, seeming not in the slightest bit concerned with his demeanour. "What could you possibly tell me that I don't already know?"

Charles leaned forward onto the desk and searched Garfield's eyes, finding nothing but arrogance. No guilt, no shame, just pure, unadulterated arrogance.

"Well for a start, Mr Garfield, they usually ask if we've made any progress in our investigation," Charles said. "And in light of the fact that you haven't, and the plans that you are quite obviously making, I'm afraid I'm going to ask you to accompany me to the station."

"What?"

"And the way I see it, we can do that one of two ways. The easy way," Charles said, and he stood from his chair, gesturing for Devon to do the same. "Or the hard way. The choice is entirely yours."

"Excuse me?"

"The easy way would be for you to come voluntarily," Charles told him. "The hard way would involve me walking you out of here in a pair of handcuffs."

"You can't do that? There's absolutely nothing to suggest that I'm responsible for my father's death–"

"We know that you were at the house, Bobby," Charles said. "Opportunity."

Garfield pulled an incredulous expression and shook his head in disbelief.

"It's also assumed that, seeing as you grew up in the house, you knew how to operate the chandelier hoists."

"What? Of course. I saw them do it a hundred times."

"And selling the house, Bobby? Selling it fast, as well. What were you afraid of? Your inheritance being drained?"

"My what? My inheritance? How dare you–"

"And seeing as you are, as you stated when we first met, a lawyer, I have no doubt that you understand that these things combined – means, motive, and opportunity – all equate to me having reasonable cause to bring you in for further questioning."

"I can answer your questions right here."

"There is, of course, more," Charles told him.

"More of what?"

"More intricacies," Charles said. "Other details that need clearing up."

"Such as?" he said, and then yelled for his wife. "Rose? Rosie, come here now, please."

"I'm not sure if that's a good idea," Devon said.

"If you're going to take this route, then I want a witness."

"I might suggest, Mr Garfield," Charles said, slowly and clearly so as to eradicate any chance of being accused of malpractice later down the line, "that this particular topic would be better off being discussed without your wife's presence."

"I want a witness," he said. "Might I remind you, Inspector, that I have just lost my father. I would hate to respond to any of your questions in a state of heightened emotions, and if I do, then I want somebody present who could, at a later date, testify to my state of mind."

"I understand," Charles said. "States of mind are a complex thing."

"Indeed."

"We dealt with somebody earlier, as it happens. Somebody who had lived her entire adult life in a confused state of mind."

Garfield shrugged as if to suggest that, right then, somebody else's state of mind was of little concern to him.

"So?"

"She'd been abused as a wee girl," Charles said, then looked to Devon. "Twelve or thirteen years old, was it?"

"Thirteen or fourteen, I think, guv," Devon replied.

"Ah, that's right. Said she was...what did she say now?"

"Pinned down and groped, guv," Devon said.

"Ah yes."

"And then she was forced to touch her abuser."

"I remember," Charles said, shaking his head again for effect. "Dreadful thing to have happened to a wee girl."

"You yelled, Bobby?" a voice said from the doorway, and Garfield, who was staring defiantly at Charles, looked up at his wife.

"Nothing," he said. "You can go."

"Excuse me?"

"I said you can go, damn it, woman," he snapped. "Leave us be."

Charles didn't turn. Her reaction could be felt in the chill that followed.

He heard her footsteps trail off down the hallway and then a door slammed.

"What are you suggesting?" Garfield asked.

"Suggesting? I'm not suggesting anything," Charles said. "I am merely stating how a state of mind can influence all kinds of behaviour. Perhaps, that's why your father died? Perhaps somebody's state of mind was... off-kilter, shall we say?"

"And why would that be?"

"You tell me, Bobby," Charles said. "Now, I have clearly stated the evidence I have before me and you have to admit that I have more than enough grounds to take you in. But as you rightly said, you have just lost your father. So I'm open to conducting an interview here. And if the answers you give me are suitable and I believe them to be true, then we'll leave." Again he leaned onto the desk. "But if they're not, Bobby, I'll drag you out of here in handcuffs and you won't see the light of day again until next week. Do I make myself clear?"

"You do," Garfield replied, totally unfazed by Charles' approach. "But I might just add one more name into the mix if I may."

"One more name?"

"I wish it to be known before I answer your questions, and answer them I will, that I believe the man you should be questioning about my father's murder..." he began. "Is none other than John Stow."

CHAPTER FORTY
August 6, 1973

The entrance that John was looking for was hidden between two shops, like a secret place for the privileged few or a terrible place buried between the walls to avoid staining the streets.

And in that doorway, a man sat. His skin was dark from both descent and dirt. His coat was in tatters and covered in grime, and he had an old blanket pulled around his legs. Beneath him, in lieu of a cushion, was a flattened, cardboard box that he must have found lying discarded behind one of the large stores John had walked past. In clear, bold letters, the word *Bovril* had been stamped or printed.

"Gonna just stand there, are you?" he asked, and John was taken a back at his gruff tone.

"No, sir," he replied.

The man nodded at his hat, which lay at his feet and contained a few, grubby, old coins.

"Gonna put something in then, are you?"

"I would, sir," he said, thinking of the envelope his ma had given him and remembering her words of wisdom. "But I'm not yet able to." He gestured at the content of the old flat cap. "In fact, you probably have more than I."

"I see," the man said, and for the first time, he took a moment to study John and his attire. "Well, best you be off then, wherever that may be. Got somewhere to go, ain't you?"

"I have, sir. In fact, I'm already here." He smiled and nodded at the door. "I have an appointment, so if you don't mind–"

"The young gentleman would like me to move, is that it?"

"Only to let me pass," John explained, and then looked up and down the street. "I dare say this is a comfortable spot for you."

"I dare say it is," the man replied, then moved to one side to allow John to pass.

A little, brass plaque on the wall marked the occupants as Swain and Swain LLP, and a small button had been provided, which, on finding the door to be locked, John presumed he was to press.

What followed was a series of doors being opened and closed, and then a petite girl, no older than twenty, descended the stairs and opened the door.

"Go on, get out of here," she said to the man and shooed him off like he was a wild dog. She stared at John, eyebrows raised, as if waiting for him to introduce himself. "Well?"

"John Stow, ma'am," he said.

"John Stow? Should that mean something to me?"

"Mr Fisher sent for me," he explained, then handed her the letter, which she perused briefly before handing it back to him. The girl took a step to one side and then ushered him inside and towards the stairs, which in light of the doorway's confined location, was the only option available. He edged past her, clutching his bag, and made his way up the stairs. The building was certainly not a reflection of The Grange and its sprawling corridors. Nor was it anywhere near as roomy as their farmhouse. The stairwell was bathed in gloom, but the door at the top was fine and rich, with a worn, brass handle and a glass window through which John saw, for the first time, a new world.

It was a world of mahogany desks and bookcases, of green

leather and baize, of sharp suits and stern faces, of clattering typewriters and ringing phones, and, of course, of cigarette and pipe smoke that seemed to hug the ceiling like the clouds in the sky.

"Go through," the girl told him from below, and he pushed the door open. He had expected the faces to turn his way, or for those fingers that danced across typewriters to stop, or for the dozen or so pairs of bespectacled eyes to stare at him. But nobody batted an eyelid. He was invisible. The girl, who wore a skirt to her knees and a blouse not too dissimilar to his mother's Sunday best brushed past him, and spoke quietly. "This way. Don't dawdle."

He followed, taking as much of the place in as he could. He had expected the shape of the room to be similar to that of the shop below, but the walls, it appeared, had been knocked through to form a long space the length of the terrace. The central space was occupied mostly by women with each desk enjoying a wall of paper files, a typewriter, an ashtray, and a teacup complete with saucer. The desks were arranged in fours, allowing four women to occupy one block. They ranged from women in their fifties wearing knitted cardigans and floral blouses with silver chains that hung from their eyeglasses and frowns so embedded into their forehead that John wondered if they needed to pull their scalps back each night before they left for home to bored-looking younger women who wore makeup, revealed their legs and who he imagined did everything possible to avoid portraying their maturer counterparts.

One seat in a block of four was empty despite there being a handbag on the floor and a piece of headed paper in the typewriter, and John presumed that it belonged to the girl.

Those two blocks of four desks saw very little daylight. Along the window wall, running the length of the space, was a row of smaller offices, each door bearing the name of the occupier whom John imagined to be higher in rank and therefore more deserving of the daylight. He remembered his mother's words with clarity.

"Don't you go reading them books in bed now," she would say. "You'll do your eyesight no good at all."

He looked at the women who were all busy typing away at God only knows what and found some truth in his mother's wisdom as nearly all of them wore glasses.

"Come along," the girl barked at him, then waited for him to catch up before knocking on a door and leaning in. "John Stow for you, sir."

"Ah," came the reply, and she moved to one side to allow John to enter and to be greeted by the man who twice had been to his home, the most recent time being only the previous day. "Come in, come in. Sit. Tea?"

"Tea?"

"You do drink tea, I imagine," Fisher said.

"Yes, sir. Of course, sir," he replied, and Fisher glanced up at the girl, who without instruction left the room.

"Now then," Fisher said, offering John a seat with a sweep of his hand and retaking his own far more comfortable chair. "In light of recent events, your path of education has been altered." He fished a file from the bottom drawer of his desk and laid it flat on the green, leather inlay. "I have spoken to Mrs Lavender, and while she was loath to provide further details, she has instructed me that she can no longer accommodate you."

"Yes, sir," John said.

"Which places me in a rather difficult position, as you imagine," he said, peering at John over the top of his spectacles. "I have, however, managed to enroll you in a program of further education. In effect, you have, unwittingly and fortuitously, managed to circumvent your final few months with Mrs Lavender."

"Sorry, sir?" John said, not following, and Fisher removed his glasses to study John with his own eyes.

"You will begin your apprenticeship early."

"Early, sir?"

"Yes, early. It was always the plan for you to take an apprenticeship at Swain and Swain once the first part of your education had been completed. But given the circumstances, the only avenue available to you is to begin early. Whether such a move proves to be an advantage or otherwise is, I might add, entirely down to you. I can't imagine the reasons Mrs Lavender had for coming to such a decision, but I will say this, at Swain and Swain you will behave in a manner befitting such an esteemed organisation. You will, at all times – be that here in the office or in your own time – represent the business. Whatever shortcomings you demonstrated with Mrs Lavender will not be tolerated here. Do I make myself clear?"

"You do, sir," John said.

"Good," he replied, pulling his glasses back over his ears. "Now, I must add that not all of Mrs Lavender's feedback was negative. She has provided an exemplary character, so I can only assume that this is a result of a minor lapse of judgement on your behalf. You will work here five days per week. You will be assigned an office, from which you will work and you will study."

"Study, sir?"

"Yes, dear boy. You may have inadvertently taken a shortcut from Mrs Lavender's tuition, but you do still need to sit your exams, do you not?"

"I do, sir, yes."

"And so you will sit them. Your time will be apportioned accordingly, between matters that I and the other partners ask of you, and your studies. You will sit your O-levels late this year, which Mrs Lavender assures me you will pass with flying colours. And then the fun starts. You will begin your degree in law."

"A law degree? Me?" John said.

"That is, I hope, agreeable to you, is it not?" Fisher said. "Unless, of course, you would prefer to take over your stepfather's farm? There's no shame in that if you do."

"No, sir. It is most agreeable."

"That's what I thought," Fisher said. "Good. Well, I see you have a bag with you. Do you have a change of clothes?"

"Clothes, sir?"

"A suit or smart trousers?" he said as the door opened and the girl reentered carrying a tray of tea. "Thank you, dear."

"Will that be all, Mr Fisher?"

"Yes, thank you," he said, and then immediately changed his mind. "Actually, no. Wait just a moment, will you?"

She stopped in the doorway and watched as Fisher stared at John.

"I sent Mrs Lavender money to have you fitted out with a suit," he said. "Did you receive such a thing?"

"Yes, sir," John said. "That is, I left it at Mrs Lavender's."

"You left it there?"

"Yes, sir. I wasn't really in a position to retrieve it," John said, awkwardly glancing up at the girl in fear of having to provide further explanation.

"I see," Fisher replied, and he looked at his wristwatch. "Well, we'd better do something about that. We can't have you going about the place looking like something we found on the street, can we? Miss Thames here will accompany you to Golds on the High Street," he explained, then spoke directly to her. "Three shirts, two suits, two ties, and a pair of shoes on my account, if you will. Mr Gold will know what to do with him."

"Yes, Mr Fisher," she replied.

"And see if you can find him something to wear while his clothes are tailored. Some trousers and a shirt from Dicks should do."

"Certainly, sir," she said.

"From there, you can take him to his accommodation."

"My accommodation, sir?" John said.

"Yes, your accommodation. You might look as if you slept on the streets, but you're with Swain and Swain now. We need you fresh-faced and free of filth and for that you need a place to get some sleep, a place to eat a good meal, and a place to keep you warm and dry. The clothing will be deducted from your monthly stipend, but the accommodation is courtesy of the partnership."

"That's very generous, sir," John said. "I've never had a place of my own."

"Oh, you won't be alone, dear boy," Fisher told him with a laugh. "Surely you don't think we're irresponsible enough to let a fifteen-year-old boy live alone in the city. No, you'll be with the others. They'll take good care of you."

"The others, sir?"

"Yes, the others," he said. "The other apprentices. Now, be off with you. I have some work to be getting on with." He checked his watch again. "I'll see you tomorrow morning at eight o'clock sharp."

"Yes, sir," John said, rising from his chair despite not even being offered a tea, which he had been looking forward to after his journey.

"And, Stow," Fisher said, returning the file to the bottom drawer, "don't be late. This is your last chance. Mess this up and I'll have nowhere to put you but back at the farm."

CHAPTER FORTY-ONE
March 30, 2024

"John Stow?" Charles repeated. "As in your boss?"

"Personally, I see him as more of a colleague," Garfield replied.

"But he is the managing partner, is he not?" Charles replied, and he reached for his notepad in which he'd made a note of his meeting with Stow. "I spoke to him yesterday morning."

"Oh really? So he's already on your radar, is he? I must say, Inspector, you impress me."

"No, as a matter of fact, Mr Garfield, he is not on our radar. I chose to speak to Mr Stow as you had recently learned of your father's death and I didn't want to burden you with more questions until I had little or no alternative."

Garfield sat back in his seat seeming somewhat pleased with the shift of Charles' attention.

"And what did the good Mr Stow have to say?" Bobby asked.

Charles mirrored Garfield's posture and crossed his legs, giving him somewhere to rest his hands.

"I think my conversation with John Stow should remain confidential at this time. But fear not, Mr Garfield, we'll get to him."

"You don't believe me?"

"It's not that I don't believe you, as such. It's just that you have this knack of diverting one's attention. It's a skill, you know? An art, some might say."

"I'm not diverting anybody's attention. I am merely suggesting that you speak to John Stow before you barge into my house and accuse me of murdering my own father, damn it." He slammed his fist down onto the desk and blood came to the surface of his face, turning it a deep red colour, which then subsided as the seconds passed.

Charles watched with interest at the man's momentary lapse of reason and self-control.

"You told me that you were here the day your father was killed, Bobby," he said. "Yet we have security camera footage showing that you passed through Hagworthingham at around four p.m. the day before he died. Can you explain the discrepancy for me? You see, I'm struggling to find any reason that a man of your obvious capabilities could possibly make such a mistake."

"So what? I went to see him. It doesn't mean I killed him, does it? Why would I kill my own father?"

"Well, before we get to the motive, I'd prefer it if we could establish if you were indeed at your father's house and not here, as you previously said."

"Yes, yes, I went to see him," he replied with a flick of his hand as if the lie was as insignificant as the dust that hung in the air.

"Yet you told me that you hadn't left the house, Mr Garfield."

"I know," he said. "I'm sorry. Maybe I was overcome by the news?"

"I doubt that," Charles told him. "You were in full control of your sense. In fact, you handled the news of your father's death far better than I can ever recall anybody doing so, and I can assure you, I've had to deliver news like that on more occasions than I care to remember."

"I don't know," he said. "I didn't think it mattered. I mean, I didn't bloody kill him, did I?"

"You didn't think it mattered? Mr Garfield, surely you of all people realise the penalty for obstructing the course of justice? We've spent two days investigating everyone your father knew. Can you see how this looks?"

"Yes, yes," he said with another flick of his hand. "Well, you know now, don't you?"

"When did you leave your father's house?"

"What?"

"You heard me, Mr Garfield, and I strongly suggest that you begin to tell me the truth. I don't expect to have to force any more truths from you, and if I do, we'll continue this in the station, where I'll have thirty-six hours to do so."

"Twenty-four, actually."

"Oh no," Charles said. "Not with what we have on you, Bobby. My application for an extension would be granted in a heartbeat once the CPS know what we have."

"I didn't kill my father," he said. "How many more times?"

"As many as it takes," Charles replied. "Now, when did you leave your father's house?"

"About eight o'clock," he replied.

"On which day?"

Garfield rolled his eyes and sighed again.

"On the Tuesday. I left at eight o'clock."

"You didn't sleep there?"

"No, I did not sleep there," he said. "Why don't you ask the cleaner girl? Ask her if she had to make my bed."

"Oh, we will," Charles said, adding an entry to his notebook. "And you returned home via the same route, did you?"

"Sorry?"

"You drove through Hagworthingham village to get home, did you?"

"No, actually," he said. "No, I used the A15 and then cut through Market Rasen."

"Any reason for the change of route?"

"I've a friend in Louth," Garfield replied. "An expert in the field of landownership."

"Oh, so you were already going ahead with the sale before your father died?"

"No, but I was considering sacrificing some of the land and how best to do so in a tax-efficient manner."

"And so you consulted an old friend?"

"Seeing how he deals with landed estates on a daily basis and I deal with criminal law, I thought him a worthy consultant."

"That's quite the favour."

"Quid pro quo, Inspector. I'm sure if ever he is in need, I shall endeavour to repay it," Garfield said, fishing a card from his wallet, which he slipped across the desk. "Call him if you want. You can even use my phone. How's that for being compliant?"

"Mr Garfield, I know that youth is not on my side, but please do not mistake my appearance for gullibility."

"I'm not following."

"A lawyer friend of yours," Charles said, reading the card. "A Henry Gallant, whom you could have quite easily called to support your claim, is providing you with an alibi. No, I much prefer to back up such a claim with tangible evidence over the word of a peer."

"What? You asked me to tell you where I was and I told you. Now you say it isn't good enough. What exactly do you want from me, Inspector?"

"The truth, Mr Garfield," Charles said, letting his voice rise a little louder than he had planned. "The truth. I want to believe you. I really do. But the fact remains that the word of a friend is nowhere near as powerful as, say, a traffic camera, for instance, which, if I'm not mistaken, there is on the way into Market Rasen."

"I know the one you're talking about," Garfield said. "And no, I didn't pass through there."

"So I have no evidence that you left your father's house on the

Tuesday night except for the word of an old friend? Is that right? Was your daughter home when you arrived here? Maybe she could vouch for you?"

"No, nobody was here. My wife was at her mum's remember?"

"Ah yes," Charles said. "Lovely lady, by the way."

"Sorry?"

"Your mother-in-law, Mr Garfield. Sorry, didn't your wife tell you? We stopped by to have a wee word. That must have been a wonderful house in its day."

"You did what? I asked you not to go and see her, yet despite my instructions–"

"We do not follow your instructions, I'm afraid. And it was imperative that I spoke to her," Charles said. "I think we've established that, as yet, we cannot prove that you were not at your father's house on the Wednesday."

"I was not."

"And until we prove it, instead of going around in circles, perhaps it's best if we move on. Now, shall we discuss your motive, Mr Garfield?"

"I don't have a motive, Inspector. The man was my father. Since my mother died, he is all I have had."

"Not forgetting your wife, of course," Devon said, to which he responded with a simple glance in her direction and a slow intake of breath.

"You see, and as I'm sure a lawyer such as yourself can appreciate, Bobby, when we come across an investigation like this one, where there is no obvious motive, as a team, we discuss the options. First of all, we identify the nearest and dearest – friends, family and the like – and then in the first instance, we like to rule them out. Believe it or not, none of us enjoys accusing the bereaved."

"I dare say," he grumbled.

"And any who cannot provide a valid whereabouts through tangible means are then investigated."

"Will you be explaining every police procedure, Inspector? I do have to be somewhere as I've already said."

"We then look at the means," Charles continued. "Could the individual in question have carried out the murder using the means that the forensic pathologist has stated? I.e. could you have killed your father? The answer of which, in this case, is a resounding yes. Now I'm not saying you did do it. All I'm saying is that, from our perspective, that little box is ticked. That's two of three."

"Well, I'd be interested to hear what you have for number three. If you think it's all about money, then you're in for a shock, Inspector. You might think that a man like me, a greedy lawyer, couldn't wait to get his hands on his dad's house and his land. Couldn't wait to sell it, I'll bet." He shook his head. "The fact is that if my dad had lived, he would have been bankrupt within the year. He couldn't have even paid for his own funeral. And the house? I already told you, it's worth nothing. The land will fetch some, but it'll do little more than cover the repairs that need to be carried out before it goes and pays off Dad's debts."

"I imagine your father would have been very reluctant to sell," Charles said, and Garfield grinned.

"Oh no. You're not going down that route. You're not saying that I murdered my own father so I could sell the lot on before it went down the drain?"

"I'm not suggesting anything of the sort, Bobby. As I mentioned before, I have to cover every eventuality. And that, which you rightly describe, is such an eventuality. It could be said that a motive that could be applied to you might be that you were after your father's money."

"Have you even seen his bank accounts?"

"I have, yes," Charles said.

"I don't suppose that you've even considered inheritance tax, though, have you?"

"I have actually. Well, a colleague of ours mentioned it."

"So you'll know that even if the land and the house were sold now, I wouldn't receive any more than what I've already got. This is not a life-changing sum of money, Inspector."

"Not for you, maybe," Charles said. "But to many, several hundred thousand pounds would go a long way."

"It wouldn't even pay my wife's shopping allowance," Garfield said.

"And that's where we hit a wall, too," Charles said. "You see, believe it or not, neither Sergeant Devon here nor myself believe that you were financially motivated to have carried out such a terrible crime."

"You don't?" he said, looking surprised.

"No," Charles said, as if the very notion was ludicrous. "No, I think if you were indeed responsible for the death of your father, then it would have to be something far greater than money."

"Sorry, what did you say?"

"What was it, Bobby? What motivated you?" Charles said. "What secret was it that was bad enough for him to die for?"

"Is that an accusation?" Garfield said. "What am I supposed to do, drop to my knees howling with grief, exclaiming that it was me?"

"No," Charles told him. "Unless it *was* you, that is."

Garfield held his own. He stared Charles in the eye from the far side of his desk and his mouth barely opened a fraction of an inch when he replied.

"I didn't kill my father," he said. "Find John Stow. He's the man you want."

CHAPTER FORTY-TWO

August 6, 1973

The cold and distant Miss Thames had become Francis by the time John had been measured for his suits, and by the time they had purchased from Dicks a pair of smart trousers and a shirt for John to wear whilst his suits were made, her smile was revealing itself with growing regularity. And so, when he asked if they could stop for tea at a lovely old building on top of a bridge before they went to the accommodation, she relented.

"Now then," a voice said, hard and gruff like an old diesel engine. "S'pose you been lucky yet, have you?"

John turned and saw the man he'd seen in the doorway. He carried an old duffle bag, which presumably contained his worldly belongings, and John couldn't help but think how alike they were – both of them with no more than a single bag of possessions.

"No sir," he replied. "I'm still poor, I'm afraid."

"Get out of it," Francis said, and again, she shooed him off, swinging her bag at him and tugging John into the cafe. "You need to have your wits about you, John Stow," she said. "Prey on young lads like you, they do."

"He must be hungry–"

"Hungry my left foot," she said. "Thirsty, more like. Give him any money and he'll be drunk by dinner time and back for more tomorrow."

He watched through the window as the man hobbled off, his head bowed low. Francis took a seat at a table, so John ordered for them both and dared to use some of the money that his mother had given him before carrying the teas to the small table where she waited patiently.

"This is nice," he said, unable to stop himself from studying the people from all walks of life as they came and went. The older men he saw mostly wore suits, or some variation thereof, whilst the younger men often wore denims and boots. Some of them were clean and well-kept, whilst others appeared to be construction workers in search of a sandwich. "Have you always lived in the city?"

"No, not always," she told him, adding a cube of sugar to her tea and stirring it in. "My father moved us up here when I was younger. He said London was no place for us girls to grow up. Not since the war."

"Oh really? What does he do?"

"Sorry?"

"What does he do? Your father. Is he in law?"

His question either perplexed her or amused her, he couldn't quite tell which.

"Why don't you tell me about yourself?" she said, and John heard Mrs Lavender's sharp tone cutting through the noise of the cafe, instructing him that the art of small talk was to always be the one asking questions, never finding oneself in a position of answering them. "Mr Fisher said your family has a farm. Is that right? Was it livestock or crops?"

He hesitated for a moment and then sipped at his tea to buy himself time.

"I suppose what I'd really like to know," he started. "Is have I done the right thing? Mr Fisher seems nice and everyone there seemed content. Would that be fair to say, Francis?"

"Content is such a generalist way of describing a feeling, don't you think?" she said. "After all, do we seek to be content or do we seek happiness?"

"Happiness, I suppose," he replied. "But sometimes being content is better than the alternative."

"And do you think you will be content here, John? Or do you think you will find happiness?"

"Happiness," he told her. "And I shan't be content until I find it."

She laughed out loud and he felt good. Despite the five years between them, he felt he had navigated the conversation well. He hadn't been rude by avoiding her questions but had not forced his own upon her either.

"I shall have to remember that," she told him, as she delicately finished her tea and placed the cup neatly back into the saucer. "Now come along or Mr Fisher will be wondering where I am."

She rose from her seat and John discreetly gulped as much tea as he could manage without spilling it. He carried the bag he had taken from home, plus the bags containing shoes, a shirt, and trousers, plus a few other accessories that Mr Gold had seen fit to add, and found Francis waiting for him on the street.

"So do you live nearby?" he asked, as she led them back up the High Street.

"You're curious, aren't you?"

"No, not really. I was making conversation, that's all."

"Oh, so you aren't actually interested. You were just filling in the time?"

"No, I am interested. I meant that–"

"You'd like to know where I live, but to what end?"

"Sorry?"

'Why, John? Why does it matter if I live in that house over there, or if I live ten miles away on a farm?" He considered the question and saw the point she was making, and so brushed it off as a failed attempt at making small talk. There would be other chances.

They began to ascend a huge, long hill. The road was made up of cobbles much like Alford marketplace, but the further they climbed, the steeper the hill seemed to get, made even more imposing by the huge cathedral to the right and the formidable Lincoln Castle to the left.

Francis, however, seemed accustomed to the climb. She walked with her head held high and with great, long strides.

"I thought the hills we have back home were steep," he said between breaths.

"It's not called Steep Hill for nothing, you know?" she replied.

"I hope you don't mind me saying, but you don't seem to be struggling with it. I thought I was fit."

"I've been walking up this hill twice a day for the past three years," she said, stopping for a breath and gesturing at a side road that seemed to have grown from beneath the huge castle walls. "That's you down there."

If she walked the hill twice per day then it stood to reason that she lived somewhere nearby. He wondered where, and if, in fact, her accommodation was courtesy of Swain and Swain or her father.

The house she led him to boasted a view across the city and he stopped before they entered to drink it in. He'd seen views from the hilltops near his home, of course, but never had he seen so many rooftops, so many chimneys gushing black smoke, and so many roads. The entire lower half of the city could be seen from where he stood. The railway line cut through the fields to his left and right, the waterways that culminated at the foot of the hill, and then formed the River Witham and everything in between.

"It's amazing," he said to her. But she hadn't heard. She was at the top of the steps of a large, red-brick house with huge sash windows and a pair of bright green front doors.

"What did I say about dawdling?" she called out, her smile

belying her tone. She opened the doors and pushed her way inside, and he followed with his stomach churning in excitement and trepidation. "This is the main living space, where you can read and relax," she said, pointing into what he supposed had been a parlour. Then she pointed to two further rooms from the broad hallway. "Dining room and kitchen," she said, then ventured up the wide staircase, and John found himself watching her with awe. Her hips seemed to rock from side to side as she walked and her legs seemed to tease him from beneath the swaying skirt. "John?" she said from the top, and he realised he had been staring.

"Sorry," he said. "Yes, I'm coming now. I was just admiring the staircase."

"Are you interested in architecture?" she asked when he reached the top step and found a selection of six large doors.

"I suppose that I am," he told her, and he stroked the bannister with his free hand. "I've never really thought about it."

She eyed him as if searching his eyes for a lie, and then turned away briskly, and shoved open one of the doors.

"This is you," she said, letting him enter before her. "You'll find you have everything you need. We have a maid that comes three times per week. She will take care of your laundry, clean your bedsheets, and so forth. What she will not do, however, is clean your shoes, make you a sandwich, and nor will she engage in any activities surplus to that of a housemaid."

The final statement puzzled John, which he made clear with a bemused expression.

"Such as?"

"You would be surprised at what some of our previous apprentices have requested, John," she said. "Needless to say that they are no longer apprentices at Swain and Swain."

"I see," he said, hoping that where his mind had wandered was not in the least bit accurate.

"Now, if that is all, I should be getting back to the office. I do still have work to do."

John nodded, staring around the room. There was an old fireplace with a mantle, a large bed, and two huge bay windows from which he could see across the city.

The double-fronted wardrobe seemed far more than he would ever need. In fact, he thought that he, Terry and his mother could fit all of their collective belongings inside it.

He stepped out of the room and leaned over the bannister to find Francis on the last step.

"Francis," he called, and she turned to look up at him. "Thank you," he told her. "I would have been lost without your help."

She smiled up at him.

"Just remember everything that I've told you and you'll be fine, John," she said. "Make some friends with the others. One of them, a Mr Gallant, is in his fourth and final year. He's the one you want to make friends with."

She nodded a farewell and he heard the front door close behind her. Back in his room, he dropped onto his bed and rolled onto his back. It was heaven. The room was more than twice the size of his old room, the bed was soft, and he had nothing to do until the morning.

The thought reminded him of when he had woken in the bed at The Grange and how he had pondered the life of a wealthy man, rich in time.

A gold coin of time, he thought, *to spend as I see fit*.

"You must be John Stow," a voice said from the doorway, and John sat up immediately to find a handsome, young man in the doorway. He wore a light grey, three-piece suit in a material that John recognised from his visit to Gold's earlier that day. From beneath it, the crisp, white collars of a fine shirt protruded and in his breast pocket, a sliver of a white handkerchief could be seen. His shoes were black leather Oxfords, much like those that Francis had selected for John. He sauntered into the room, causally studying the pelmets and the drapes, as if comparing them to those in his own room. "How are you settling in?"

"Just fine so far," John replied. "Thank you."

The young man peered through the window and then back at John.

"Oh, forgive me," he said, rushing across the room with his hand extended. "Henry Gallant. They might have mentioned me?"

"They?" John said.

"Mr Fisher and Franky," he explained. "Sorry, Francis." He pulled a boyish grin. "She doesn't like to be called Franky."

"So why do you?" John asked, to which Henry Gallant cocked his head.

"Have you met the others?" he asked after a while.

"Not yet. You're the first."

"Then come," Henry said, clapping his hands once. "There's no time like the present."

He left the room and John trailed after him, smoothing his clothes as he descended the stairs. Henry seemed excited to introduce him to the rest of the apprentices, and he hurried to the kitchen door, shoving it open with the same gusto he had demonstrated on leaving John's room.

"Listen up," he called with some authority. "This here is our newest member."

The faces in the room entered into a combination of polite nods, smiles, and indifference. Each of them looked him up and down but said nothing.

"It's a pleasure to meet you all," John told them, and seeing his nervous state, Henry took over.

"This is Dickie," he said, presenting a red-haired lad who could only have been a few years older than John. Then he proceeded to point and name the other two. "This is Jack, and finally, this is Edward."

He seemed to have presented them in order of age, and it was the youngest, he who had seemed indifferent to John's presence, who was the first to speak.

"How old are you?" he asked.

"I'll be sixteen soon," John told him.

"Another baby?" Jack said and looked at Henry. "Does this mean that Edward and I might delegate the drawing up of tenancy agreements? They're becoming quite tiresome."

"It does," Henry said, then elbowed John. "Don't worry. We all have to start somewhere."

But the drawing up of tenancy agreements, whatever that entailed, was not what concerned John. He looked Jack in the eye.

"Sorry, did you say another baby?"

"He means to say that you're a newbie," Henry said. "Never mind him."

"Yes, I know, and it's fine. But do you mean to tell me there's another? That I'm not the only new starter?"

"No, they always draft us in pairs. The boss likes healthy competition in the first year," Jack said.

"Not to mention that one of us is always booted out at the end of the year," Henry added and then peered through into the hallway. "Speak of the devil." He waved at somebody out of view and then made room for the newcomer, whose shoulder he draped his arm across and then made the introductions. "John Stow, may I present your adversary, Bobby Garfield."

CHAPTER FORTY-THREE
March 30, 2024

"Before we talk about John Stow," Charles said, "there is a matter I'd like to discuss. You see, while I can't, at this stage, rule out a financial motive entirely, I am inclined to pursue a motive closer to the heart."

"Right," Garfield said. "So you can't nail me on the finances so you're trying to pin anything you can on me? This is bordering harassment, Inspector. You're more than aware of the situation I am in. My father has been dead for a matter of days and you might as well be shining a lamp in my eyes."

"I am aware of your situation, Bobby, which is why I have agreed to conduct these questions here and not down at the station. But I am also aware that you are a lawyer. Your knowledge of criminal law is extensive, and therefore you of all people should understand that even if I were to pursue this John Stow, which I will, by the way, any defence lawyer worth their salt would raise a flag against any possible leads that I have not followed. It would have a negative effect on the credibility of the investigation, casting a shadow over any future prosecution. You understand that, don't you?"

"Leads? You don't have any leads, Inspector. You're clutching at straws."

"I believe that your father died because either he had angered somebody or because he knew something. Something that he threatened to reveal, perhaps?"

He searched for a sign in Garfield's eyes but saw nothing of the sort.

"A secret?" Garfield said with a smirk. "My dad was ninety-eight years old. You don't live that long without picking up a few secrets along the way."

"Tell me, Bobby. What do you know about Joanne Childs?"

"Who?"

"Joanne Childs," Charles repeated.

"The cleaner?" he said, pulling a face. "What, you think she had something against my dad? The man who paid her to rock up once a week and run a duster about the place?"

"I'm not making any claims against you, Mrs Childs, or anybody, Bobby. I am merely exploring all possible paths."

"Well, I suppose it was her who found him, but I still think you're looking at the wrong person. you need to look into John Stow."

"And I will," Charles said. "My problem is that we found an old complaint filed by Mrs Childs when she was just a young girl. No older than thirteen or fourteen, in fact."

Garfield narrowed an eye and cocked his head to one side.

"Right? What type of complaint?"

"It is of a sexual nature," Charles said. "Which is why I suggested that your wife doesn't necessarily need to be present."

"A sexual nature? You think she and my father were having an affair? A ninety-eight-year-old–"

"The complaint was against you, Bobby," Charles said. "You could only have been fifteen or sixteen at the time."

"Against me?" he said, to which Charles nodded. "You can't be serious? Not that time she made all that rubbish up, surely?"

"What time would that be?" Devon asked, and Garfield let his head fall back and sighed heavily.

"Look, there was an incident once. It was nothing really. The two of us were playing in my bedroom. Her mum used to bring her to the house, you see. Joanne used to play with my toys or whatever, and sometimes she'd help her mum with the dusting."

"So you are familiar with her then?"

"I am reminded of her, yes," Garfield said. "The two of us would sometimes play together. I'd show her my books and whatnot, and maybe even my train set."

"I see," Charles said. "And did these playing sessions sometimes get physical?"

"Physical? What on earth are you implying?"

"Well, you see, Mrs Childs recalled the event with some clarity of mind. There was very little hesitation, and she had very little trouble remembering you, Bobby."

"Well, she would, wouldn't she? She probably fancied me."

"Excuse me?"

"Oh come on, let's not beat about the bush. We're all adults now. She was thirteen, I was fifteen, and she had this infatuation thing going on. I didn't like playing with her, but my dad made me. He said we should be kind to those less fortunate. So I tolerated her."

"And did your father ever tell you to do anything else?"

"Like what?"

"I don't know. Show her who's the boss, maybe?"

"Show her what? She already knew who the boss was. Why on earth..." he started. "Look, this incident was nothing more than her trying to kiss me and me pushing her off."

"She told us you groped her, Bobby."

"She said what? I groped her? She was thirteen. There wasn't anything to grope. And anyway, it could only have been when I shoved her off me. I wasn't groping her, Inspector, I was pushing her away."

"So you remember it well, do you?" Charles said, and again Garfield's expression dropped.

"Like I said, I am reminded."

"And what about the part where you made her touch you?" Devon said. "Was that when you were pushing her away as well?"

"She amended her complaint, didn't she? What does that tell you? It tells *me* that she had made it all up to begin with."

"Of course she could have just been scared," Devon said. "Her mother might have feared losing her job, or worse."

"The part that I can't get past, Bobby, is that your father made you assert your authority over her."

"All right. Yes, he made me demonstrate my position. That was just Dad being Dad," Bobby said. "He said that I should know how and when to draw the line and he was right. The people that served us were human beings, after all."

"At least we can agree on that," Devon said.

"Knowing where that line is, that's key to good leadership," Bobby said. "You can laugh with them and have a joke, but there's a line that should never be crossed."

"And where was that line with Joanne Childs?"

"Forget Joanne Childs," Bobby said.

"Right, yes," Charles cut in. "John Stow. You seem incredibly keen on pushing him to the forefront of this investigation, yet so far you're the only one to have mentioned his name."

"Well, then I suggest you look into him a little deeper," Garfield said. "That man has made it his life's work to destroy me."

"It looks to me as if he has failed, Bobby," Charles said. "You're a partner in a leading law firm, you've a beautiful wife, a nice house, not to mention you're inheriting your father's house." He glanced across at Devon, who nodded her agreement. "You haven't done too bad considering Mr Stow's apparent efforts to bring you down."

Garfield leaned on the desk and jabbed a finger in Charles' direction.

"You don't know the half of it," he said. "That man and I are sworn enemies. Always have been, always will be."

"I don't know the half of it, no?" Charles said. "Then while my colleague here runs some checks into your route home from Hagworthingham, why don't you tell me all about John Stow? Convince me and we might just leave you in peace, Mr Garfield."

CHAPTER FORTY-FOUR
August 7, 1973

"You've got a nerve," Garfield said from the doorway. On their first day at Swain and Swain, he had discovered that John had not only arrived to work a full hour ahead of the proposed eight o'clock but had also offered to help Francis with some of her work, which was mostly filling and addressing envelopes with letters that she had already typed. "What do you think you're doing?"

"Making myself useful," John replied. "It's nothing really, but I suppose in helping me, Miss Thames must have fallen behind in her work. It's the least I can do."

"You know what I mean," Garfield said, closing the door behind him. They were situated in one of the rooms that overlooked the street, and from which, if he ducked down and peered through the window, John thought he could see their house looming in the streets above.

"No, Bobby, I most certainly do not," John said.

There were two desks in the room standing side by side save for a gap just large enough for a man to edge through, and Bobby marched to the seat behind the other.

"Here. Bloody Swain and Swain. This is my apprenticeship. My dad got me this placement."

"Oh, I did wonder," John said. "Whereas I earned my place here."

The comment only served to rile Bobby, and John laughed to himself as he filled another envelope and began, with his best handwriting, to add the address.

"You haven't been at school for three years, John. You can't even have sat your bloody O-levels."

"Not yet I haven't. I believe I'm due to start in a month or two."

"How? One day you were at school then you weren't. We didn't see you again."

"Oh, I see," John said, feigning interest. "Mother thought a private education would be preferable."

"You what?"

"A private education, Bobby. She wanted me to have a start in life."

"But how? She's a bloody farmer's wife."

"She believed in me," John told him. "I suppose she saw my true potential."

"Your true potential? Give over, Stow. And why are you speaking like that? You sound like you've swallowed a silver bloody spoon."

John grinned, unashamed, and smiled inwardly at how Mrs Lavender's tutorage was coming into play.

"What about your father? I would have thought that with his wealth he might have given you a private education," John said, as he added the envelope to the pile. "Unless, of course, he didn't believe in you. I mean, it's understandable given your track record. You were, after all, held back for a year at school. That must have come as quite a disappointment."

"You're sailing perilously close to the wind, Stow," Garfield hissed.

"Oh really? Did your two goons also win an apprenticeship here?"

"Mason and Pepper?" Garfield said. "Get away with you. They'll be lucky if they can tie their shoes by the time I've got my degree." John smiled and began another of the letters. "So this is it, is it? You and I, side by side for the next year?" Garfield said, and let his arms flop onto the desk. "And here's me thinking that I'd never have to see your ugly mug ever again."

"I have to say that I was also surprised to see you, Bobby," John said. "But I have had the evening to give it some thought while you and the others were playing cards downstairs. And of course, I've had the morning to run through it all in my head."

"And?" Bobby said. "What, pray tell, did you come up with after all that time? Are you going to run?"

"No, I'm not going to run anymore, Bobby. I was never really running from you anyway, was I? No, I don't really have a plan as such," John said, stuffing another letter into an envelope. "Except that I feel we should move forward in a manner more appropriate to our positions."

"You what?"

"I feel that we should channel our energies into our roles here," John explained. "Your father wants to secure you a career for when the day comes that he is forced to sell his land."

"That'll never happen," Garfield said.

"Really? Then why are you here?" John asked, to which Garfield said nothing. "You needn't think that you're alone. It's happening all over Britain, you know? Large estates are being carved up left, right, and centre. Your father might call himself the squire, but he's not, is he? Not really. Nobody respects him. The only reason they do as he says is because it is both within his power, and his temperament, to remove their livelihoods at a moment's notice."

"You need to be careful, Stow—"

"You see, that's just it, Bobby. I don't, do I? You're nothing without Mason and Pepper. I showed you that three years ago the day I walked out of that schoolhouse for the last time." He stood and pulled his chair back to give him room to move and then collected the pile of envelopes from the desk. He edged through the gap and then leaned over Garfield. "Look at me, Bobby. What do you see?"

Garfield's eyes wandered across his face then loitered on his lips.

"I see a little boy who's out of his depth," Garfield said. "And one who carries the scars to prove it."

John pointed to his lips and the gentle bruising around his eye.

"Don't you see, Bobby? Don't you see that after all that you did to me not thirty-six hours ago, all I have is a swollen lip and the makings of a black eye, both of which will be healed in a few days' time?" He shoved off the desk and started towards the door.

"I wonder what Miss Thames will think of you when she learns about your little escapade in the hills?" Garfield said, and John stopped in his tracks. "I wonder if she'll be so keen to help you when she learns about that poor little girl you helped yourself to?"

"I imagine that she would be most discouraged," John told him. "But not nearly as discouraged as she would be when she learns about you."

"What's that supposed to mean?" he said. "What about me?"

"You know I had nothing to do with what happened to that girl. I was bloody twelve years old when it happened."

"Were you? I don't recall. All I remember are the rumours of old Jimmy Sutherland hiding in your stepdad's farm. Coincidence? I think not."

"Before you decide to sully my name with a story that you cannot possibly prove, Bobby–"

"Oh, can't I?"

"No, you can't. Because it isn't true. These are lawyers, Bobby. Men and women who deal with tangible facts. They're not going to take the word of some half-wit boy who was kept behind for a year at school because he wasn't smart enough to be entered for his exams. If you even mention my name with that incident, then you'll find yourself backed into a corner from which you cannot possibly escape."

Garfield's smug expression had faded during John's monologue, and he was clearly giving the words serious thought. So John finished with the speech that had played over his mind during that first night in the new house, with its new room and new possibilities.

"Remember this, Bobby. It's just you and me now. It's no longer a battle of brawn. Mason and Pepper aren't here to back you up. This a battle of wits and brains, and you know as well as I do that you were never particularly blessed in that department. I know everything about you. I know everything about your mother, and most importantly, I know everything about your father," John told him as he opened the door.

He stopped once more and smiled back at Garfield's evident concern.

"So, may the best man win, Bobby. May the best man win."

CHAPTER FORTY-FIVE
March 30, 2024

To walk away from a man as cold as Bobby Garfield was as painful as it could be. There was more to the man than he had let on, yet with irrefutable evidence that he had indeed driven home through Market Rasen before his father had been killed, Charles had not only been forced to leave Garfield to grieve, but his character reference of John Stow left him unable to pursue any other line of inquiry.

"He's playing me at my own game," Charles said over the car's Bluetooth system, and he heard Devon's heavy breathing as she sought to understand the comment. "He's given us a lead. Well, a hint of a lead anyway. He knows if we don't follow it up, that his defence will pull our case apart. They'll question why we didn't follow up on John Stow."

"Meanwhile Bobby Garfield remains free," Devon said.

"How positive are you that that was his car on the ANPR?"

"One hundred per cent, guv," she replied. "He wasn't at the house."

"No, he wasn't there. But that's not to say that he didn't have a hand in this."

"What are you saying?"

"I'm saying that he's smart," Charles said, as he pulled up outside the address Vanessa had sent him. "Get onto his alibi, will you? That solicitor he mentioned. I want to know what was discussed."

"Righto," she replied.

"And talk to the others. I want a briefing first thing tomorrow. In the meantime, find anything and everything you can on John Stow. Let's rule him out or rule him in."

"No problem, guv," she replied, as Vanessa approached the car, hands in pockets. "Enjoy your evening, yeah?"

"I'll do my best," he replied. "But I can't make any promises."

He ended the call and climbed out of the car, kissing Vanessa on the cheek.

"Well?" she said, presenting a row of neat, brand-new houses. "What do you think?"

"Well, I hardly need to ask which one it is, do I?" he said. "They're all the same."

"They're not. Look, my one has the green front door."

"Your one? Moved in already, have you?"

"You know what I mean," she said and then linked her arm through his. "Come on. The agent is inside already."

She dragged him towards the house and he let her enthusiasm run riot for a while. It had been a while since she had been that hyped up about anything, but still, he couldn't quite shake the feeling that as happy as she seemed, he was on the brink of losing her.

"Hello," she called, as she pushed open the door.

"Ah, good to see you both," a man in a blue suit said, as he stepped over to shake Charles' hand. "Tim Manilow."

"Manilow, eh? Any relation?"

"To who?"

Charles placed him in his early twenties. Along with his blue suit, he wore brown shoes, which had at least been polished, and a white shirt with a blue tie. At least he had made an effort.

"Ah, nobody," Charles said, not wanting to show his age too much. "So this is it, is it?"

"Two bedrooms, semi-detached, open-plan kitchen with a spacious garden," Tim said, and Charles peered through the kitchen window into the garden.

"Spacious, you say?"

"Dad," Vanessa said. "It's big enough."

"Aye, you're right," he replied.

"The bedrooms are a nice size, too," Tim added. "If you'd like to follow me upstairs."

"Are the utilities included in the price?" Charles asked.

"Unfortunately not," he replied and presented the entrance to the master bedroom. Void of furniture, the space looked big. But once a double bed had been dropped against the wall, there would be barely enough room to shuffle around the edge. "Built-in wardrobes, as you can see, and this is my favourite part." He opened a door to one side, revealing a cosy, little bathroom. "En-suite."

"Ah nice," Charles said. "That'll give you two bathrooms to clean."

"Dad," Vanessa said again, then spoke directly to the agent. "Sorry about him. He'd prefer it if I had an outdoor privy."

"Aye, there's nothing wrong with an outdoor privy, I can tell you. Didn't do us any harm, you know."

Tim smiled politely and led them through a brief tour of the main bathroom and the spare bedroom.

"It's heated by a gas combi boiler and is insulated to a grade B standard, so it's an efficient property. None of those leaking windows and roofs."

"Very good," Vanessa said, and she nudged Charles to drum up some enthusiasm. They made their way back downstairs and reconvened in the small lounge. "Look, Dad," she said, pointing through the window to the front. "There's a playground for the kids."

"Kids plural?" he said.

"And a school up the road," she added, ignoring his comment. "The bus routes are good, and there's plenty of parking for when you come."

"Aye, I can see," he said. "It just feels a little small, doesn't it?"

"For a starter home, it's actually on the larger side," Tim said. "Some of them are much smaller than this."

"You wouldn't be able to get much furniture in," Charles said. "A little sofa and a TV and that's your lot."

"I don't need much more, do I?" she said, and her expression told him that she sensed his hesitation.

"Aside from that, it's lovely," he told her. "Better than I was expecting at any rate."

"You like it?" she said, with hope in her tone.

"Aye, it's not bad. But I think we should take a wee look around."

"What for? It's perfect."

"I just think it's good to get a feel for the market, that's all," he said. "I'm not saying no—"

"This place won't be available for long," Tim said. "With the economy the way it is, rental properties are being snapped up, especially at this end of the range."

"And what end would that be?" Charles asked.

"The affordable end," Tim said. "It's clean, in a respectable neighbourhood, and with the links to the city and local amenities, it's ideal. I'd be surprised if I still have it by the middle of next week."

Vanessa looked at him hopefully, and as young as Tim was, he knew when to stop talking. He'd make a good salesman in a few years' time.

"And the deposit?" Charles asked.

"One month's rent," Tim said. "Non-refundable, I'm afraid."

"Aren't they always?" Charles replied. "All right. You're sure this is what you want, is it?"

She grinned from ear to ear and that alone was worth a year's rent.

"I'm positive, Dad."

"You don't want to find something close to me?"

"Dad, it's a ten-minute car journey. If I found something closer, it would be half as nice or twice as expensive."

"All right," he said in mock defence and then turned to Tim. "And how exactly do I pay this deposit?"

"Really, Dad? You like it?"

"Really," he told her. "If it's what you want, then we'll make it work." He looked back at Tim. "God knows I'll regret it sooner or later."

"She's lucky to have a father like you," he said.

"No," Charles replied. "No, I'm the lucky one. You don't get many second chances in life."

CHAPTER FORTY-SIX
December 23, 1973

There was a feeling of relief in Lincoln's historic Usher Gallery. For many, the relief was that another year had passed and they could enjoy some time with their families. For John, however, the relief was unique to him – a smattering of As and Bs among his exam results.

A string quartet had been booked for the first half of the Swain and Swain Christmas party, which appeased the more mature individuals such as Mr Fisher and the other senior partners, along with their wives and prestigious clients who seemed to take advantage of the firm's generosity. Canapés were served on silver-plated trays by hired footman, champagne was offered freely, and by the time the nearby cathedral announced the eighth hour, the room was filled with dinner jackets, elegant dresses, and polite chatter.

It was the first time John had seen the company in its entirety. So often, the partners would be out of the office, never seeming to come together at once. The apprentices had gathered on one side of the hall beside a statue of a near-naked hunter with his dog. Henry joked at the size of the leaf that covered the hunter's modesty, which raised a few laughs, and John found himself joining in, despite not really understanding the humour.

It came as no surprise that each of the apprentices had arrived alone. The division of work that Mr Fisher had described to John on that very first day had been accurate, although the volume of work assigned to him was enough for two or three apprentices, and on top of that, John had to find time for his studies, which had left very little time to meet anybody. He arrived home from work past eight o'clock on most evenings, and after snatching a bite to eat from the kitchen, he usually spent another three hours reading. And all the while, the other apprentices, Henry, Jack, Richard, who was aptly named Dickie, and of course Bobby, all laughed and joked, played cards and at times even played records on Henry's turntable. The only member of their little party missing tonight was Garfield, whom John had seen getting ready and so knew that his arrival was imminent.

"I think it's time," Henry said, during a break in the laughter.

"Time for what?" John asked, to which Henry pointed across the room to where Mr Fisher and his wife were in deep discussion with a bald man with a gold pocket watch and a top hat.

"Time to dance," Henry said.

"Dance?"

"Yes," Henry said. "It's custom for the youngest apprentice to dance with the senior partner's wife. It's the way the ball is opened."

"Me, dance with Mrs Fisher? I presume this is some kind of joke? She doesn't even know me."

"It's no joke, John. Heritage is what it is," Henry said, reaching out and taking John's champagne from him. "I'll hold this."

"But–"

"You can't let her down, John. She'll take it personally," Henry said. "Look, nobody has danced yet. They're all waiting for you both to get it started."

"He's right, John," Jack added. "It's pretty bad form to start dancing before the lady of the evening has opened the ball. You won't just be letting her down, you'll be letting us all down."

A fire rose from John's stomach to his throat, where it sat like lava. The quartet brought the melody to an end and as they turned the pages of their music books, Henry nudged him forward.

"Come on. It's not as bad as you think. It's like the first dance at a wedding. People watch you for the first thirty seconds or so, then after that, they're all dancing themselves."

"And you did it, did you?" John asked.

"I did it, Jack did it, and Dickie did it," Henry said.

"What about Bobby? Shouldn't he do it?"

"Bobby isn't here yet, is he?" Jack explained.

"And now I understand why," John remarked. "He's a sly bugger is Bobby Garfield."

"Look, it's a mark of respect, John. Mr Fisher will appreciate it. He'll look at you in a whole new light. He'll have respect for you."

"Unless, of course, you'd rather wait for Bobby to arrive and for Mr Fisher to respect him more?"

"No," John said, straightening his suit jacket. "No, of course not."

The quartet began with three sombre, descending notes that John recognised in an instant, and then they entered into the lively Emperor's Waltz as he made his way across the room.

She wore a green dress that hung from her shoulders rather than hugged her figure. Her shoulders were bare with upper arms broader than John's thighs and bosoms bigger than his head. Yet considering her formidable size, her face seemed to belong to another body. It was long and thin like a horse. He had overheard some of the legal secretaries in the office talk of it once. She had complained about how delivering three children had destroyed her body, and she somehow still carried them on her hips.

The bald man was the first to notice John's approach and he peered between Mr Fisher and his wife to gaze at him.

"Ah," Mr Fisher said, "and this is our youngest member, John Stow." He leaned in towards the old man. "He's going places, you know."

"Oh, is he now?" the man replied. "Well, I shall be keeping an eye on you, young man. What did you say your name was?"

"Stow, sir," John said. "John Stow."

"Stow, Stow," the man mused. "Wasn't there a barrister named Stow?" he said to Mr Fisher.

"No, he was a Snow," came the reply. "No, as far as I know, this young man will be the first practising *Stow* in the county. He passed his O-levels with flying colours, you know? The results came through only yesterday."

"Very promising."

"And if he's lucky, he'll be embarking on his degree sometime next August," Fisher said. "Of course, there are a few matters to be decided beforehand."

"Well, I'm glad to hear it," the man said and then smiled as if he expected John to say something. But it was Mr Fisher who broke the awkward silence.

"How can we help you, Stow?" he said.

"Well, I was wondering," John said, turning to Mrs Fisher. "That is, I was wondering if you'd care to dance, ma'am?"

"Dance?" she said, her eyes widening in horror. "Whatever for?"

"Well, I suppose everybody is waiting for us," John said. "You know? To open the ball. They won't dance until the lady of the evening permits it."

"What a jolly good idea," the old man said.

"Well, I'm not sure if being called a lady of the evening is suitable," she replied, and her eyes narrowed, making her face look even more horse-like. And then she relented. "But how could I refuse such an offer?" She handed her glass to Mr Fisher and allowed him to lead her to the centre of the room.

He sensed rather than heard the chatter come to a stop and the eyes of close to one hundred people all turn to him. And he felt his face begin to burn under its blush.

Somewhere behind him, he heard Bobby's unmistakable laugh, and he was joined by the others, Henry, Jack, and Dickie. But it was too late to back out now.

He thought of Mrs Lavender and all she had taught him. He recalled how he had danced with Rose under her mother's tuition, over and over to that very tune.

He held Mrs Fisher and silently they waited for the melody to run its cycle, before stepping into the next, and to John's surprise, they received some applause, albeit somewhat subdued.

They moved together and John held her tight, and above the music Mrs Lavender's voice guided him. *One two three, one two three...*

"I'm impressed," Mrs Fisher said, as they travelled across the floor. "I imagine that not many young boys are taught to dance properly these days."

"Oh, it's nothing," he told her.

"It's more than nothing," she said. "I think it shows great personality. Too many of today's youth spend their time listening to all that new-fangled nonsense."

"Oh, I think there's room in the world for all kinds of music," John told her, as they circled past Henry and the others. "But I agree. It's important not to forget the way things used to be."

"You do surprise me," she said, as the music softened and then came to an end. He bowed slightly, enough to show respect. "Thank you, John Stow. You know, I think I should dance with one of the apprentices every year. Perhaps it will become a tradition." She laughed aloud, oblivious to the trick he had fallen for. "But I must say, Master Stow, you have set the bar high. Very high indeed."

By the time he returned to the statue of the hunter and his dog, the dance floor was filled and the quartet had entered into Tchaikovsky's Waltz of the Flowers.

Henry stood with his mouth slightly open and both Jack and Dickie were equally as dumbstruck. But it was Bobby who spoke first.

"What the bloody hell was that?" he said.

"What was what, Bobby?"

"That," he said and nodded at the dance floor. "The dance."

"That was a waltz," John told him. "Do you not waltz?"

"No," he said, shaking his head. "No, you see. I'm not sure if anybody told you this, but this is *nineteen* seventy-three, John, not *eighteen* seventy-three."

"Oh," John said, taking his glass back from Henry. "Pity. I think she rather enjoyed it."

"Yeah, right."

"It's a shame you weren't here on time. You missed an opportunity to impress Mr Fisher and his client." Bobby's grin faded, while John's grew. "Why were you late, anyway? I'm sure the partners all noticed your absence."

"I was meeting somebody," he replied.

"Oh really?"

"My date," Bobby said. "I think the partners will forgive my tardiness when they see who I am chaperoning."

"Oh yeah? Don't tell me that Francis has finally given in to your persistence?"

Garfield laughed aloud and sipped at his champagne.

"I wouldn't be seen dead with a bore like Miss Thames, Stow, and you know it," he said.

"So where is this delight and how much have you paid her to accompany you?"

"She's powdering her nose if you must know," he said and then pointed across the room to the double entrance doors. "Here she is now."

John and the others turned to face her as she strode around the edge of the dance floor with a confidence like no other. In the setting of that fine hall, she could have been a princess or a queen. Her long curls hung onto her shoulders and swayed gently as her hips rocked from side to side, and she came to stop before them all.

"Gentleman," Garfield said. "May I present my guest for the evening? Miss Rose Lavender."

CHAPTER FORTY-SEVEN

March 31, 2024

Charles wrote a single word beside Bobby Garfield's name.

Alibi.

He circled the word and was about to strike a line through the name but was reluctant to do so.

"You okay, guv?" Devon asked.

It was Sunday morning and the incident room was quiet and smelled of coffee, unlike the usual stench of printing ink, sandwiches, and human bodies.

He found a clear space on the board and in block capitals, he wrote, *John Stow*.

"They're all old," he said.

"Sorry?"

"Their ages," he replied, then tapped the names on the board one by one with the end of the marker. "Hugo was ninety-eight, Bobby Garfield is nearly seventy, and John Stow must be around the same age."

"Sixty-six, guv," Chalk said. "I wouldn't call them old. Well, not Garfield and Stow anyway."

"Is that supposed to be a compliment?" he asked with a smile. "I'm not far behind them, you know? But everybody involved in this investigation seems to be more mature, shall we say, than the average individual we deal with. What does that tell you?"

"It tells me that human nature is a funny thing, guv," Devon said, but Charles wanted to hear from Forsythe, who had been quiet since he arrived.

"Anything to add?" he asked.

"No, guv," Forsythe said quietly.

"Is there somewhere you need to be? Family, maybe? Kid's football match?"

"No, guv," he said. "I'm here. I'm just thinking, that's all."

"Sharing is caring," Charles replied.

"It's nothing," he said. "Actually, do you mind if I grab a coffee? I just need a minute."

Charles watched him stand, close his laptop, and then walk towards the door.

"You take your time, Forsythe."

"Cheers, guv," he replied from the doorway and then slipped out.

Charles turned to the two remaining members of his team.

"Is there something I should know?"

"Not that I know of, guv," Devon replied.

"Nor me," Chalk said. "Family stuff, maybe?"

"Aye," he muttered. "Aye, that'll be it." He inhaled long and hard and turned his attention back to the investigation. "Joanne Childs is fifty-eight. The youngest person in this investigation is Dorothy Garfield, and as far as I can tell, nobody has even mentioned her."

"Are you saying we should be talking to her?" Chalk asked.

"No, I am not saying that we should be talking to her. Christ, with a father like Bobby Garfield she'd have learnt her lines a long time ago. No, what I'm saying is that mature adults do not wait until they are in their autumnal years to murder a ninety-eight-year-old man. Not unless they were provoked. Now, we've been through Joanne Childs, and I'm sorry, but I cannot write her off just yet. She may have an alibi, but if you ask me, she has a part to play in this yet." He tapped Bobby Garfield's name on the board with the pen. "Same goes for Bobby Garfield."

"His alibi checked out," Devon said. "I got in touch with the solicitor he told us about. He confirmed the meeting and, of course, his car was seen coming into Lincoln from Market Rasen before his father was killed."

"Aye, but still, he's involved. He's a slippery bugger and he knows the law."

"You asked us to look into John Stow, guv," Devon said, and Charles had the feeling that she was urging him out of his thoughts and into the present.

"Aye," he said. "Aye, go on then. What do we have?"

It was Devon who spoke, assisted by Chalk who had laid out the facts before her.

"John Stow, sixty-six years of age, unmarried. Born out near Maltby-le-Marsh, until his father died in the late sixties. There's not much between then and a few years later when his mother, Mary Stow, remarried, to become Mary Frobisher."

"So John kept his father's name, did he?" Charles said, then brushed their inquisitive stares off with a shake of his head. "Sorry, go on."

"They moved to Terry Frobisher's farm shortly after the wedding, where John attended the local school until nineteen-seventy."

"Nineteen-seventy? What does that make him, twelve or thirteen?"

"Twelve, guv," Devon replied.

"Right, so then what?"

"Then, nothing," she said. "Nothing at all, in fact, until he registers for an apprenticeship with Swain and Swain three years later."

"Three years?"

"Can't find a thing, guv," Chalk explained.

"He had a private education," Charles said, much to their surprise. "What? Aren't I allowed a little inside knowledge?"

"How do you know that?"

"He told me," he replied. "It was a plant name. Lavender, that's it. A Mrs Lavender. He's a rags-to-riches story. Nice man, if you ask me."

"Lavender?" Chalk said, immediately flicking through her notes. "I know that name. I've heard it." She paused her flicking, then dragged a sheet of paper to the top of the pile. "Rose Lavender," she said and slid him the sheet. "Only now she's Rose Garfield."

"Christ, we met her," he said to Devon. "Rose's mother. Mrs Lavender. The old lady at the house."

"I remember," she replied, and he tapped his finger on the desk.

"Another one on the wrong side of eighty," he said.

"It does give us a link to John Stow," Chalk said.

"Ah, John Stow," Charles said, quietly. "A name that keeps raising its head."

"Who, might I add, Bobby Garfield has raised as a potential suspect, knowing that, should we fail to investigate Stow, any case against Garfield will be thrown out on the grounds of reasonable doubt," Devon said.

"That's about the size of it," Charles agreed. "Like I said, Bobby Garfield is a lawyer. He's doing what he does best."

"As is John Stow, guv," Chalk added. "In fact, Stow is the managing partner whereas Bobby is a mere partner. I wonder if that suggests some kind of grievance, or historical matters that we are, as yet, unaware of."

"What are you saying?" Charles asked.

"Nothing really, it's just that you're talking about Bobby Garfield like he's guilty, and just because you've met and liked John Stow, he's innocent. I think we should look at him with fresh eyes."

"Give Bobby Garfield the benefit of the doubt, you mean?"

"Something like that, guv," she said.

"You haven't met him yet, have you?"

"Bobby? No, guv."

"Wait until you do," he told her. "The man has a way of getting under your skin, believe me."

"And John Stow?" Devon said. "What does he have? A way of getting into your heart?"

"Are you two ganging up on me?" he said. "What is this?"

"I just think that if Bobby Garfield is using the legal processes and procedures to his advantage, then perhaps we should," Devon said. "What harm can it do?"

It was interesting, to say the least, that Devon should choose such a path, and as loathe as Charles was to accommodate an unnecessary investigation into John Stow, with all the delays it would cause, he knew she was right. Besides, she needed a chance to shine. She'd earned that much.

"Do we have anything on John?" he asked, to which she smiled.

"Oh, yes," she replied. "Means, motive, *and* opportunity."

CHAPTER FORTY-EIGHT

December 23, 1973

"May I have your attention please?" Mr Fisher said when the guests were clapping at the quartet's performance. It was closing in on ten o'clock and the champagne continued to flow. A few of the guests had moved onto cocktails, while others had taken to the provided chairs, perhaps to recover. "Before the quartet pack their instruments away and go home to be with their families, I think we should convey our gratitude."

And with that, the audience began to clap and cheer. Even those who were seated stood. And when the applause was fading, Mr Fisher resumed control of the room with a single raised hand.

"And it is custom within organisations such as Swain and Swain, for the managing partner to give a speech, I am honoured that this year, the pleasure shall fall to me. For thirty years I have enjoyed the company of Swain and Swain employees, some more than others. And this year is no different. As I take the reins of our esteemed organisation, it falls to Mr Forsdyke to join the team of partners who support me. Congratulations, Mr Forsdyke."

Forsdyke, whom John had only seen but never spoke to, gave

thanks for his moment with a smile and received an admiring kiss from his petite wife.

"Mrs Clark, whom you will all know as our fearless senior legal secretary," he began, and then added, "or perhaps that should be fearsome, will be leaving us. Mrs Clark is to date our longest-serving employee. I remember when I first joined the firm as a Junior Lawyer, it was Mrs Clark who welcomed me, and I use the term loosely, and set me onto the right path." From a table to his side, he retrieved a bunch of flowers and then beckoned her to join him on the stage.

"Thank God for that," Henry muttered, catching the apprentice's ears. "Maybe we can push to have a wireless in the office when she's gone."

"That would be fun," Jack said. "It might ease the burden of those long days."

"And I am extremely happy to announce," Mr Fisher continued, "that taking the reins of our team of legal secretaries will be Mrs Brown. Congratulations, Mrs Brown."

Mrs Brown was a stout woman who wore pearls both around her neck and from her ears and who John had never once seen smile. Her voice could cut glass and her glare could freeze water. She nodded once at the room, when all eyes fell upon her, and not a single facial muscle twitched.

"Well, there goes that idea," Henry said quietly.

"Now, as you all know, aside from my academic accomplishments and, let's face it, my charm, my contributions to Swain and Swain venture way beyond the day-to-day running of the office and our esteemed clients."

He paused to allow room for a few laughs, which were accompanied by more than a handful of stifled comments at the mention of his charm. Fisher then looked over to the side of the room, where his eyes fell directly onto John.

"Not all of you will know this, but myself and my predecessor, the late Mr Holly, were, in fact, responsible for the creation of our apprenticeship program. We felt that by identifying great skills early on, and through a series of nurturing, mentoring, and guiding, we could produce some of the country's finest lawyers. And I am pleased to say that the result speaks for itself. Mr Forsdyke, our newest partner, began life at Swain and Swain as an apprentice, as did Mr Frost, Mr McLaughlin, and Mr Haringer. And there are others, many more, in fact, who for reasons of their own have flown the nest. The program is, without doubt, one of my proudest achievements. But it is not for the faint of heart," he said, shaking his head. "Each year, two individuals are brought into the program, only one of which will see a second year and enjoy an education in law paid for by Swain and Swain. Ladies and gentlemen, the eldest three apprentices you see to the side of the room have won their places through hard work, intelligence, and determination, traits that, if nurtured will surely bring them every success. The youngest, John Stow and Robert Garfield, are still doing battle. Who of them will be in attendance next year is still to be decided." He stared at John again. "And right now, it is anybody's game."

"That's your cue to leave," Garfield muttered. "If you want to avoid the embarrassment, that is."

"Bugger off, Garfield," John told him, smiling at the room of curious eyes that seemed to study them both as if guessing who might be staying.

"And so, this year, it gives me great pleasure to pluck from that plethora of prowess, that pool of great talent, a young man who I am sure will continue to uphold the Swain and Swain name, and whom I hope will one day go on to stand where I am tonight. Ladies and gentlemen, I give you Mr Henry Gallant, who is from this moment no longer to be considered an apprentice but instead a junior lawyer. Congratulations, Mr Gallant," he said. "Now, we've heard from our dazzling quartet, but it might come as a surprise to some of you that I am keenly aware that at least two-thirds of us, myself not included, are young enough to appreciate some popular music. Don't let it be said that Swain and Swain is an organisation that is stuck in the past. Oh no. Even us old duffers know how to party, you know?" He took a few steps back to where a pair of twenty-foot-high drapes covered the far wall. "Ladies and gentlemen, for the remainder of the evening, we shall enjoy the music of..." he said and pulled at the drawstring. "Lincoln's finest homegrown pop band, The Songbirds."

The curtains fell open to reveal something that John had only seen photographs of in magazines. There were four men, each of them no older than twenty-five. Three of them held a guitar of some description, while the fourth sat at a drum kit, and without any further introduction, they launched into a Beatles song that was on Henry's latest LP.

The dance floor was immediately set upon by the younger portion of the guests, and not one of them held the other the way Mrs Lavender had taught him. They jived and bucked freely, waving their arms, and kicking their legs. Both Dickie and Jack ditched their champagne glasses and made a beeline for the floor leaving John with Henry, Garfield, and, of course, Rose.

"Congratulations, Henry," John told him and shook his hand respectfully.

"Thank you," he replied. "And listen, sorry about the little trick earlier. It was just a bit of fun."

"Don't mention it," John said. "It was actually rather fun."

"To be honest, none of us expected you to go through with it, least of all pull it off the way you did. How the hell do you know how to dance like that?"

John leaned into him, catching Rose's eye behind Garfield's back.

"I had a good teacher," he explained.

"You had dance lessons? I thought you were raised by sheep," Henry said, and he tapped Garfield on the shoulder. "Here, Bobby, I thought you said he was raised by sheep."

Garfield eyed John and grinned.

"Sheep, cows, chickens," he replied with a casual shrug. "It was an animal of some description if I recall."

"It wasn't just dance lessons," John explained to Henry, keeping Garfield's ear before he was lost to the music.

"No?" he said.

"Oh no," John said, and feeling the weight of Rose's glare, he stared directly into Garfield's eyes. "She taught me all about life. She taught me manners, how to eat, how to dance, how to walk, how to stand, and most importantly of all, Bobby, she taught me how to please a woman."

"Well, you couldn't have listened very hard in your lessons on manners," Rose cut in. "If you speak of a poor young lady like that behind her back."

"Oh, she was no poor young lady, Miss Lavender," John explained. "She was the finest woman I ever did see."

"Oh really?" she said, an eyebrow cocked in amusement. Garfield, sensing something awry, stared between them suspiciously.

"She was. In fact, so fine was she that no collection of adjectives in the English dictionary could describe her beauty," he said, and he held his hand for her to take. "Would you care to dance, Miss Lavender? I'm quite sure that your chaperone has neither the gumption nor education to accompany you, and I'd hate to see you miss out."

"She can't," Garfield said, and after a cursory glance at his wristwatch, he snatched Rose's hand before John could touch her. "We're leaving."

"So soon?" Henry said. "The party is only just getting going."

"We don't want to miss the last train," he explained.

"The last train?" John said, and he watched as Rose held her tongue.

"Back to Sutterby," Garfield said. "We're spending Christmas with my father and Mrs Lavender, Rose's mother."

"Christmas?" John heard himself say in a boyish voice and

then cleared his throat. "That sounds rather organised for a courting young couple. Surely you've only just met?"

"What are you talking about, Stow?" Garfield said. "Rose and I are to be married."

"Married?"

"When I'm eighteen, that is. Our parents arranged it years ago," Garfield explained. "It's a mutual agreement between two esteemed families. A bond between Hagworthingham and Sutterby."

John did his best to hide his surprise but the news could have floored him. He felt himself rock on his feet.

"So your father truly does live in the past," John said. "I thought all those arranged marriages had stopped years ago, along with titles like squire and–"

"Well, thankfully for Rose and I, our families still hold onto those traditions," Garfield said, and the smug grin that John had come to loathe reformed.

"Will you be travelling back to the Wolds for Christmas, Mr Stow?" Rose asked, and for a moment John thought he saw a flash of hope in her eyes.

"No," he said, suffering a pang of dejection. "No, I'll be staying at the house here in Lincoln. I'll be alone this Christmas. Lots to do, you know."

"They do sell third-class tickets, you know?" Garfield said. "I'm sure if you scraped enough pennies together–"

"Thank you, Bobby," John said, cutting him off before the insult widened the wound in his gut. He took Rose's hand from Bobby. "It was a pleasure to meet you, Miss Lavender," he said. "I wish you the merriest of Christmases."

And with that, he turned and walked away, never once looking back.

CHAPTER FORTY-NINE
March 31, 2024

Being a Sunday, the city was quiet, which meant that the old man with the scraggly beard had his choice of shop doorways to occupy. Charles dropped three pound coins into his hat.

"Get yourself a coffee, my friend," he said.

"God bless you," came the reply, and the man's eyes followed them to the doorway of Swain and Swain. Charles pushed the buzzer and then glanced back to find the old man nodding his appreciation and pocketing the few coins.

"Swain and Swain," a voice said.

"Ah, hello. I'm here for John Stow," Charles said, and the lady must have recognised his voice as the buzzer rang out and the door lock clicked open.

At the top of the stairs, they pushed through into the office, where a familiar face greeted them.

"Mrs Hyke, was it?"

"That's right," she replied. "If you'd like to follow me."

"You know I don't have an appointment, don't you?" he said playfully.

"I know," she replied. "I also know that anything regarding the welfare of Mr Garfield's father is a priority." She smiled knowingly as she opened the door to the meeting room Charles had used before. "Tea or coffee?"

"Not for me," he said, and Devon dutifully declined.

"Bit stuffy, isn't it?" she said, when Mrs Hyke had left them to it. "Makes the incident room look like an open-air theatre."

"Imagine it back in the day," he told her. "When everyone smoked at their desks."

"Oh God, I can't imagine anything worse. All those books and all the wood-panelled walls. Must have been unbearable."

"As was the incident room," Charles said. "I used to go home at night and my clothes would reek of cigarettes. Nothing you could say, of course. That's how it was."

"Funny how times change, isn't it?" a voice said from the doorway, and they turned to find John Stow standing there in a three-piece suit, despite the weather. "Chief Inspector Cook, wasn't it?"

Charles extended a hand.

"Thanks for seeing us," he said, as Stow offered them seats with a sweeping gesture. "We'll try not to take up too much of your time."

"Did you try to reach me at home?"

"Why would we go to your home?" Charles said. "You're a managing partner in the biggest law firm in Lincoln. You're not married, you have no children, and I'm no expert, but I would hazard a guess that you didn't get to your position by sitting at home reading the Sunday papers. Am I right?"

Stow seemed impressed but Charles wondered if he'd picked up on the research they had carried out.

"Very intuitive," he said eventually and then clapped his hands once. "I'm afraid that I am guilty as charged. My work is my life, Inspector, and perhaps that's why we both find ourselves sitting in a meeting room in my office on a Sunday morning."

It was a smart response and one which Charles hadn't foreseen. All he could do was smile in reply and then press on.

"We have had to expand our search for Mr Garfield's murderer," Charles explained. "And one way or another, we find ourselves with many questions, all of which seem to lead to you."

"I see," Stow said, and Charles imagined him sitting before one of his powerful clients, inciting confidence in his skills and demeanour. "Well, I'm sure that if your questions lead to me then the answers should be fairly straightforward."

"I'm sure," Charles agreed. "Before we begin, could you please just state where you were the day that Hugo Garfield died?"

"Was that the Wednesday?"

"It was, yes. Around lunchtime."

"Around lunchtime," Stow said. "I had various errands to run, so I cannot state a specific time and place."

"Where, Mr Stow. Lincoln? Scotland? Skegness?"

"I was at home. My mother's house," he replied. "I stopped by to see her and my stepfather."

"I see. And your mother lives in Hagworthingham? Is that right?"

"Close," he said. "We're just outside the village."

"On a farm?"

"That's right."

"And can anybody corroborate that, Mr Stow? It might help us to move on."

Stow cocked his head, his keen eyes never leaving Charles'.

"I believe I can provide proof of my whereabouts," he replied.

"You see, that's where things get a wee bit hazy, Mr Stow," Charles said. "You see, my colleague here has identified a security camera in Hagworthingham that your car passed by on the Tuesday. But I'm afraid there was no return trip until the Thursday morning. The day we first met, as it happens. Can you explain that?"

"That sounds about right," he said. "I'm sorry, is there a point to all of this? I'm feeling a little interrogated. I'm not used to sitting on this side of the fence as I'm sure you can appreciate."

"I'm sure," Charles said politely. "Would you say that you're familiar with the Garfield house?"

"Would that be the outside or the inside?" Stow asked. "The outside, I can probably describe in detail, from the ivy on the walls to the chimneys on the roofs. But as for the inside, I couldn't even tell you how many bedrooms there are or where the kitchen is."

"So you were not a frequent visitor?" Charles asked.

"As far as the Garfields go, I was not, nor am I still, a frequent anything, Inspector. In fact, I can count on one hand the number of times I have visited the house."

"One hand?"

"One finger, to be precise."

"I see," Charles replied. "There are some matters I want to discuss with you, Mr Stow. But before that, could you answer me one simple question?"

"Certainly," Stow said. "I'll answer it the best I can."

"It concerns you and Bobby Garfield," Charles began. "Would it be fair to say that the pair of you are…"

"Are what, Inspector?"

"Rivals, Mr Stow," Charles said. "And if so, why might that be?"

CHAPTER FIFTY
August 16, 1974

The day marked a monumental occasion. A full year had passed since John had first walked through the doors of Swain and Swain. And although his career had barely begun, it felt like a lifetime had passed. His sixteenth birthday had been and gone, which he had celebrated by reading a letter from his mother alone in his bedroom. Henry Gallant had already traversed the realms of junior lawyer to become a full-fledged lawyer and Jack had taken command of the apprentices. Miss Thames was now Mrs Hyke, putting pay to any ideas John might have harboured of courting her.

But there remained two dubious events that would steer John's path. The first was the wedding, which Garfield spoke of freely, describing the planned events to rival that of Princess Margaret and Antony Armstrong-Jones, which according to those who remembered it, was scandalously ostentatious.

The second dubious event was announced after a full three hours of sitting in the office that he shared with Garfield. They had known it was coming, and that, at the end of the day, one of them would be leaving Swain and Swain. And as if he knew of the torment they would be suffering, Jack had ensured that each of their desks was piled high with notaries, meeting minutes, memorandums of association, certificates of incorporation, and share certificates, all of which they were to pore over and administrate in order to direct appropriate communications via the legal secretaries.

It was like the final test in a year-long exam, but one in which the examinees knew not when the bell would ring to mark the end. But it was clear that Garfield felt the same. He had made a large dent in his pile, made pages of notes, and with furtive glances at John's much larger stack, had developed some permanency to his grin.

"You've got your train fare, I presume," Garfield said, which John ignored. "You know, I think they're running every hour these days, so you'll be home before dark. That is, of course, if your stepdad can get his old pony and trap into shape."

"Bugger off, Garfield," John told him.

"Oh, I'll miss that," he said. "You know, I was talking to Rose just the other day, about—"

"I said, bugger off, Bobby," John hissed. "If you know what's good for you, that is."

"Well, well," he replied, "there's the old John Stow. The one I used to know. What's happened to the plum in your mouth? Did you choke on it? I must say, I did wonder how long you could keep it up for. You don't honestly think that people fall for it, do you? You don't honestly think that by speaking all hoity-toity like you do that anyone will see you as anything other than what you actually are – the son of a farmer. Born in a stable. Raised by sheep." He sneered at John with a look of disgust on his face. "A no good, dirty, peasant."

While the insults spilled from Garfield's lips like faeces from a lamb's backside, John was forming his response, which was far less fictitious than Garfield's and would leave him pondering his choice of words. But as he opened his mouth to provide his retort, the door opened and in walked Mrs Hyke.

"Good afternoon, Mrs Hyke," John said, parking his well-constructed monologue. She eyed the two piles carefully and then removed those files from each desk which had been completed. The result was evident. All that remained of Garfield's pile were four files, whilst on John's desk there were still more than he cared to count. She said nothing and then left the room, leaving Garfield every reason for his grin to bask in the sunshine. He sat back in his chair and placed his hands behind his head.

"It's funny," he said. "Do you remember that first day we were here together? In fact, it was in this very office." He shook his head and smiled. "I could have sworn you said to me something about best men winning. Ring any bells, Stow?"

The day had been designed, over the course of two decades, to provide maximum competition, and such behaviour was par for the course. The year had been long and gruelling. Garfield had been insufferable, especially since he had announced that he and Rose were to be wed. But to top the whole affair off, the icing on the cake, as it were, was the condition that on this day, the last of that first year, both he and Garfield were to arrive at work packed and ready to leave. The condition was, of course, designed to prevent disgruntled losers from destroying the house or stealing property, which John presumed was the result of previous former apprentices. But it softened the blow not a smidgen.

He stared at his bag beside his desk. Since arriving in Lincoln, he had purchased several new suits, including those two that Mr Fisher had procured on his behalf. There were other clothes also – clothes for dining, for relaxing, and even for travelling, all of which marked him out as a future gentleman. A man of substance.

Garfield eyed the bag too and smirked.

"What's that?"

"It's my bag," John replied.

"Is that it? That's all of your stuff? It looks like something you might find in a ditch."

"It was my stepfather's," John explained. "He gave it to me when I first came here. I'd had no call for a bag until then."

"But it's barely big enough for a pair of shoes, let alone all of those suits."

"I didn't bring them," John said.

"You what?"

"I didn't bring them. I left them at the house."

"Are you nuts? They must have cost a fortune."

"They did," John told him. "To me, anyway. But if I'm to leave, then I shall have no use for them. Perhaps the next apprentice will find some use for them. Perhaps they will give him the start that I never had."

Garfield shook his head.

"You really are a tramp, aren't you?"

"When I left home, exactly a year ago, Bobby, I told my stepfather that if I returned with no more than I left with then I would be unchanged. I would be no better off and no worse off. As it stands, I'll be going home with this suit, these shoes, and this shirt. So I will have gained something."

"And what will you do?" Garfield asked. "Will you go back to working on the farm?"

"I don't know," he replied. "And you?"

Garfield laughed and then finished with a sigh.

"You know that my father has been a client of Swain and Swain for more than two decades, don't you?"

"So?"

Garfield rolled his eyes.

"And he makes a significant donation to the apprenticeship fund."

John wasn't surprised. But he was reminded of a conversation he had once had with Mr Matheson, the old school teacher, in which he had naively claimed that all men were equal. And to follow on, Mrs Lavender's words came to him, when she had told him that a rich man is not wealthy and that every man must have his price.

The door opened once more, and Mrs Hyke leaned into the room.

"Mr Fisher will see you now," she said calmly, and Garfield rose to his feet, anxious to get the ordeal over with. John followed slowly. The banks of legal secretaries were renowned for their focus. Rarely did they ever raise their heads from their work. It had been that way since long before John had first entered the room.

But on this day, the typing stopped, cigarettes were snuffed out, and they all watched as John and Garfield made their way through the office.

Mrs Hyke held the door open for them and Garfield entered first, taking the seat closest to the wall. John followed and heard Mrs Hyke whisper as he passed her.

"Good luck, John," she said and smiled briefly before closing them inside.

"Now then," Mr Fisher said, which was a standard greeting in those parts, yet sounded altogether wrong when spoken with anything but a Lincolnshire accent. He gestured for John to take the seat beside Garfield and then made a show of clearing his desk, save for a single file. "Do you know what this is?"

"A file, sir," Garfield said, to which Mr Fisher appeared to become perplexed.

"Do you know what's in it?" he asked.

"I can only assume," John began, "that it's the summary of our time here at Swain and Swain. I would imagine that it is a combination of subjective analyses. Perhaps some feedback from the individual partners and apprentices, plus I would imagine that Mrs Brown might have been asked to provide some input. And then there would be some objective reports on our performance, our accuracy, our timekeeping, and so forth."

Garfield shook his head.

"Quite right," Mr Fisher replied. "But if you were to summarise this file?"

"If I may, sir," Garfield said. "For one of us, by which I mean either myself or my esteemed colleague here, it is a golden ticket."

"And for the other?"

"A hangman's noose, sir," Garfield said. "A loaded gun, if you will."

"Well, I'm not sure that I would have phrased it quite so, but the sentiment is there," Mr Fisher said. "It is time for one of you to leave Swain and Swain. Now, you have both worked extremely hard and every year that the apprenticeship program concludes, I am overwhelmed at the progress you boys make. But the fact remains that only one of you can remain, and before I deliver the news, I might just add that whichever of you leaves will receive a glowing reference from me. You should find that suitable to gain employment from anywhere in the county. So all is not lost. This is not the end for either of you. But one of you must tread a different path from this moment on."

He reached into the top drawer of his desk and retrieved an envelope. It was no different to the thousands of envelopes John had seen during his time at Swain and Swain. But he thought at that moment that it might be the last.

"Inside this envelope is a train ticket to Hagworthingham. It is an open ticket valid for today. First class, too, I might add. That's how highly we think of you both."

"Thank you, sir," John said, wishing he would just get on with it and say his name so he could leave.

"And so without further ado," he said and turned to Garfield. "Robert Garfield, a summarisation of the feedback I have gleaned from my colleagues states that you are arrogant, snobbish, and self-righteous."

"Sir?"

"All of which I might add are traits that I am not unfamiliar with. In fact, I believe Mr Forsdyke and Mr Randell, both of whom are now partners, share the same traits."

"Oh good, sir," Garfield said, clearly relieved.

"It is reported that you are able to produce good work in a timely fashion. Your attention to detail, however, needs to be improved, as do your English language skills, your numeracy, and your handwriting. All of which are perfectly addressable and should be the focus of your attention from here on in."

"Yes, sir," Garfield said. "Thank you, sir."

"How many of the tasks set for you today did you complete?"

"All but four, sir," Garfield announced proudly, to which Mr Fisher nodded and noted something down in his file.

"John Stow," he continued. "Appeasing, humble, personable, and lacking in confidence. Those are the words used to describe you by members of this organisation whose opinion I value wholeheartedly."

"Yes, sir," John said, and that fire in his belly began to climb towards his throat.

"I should add that whilst humble and personable traits might befit a farmer's son, or shopkeeper, for instance, I dare say they have no place in a legal practice, and they should be your areas of focus."

"Understood, sir," John said, and the room swayed.

"However, your numeracy and language skills are second to none. Better, I might add than some of our younger legal secretaries, and you know by now that legal secretaries prize their use of the English language. Indeed, if it wasn't for Mrs Brown and Mrs Clark before her, I dare say Swain and Swain would be receiving returned mail from our clients marked with a red pen to highlight our mistakes."

"Sir," John said, the humour doing very little to soften the blow.

"And how many of the tasks set to you today did you accomplish?"

"Twelve, sir," he said.

"Twelve?" Mr Fisher said. "Compared to Mr Garfield's twenty-two?"

"Sorry, sir. I did my best. I'm sure of that."

"May I ask why you only managed twelve of the twenty-six tasks set?"

John shrugged.

"I don't know, sir. I re-read them twice to make sure I hadn't made any mistakes."

"Why?"

"I suppose because I lack confidence in myself, sir. I think your colleagues were quite right in their analysis."

Garfield was doing his best not to beam, and failing. Mr Fisher nodded and then sighed heavily.

"Do you have your bags?" he asked, and John nodded to the old, leather bag at his feet. "Well, then, I'll walk you out."

Time stopped.

There it was. The result he had expected to hear came in the form of those four words. *I'll walk you out.*

Garfield let his head fall back and he sighed loudly, almost groaning. But some part of him, some part of his centuries-old family must have held some semblance of honour, as he stood alongside John and held out his hand.

"Bad luck, old boy," he said.

John stared at the hand that had punched him so many times in the past. He stared at the cruel lips from which countless insults had fallen and at the eyes that one day, in the not-too-distant future, Rose would gaze into and say the words, *I do.*

He shook the hand. Not because he felt obliged to but because that was the honourable thing to do. So he could walk out of the room with his head held high.

They watched him go. The legal secretaries, some of whom, Mrs Hyke included, he had grown quite fond of. But nobody said a word. Cigarettes in ashtrays cast lines of spent smoke straight up to the ceiling, and once more, the typewriters came to a stop, much like the minute's silence that Terry and he had attended in Alford a few years before.

Mr Fisher was waiting on the footpath outside.

"Do you have everything?" he asked when John finally left the building and descended the few steps.

"Yes, sir. I think so."

They walked slowly and it was odd to see Mr Fisher so relaxed. He walked with his hands in his pockets and seemed to scuff the heel of his shoes on the footpath while deep in thought.

"Well, if it ain't the young lad," a voice said, and John turned to find the man who lived in the doorways on Guildhall Street. "S'pose you been lucky yet, have you? Look at you. You've a bag and nothing more and I've a bag and nothing more. How about that? Got to be worth something, ain't it?"

Not wanting to appear weak in front of Mr Fisher, John ignored the man and walked faster but stopped when he realised he was walking alone. Mr Fisher had bent in front of the man, opened his wallet, and placed a note into the old hat, folding it over so the wind wouldn't carry it off.

"Much obliged, sir," the man said, and Mr Fisher, replacing his wallet into his pocket, nodded his goodbye.

"You gave him money, sir?"

"Of course, I did," Mr Fisher replied. "You should always look out for those less fortunate than yourself. You of all people should understand that."

"But, Francis...I mean, Miss Thames always shooed him off."

"Miss Thames has never had to fight for what she has, John," he told him. "Do you know that man's background?"

"No, sir."

"He could have fought for this country. He could have done any number of things that you and I will never know of. Good things. Brave things. Who are we to ignore his pleas simply because his position has altered? It's not our place to judge, John. Remember that."

"I suppose," John said, feeling ashamed of his behaviour.

"I should mention that you are no longer under the influence of your benefactor. You understand that, don't you?" Mr Fisher said.

"I suppose I'm not," John said. "I suppose that I've failed him, haven't I?"

"I wouldn't put it quite like that."

"But Mrs Lavender cast me off and now you are too, sir. I just wish that I knew who he was so that I could thank him for the opportunity."

"And that, I am afraid, is not within my power," Mr Fisher said. "I suspect that by now you are familiar with what is called a non-disclosure agreement?"

"I am, sir, yes."

"I suspect that one day he might find you and make himself known, but that is his prerogative."

"But why, sir? Why did he do all of this?"

"Ah, I'm afraid only he knows the answer to that."

"And what do I do now? Should I apply to another firm? Because I doubt I shall enjoy working for anyone else now that I've worked for you, sir."

"Apply for another firm?" he said. "No, I shouldn't if I were you." He studied the sky and let the sunshine warm his face. "No, if I were you I would go back to the house, unpack your bag, and just relax. You've earned a good rest, John. Because this is where the work really starts. I hope you understand that?"

"Sir?" John said. "I'm sorry I don't understand."

"Well, it's quite simple, John. Should I spell it out for you?"

"But I thought—"

"My dear boy," Mr Fisher said, and he stopped to place a hand on his shoulder. "Do you recall what I did with the train ticket to Hagworthingham?"

John thought for a moment, recalling the envelope on the desk.

"You left it on your desk, sir," John said, and he let Mr Fisher turn him so that together they faced the entrance to the office further down the street. A taxi had been summoned, the driver of which was loading Garfield's luggage into the boot compartment. "I don't understand. Do you mean that..."

"If I had been the managing partner when Mr Forsdyke was an apprentice, he would have suffered the same fate," Mr Fisher said, watching as a tearful Bobby Garfield stared at him from beside the car, all the joy gone from his face, and then climbed into the back seat. "Arrogance and self-righteousness have no place in this world, let alone at Swain and Swain, my boy." He winked at John. "Welcome to the club, John."

CHAPTER FIFTY-ONE
March 31, 2024

"So Bobby was thrown to the wolves, as it were?" Charles asked, to which Stow simply nodded. "Yet he's now a partner. What was that, some kind of reincarnation?"

"He's a good lawyer," Stow said. "And you know what they say about keeping your enemies close."

"Aye, I do," Charles said. "Although, if you don't mind me saying, keeping them close is one thing but employing them?"

"Like I said, he's a good lawyer. Not so much in the academic sense. You'll find his name has more entries in our reference library than most others, but he is tenacious. If there's a way to win, then he'll find it."

"Whereas a lawyer such as yourself would memorise facts and precedents? You could recall them at a moment's notice?"

"That's right," Stow said. "But it takes all sorts, does it not?"

"It does indeed. But I have to say that this little feud between the two of you—"

"Let's not escalate this above what it actually is, Inspector. Whatever it is between Bobby and I, it is not a feud, I can assure you."

"A lifelong rivalry then?" Charles suggested. "Whatever it is, it's enough that we looked a little deeper into your history."

"Hence your opening statement," Stow said, and with every sentence the man spoke, his friendly tone was fading.

"You know how we work, do you not? You know what we look for during investigations such as Hugo Garfield's murder?"

"A motive? Of course," Stow replied. "You identify individuals who were close to the victim then eliminate them through a process designed to place each one in another location without means or opportunity. Those who you fail to eliminate are therefore worthy of an investigation. Tell me, Inspector, how did Bobby fare during this process?"

"He passed," Charles said. "Why do you ask? Is there something I should know about him?"

"I would imagine that if you've spoken to him, Inspector, then you'll be fully aware that Bobby Garfield is a curious man."

"A curious man, indeed," Charles agreed. "In fact, we've spoken to him at length."

"In that case, I might add that if you've spoken to him at length, and you now find yourself in a position where I might be able to further your inquiries, then I can only assume that Bobby has put you my way. In fact, I'd venture further and suggest that Bobby Garfield has dreamed up a line of inquiry which you cannot ignore."

"That's very intuitive of you, Mr Stow."

"Not really," he replied. "He does it all the time. In fact, I would go as far as to say that it's his signature move. Can't find a suitable defence? Then shine the light onto somebody else. Give the jury something to chew on. Something to cause a little doubt, because as you well know, it is not the purpose of the defendant to prove innocence but the prosecution to prove guilt, and where there's doubt, guilt cannot be proven."

"And how does he tend to do that?" Charles asked.

"Any way he can, Inspector. Like I said, he is a tenacious man, and if it means that he must dredge through decades of accounts to find something worthy of resurrecting, then he will." He leaned forward and jabbed a finger at Charles. "That man will go to any lengths to win."

"But he didn't win, did he?" Charles said. "He lost against you."

"He did," Stow said, with no suggestion of a glower.

"But there were more, weren't there?" Charles said. "More battles to be fought. Am I right, John?"

"You are," he replied, without hesitation. "There were many battles over the years if that's what you want to call them."

"And was Rose Garfield one of those battles, John?" Charles asked. "Or should I say, Rose Lavender?"

Stow turned towards the window and ran his tongue across his teeth.

"Do you want to tell me about her, John?" Charles asked. "Is there something between you and Rose? Something big enough to reopen an old wound, perhaps?"

CHAPTER FIFTY-TWO

December 23, 1984

The night was cool and still and Lincoln was bustling with last-minute shoppers, drinkers, and workers. Pulling his coat around him, John stepped into the night and savoured the fresh air. It seemed to him that everyone and their dog had taken up smoking, and the cool air was refreshing in his lungs.

He could still hear the band, which seemed to be louder than the previous years, and the music they were playing was far more raucous than ever before. They had played the classics of course, including a number of Beatles and Stones songs, which were guaranteed to fill the dance floor, and some of the more recent hits from the likes of Prince and The Police. The quartet had played their part and it pleased John to see the youngest apprentice and Mrs Fisher open the ball with a waltz. Nobody had said anything about the tradition but he caught Henry nodding his appreciation from where he entertained a number of clients.

But enough was enough. The music was too loud, the room too smoky, and the year too long. It should have been a night of celebration. He should have been on his knees on the dance floor with champagne in one hand and a cigar in the other or being lifted into the air by his colleagues.

But the night called to him, the peace summoned him, and it felt good to disappear into that throng of shoppers, drinkers, and workers. He found himself at ease and for once actually had the time to saunter while those around him fought for the space ahead, edging and bumping, darting this way and that. Once again, he held that gold coin of time. Even if it was only for a while, he would hang on to it and clutch it with both hands.

He stopped on High Bridge with the old Tudor building behind him and the river stretching off towards the Fens and the Wolds and the coast beyond. It was odd, he thought, that he could drop into the icy water beneath him and float nearly all the way home. If he alighted at Bardney, half of the journey would be complete – unbearable, unrealistic, and deadly, but complete nonetheless.

He was reminded of a song he had heard on the wireless that Henry had insisted on installing in the office. It was by an American chap, as was so much of the music these days. The Times They Are A Changing, he recalled, and couldn't help but agree. The artist was, in John's opinion, no poet or seer of the future, and John doubted he would become a household name, such was the tumultuous nature of the music industry, which seemed to move like the river beneath him endlessly and unforgiving. But he was right. The times were indeed changing. The world moved faster than it ever had. People had less time for each other, less time for manners, and less tolerance of needs. Christmas was losing its purpose, which was evident in the volume of shopping bags that passed before him and the men who shouted abuse as they ventured from pub to pub. Even the women these days seemed to have found a voice and were just as guilty as the men of stumbling through the city centre.

A busker, one of those vagabonds whose arrogance depicted that the general public should enjoy their music, and if not, endure it nonetheless, ended his song. He entered into something a little more pleasing to the ear. A classical piece that John recognised well, and it brought a smile to his face.

"Ave Maria," he said aloud and to himself, and he wondered how many of the people who flowed past him from left to right and right to left also knew the piece, or if they were left wanting another of those cheesy Christmas pop songs.

It was as if the busker played solely for him and he closed his eyes, remembering a time when that old turntable in Mrs Lavender's room had crackled and popped before those same notes had filled his mind with joy.

"A penny for your thoughts," a voice said, soft and creamy in tone but harsher than in his memories.

And there she was, draped in fur, with that porcelain skin shining in the streetlight.

"Rose?" he said.

"Good evening, John," she replied, and she came to his side, leaning against the bridge, just as he did. "I thought it might be you."

"Thought?" he said. "Have the years been unkind to me, Rose?"

"Hoped," she said with a laugh. "And no, they haven't."

"Would it be impertinent to suggest that you're still as beautiful as you were ten years ago?"

"Not impertinent, no," she said. "But perhaps it's a little inappropriate." She held up her left hand to reveal a brace of rings on her third finger, the first of which was a gold band encrusted with glittering diamonds. The second had just a single diamond in a golden clasp and could have paid the shopping bills of any dozen of the shoppers that to-ed and fro-ed.

"How lovely," he said. "Well, I hope that you are very happy."

"Define happy," she replied coyly.

"Does he treat you well, Rose?" he asked, to which she responded by shoving her hands into the pockets of her fur. "I see."

"And you? Is there a special somebody to whom I might cast my unending jealousy?"

"There's not," he said, forcing the words out with as much enthusiasm as he could. "I am as free as the wind."

He pushed off the balustrade and then turned to face her, and for the second time in a decade, he held out his hand.

"I wonder if you would care to dance?" he asked, exactly as her mother had taught him.

"Dance? Here?"

"It's our song," he replied, still holding his hand out. "This is the song your mother played when you taught me to dance."

"You're mad."

"It's Christmas, Rose," he told her. "And how can you possibly tell me that this is inappropriate? What are the chances of us meeting here tonight when the band is playing our song?"

"It's a busker, John."

"Not in my head it isn't," he said, and his persistence ground her into submission. She took his hand and he held her, while all about them the shoppers and the workers, and the drinkers went about their lives. Time stood still for him. They waited for the melody to come around, and he led. They could have been centre stage in a show or atop the highest mountain because not a single other soul in the world existed.

Until she uttered four words.

"He's nearby, you know?" He heard them and he didn't break step. "He's a lawyer at Bain and Co. They're having their Christmas drinks near the castle."

"Won't you be missed?"

"Not likely. He's busy entertaining clients. I've played my part."

"Which is?"

"I'm the glamorous wife, John. They've seen me and now they're talking shop," she said. "You'll excuse me for saying that listening to lawyers discussing contracts and law isn't at the top of my most exciting things to do."

"I wholeheartedly agree," he said.

"And so I find myself redundant."

"Not to me you're not."

"Free to peruse the shops and to drink in the Christmas spirit."

They were cheek to cheek until she moved to stare at him, and although he smelled the wine on her breath, her eyes were as clear as a mountain pool.

"There are benefits to being free," he told her.

"Just as there are drawbacks," she replied. "Sometimes a tether or two can help us appreciate what we have."

"And are you tethered?" he asked. "Is there a young Bobby Garfield somewhere? Or a Rose, perhaps?"

She shook her head and nestled into him again.

"I'm afraid that wasn't meant to be," she said sadly.

"I'm sorry."

"There's no need to be. These things aren't for us to decide, are they?"

"Then who gets to bear that particular burden? Not God, surely?"

He recalled the time they had spoken of God and those they had lost.

"No, not God," she said. "But whoever it is, it certainly isn't me."

The busker picked the final few notes to little applause, save for John's grateful nod cast from Rose's delicate shoulder.

They stayed that way for a moment and John savoured it. He inhaled her, breathed her, and remembered her. He remembered the way she had looked that very first time she had entered Mrs Lavender's room. He remembered her since, in the frocks, the dresses, and with nothing at all but their sweaty cocktail.

"Kiss me," she said and he was fifteen years old again, unable to move, speak, or even think. "I just want to feel it once more. The freedom." Her tongue moistened her lips and the breeze caught her loose curls.

"Will I have to run naked through the city?" he asked, and she bit down on her lower lip.

"Not this time," she replied. "No, this one is for me."

CHAPTER FIFTY-THREE

March 31, 2024

The interview, as informal as it was, was progressing. Stow had long since dropped his charm and adopted an altogether more stoic demeanour. It was a defence mechanism, of that Charles was sure.

"While Sergeant Devon contacts your mother to confirm your whereabouts, John," Charles began, "I think that now would be a good time to discuss the farm, don't you?"

"I am at your mercy, am I not?" he said, linking his fingers and laying his hands on his lap. "Although I should warn you that Franky will be leaving shortly, so if you'd like a drink–"

"I'm fine, thank you," Charles told him. "So you moved to the farm when exactly?"

"After my father died," Stow replied. "Mother was struggling. She picked up a little job in a nearby village. If I'm honest, I can barely even remember those days."

"But she met your step-father?"

"She did," he said. "Terry is a good man. Not many men back then would have taken us on, but he did."

"You went to live with him?"

"We did, but listen, is all of this necessary?" Stow said. "I fail to see how digging up my past is going to help you find Hugo Garfield's murderer. I mean, I was still in short trousers."

"I just want to build a picture, that's all," Charles said. "The thing is that with this investigation, everyone I speak to has, at some point or another, referred back to a time in the past. An event, so to speak, and given that, if you don't mind me saying, each of you are mature adults, I'm led to believe that whatever the reason for Hugo's death lies in the past somewhere. Something happened, John. Something big enough to warrant the murder of Hugo Garfield. Now, whether that be revenge, or power, or money, I don't know." He sat back in his chair and mirrored Stow's posture. "But I intend to find out, and if that means that I have to dig into your past, Bobby's past, Hugo's past, and anybody else's for that matter, then so be it."

"You're very articulate, Inspector."

"I'm glad I'm able to make myself clear," Charles replied, and he nodded for Devon to leave them so she could verify his whereabouts. "You see, the farm in question, Frobisher's farm, I believe it's called?"

"Correct."

"As I understand it, the land belongs to the Garfield estate. It's what is known as a tenant farm, is that right?"

"Very good."

"And therefore, your stepfather, Terry, has rented the land from Hugo Garfield for a sum of money since before you moved there."

"He took over the contract from his father. It's been in the family for more than a hundred years now, I believe."

"That's quite the business relationship."

"It's an agreement," Stow replied curtly.

"See, here's the thing," Charles said, hoping to provide some kind of background to the avenue of questioning. "When Bobby Garfield suggested that you might have cause to harm the Garfield family, he gave us no real reason as to why."

"He's well aware of the repercussions of slander," Stow said.

"Agreed," Charles replied. "But as you can understand, my team were then required to see if we can find a motive. You have to believe me when I say that I was pushing back on the idea that you could be involved. I didn't want to be here taking your valuable time, John."

"Which suggests that they found something with enough substance that you were forced to set aside your personal opinions and venture down this route," Stow said.

"They did," Charles agreed. "We know about the farm being sold."

"I see. So?"

"Well, it must have been hard news to learn, John. The family farm, which as you said has been in the family for more than a hundred years being taken away. How old is your mother now, if you don't mind me asking?"

"Do you need to ask?" Stow said, to which Charles smiled.

"No, I don't," he said. "She's eighty-three and Terry, your stepfather, is eighty-eight. That's a hell of an age to be working a farm."

"He doesn't work the farm himself," Stow replied. "Well, he keeps a small field for their own produce but the rest is sublet."

"So that provides an income, does it?"

"It helps," Stow said.

"The point I'm trying to make is that for a couple in their eighties to up sticks and move to a new house with no income, and as far as I can see, no real private pension plan to speak of, that must be harrowing. They're about to become destitute, are they not?"

"Of course not," Stow said. "I wouldn't see my mother fall into ruin, would I?"

"Ah," Charles said. "That's exactly what I thought. You see, one of my team, a Detective Constable Chalk, to give her a name, is a wonder with research. Absolutely thrives on it, she does. She looked into Hugo Garfield's accounts. The same accounts that Bobby Garfield was poring over when we first visited him at his home in Lincoln."

"I presume this line of sporadic questioning will culminate in a point?" Stow said.

"Oh aye, it will," Charles said. "But let's go back to nineteen-eighty-four, shall we? What happened, John?"

CHAPTER FIFTY-FOUR

December 24, 1984

The roads were as familiar to him as his reflection in the mirror. Yet in all his years in Lincoln, he could recall the journey only once – the time when he had been a little more than a fifteen-year-old boy in the passenger seat of his stepfather's truck, off to seek his fortune.

The winter sun was low in the sky and the bare trees that dotted the fields were skeletal against the hues of blue and grey. It had been one of those days where the sun shone brightly as if to lure a man from the warmth of his fireside, only for the bitter cold to bite into his bare skin.

The village was unspoiled and yet it seemed not to welcome him but to turn its back, if ever buildings could. Grey smoke rose from chimneys, and people, strangers to him now, crossed the road and hurried along the footpath, perhaps making final preparations for Christmas with their families.

He turned into the lane and brought the car to a stop. Excitement, trepidation, anxiety, and hope all combined to wet his palms and send his heart into a thumping drum inside his chest. A layer of sweat had formed on his back, despite the cold, and even his feet twitched inside his Oxfords.

The house was in view now, across the fields that he had worked so many times. And a single light shone like an all-seeing eye watching his arrival. The kitchen window. It was three o'clock. They would be hunkering down for the evening. Perhaps Terry would be fetching in wood for the night while Ma prepared dinner.

He wondered if she had a new pinny and then smiled at the thought of her before pushing the car into gear and moving slowly forward.

He brought the car to a stop in the courtyard and switched the engine off. Little had changed. The same cast-iron sheep stood outside the back door for Terry to scrape his boots, the same curtains hung in the kitchen window, and even the same locks and chains secured the outbuildings.

The door opened and light from inside spilled onto the gravel and mud. He was still strong and fit and lean, and his curious eyes still drank in the scene without revealing a single thought. He squinted and ducked to see into the car and his brow furrowed as he drew nearer. But John could contain it no more. He climbed from the car and stood with the door between them, basking in Terry's surprise.

"Hello, Terry," he said.

"Well, I'll be," Terry replied, shaking his head. He opened his arms and his leather face accommodated the smile John had seen so often in his dreams. They embraced and then he held John at arm's length to appraise him. "Just look at you. Just bally-well look at you." He turned to the car, narrowing his eyes. "A Jaguar?"

"An XJ6," John replied. "It goes well."

"My my," Terry said, and he tutted, shaking his head again. "Just look at you, John. Just look at you."

"How is she?" John asked, and Terry's expression saddened.

"She's all right, John. She's bearing up," he said. "Come on, let's get you inside."

John popped the boot lid open and Terry came to help.

"Is that my old bag?" he asked.

"It is," John said proudly, and he handed it to him, before reaching for his much larger holdall. "You'll be pleased to learn that it has served me well."

"I remember the day you left here, John," Terry said. "With nothing more than this bag. And do you know what you said to me?"

"If I come home with anything more, then I will have gained?" John said, and Terry nodded.

"And boy have you gained. Come on, or your ma will be wondering what I'm up to."

He led the way and John followed him through the back door and into the kitchen, where a wall of warmth hit him from the open fireplace.

"You there, Mary?" Terry called out.

"I'm in the parlour," she called back, and Terry put his fingers to his lips for John to keep quiet. "I thought we'd have Christmas dinner in the parlour," she replied, her voice growing nearer. "We barely have use for it any more."

"Well, you might want to lay an extra space," Terry called out and winked at John.

She stepped into view and stopped dead. Her mouth hung open and her eyes danced across him as if in disbelief.

"My boy," she said, and ran the few steps to him, jumping into his arms. "Just look at you."

"Hello, Mum," he replied, staying within her arms but holding her face away so he could see her. "Happy Christmas."

"Oh, my dear boy," she said and then pulled away to stare at Terry. "Did you know about this?"

"Not a clue," he replied. "I found him outside parked up in his Jaguar."

John smiled at her.

"You always wanted a Jaguar."

"There's lots of things I wanted," he said.

"It's been ten years, John. If it wasn't for your letters, I might have thought something had happened."

"Oh, something has happened, Ma," he replied. "Something wonderful has happened."

"No? You're getting married. Who is she? A city girl?"

"No, Ma," he said. "Not that. I've been made a partner at the firm."

"A partner?"

"The youngest partner we've ever had. I'm twenty-six, Ma. The youngest before me was thirty-three." He smiled emphatically at her. "I've made it, ma. I've really done it."

She beamed from ear to ear.

"I never doubted it for a moment," she said. Her hair was greying and she'd lost weight, but she was still the same woman. Yet it was almost impossible not to reflect on her demeanour towards him. All he remembered of the fifteen years he had lived with her were the scoldings, the moods, and the brooding atmosphere. And although her eyes were still cold and hard, she had softened with age like a fine wine. "Not a single moment."

"I thought I might stay," he said. "If you'll have me. Just for a day or so. Then I'll need to get back."

"You can stay as long as you like, John," Terry said. "I'll just take your bags up to your room."

"It's how you left it," she said when Terry had left. "He wanted me to change it, but I stood firm. Not a thing is out of place."

"Nothing's changed, Ma," he said, his eyes roaming the room, drinking in the scene like he was a fifteen-year-old boy once more. "Not a thing. I thought you might have changed something. Decorated or something."

"No need," she replied. "There's nothing wrong with it. Why bother?"

He eyed the old dress she was wearing beneath that same old pinny and remembered it well.

"You have been receiving the money I sent, haven't you?"

She nodded.

"And grateful we are, too," she said.

"You haven't spent it, have you? Please don't tell me you've saved it. It was meant for you, Ma."

"Oh, it's spent. Don't you worry about that," she replied, and then fussed about the oven, turning her back on him.

"Ma, is everything okay? If you need more, then you only have to ask–"

"It's fine," she said. "Everything is just fine." She stood and leaned on the kitchen worktop to stare out of the window into the dying day. "Come on, tell me about life in the city."

"It's not, Ma, is it?" he said. "It's not fine,"

"Oh, John," she replied and closed her eyes to him as he came to her side. "Ma, whatever it is, we can sort it. Just tell me."

"You can't, John. It's too late for any of that now."

"For any of what?" he said, and then a thought struck him. "Ma, you're not sick, are you?"

"No," she said.

"Promise me, Ma. If you are then we'll find someone to help us."

"I'm not sick," she said, and her weak smile conveyed the gratitude she couldn't bear to say. "It's the farm."

"The farm? What about it?"

"Squire's put the rent up," she said. "We got the letter this morning. Hand posted, would you believe?"

"I'm not following," John said. "How long have you got? Why?"

She stood, tossed her cloth over her shoulder, and sighed heavily.

"We can't pay it. We've got 'til March. Then we're to find somewhere."

"Three months?"

"Don't say nothing, John. Not to Terry. He won't want you to worry."

"I'll go and see the squire," John said. "Although I can't believe the self-righteous bugger still calls himself that."

"No, it'll only make things worse, John. Just leave it. We'll have a nice Christmas together. It'll be like old times."

"And then what?" John said. "What will you do then?"

"We'll muddle on by, I expect."

"But, ma, he can't just throw you out on your ear," John told her, and he paced to the back door and back. "Hugo Garfield has overstepped the mark this time, Ma. I'm a partner in a law firm. I can make things happen. I can find a loophole or a clause, I don't know. I'll need to see the contract."

"John, John, John," she said, and any sign of the brawler she had once been was gone. "It wasn't Hugo. He don't manage the tenants no more, not that there's many of us left."

"So who does?" John asked. "Ma, who manages the tenants on his behalf?"

She pulled her lips into her mouth as if wondering if she should even tell him, but then relented.

"It's his boy who does it all now," she said. "Bobby Garfield. He's a lawyer, just like you."

It was as if she had sucked the very breath from his body.

"Bobby Garfield?"

"Squire's knocking on, John," she said. "Suppose he had to pass on some of the duties someday, didn't he?"

John nodded and watched as she moved about the kitchen. She could have done it all blindfolded with one arm tied behind her back. He saw it – the kitchen, the house, and the farm, for what it really was, and them, Terry and her, they were as part of that old place as the old dresser was and the old wattle and daub walls and the old stone floor.

"You're not leaving," he said.

"Oh, John. It's not that bad–"

"You're not leaving, Ma," he said. "I'll pay."

"You can't do that. You do enough already–"

"I'm paying, Ma, and that's all there is to it."

She shook her head sadly.

"And next year and the one after that? Rent ain't coming down, is it?"

"You're not leaving, Ma," he said. "You belong here. Terry belongs here. One way or another, I'll make it work. I have a position now and I'll be damned if I let those Garfields get the better of us any more."

"Oh, John–"

"Things are going to change, Ma," he said. "You mark my words. One of these days, Bobby Garfield is going to be sorry he ever tried to cross us."

CHAPTER FIFTY-FIVE
March 31, 2024

"And you've been paying it ever since, have you?" Charles said. "In addition to your Lincoln home, you've been subsidising your mother and stepfather's rent, which I might add, is not a sum to be sniffed at."

"What would you have done?" Stow replied. "Tell me, Inspector. If you had the means, would you have seen your own mother fall into, what was the word that you used? Destitution? Would you have seen them lose everything they've worked for, for the sake of some petty feud between Bobby Garfield and me? How would she feel if she discovered that was the reason they had been on the breadline for the past forty years? Not because of the economy, not because of the government's ridiculous red tape and inability to understand that British farmers are suffering, but because of me, her only son and some long-winded argument with the local rich boy who–"

"Who what?" Charles said, to which Stow said nothing, instead choosing to take a breath and collect his thoughts.

"I paid the difference. Whatever the outstanding balance was, I paid it."

"Well, see now, that makes sense, John. I noticed that

Frobisher Farm is not the sole tenant on the estate. There's another rented to the Mason family, too, and more. But none of those seemed to have experienced the hikes in rents, certainly not to the degree that Frobisher Farm has."

"Like I said, Bobby Garfield is a tenacious man. If he wants something, he'll get it."

"And if that something is your demise?"

"Then he'll go to any lengths to get it, Inspector," Stow finished for him.

Charles contemplated the conundrum, doing his utmost not to let the back and forth between Garfield and Stow sway his own mind. He had to remain objective, which in matters of the heart, recent matters, was easy enough. But when it came to matters that had been brewing for decades, there was far more to lose for both parties.

"Would I be right in my assumption that your main defence will be along the lines of Bobby Garfield's lifelong ambition to destroy you, John?" he said, laying his cards out on the table in a line. Whatever the question lacked could be surmised from his tone and choice of words.

"You would," Stow replied. "Which puts you in a slightly challenging position, does it not?"

"You're playing the same game as Bobby Garfield, John," Charles said. "Which is interesting in more ways than one."

"How so?"

"Well, Bobby Garfield knows that should he be charged for his father's murder he would, of course, provide a plea of innocence and thence be required to stand trial, hedging all of his bets onto the doubt caused by the lines of inquiry he has provided surrounding you, his lifelong rival." Stow nodded his agreement, but Charles hadn't finished. "And in response to that, what you're suggesting is that should you stand trial, Mr Stow, you would also be counting on reasonable doubt caused by lines of inquiry surrounding Bobby Garfield, no doubt providing evidence of unfair tenancy agreements, his suffering at you not only winning the apprenticeship way back in the eighties but subsequently becoming the managing partner. The problem is that this then detracts from the issue of who killed Hugo Garfield, and focuses on which of you has more to lose, and which of you is willing to go furthest to win."

"I have to say, Inspector, you are extremely astute," Stow said.

"But here's the thing that I think you're missing, and if it helps it's not just you. You're both missing it. I am, as you say, astute, and I have the benefit of being rather separated emotionally from the mess that you both have found yourselves in," Charles said. "Which, in a roundabout way, leads me to believe that the root of this issue lies somewhere deeper." He hit his chest with his fist. "It's a matter of the heart, John. There's nothing that a man doesn't fight for more than the love of a woman."

For the first time, Stow showed a sign of weakness. He licked his lips, narrowed his eyes, and cleared his throat, all of which were signs that he was masking his true thoughts. Yet had his true thoughts been innocent, he wouldn't have moved an inch and he wouldn't have made a sound.

"I'm going to be honest with you, John," Charles said. "Out of the two of you, it is you who I am inclined to pursue in this matter. Not that I find Bobby Garfield anything other than reproachful, but merely because we have found evidence that places his car entering Lincoln before his father was murdered. Now, as you well know, anybody could have been driving that car, and if need be, we will investigate his alibi further, but for now, my attention lies solely with you." He laid his hands on the table and considered his words carefully. "I am a fair man, John. I hope you have no reason to think otherwise."

"From what I know of you, Inspector, I would agree," Stow replied.

"Thank you. So when I tell you that we can place you in the

area of the murder on the day of the murder, and can prove that you have at least some knowledge of the house and its workings, then you would understand, I hope, that I have enough right now to ask you to accompany me to the police station. Would that be a fair analysis?"

"Should I see things from your perspective, Inspector, yes, it would."

"Thank you again," Charles replied. "But before we venture down that path, from which I am quite positive, this friendly relationship we have developed will never recover, I'm going to give you one chance to tell me if there is any other reason for the feud between Bobby Garfield and yourself. One chance, John. That's all you have left."

"One chance? Out of hundreds of episodes of bullying and humiliation?" Stow said. "You didn't know him when we were young, Inspector, and you have barely scratched the surface of who he is now."

"Well, in the interest of keeping this concise, I'll narrow it down, shall I?" Charles added. "Rose Garfield." He sat back, laying his hands on his lap once more. "Or should I say, Rose Lavender?"

CHAPTER FIFTY-SIX

December 23, 2023

It was hard to believe that fifty years had passed since John had attended his first Swain and Swain Christmas ball.

He almost couldn't bring himself to utter the words, but once he had started, he found comfort in them somehow, just as he found solace and reassurance in the office's wood-panelled walls and the nostalgia in the volumes that had sat on the bookshelves for all that time.

"Fifty years?" he said into the microphone to his polite audience, and then let them ponder the magnitude of the statement. "I was apprenticed at fifteen," he continued. "And I'm sure you all know well enough the humiliation I endured that evening when I was tricked into dancing a waltz with Mrs Fisher who at the time was the managing partner's wife. How times have changed since. And as I have no wife to call my own..." He pointed at the group of trainee solicitors standing to one side of the ballroom. "You should count yourselves lucky that that particular tradition should continue in the arms of the wonderful Mrs Garfield."

Rose smiled briefly and then clutched Bobby's arm in a show of solidarity that John saw through with ease.

"Hear hear," somebody called from the crowd, and John raised a hand before others joined in and dislodged his grasp on their attention.

"It took me ten years to make partner. Ten years. From a young boy who knew nothing to a young man who, through sheer grit and determination, focus and hard work, suddenly had a bright future. And I think that's the key here," he told the audience. "I think that it is that same grit and determination, that unwillingness to let the other side win, that has kept Swain and Swain going for all these years. Not my own determination, which I can only apply to my individual career, but to us all. To you all. And to the generations to come."

He peered at the trainees again, remembering the first time that he had stood there in wonder as Mr Fisher had given his speech, praying that one day, he would have that same chance. He wondered if they too shared that same feeling, or like so many of today's youths, the opportunity they had been given was lost on them.

"And now it is time for me to hand the baton over," he said, and the hum in the room faded. "Thankfully, we are all too young to remember the Second World War, although many of us were raised in its wake. But there is one prominent episode that took place during that terrible time that I'd like to draw your attention to if I may. I'd like to speak of France and her decision to relinquish its most prized asset to Germany. Please, this is not a history lecture. There is a point to which I am heading. We are led to believe that the sheer force with which Germany swept through Europe terrified France into submission. I beg to differ. I believe that the powers that be recognised the beauty of cities like Paris, and for the greater good, for the sole purpose of generations to come being able to enjoy them under whatever regime that might be, they conceded. They handed over their fabulous city, and it *is* fabulous. I've been a few times and I can say that Paris is astonishing. But it wouldn't have been there for me to see, had that decision not been made. Had France dug her heels in,

Germany would have flattened the entire city, just like it had done in other parts of Europe."

He recognised the faces in the crowd, each of them captivated. Francis Hyke dabbed at her eye and beamed at him.

"And that's what I'm doing," he said aloud, but to her. "There are many great lawyers within Swain and Swain, some younger than me, and whether you believe it or not, some who are older by a year or two. But there is one man among them for whom I have the utmost respect. A man who I believe can lead Swain and Swain into its next phase. To bring on new lawyers, to accommodate the future far better than I ever could. I, ladies and gentlemen, and for those of you who failed to decode my metaphor, am France."

He smiled at the silence in the great room, where for fifty years he had been almost deafened by the volume of the band and the guests.

"If you believe the records and the hype, then you'll believe that France surrendered after just six weeks. I'm pleased to say that it will be a few months before I hand over the keys to the office. But hand them over, I will. And that leaves us with just one crucial piece of information to impart. Who, in this rather long-winded speech, gets to play at being Germany?"

Although forty years had passed since that first Christmas when John had stood upon High Bridge, nothing had really changed. Shoppers, drunks, and workers still filled the streets despite the late hour, and there was even a busker nearby, just as there always was. But the busker was not the same, and John wondered briefly, as he listened to the gentle acoustic guitar, where that man was now. Had he made it in the harsh and fickle music industry? Was he a household name, or had John, unbeknownst, heard him on the radio? Perhaps busking had been a means to an end and he now worked in an altogether different industry.

"If I didn't know you so well, John, I would have said that you did all that to see me," a voice said as he peered down into the River Witham. The voice was accompanied by a fragrance, familiar and fresh as ever it was. He felt her sidle beside him, and then eventually, he looked at her. "You would give up your entire career just for a chance to kiss me?"

"I would run naked through the streets for the chance to kiss you," he replied, and she closed her eyes as she smiled. "I suppose he's still giving his acceptance speech, is he?"

"You know Bobby," she replied. "He'll be up there all night given the chance."

"And you won't be missed?"

"Oh no, my job is done for the night," she replied.

"Well, you'll have to continue the tradition of dancing with the youngest apprentice," he told her. "This time next year, you'll be married to the managing partner. There'll be no escaping the responsibility."

She laughed once but it faded fast.

"Maybe," she said quietly. "I'm more interested in our tradition."

"Which tradition is that?"

"Our tradition," she replied, and they each turned their heads. They were inches apart yet worlds away. "Do you remember that first year we met here?"

"How could I forget?" he said, and he thought he saw a blush creeping onto her cheeks. "It was nineteen eighty-four. Water passed beneath our feet. You pretended not to be cold–"

"And you acted like I was lost to Bobby Garfield," she finished. "You gave up."

"Nothing's changed," he said, and he glanced down at the water.

"We did it again ten years later," she said. "And every ten years since. That's our tradition, John. That's what I don't want to lose."

"I'm not sure how many decades I have left," he said. "In fact, I'm running out of them. We all are. At some point, I have to make the decision to walk away before things are spoiled forever."

"Are we talking about Swain and Swain now?" she said. "Or me?"

"I asked myself that same question" he replied, and laughed aloud, before concealing his thoughts.

"Why did you do it, John? Why did you give in to him?"

"I didn't give in—"

"Then what was all that about France and Germany?"

"It was a metaphor," he said. "And it was rather apt, I thought." He shoved off the handrail to stand straight and then held a hand out. "Dance with me," he said. "For old time's sake."

She hesitated, and considering they had danced there every ten years for the past four decades, her hesitation had little to do with the embarrassment of dancing in public, and more to do with her reluctance to begin the end of their tradition.

But she took his hand and John caught the busker's eye.

"Oh really," she said, as the busker began the opening bars of Ave Maria. "How much did you have to pay him to do this?"

She rested her head on his shoulder and they swayed back and forth.

"Oh, enough that he can probably pack up and go home when we're done," John replied, and he felt her grin against his chest. "Do you suppose that had I been born into money, that things might have worked out differently?"

"Born wealthy, you mean?" she asked and raised her head to see him. She was a marvel, even at their age, her skin was near flawless, and her eyes so vivid, as if the strains of life had done little to ease their lustre.

"No, that's an entirely different thing," he told her. "Bobby is the wealthy one. He has the money, the girl, the daughter, the life. Me? I'm just rich."

She smiled sadly and laid her head back down on his chest.

"John?" she said, and he squeezed her hand in response, savouring her touch and not daring to speak with tears in his eyes. "You're wealthier than you think, you know?"

CHAPTER FIFTY-SEVEN
March 31, 2024

Charles was enthralled. Dumbfounded. He gazed at John Stow, a man who commanded the room with very little effort yet somehow managed to retain his humble beginnings and his heart.

"You met her in the same spot at the same time every ten years?" he said, to which Stow nodded happily.

"It was our thing. Our tradition."

Charles shook his head.

"And you handed over the keys to Swain and Swain to Bobby Garfield? Despite everything we've discussed, did you not think it a pertinent fact, John? Do you see how a jury might consider that as withholding information or even obstructing the course of justice?"

"I knew you'd get there," he replied confidently. "In the end at least." He checked his watch and then tugged his sleeve back into place. "Besides, I still have a few hours left at the helm, so it wasn't really a lie now, was it?"

"A few hours?"

"Bobby Garfield begins his reign tomorrow, Inspector."

"Tomorrow?"

"And what will you do? Slip into retirement, I suppose? Happy in the knowledge that Hugo Garfield is dead?"

"Ouch," John said, and playfully he pulled a hurt expression to accentuate his point. "And anyway, who said anything about being happy?"

"If you're not happy, then what are you?" Charles asked.

"Beat?" Stow suggested. "Tired, even? I don't know anymore." He sat back and with a neatly manicured finger, loosened his tie, and then took a few moments to pop the top button of his shirt. "Do you know, in the fifty years that I've been coming to this office, I don't think I've ever been here in such a state of undress?"

"Well, if that's a state of undress, John, I'm afraid you'd find the sight of our incident room nothing short of indecent," Charles remarked, which raised a weak smile.

Stow inhaled long and hard and seemed lost in the world outside the window. The morning was growing late and the street was far busier than it had been. And still, the old man in the doorway remained there, safely tucked into the niche with a blanket around his legs.

"Do you know, that man has been living on the streets for as long as I can remember?"

"It's a way of life for some," Charles replied. "Not you though, I expect. I imagine your retirement to be far more comfortable."

Stow laughed once and then let it fade away.

"Do you think it'll bother you in the years to come?" Charles asked. "Being beaten, I mean. Do you think you'll ever be able to let it go?"

"Let what go, Inspector?"

"Bobby Garfield beating you," Charles replied. "Won't that get to you? Or is that it? Is that the reason for all of this?"

"Bobby beating me?" He laughed aloud this time and was clearly unwilling to let it fade.

"Have I said something to amuse you?"

Stow sighed but carried on smiling.

"Swain and Swain has earned me a good pension. My mother will want for nothing, and Terry too. I'm sure I'll find a way to fill my days."

"You're an enigma, John," Charles said. "And if I'm honest, it's not helping your cause."

Stow turned his back to the world outside and faced Charles.

"Inspector, for the first time in my life, I can see freedom," he said, then held his hand palm up, as if picturing some imaginary object before him. "It's right there, within reach. I could just reach out and touch it."

"Well, from where I'm sitting, that freedom you speak of is getting further away, John. In fact, with every word you speak, my desire to escort you to the station grows stronger." Charles stood from his chair and came to stand beside Stow. Charles faced the windows, while Stow stared at the office through the glazed meeting room walls. "You're running out of time," Charles said. "I said I'd give you one chance to explain your side of the story, yet you seem content on leading me further into this world of yours. I walked in here unsure if I had reason to arrest you, John. But now? I think I'd be remiss not to. In fact, no, I'd have to be a damned lunatic not to."

"Shall I tell you what my plan was, Inspector? My endgame, so to speak."

"I think you should, John."

"My plan was to enjoy cooked breakfasts with my mother and Terry," Stow said suddenly and then turned his head to stare at Charles. "To walk in the hills as free as a bird. A wealthy man at last." He plunged his hands into his trouser pockets and rocked back and forth on his heels and toes. "And where would Bobby Garfield be?"

He stopped and raised an eyebrow while Charles digested the question.

"Here, I suppose?"

"Exactly, Inspector. The man is so blinded by his tenacity that he hasn't even seen it. I've handed him the keys to the empire. He's the new managing partner of Swain and Swain. Do you honestly think that he would give that up? Do you really think he would have rejected the offer?" He shook his head. "No, of course not. The man will be working until he dies. He'll be so fuelled on power and position that the rest of his meagre life will pass him by, while I should be breathing the fresh air and eating good food." He turned again to face the window and Charles saw him as if the for the first time. "I should have won the battle between Bobby Garfield and John Stow, Inspector? Me. I should have come out on top."

"You tricked him? You used his ego to you own advantage?"

"That's how it's been for as long as I can remember, Inspector," Stow said, and then his smug expression soured. "A perpetual pulling and pushing of power and manipulation. But it's ended now. It's over." He looked at Charles sadly. "And I'm glad for that, at least."

"You speak as if you lost, John," Charles said. "Sounds to me like you're the one who came out on top."

"Yes, well," Stow said. "I should have. But sadly Bobby Garfield has one thing that I do not." He held Charles' stare for a few moments. "Tenacity to the extreme, Inspector," he said. "Bobby Garfield will sink to the lowest depths of hell to win. And that's exactly what he did."

CHAPTER FIFTY-EIGHT
March 26, 2024

So few times had John driven up the driveway to the old farmhouse, that each time was an absolute pleasure. Yet, should he have stopped and taken a photograph in the same place every time, they would appear identical, save for the ever-changing plants, trees, and the sky.

He parked in his usual spot, where once upon a time, Mr Fisher had parked his old Mk II, and then he sat for a moment, wondering what he might say to his mother, how he might explain the circumstances, and convince her of the future he had planned for them.

It was Terry who, as usual, hadn't missed his arrival and appeared at the side of the house. It was good to see him wearing clean clothes – a check shirt, tan corduroys, and, of course, boots. His hair was fully grey now and still as wild as it had always been.

But it was his smile that warmed John. It was as unchanging as the house, growing fuller and richer with every passing season.

"You're still on your Jaguars, I see," he called out, as John climbed from the car, and they embraced before Terry held him at arm's length as he had often done. "It's good to see you, John. Bally-well good to see you."

"Likewise," John replied, and for the first time, he sensed a shift in the dynamics between them. Where once, Terry, with his farming strength and lithe body, had overpowered John with ease, now even his embrace felt weak. He seemed shorter somehow if that was possible. "Is she around?"

"Of course she is," Terry said. "Here, let me get your bags."

"It's fine," John told him, not wanting to see Terry struggle with his bags. "I'll come and get them. Come on, let's have some tea or something. It's been a long drive."

"Aye right you are," Terry said, and he put his arm around John, and then walked him to the back door.

"Looks just the same, Terry," John remarked.

"If it ain't broken," Terry replied. "Don't try to fix it."

"My boy," a voice said from the doorway, and John's mother stepped out into the courtyard. "My dearest boy." She walked over to him and swallowed him in her arms, leaving Terry to stand by and marvel at them. But John pulled him in and the three of them stayed that way for a moment.

"I have some news," John said, and they both pulled away to see him. "I have some fantastic news."

"Oh, John," his mother said. "Have you finally met somebody? I always prayed that you would have somebody to care for you–"

"I haven't met anybody, Ma," he said. "I'm retiring."

"You're what? Retiring?" Terry said. "To do what?"

"To be with you both," John replied. "So we can spend time together. Time that, by rights, we should have had years ago, and we would have had I not chosen my path."

"If you hadn't gone, John," Terry said, "I don't think any of us would be here."

"That's just it," he said. "I can now. You can give up work entirely."

"Oh, you might be able to just give it all up at the drop of a hat, John, but me? No. I'll be out here until my dying days, I reckon. Even if it is just the one field now." He gave a little laugh. "Man's got to eat, John. And he has to pay the rent, too."

"You don't understand, Terry," John said, and he fought to control the emotions in his voice, as he prepared to say the words he had longed to say for an entire lifetime. "The farm is mine. I bought it."

"You did what?"

"I bought it," he said, and he dragged them to the edge of the fields, where he spread out his arms. "Everything. Every piece of your sweat-soaked soil, Terry. And, Ma, the house that you have taken care of for my entire lifetime. It's ours now."

"You bought it from Garfield?"

"Yes. Well, the contract hasn't been signed, but it will be. We made an agreement to end the rivalry once and for all."

"You made an agreement with the Garfields?"

"It was easy, Ma. The answer was staring me in the face for years. Ever since I was made managing partner, in fact."

"John," his mother said, and she wore that look of dejection. "John, come inside."

"No, Ma," he said. "Listen to me for once, will you? Everyone wins. I step down as managing partner, placing Bobby in control of the firm. In return, he vowed to slice the Garfield estate up." He grinned as he approached her and took her by the hands. "The estate needs the money, Bobby gets what he's always wanted, and we get the land. I mean, it cost me nearly everything I had, but it's worth it. Don't you see? We can rent the land to local farmers. People like us, Ma. Real people. Good people. We can make this work, I know we can."

"John, no," she said and gave his hands a squeeze before letting them go.

"What?" he said. "What is it?"

She opened her mouth to speak but words failed her, and she turned away, dabbing at her eyes with the corner of her pinny.

"Terry?" John said, recognising the sorrowful expression he

now wore. "Terry, what's happened? Why aren't you both happy? This is our chance. This is what we've been working toward. This is why I went away so that I could take care of you both. So we could be together in comfort." He heard his voice trail away, heard but disregarded. "Doesn't this please you? Have I done wrong, Ma? Terry, tell me. Isn't this what you want?"

"It's a nice idea," Terry said, his deep voice grumbling like an old diesel generator. A grateful smile flashed and then faded like lightning on the horizon.

"So what then?" John said as Terry withdrew a piece of folded paper from his pocket. "What's that?"

Instead of unfolding the paper, Terry simply handed it to him and then stepped over to John's mother to put his arm around her shoulders, leaving John to open the letter himself. He read the first few printed lines aloud.

'Dear Mr Frobisher, it is my duty to inform you that the notice period served is now expiring. Please ensure you have vacated the property, namely Frobisher Farm, by April 1, 2024. An asset register and survey will be conducted during the course of the next few days, but from the date specified, all assets and land (512 acres) belonging to Frobisher Farm will cease to be registered to The Garfield Estate and Property Management Ltd...'

"This is it," John said, flicking the letter. "This is me. I've bought it. We don't need to vacate. It's ours. This is simply a solicitor following the process—"

"Read the last bit, John," Terry grumbled.

'*A legal representative of the new land ownership trust will be scheduling a visit with you on the last day of your tenancy. We wish to thank you for your business and wish you luck in your future endeavours. Signed Henry Gallant, Land Agent and Solicitor.*'

"A land ownership trust?" John said. "What the bloody hell is this?"

"John!" his mother snapped at the use of the B-word.

"I'm sorry, Ma, but no. This is unacceptable. I'm not a trust. I haven't arranged for anybody to come and see you on the last day of your tenancy."

"John, John, John," Terry said, extending his free arm and inviting him into the hug. "He's played you. He's played all of us."

"No," John said. "I've given him my fortune to make this work. My life's savings."

"He's won, John," Terry said. "Just let it be, eh? I mean, who do I think I am? I can't be out here any longer, can I? I can barely get up the stairs each night."

"No," John said. "No, bloody way. I'm not having it."

He turned on his heels and marched back towards his car.

"John," his mother called out. "John, where are you going?"

He tore open the car door and stopped to look back at them both.

"I'm going to see him, Ma," he said. "I'm going to put an end to this once and for all."

CHAPTER FIFTY-NINE
March 31, 2024

"He outsmarted you?" Charles said and almost laughed at the idea. Not too long ago, he had admired the man before him, but the more of his story he divulged, the more he began to doubt his initial judgement. "You lost your position in the firm, your home, and your family's home. What about your savings? What about the money you had paid for the land?"

The door burst open at that moment and Devon halted at Charles' raised hand.

"The money is in escrow. I'll get it back after jumping through a few hoops, but that's not the point is it?" He stabbed a finger at the desk. "I've been paying into that farm for decades. That was my mother's home. So, the money, Inspector, is not the point, is it?"

"No," Charles said. "No, it most certainly is not." He glanced up at Devon, who gestured that perhaps they should speak outside.

"Oh, for God's sake, woman, whatever it is, you can say it in front of me," said John. "It does, after all, concern me?"

She looked to Charles, who nodded, and gestured for her to join them.

"What do we have?" he asked, and she laid her notebook on the table.

"I spoke to your parents, Mr Stow," she began. "They can confirm that you arrived there on the Tuesday, the day before Mr Garfield died."

"I've already explained that to your boss," he replied.

"They also explained that you left to pay a visit to the Garfield house in the early evening."

"Again," he said. "I've explained this."

"And then they explained that you didn't return," she added, and he rolled his eyes. "In fact, you haven't been back since."

Stow said nothing. He stood from his seat and stared out of the window once more.

"John?" Charles said. "This is the part where you explain where you were."

"I can't," he said. "Not yet, anyway."

"Well, that doesn't give me much leeway, does it? I'm trying to help you, here."

"I don't..." he started, a little too aggressively, before checking his tone and glancing over his shoulder to stare at Charles. "I don't need your help." He turned back to the window. "Besides, that's not enough, and you know it. None of what I have said is enough until you get me to a station to be interviewed formally—"

"Well, that can be arranged," Charles told him, and then let his won tone soften. "Until now, I've allowed you the decency to remain in your office. The office in which you have worked for fifty years, John. If you want to leave here for the final time on your own terms, then I'd appreciate it if you could show Sergeant Devon here a little courtesy."

"Of course," he said, then turned to nod at Devon. "Please. Go on."

"Should you choose to deny your presence at the Garfield house, Mr Stow," Devon continued, "then I would reconsider." She flipped a page in her notebook. "In addition to your vehicle being caught on CCTV entering Hagworthingham prior to the murder, CSI have also confirmed that a near-full set of fingerprints have been lifted from the broken glass we discovered in the bins. The prints are yet to be identified, but we do have reason to believe they belong to a male. Given that Bobby Garfield has been alibied and Joanne Childs is a female, then…"

"Then what, Sergeant?" Stow said.

"Are they your prints, Mr Stow?"

"They are. Of course they are."

"So there's your opportunity," she said.

"And we've established a motive," Charles said.

"Is that it? Really?" he replied. "All those years of him breathing down our necks, controlling us like some kind of rich puppet master, and you can really find nobody else with the desire to murder the old man?"

"Well, I'm all ears if you want to mention any names," Charles said. "I don't think that, at this stage at least, it would help your particular cause, but if there's somebody you think I should be looking into?"

Stow glared at him and then at Devon.

"Anybody at all," Devon said.

"There's nobody," he replied. "But will you do as you said?" he asked, and seemed to humble before Charles' eyes. "Let me leave of my own accord?"

"You don't want to say goodbye? I would have thought the firm would have laid on a leaving party after fifty years, John."

"They have," he said softly. "It's tonight. At the Usher Gallery."

"Very nice," Charles told him.

"It's where we hold most of our events," he replied, and then let his voice fade as if recalling a particular time.

"I'm afraid to say that you won't be going, John. They'll have to make do without the man of the moment."

"Oh, they will," he said and then glanced about the old

meeting room before taking a deep breath and giving Charles the nod.

"John Stow," he began. "I am arresting you on suspicion of the murder of Hugo Garfield. You do not have to say anything. But it may harm your defence if you do not mention when questioned something which you later rely on in court. Anything you do say may be given in evidence. Do you understand what I have said, Mr Stow?"

He held his head high, closed his eyes for a moment, and then spoke.

"I do," he replied, and Charles caught Devon's eye.

"I have a car waiting for him at the end of the road, guv," she said, as if reading his thoughts.

"Thank you. Let him walk out alone," he said. "I don't think this one is going to run very far."

"That's decent of you," Stow said and nodded approvingly. "Thank you."

"Oh, don't thank me just yet, John," Charles replied. "I can place you at the scene with a motive." Charles stared him in the eye. "You need to start talking, John." He checked his watch. "We'll be in an interview room in under an hour. I suggest you think about telling me exactly what happened when you paid the Garfields a visit. No more lies, John."

CHAPTER SIXTY

March 26, 2024

In all the years that he had walked past the Manor House, peered at it from the window on their staircase, and even seen it in his dreams, only once had he ever stepped foot onto the grounds.

But that was about to change.

A sign hung from one of the two giant doors directing visitors to the brass bell that had been installed.

But John thumped on the old oak with his fist and then stepped back to wait. Footsteps inside clicked across a wooden floor, and he was greeted with a smile that on any other day, he might have enjoyed.

"John?"

"Move out of my way, Rose," he said, and he politely pushed past her.

"John, don't," she called after him, but he wasn't listening.

The staircase might have been a sight to behold and the great, stained-glass window that shone a kaleidoscope of colours onto the parquet night have been a marvel to behold, but he couldn't give a tuppence for the architecture. Not then. Two doors led from the broad hallway, one on either side, and from one the sound of laughter came – and music. He pushed into the room and took in the scene.

A large fireplace dominated the room, around which three large sofas had been arranged. In the spaces on the walls where there were no books or shelves, large paintings hung in gilded frames, of which John was almost certain were genuine gold leaf presenting the Garfield ancestry.

On one of the sofas, Mrs Lavender was sitting. She wore the same old dress he had seen so many times, and a familiar, disapproving scorn was etched into her face. Beside her was a woman in her late thirties and although John had never laid eyes on her, there was little doubt she was Rose's daughter.

Opposite her, Hugo Garfield peered up at him through his spectacles, crinkling his nose as if the lenses were not quite up to scratch.

Beside him sat Bobby Garfield, and by the expressions on their faces, their ability to foresee the future had drastically improved.

"You," John said, a single word that conveyed so much hatred that any suffix seemed superfluous. But he found the words, anyway. "You unscrupulous bastard."

"Now, now," Bobby Garfield said, rising to his feet and holding his hands out in defence. "I'm sure whatever this is about can be resolved in a gentlemanly manner."

"After all this time," John said, taking a few slow steps into the room.

"John don't," Rose called from behind him, and again he ignored her. "Now is neither the time nor the place."

"You should listen to her," Garfield said, as he backed away from the sofas.

"You gave my family notice, Bobby."

"I think you'll find that wasn't me."

"We had a deal, Bobby," John said. "All we had to do was sign the contract."

"Business is business," he said. "I'm afraid you were outbid, John."

"Take it back," John told him. "Retract the sale. That land is mine."

"No, it was never yours," Garfield corrected him. "And if accuracy is your thing, which apparently it is, it was never *going to be yours*. Your stepfather was a tenant. A temporary custodian."

"What are they supposed to do? Where are they supposed to go, Bobby?"

"I don't know. Perhaps they could do as the Masons did and take early retirement, who I hear have a very nice life over on the coast. Simple but nice. Mablethorpe, I believe."

John looked to Bobby's father who nodded and then stared at John again.

"You've got a nerve, Bobby Garfield."

"I also had five hundred and twelve acres of land that either needed to pay towards the upkeep of the estate or be sold off," he replied. "And of late, your stepfather's rent hasn't really touched the sides."

"What are you talking about? *I* pay the balance. *Me*. Not them. I send money to the Garfield estate every bloody month."

"I think we've pushed the boundaries of acceptable language enough for one day," Hugo Garfield stated.

"How much do they owe?" John said, to which Garfield winced.

"May I direct you to our guests, John? I'm sure that, as entertaining as this is, my mother-in-law would prefer to enjoy the occasion without your profanities and vulgarities."

"How much, Bobby?"

"You don't give up, do you?"

"Never," John said. "Tell me how much they owe."

"I'm sure that whatever backstreet slum provided your so-called private education, John Stow, that your teacher would have instilled the concept of vulgarity and how to avoid it. We do not discuss money publicly. I certainly do not at any rate."

John glanced back at Mrs Lavender, who sat with her adult granddaughter, clearly enthralled by the debate.

"I certainly did install the concept of vulgarity," Mrs Lavender said, and all eyes fell on her. "And my house is not a backstreet slum, Robert. It may be in need of repairs but a slum it is not."

"What?" Garfield said. "I think you must be mistaken—"

"I educated this young man myself," she said.

"You?" Garfield said, laughing it off as if the whole thing was some kind of wind-up. "Be serious."

She nodded.

"You see, when I lost my daughter, Polly, I found myself both without purpose and without an income. Mr Stow here provided a remedy for both."

"But how on earth could his mother have afforded—"

"Now who is being vulgar, Robert?" she said. "It is as plain as the nose on my face that Mr Stow is not prepared to leave this house until the matter is settled, and nor should he. Which leaves you with two options. You can either stay here to discuss the matter publicly or you can take the conversation elsewhere."

"Why did you never say?" Garfield said, then turned to his wife for an explanation.

"You have a study, I presume," John said, hoping to draw the attention away from the women, to which Garfield responded by turning and leaving the room. John nodded his thanks to Mrs Lavender but received nothing in return except a wide-eyed look of awe from Rose's daughter.

"Now it makes sense," Garfield said, the moment John entered the study. "You and Rose. The little connection you have."

"I'm not here to discuss your wife, Bobby."

"Well, discuss it you will," he said. "You must think me backwards, John." He tapped his temple with a fat forefinger. "I remember what you told us. Me, Henry, and Rose. At the

Christmas ball all those years ago. About how your private education covered all manner of things."

"Bobby—"

"I may have been blind to it, John. But I'm not going to let you walk in here and make demands. And if I was open to negotiation, I certainly am not now."

"How much do they owe, Bobby?" John asked, keeping his voice low and calm. "I'll pay it and whatever it takes to better the bid." Garfield laughed the question off with a shake of his head, so John leaned across his desk, jabbing his finger at him. "Look, you can obsess over the past as much as you like, but it will be to no purpose save for sending you into an early grave. Look at you," John said. "Your face is bright red, you're still overweight, and I'd happily wager that your father outlives you despite the fact that he looks as if he's on death's door. Whatever happened happened. I can't change that, your mother-in-law can't change it, Rose can't change it," he said, and Garfield winced again. "And you certainly can't change it."

Garfield loosened his collar and wafted some air into his shirt, and then sat back in the leather chair behind his desk. From a drawer, he retrieved a lined notebook and then opened it to a particular page. Then, staring directly into John's eyes, he turned the book around and shoved it towards him.

The figure was higher than John had imagined and he scanned the numbers in the lines above.

"Is this a joke?" he said, to which Garfield said nothing. From his pocket, John withdrew his chequebook and pen and then helped himself to the visitor's chair. He made out the cheque, tore it from the book, and slid it across to Garfield, snapping the lid back onto the pen. "That's what they owe. Perhaps now we can discuss the sale?" John said, and he gestured towards the lined notebook. "Where do I need to be to outbid the buyer?"

Garfield studied the cheque and held it up to the light before opening a small, lockable tin and discarding it inside as if he were disposing of yesterday's newspaper. He locked the tin and placed it into the bottom drawer, which he then locked and dropped his keys into his pocket.

"Changes nothing," he said.

"Sorry?"

"It changes nothing," Bobby said and nodded at the drawer with the tin and the cheque. "The land is sold."

"The land can't be sold, Bobby. Surely there's a cooling off period or some way I do this?"

Garfield stood, and from an occasional table to one side of the study, he poured two glasses of whiskey into crystal tumblers.

"Same as Mason's farm and Talbot's," he said. "It's all gone."

"You're selling up completely?"

Garfield set one of the glasses on the desk before John and then returned to his seat.

"You said it yourself, John. The days of estates like this are well and truly over. If we're to keep the house, then the land must go."

"But you took the cheque for what they owed. We had a deal, Bobby," he said. "I step down from the firm and you allow my mother and her husband to live out their days in peace."

"I made no suggestion that I would reevaluate my position, John. It's out of my hands, I'm afraid."

"Then perhaps you can tell me who bought it? They might be willing to listen to reason. Please, Bobby. This is my family. Whatever differences we've had, surely they do not extend to facilitating the demise of my family. Me, yes. In fact, I could almost understand it. But my family? Who is it? Is it somebody local?"

"I wouldn't tell you even if I knew," Bobby said. "My dealings have been with his land agent and solicitor," Garfield said.

"Henry Gallant?" John said. "I can't believe he's taken your side in all of this."

"A call was arranged for yesterday morning. I deliberated, as you can imagine. I mean we could have developed one of the farms. You see it everywhere these days, don't you? Masses of ugly houses spoiling the landscape."

"But you sold. You sold before even consulting me, when you knew full well I might have been able to save them."

"It was a difficult decision," Garfield said, and he sank his drink, placing the glass down far harder than was necessary. "Made easier by something I saw while walking through Lincoln one night last Christmas."

He smiled the unforgiving smile of a man who wasn't about to relinquish a penny of his winnings.

"What did you see, Bobby?" John said, but Garfield said nothing and instead chose to stare into John's eyes. John slung his glass at the wall and reached across the desk for Garfield's throat. "What did you see, Bobby?" he yelled. "What? Tell me!"

"You have had all that you will ever get from me and my family, John Stow," Garfield grumbled quietly and then peeled John's hands from his collar. "Now get out of my house."

CHAPTER SIXTY-ONE
March 31, 2024

"That explains the fingerprints on the glass," Charles said, and John Stow sat back in the chair. The interview room was far more formal than the Swain and Swain meeting room had been, and far colder too. The posters on the walls were of little interest to Stow, who seemed content to stare at his fingers on the table before him. "What did you do after that?"

"I went back to the farm," Stow replied.

"Did you speak to anybody else before you left?" Devon asked. "You mentioned that Rose Garfield and her mother were present."

"No," he said. "I said nothing to them. I was in no mood for chit-chat, as you can imagine."

"You didn't say goodbye?" Charles asked. "Not even to Rose?"

"I wanted to get out of there," he said. "I was seething and anything I might have said would, I'm sure, have been less than polite."

"So you went back to the farm, where you stayed the night? Is that right?"

"It is, yes," he said. "My mother was upset. As was Terry,

although he did a good job of hiding it. He's not an emotional man. I ate with them and we made plans."

"What type of plans?"

"The future," Stow replied. "Where we were to live. How much money we had to live on. You have to remember that I put every penny I had into buying that farm. So until the funds are released, I have nothing."

"Oh, I don't believe that."

"Believe it," he said. "I might have a little tucked away in an account and there are some investments I could take out of, but not enough for us to live on for any more than a year. We had choices to make. Difficult choices. You see, I've been paying into that farm since ninety-eighty-something, topping up the rent, or so I thought, with a view of one day owning the land. If I could just keep Terry and my mother on the farm until the day came, it would be all right."

"And the day came," Charles said.

"The day came, all right. It came and it went, leaving me as good as penniless in the process," Stow said. "I went to bed that night, in my old bedroom, and I planned. I knew that, whatever happened, my mother and Terry couldn't be left destitute."

"You planned your revenge?"

"I planned my suicide," he said, with a hint of sadness in his voice. He leaned back in his chair and let his arms fall to his side, and then glanced at the recording, with its little digital readout stating the elapsed time. "I was gone before my mother or Terry was awake."

"Gone where?"

"Walking," he said. "I walked the hills and the lanes and the tracks. Remembering. That's what I was doing. I was remembering every time Bobby Garfield had hurt me. Every ditch he had thrown me into, every patch of grass on which I had curled into a ball and let them kick me into submission. I remembered it all."

"Why?" Devon said. "Why put yourself through all of that?"

"I needed the fire," he replied, and he pressed a fist against his gut. "I needed a fire to help me through it all. To help me do what I needed to do."

Charles glanced sideways at Devon who remained expressionless. They waited for Stow to speak more, knowing that any encouragement would only stall the flow.

"I took a length of rope from Terry's store. I knew where I would do it." He looked up at Charles and his eyes filled with angry tears. "From Garfield's gate."

"Why there? Why do it at all?"

"Because if I die, Inspector, my mother and Terry could at least benefit from the insurance. It was the only way I knew that they'd be okay."

"But suicide?"

"I promised them that I'd make everything okay," he said. "I couldn't fail them. I couldn't fail my ma. Not in her last years."

"But clearly you didn't go through with it," Devon said, and Charles heard the change in her tone. She too had been through a similar process and survived to tell the tale. There was an understanding in her eyes. Like she knew how he must have felt.

"You had lost everything," she said. "Your home, your savings, your job. And you wanted to protect your mother from suffering."

"I found myself at the gates," he said, nodding at her. "And I stared up at the Garfield house much as I had done when I was a boy. Although, I wasn't scared this time. Not like all those years ago. I knew what I had to do." He leaned forward, adopting a stance that Charles recognised as professional. He was engaged and ready to speak freely. "It was early. The house was still. And as I stood there, I had an idea. It was a terrible idea really, but you know how it is when you're in that state of mind."

"I do," Devon told him, offering him a reassuring smile. "What was your idea?"

"The idea was that I wouldn't do it at the gates. I'd do it

inside. I'd hang myself from one of those chandeliers. If Bobby was going to take our home from us, then I'd ruin his forever. Even Bobby Garfield wouldn't have the gall to ignore the image of me hanging inside his house," he said. "I'll never forget how it made me feel when I stepped inside. I was David and somewhere inside the house was Goliath. I heard the cleaner upstairs, toing and froing with the vacuum cleaner, and Bobby's car had gone, so I knew Hugo would be alone. But the further into the house I went, the more the plan began to make sense. Mother would get a payout from the insurance and if I set it up right then Bobby might even be dragged into the mix. Imagine that. Who would have won then, eh?"

"John, before we continue, are you sure you don't want to call a colleague?"

"I don't need legal support," Stow replied, slightly irritated by the distraction. "I went to the study. I'd seen it the previous night. The little rope mechanism to lower the chandeliers. So I tied my rope and I tied it well, exactly how Terry had shown me once when we had old Barney."

"Barney?"

"His horse," Stow explained. "Then I tied the noose and placed it around my neck to test it."

"To test it?"

"I wanted to make sure it could take my weight," Stow said. "But I needed something to stand on. The desk was too far away, so I removed the noose and was about to drag it beneath the chandelier when I heard someone. Hugo, I think."

"You heard him?" Charles said and then waited a moment for the atmosphere to settle. "What was he doing?"

"In the library outside. I heard the fireside tools rattle," he said. "I suppose he was stacking logs, or something."

"And did he see you?"

"No," he said and then took a deep breath. "No, but it did give me time to think about what I was doing. Made me see sense.

Funny, isn't it? Things could have been a whole lot different. I froze when I heard him and I prayed he didn't come into the study. I just stared at the rope and the chandelier and-"

"And what, John?" Charles asked, to which he shook his head.

"I just saw how ridiculous the whole thing was, I suppose. How much of a waste it would have been if I went through with it."

He seemed lost in thought like he was regretting his decision.

"But you didn't go through with it. These things happen for a reason, John," Devon said. "And you're still here."

"I know," he said with a weak smile. "You're right. For better or worse, I'm still here." He stared at them from across the table. "And so is Bobby Garfield."

"John, I'm going to ask you a simple question," Charles said. "I just need a yes or no answer."

"Go on," he replied, regaining control over the emotions that he had set free.

"Did you murder Hugo Garfield?"

"I did not," he replied and then ran his tongue across his teeth. "Although part of me wishes I had."

CHAPTER SIXTY-TWO
March 31, 2024

When he thought of everything he had been through in his life, the sacrifices he had made, the decisions he had worked through, he wondered how on earth it had come to this. John Stow, the man who had risen from a life of poverty to great wealth. And it *was* wealth. Not just financial but the type Mrs Lavender had alluded to. Unquestionable wealth. He was a man who wanted for nothing.

Every one of his needs had been met. Save one.

He sat on the edge of the bench on the blue, plastic mattress and thought of the men who had laid there before him. The drunks, the thugs, the druggies, and the desperate.

And there was him.

It wasn't his first time in a cell. In fact, he'd been inside more cells than most criminals. But always, the door had been open to him. He'd been a visitor, there to discuss the options of his client, who had nearly always been guilty.

The inspector had been a reasonable man, making use of John's knowledge of the law and processes to his advantage. He had laid out the facts. John had indeed been to the house during the previous evening and had remained in the area until well after

Hugo Garfield had been killed. He had knowledge of the land, and of the individuals, but most importantly, he had a motive. More than a motive, in fact. He had a lifelong ambition to bring Bobby Garfield to his knees.

The facts were irrefutable. The truth would therefore have to be convincing enough to sway a jury, which no doubt Bobby would have some kind of influence over.

Finally, he'd been beaten. Finally, Bobby Garfield had had the last word. And the thought of it brought a smile to John's face.

How long did he have left anyway? Ten years? He wasn't like his mother or Terry, who had the fortune of the fresh air and clean living to see them into their eighties. No, John had sacrificed his winter years for the wealth he had so desired.

The lock on the door clicked open and John stood in the hope that he could be led into an interview room where he could begin to fight his cause. But instead of being summoned, a man entered the cell and the door was locked behind him. He wore the clothes of a vagrant, yet did not smell as foul as some that John had met. And his face was familiar as he stood there before John, studying his posture, his clothes, and his forlorn expression.

"Hello, John," he said.

"You?" John said, and the recognition hit him hard. "What on earth?"

"Ah, so you remember me, do you?"

"Of course, you're..." he began, then felt the shame. "I'm, sorry, I don't know your name."

"S'alright," he said. "Nobody else does. Why should you be any different?"

"I don't understand," John said. "Why are you here? What could you have possibly done?"

"Oh, I've done nothing to be ashamed of, John. I'm here to see you," he replied and gestured at the blue mattress as if seeking permission to sit.

"Of course," John said, and he scooted along a few feet to make room. "Sorry, what do you mean you're here to see me?"

"It's not difficult, John," he said. "Surely you can see that?"

John shook his head and stood to pace a few steps.

"Look, it's been a...strange day."

"An awful day, John," the man said, and he looked around the bare room before resting his eyes on John. He was a dark-skinned man with shiny, brown eyes, but those submissive traits that so many homeless men adopt were missing – the averting of the eyes, the downcast look, and the sagging shoulders. In fact, now that John came to think of it, for all the years he had walked past the man, dropped a pound or two into his hat or nodded a greeting, never had he shared the downtrodden attributes that many do as they stand at the lowest platform of society seeking a hand up.

"Who are you?" John said.

"So you don't remember me?"

"If I remembered you, sir, I would at least do you the honour of using your name."

"How well you speak," the man said. "The Queen's English, if I'm not mistaken." He smiled a little, revealing white teeth. Not stained, yellowing teeth, but white. Whiter than Rose's, even, despite his age. "And such confidence, too. Look at the way you stand. You, sir, have become a great man, have you not? The managing partner of Swain and Swain." He shook his head. "My my."

"Is this some kind of joke?" John asked.

"Oh, it's no joke."

"Then I suggest you endeavour to explain yourself, or I'll be forced to call the officer to have you removed."

"How many coffees have you bought me over the years, John Stow?" the man said, and there was something in the way he used John's full name that stirred something inside.

"I don't recall. Hundreds maybe."

"Plenty," the man agreed. "Took a while though, didn't it? Needed old Fisher to show you the way, didn't you? Before you put your hand in your pocket?"

"I was new to the city," John explained. "My mother warned me to take care."

"And good advice it was, too. It was the girl though, wasn't it? The Hyke girl. Course, she wasn't a Hyke back then, was she? She was a Thames back then, wasn't she?"

"Sir, I'm afraid this charade is growing tiresome."

"Showed you how to look the other way, did she not?" He grinned. "I remember. I remember it all, John. Course I have nothing much else to muddle my mind with, do I? Not like you, John Stow. All those high-powered lawyers at your disposal. With so many secretaries, admins, and God knows who else in your employ. How far you've come."

John backed away from the man until he felt the cool steel door behind him.

"I asked you once," he continued, "if luck had found you yet. Do you recall, John?"

To his surprise, John did recall. In fact, he recalled every interaction they had had in that first year. The times when John had only the money from his father to his name, and the times that followed in that first year, when he kept a small parcel of folded notes in his wallet yet had not dropped a single penny into the hat.

"Like I said, I was new to the city. I allowed myself to be guided by Francis."

"Francis?"

"Miss Thames, as she was known back then."

"I wonder if some understanding of morals shouldn't have been included, John," he said. "In your education, I mean."

"Sorry?"

"Your education. Mrs Lavender?"

"How on earth–"

"And Rose. Sweet Rose."

"Listen, unless you stop all this nonsense and explain yourself, and what you mean by visiting me here, I shall be forced to call the officer."

"Course, you always had morals, didn't you, John? You were always a good lad, deep down. Knew right from wrong, didn't you? Even back then."

"Back when?"

"When you brought me that pie. A beer, too, if I recollect." He shook his head in wonder. "My God, I needed that."

And there it was. Recognition. It was as if two strong hands held John's eyelids wide open and he could see the man for who he was, despite the desire to simply reject the idea.

"You?" he said, to which the man smiled.

"As I live and breathe, John Stow."

"My God."

"Close," he said. "But not quite." He stood from the bench and faced John, polite enough to keep his distance but close enough for John to see the sincerity in his eyes. "You helped me, John Stow, and so I helped you."

"I don't understand."

"Your education, John," he said with a tinge of anger in his tone. "Who do you think paid for it?"

"You?" John said, and again the man grinned. "I don't believe you."

"Well, you should," he said angrily. "I've watched you, John Stow. Every day of my miserable life, I've watched you. Seen you grow, I have. From a young, naive boy into this." He took a step closer. "And how proud you make me."

"You're my benefactor?" John said. "You? But you're—"

"A penniless tramp?" he said, using that word that John refused to adopt. "A beggar on the street? What was I supposed to do, John? Where was I supposed to go? One mention of my name and I would have had half the county's police force on my back. A black man like me? I wouldn't have stood a chance, John."

"You could have gotten away?"

"Gotten away? How? I've no passport. No documents." He shook his head again, this time in submission. "No, John. The day Polly Lavender died, that day you found me in your stepfather's granary, my life as I knew had ended. I could be torn apart by Garfield's dogs or I could disappear. I chose the latter."

"Polly Lavender? The girl?"

The man nodded slowly and stepped forward once more.

"Rose's sister, John," he said, and John found himself using the wall to support his weight. "Didn't you know?"

"No," he said. "I just knew it was a girl. I was a boy. Nobody said a name."

"No, and why would they? Why would they when Hugo Garfield had them all by the scruffs of their necks?"

"Hugo Garfield?" John said, and through all his years in law, he had come to know that coincidence was a rare occurrence.

"S'right, John," the man said, his voice deep and low. John could see him now, as he was back then. Without the scraggly beard, and with fear alive in his eyes. "We were to be married. Did you know that?"

"Sorry, what?"

"Mrs Lavender and me. Ivy and I. That was to be our wedding day. That was to be the day that a well-to-do English lady broke all of society's rules and married a black man. Didn't matter that I was rich, did it? Didn't matter that I could have kept Ivy and Rose in good health. What mattered was the colour of my skin, John. And you? You gave me a chance. You gave me life."

"Are you saying that Hugo Garfield fabricated your demise?" John asked. "All because of the colour of your skin?"

"Do you remember what it was like back then, John? In nineteen-seventy?"

"I was a boy," John replied.

"What was a black man like me doing in the middle of the English countryside? You should have seen how they all looked at me. Ivy and the girls were the only ones who saw me for who I am. I should have been working in a factory by rights. Heaven forbid I should have made something of myself. Heaven forbid that white men might work for a black man." The man closed the distance between them and then raised his fist into the air. "You saw me, John, didn't you?" he said. "You saw past the colour of my skin, and for that, I gave you all I could." He slammed his hand against the door beside John's head. "Fisher. Now he was a good man. He saw me too." He rubbed his thumb and forefinger together. "He saw the money, see? He knew what I really was. All I had to do was get him on side then I could become invisible." He hissed air through pursed lips to accentuate this point. "Gone. A vagrant. A tramp. Don't matter what colour your skin is when you're sitting in a shop doorway, does it? Nobody looks anyway. Nobody sees you, John."

The little flap in the door opened and the officer peered through, but the man held his hand up for the officer to wait a second or two.

"Who arrested you?" he said to John. "What's his name?"

"Chief Inspector Cook," John told him. "Charles Cook."

"Find him, will you?" the man said to the officer. "I have something he'll want to hear."

The officer closed the flap and they heard his boots trail off.

"Where would you be, John?" the man asked. "Where would you be if you hadn't saved me that night? A farmer?" He shook his head. "No, I don't think so. You were meant for great things, John Stow. You lived the life I was supposed to."

"But why didn't you say? All these years I've been tossing you a few pounds for a hot drink. Why didn't you tell me?"

"And what would you have done? What could you possibly have done to make my life any better? The moment I raise my hand, John, I'm done for."

"Then what are you doing here?"

Footsteps approached the cells from the outside and the man's grave expression gave way to a sad smile.

"Raising my hand, John Stow," he said. "It's time."

A metal bolt slid back and a key turned in the heavy lock.

"What? No. No, you can't," John said, and he pushed the man away from the door, hearing it open behind him. "Not now. Not after all this time."

But the man stared over his shoulder and John turned to find Chief Inspector Cook in the doorway.

"What is it?" he asked, his echoes of Celtic tones sounding almost musical. "Who called for me?"

The man for whom John had bought a lifetime of hot drinks, nodded a good morning to, and, at one stage, ignored pushed him gently to one side.

"I did, sir," the man said.

"No, you can't do this," John pleaded, but the old man's voice was heavier and angrier.

"I know you," the inspector said. "You're the man in the doorway. "You're—"

"My name is Jimmy Sutherland, Inspector Cook. I've been on the run since nineteen-seventy," he said flatly.

"Is that right?" Cook replied, a little suspicious of such an audacious claim. "What are you running from, Mr Sutherland? What is it that you are wanted for?"

"The rape and murder of Polly Lavender on March the ninth, nineteen-seventy. I wish to clear my name of the crimes," he replied. "And confess to the murder of Hugo Garfield."

CHAPTER SIXTY-THREE

March 31, 2024

While Devon prepared the second recording of the afternoon, Charles sat quietly, watching the old man before him. The duty solicitor that Charles had insisted on being present prepared his notes, but Sutherland remained calm. His beard was long and scraggly but his skin was clean. Unlike many of the homeless Charles had seen and spoken to over the years, his fingers were clean, his nails had been trimmed, and even his teeth appeared to be cared for.

His clothes, which consisted of a heavy duffle coat, thick trousers, and leather boots, were grimy yet did not reek of the streets as Charles thought they might. It was as if his attire was merely a disguise.

A long buzzer marked the beginning of the recording and Charles introduced the date, time, location, and then his name and rank, before beckoning for Devon to follow suit. Only once the duty solicitor, a man named Benedict Charlton, and Jimmy Sutherland had introduced themselves did Charles begin.

The question was, where to start?

"Before we begin, it is my duty to reread you your rights, Mr Sutherland," he said. "You are under arrest on suspicion of the murder of Hugo Garfield. You do not have to say anything. But, it may harm your defence if you do not mention when questioned something which you later rely on in court. Anything you do say may be given in evidence. Do you understand?"

"I do," he said, his voice loud and clear.

He sat straight in the chair, no slouching, no crossed legs, and no fumbling with his fingers as so many would do.

"You have given an informal confession to the murder, but as I'm sure you can appreciate, we do need to formalise your account. It's worth mentioning that your DNA and fingerprints are, as we speak, being analysed against evidence taken from the crime scene."

"What about Polly?"

"I think that, in this instance, Mr Sutherland—"

"Jimmy, please."

"Very well. In this instance, *Jimmy*, given the complexity of the investigation, we'll be working our way through the Hugo Garfield murder first. We can look into the young girl's death when we have this one all wrapped up. That said, I have taken the liberty of tasking my two detective constables with accessing the archives to see what evidence remains. But before we begin, I'd like to understand why you might want to murder Hugo Garfield. What motivated you to do such a thing?"

"That's quite simple," Sutherland said. "The man is a monster. The family are monsters."

"Can you elaborate on that? I mean, in this line of work, you meet some pretty horrific characters, but I can't say that I've ever considered murdering them on the basis of their personalities."

"He destroyed me," Sutherland said. "That's what they do. They destroy people."

"They?"

"The Garfields," he replied. "Bobby included."

He spoke clearly and with confidence as if his time on the streets had had little effect on his mind. He was a lean man with skin as dark as any Charles had seen. Small freckles dotted his upper cheeks and his nose, but what fascinated Charles were those big, bright, brown eyes. They bore intelligence, they held secrets and wisdom, and they shone like stars in the night sky.

"How did Hugo Garfield destroy you exactly?" Charles asked, to which Sutherland sat back in his chair and laid his large brown hands on his thighs.

"I'm afraid, for that, we might need to deviate a little, Inspector," he replied.

"Polly Lavender?" Charles asked and Sutherland nodded.

"It was the ninth of March, nineteen-seventy," he began and then smiled fondly at some distant memory before looking up at Charles. "My wedding day."

"Your wedding day?" Charles replied, and he glanced down at the man's hands, seeing no sign of a ring. "My my."

"I'm well aware that a man like me has no place in the British countryside, Inspector," he said. "And back then, the sentiment was driven home with vehemence."

"If you're referring to the colour of your skin, Jimmy, then I might suggest that times have changed."

"That may be, but I can assure you that barely a man in that village wanted that marriage to go ahead, none more so than the squire."

"By which, you mean Hugo Garfield?"

"As black as I am," he continued, unperturbed, "there's nothing I enjoy more than fresh air, dark nights, and the sound of nature."

"Alluring, isn't it?" Charles said, to which he nodded slightly.

"I was awake in the early hours, thinking of the day ahead and the times we would have. It was cold but I opened the window in the room I had rented. Have you ever listened to the noises at night, Inspector? They're quite different to the daytime sounds. Quite beautiful in their own way."

"I can't say I have," Charles admitted. "But I can imagine."

"Owls," Sutherland said, "bats, and all manner of nocturnal creatures. Faceless in the dark. It's quite something, you know?"

"I see," Charles told him.

"But there was one sound that was not faceless. A sound that I can still hear to this day," he said, and any joy the memory of that night had induced faded, pulling the skin on his face taut against his skull. "A girl's scream."

CHAPTER SIXTY-FOUR
March 9, 1970

Jimmy sat bolt upright in bed, listening hard for a repeat of that awful sound.

And there it was. A cry of desperation from the fields behind the roadside bed and breakfast. He pulled on his trousers and his old boots, dragging his shirt over his head as he left the room and crept down the stairs.

The moon was bright and the field was a bare expanse of smooth cultivated soil, marred only by a distant barn. He listened but heard nothing, not even the owl. It was as if whoever or whatever was out there bore an evil that even the creatures dared not confront.

He walked at first for fear of making a noise, drawn to that old distant barn like a moth to a flame. The village behind him was dark. A few lighted windows stood out, but any movement was the result of the same cold breeze that licked at the sweat on Jimmy's back.

Then he ran.

The closer he got to the barn, the stronger the sensation in his gut became. That feeling of an iron grip clamping down on his stomach with sharp, claw-like fingers. He prayed while he ran. He prayed that he would make it in time. He prayed that whatever man was behind it was still there. And he prayed that whoever had issued that awful scream might still breathe.

But when he burst through the barn door, the moonlight displayed his unanswered prayers in all their brutal glory. He dropped to his knees beside her and searched for a breath, a sign of life, anything. Her knees had been drawn up and fallen to one side, and her hair lay lank across her face. So he straightened her, as her mother might have done, and he smoothed her hair.

And then he saw them. His shoes. The shoes he was to wear in just a few hours, and his hat, and even the hellebore he was to pin to his lapel.

He understood right then. He understood the girl's sacrifice. His clothing would cast suspicion. His bootprints across the field would lead them to the bed and breakfast.

The torches across the field arrived with startling speed and the rousing of the local men even more so.

There would be no wedding. There would be no future. And for the last time, he had heard those sounds of the night through his open window.

He smoothed her hair again, wiping away his tears with his shirt cuff. He kissed her hand and prayed for her. He prayed that wherever she was on the next part of her journey that somebody held her hand to guide her.

The dogs called out, jostling for the alpha position, and marking the end of Jimmy's life.

It was a game of high stakes. Polly Lavender had been nothing more than a pawn in a game that Jimmy had unequivocally lost.

But more importantly, Hugo Garfield had won.

CHAPTER SIXTY-FIVE
March 31, 2024

"That's quite the compelling story," Charles said.

"It's the truth," Sutherland replied. "And the truth is often compelling."

"And you've been on the run ever since, have you? What is that, fifty years? Must be some kind of record, eh, Devon?"

Devon shrugged, clearly not sold on the man's tale of woe.

"And you've never thought of giving yourself up?" Charles asked. "In all that time, you never once considered handing yourself in and telling your side of the story?"

"I'm a black man in a white world, Inspector."

"This isn't nineteen-seventy."

"That may be," Sutherland said. "I suppose the longer I stayed beneath the radar, the harder it became."

"Until now," Charles said, and he glanced down at the man's hands once more. "Where do you sleep, Jimmy?" Sutherland examined his hands and smiled softly. "You're as homeless as I am.
"

"I have what you might call a long-term understanding with Swain and Swain," he said.

"A long-term understanding, eh?"

"I don't expect you to understand, Inspector. In fact, when I tell my story aloud, I can barely believe it myself. But it is what it is and I have few memories to be ashamed of."

"I don't know about you, Sergeant Devon, but I don't have a lot on tonight."

"Me neither, guv," she replied. "In fact, I'm quite intrigued."

"Perhaps some coffee, then?" Charles suggested. "Jimmy?"

Sutherland eyed them both and then relented with a nod of his head, the cue for Devon to disappear for a short while.

Charles announced her brief departure for the benefit of the recording and then sat back, crossed his legs, and linked his fingers, a sign as good as any that he was ready to listen.

Sutherland closed his eyes. His nostrils flared as he took a deep breath and then his face came alive.

"I had a choice, Inspector. Stay and let Garfield destroy me or run. Either way, I would lose everything, but running was the only real chance I had."

"And where did you run to? From your previous account, I understand that it was dark. A black man in nineteen-seventy running through the countryside? Can't have been easy."

"I was fortunate," Sutherland said. "And I did have one thing on my side."

"And what was that?"

"Money," Sutherland said. "Plenty of it too. It was tied up, of course, and I knew I would have no chance of accessing it, but my lawyer could. And he did."

"Your lawyer?"

"Mr Fisher," Sutherland replied. "He was able to assist me in my hour of need. I had a room in the name of Swain and Swain and a small dividend from my investments served my purposes. But the real task was repaying my debt."

"Your debt? Which debt is that?"

"John Stow," he said after a short pause. "My saviour."

"I'm not following," Charles said, finding himself leaning forward in his seat. "The same John Stow—"

"That recently resigned as the Managing Partner of Swain and Swain," Sutherland finished for him. He bit down on his lower lip in thought and then considered an explanation. "You see, when I decided to run, I knew I wouldn't get far. I had to lay low for a while. I had to let the chaos die down, you see? So I found an old granary at Frobisher's farm. It was March, so the place was almost bare. All I had to do was stay there for a few days, and then make my escape."

"A few days?"

"It didn't come to that," Sutherland replied. "He must have been twelve years old when he found me. But he wasn't scared. Not like some might have been. In fact, he helped me."

"He helped you? A twelve-year-old laddie?"

"He brought me food. It was a pie and a bottle of beer," Sutherland said with a laugh and a shake of his head. "He even showed me the way to the road. Said that trucks use it to and from the coast to the city."

"Sounds rather fanciful if you ask me," Charles said.

"It does," Sutherland agreed. "I never ever forgot that act of kindness. When all around me, the men and the dogs were closing in, he risked everything to help me. And so I repaid him the only way I could."

"With money?"

"Not directly," Sutherland said. "I couldn't very well write him a cheque, could I? But I could give him a start in life. An education, as it were. And in the process, I could ensure that my bride-to-be had an income."

"Rose Garfield's mother?" Charles said. "Polly Lavender's mother."

"She was a fine woman, Inspector. A fine, fine woman. She risked everything too. The county would have turned its back on her had she married me, but she didn't let them get to her. She never backed down. She must have been heartbroken. Rose too. The girls were like daughters to me and I'd have been a good father too, given half a chance."

"So, let me get this straight," Charles said. "You paid for John Stow to be privately educated by Ivy Lavender?"

"That's right," he replied. "And when that education came to a rather unfortunate end, I arranged for him, through Mr Fisher, to begin an apprenticeship at Swain and Swain."

"And you've sat outside that office every day ever since?"

"Not every day," he said. "But often enough. I wanted to see him grow, you see? I wanted to see the fruits of my investment."

"You do realise that until your confession he was a prime suspect in Hugo Garfield's murder, don't you?"

"Oh come on, Inspector. You don't believe it was him, do you?"

"The evidence stacks up," Charles said. "Which I might add is a darn sight more than I say for your account."

"What do you want to know?" Sutherland asked. "Do you want to know how I watched John go into the house that morning? And how I followed him inside? Do you want to know how I dragged the old bastard from his rose garden and strung him up by the neck, leaving him hanging there from a chandelier?"

"That would be a start," Charles said. "Where did you get the rope?"

"It was already there," Sutherland replied almost immediately. "Even the noose was tied. It seems I arrived just in time for John to have second thoughts."

"Convenient," Charles said. "But why go there in the first place?"

"Why?" he laughed. "That's easy. I was sitting outside the office, in my usual spot, when I saw John leave. He didn't acknowledge me, which was unusual. He seemed quite distracted, so I made some inquiries. I wanted to check he was okay."

"You made some inquiries?" Charles said, a little disbelievingly.

"I may go under the guise of a vagrant, Inspector, but I can assure you people know who I am. My money has, after all, been good for Swain and Swain for more than half a century."

"Somebody in the firm?"

"Mrs Hyke," Sutherland said. "Or as I once knew her, Miss Thames. Assistant to Mr Fisher, and seeing as the old boy died a few years ago, she's my main source of information. She's quite loyal, you see? She has access to everything I need and slips beneath the radar, so to speak."

"Clearly."

"She's been good to me over the years has Mrs Hyke," he said. "But never more so than that day last week."

"And what did you learn?"

"Oh, I learned a lot," Sutherland said. "I learned that Garfield is as devious and untrustworthy as his father and that John was about to lose everything he had ever worked for."

"You learned about the sale of the land," Charles said, to which Sutherland nodded. "I know how these things work. I could see what Bobby Garfield was doing from a mile away. John walked right into it. Mrs Hyke told me that he was going to his parents' house, where I imagined he was going to deliver his good news."

"But you knew what they would have to say?" Charles asked. "So what then?"

"I had to get there. I had to stop him. But I couldn't. I can't drive, Inspector, one of the burdens of my predicament. By the time I got to the Garfield house that night, I was in time to see John leave. I never did see a man so broken."

"Did you speak to him?"

"No, of course not. You have to understand that until an hour ago, John Stow didn't even know I existed. So if you think this is all some story that we've concocted to set him free, then you're wrong. But I was worried about him. I followed him," he said and then laughed again. "I even slept in the granary again. Can you believe that?"

"And you followed him in the morning?"

"I did," he replied. "Though God knows what he had in mind. Through the hills and all over he went with me trailing behind. I could have been three steps behind him and he wouldn't have known, so lost in his own thoughts he was." He stilled and stared at Charles as Devon returned with three coffees. "Then he went to the Garfield house and I had an idea of what he might be doing."

"And what might that be?" Devon asked as she took her seat.

"One of two things," Sutherland replied. "And either one of them would have been a disaster."

"So you waited outside?" Charles asked. "What did you do? I mean, you couldn't have intervened if you only just made your identity known to him."

"That was the hardest ten minutes of my entire life, Inspector. I waited for him and when he didn't leave the house, I went inside."

"And what did you find?" Charles said. "Tell me what you saw when you entered Hugo Garfield's study."

"It wasn't what I saw, it was what I heard," Sutherland replied. "Have you ever heard a grown man cry, Inspector?"

"I have as it happens," Charles replied, to which Sutherland simply shook his head.

"Not like this, you haven't. I stood there in the library listening to his sobs. You have to remember that I have spent every day for the past fifty years making damn sure that John Stow made a success of his life. So to hear him crying like that was nothing short of painful."

"But you didn't make yourself known to him?" Charles asked. "You didn't stop him."

"What was I supposed to do, walk in there and tell him who I was?" Sutherland said. "No. No, Hugo came back into the library so I had to hide. But suffice to say that his presence gave John enough time to reflect on what he was going to do. Hugo returned to the garden and John ran out of the house moments later."

"Leaving you alone with Hugo," Charles said. "Did you follow him?"

"Hugo? No, I went into the study first."

"And what did you find?"

"I found a way to end it all, a way to set John free, and to destroy Bobby Garfield in one hit," Sutherland said.

"You realise that you'll be charged with murder pending further enquiries, Jimmy?"

"I do," Sutherland replied. "And John will be released?"

"Aye, for the time being, he will," Charles said. "But I still don't see why you would go to such lengths after all this time."

"I doubt you or anybody would," Sutherland said. "You see, on March the ninth, nineteen-seventy, Hugo Garfield set all of our lives on a course over which we had very little control," Sutherland said. "All I've done is rewrite our endings." He grinned a little, revealing a gleaming front tooth. "The Garfields lose, Inspector," he said. "John Stow wins."

CHAPTER SIXTY-SIX

It was gone five o'clock when they pushed into the incident room, and when Charles dropped into his chair he felt as if he'd tackled his back garden in spring after a particularly long and frightful winter.

"How did it go?" Chalk asked.

"Oh, about as good as it gets," Charles replied heavily. "Where's Forsythe?"

"He's having a mysterious conversation in the stairwell," Chalk replied.

"Forsythe? Mysterious? He's about as mysterious as a bucket," Devon added.

"Well, he wants me to think it's mysterious. He keeps having these hushed phone calls and then ending them when I get close."

"I thought he was happily married."

"Married, yes," Chalk replied. "Happily? I don't think so. Oh, and Vanessa was here earlier."

"Vanessa? As in my daughter Vanessa?" Charles said.

"Saw her in the car park when we got back from the archives," Chalk replied.

"Well, what did she want?"

"I don't know," she said. "I told her you were busy and Forsythe saw her out. Said I'd pass the message on."

"Forsythe saw her out, did he?"

"I had my hands full, guv."

"And the message is?" Charles asked. "What did she come here to tell me?"

"Oh, only that you're supposed to call her, guv," she said. "Anyway, have we charged this Sutherland character?"

"Not yet," Charles replied. "He might have confessed but CPS will want more than that, I can tell you. They'll want to know that every part of his statement is accurate."

"Well, as it happens, I've done some digging," Chalk said, seeming rather pleased with herself. "You said he sits outside the Swain and Swain office most days, right?"

"Right?" Charles said.

"So I got hold of the CCTV from the council," she replied.

"You did what?"

"Tall, lean, black man?" Chalk asked.

"That's him."

"Sits about twenty yards from the office?"

"Just spit it out, Chalk, will you?"

"He was there all week," she replied. "Except for the day before and the day that Hugo was murdered."

"That doesn't prove anything."

"Well, it kind of does," Chalk said. "He was there on the Wednesday morning and then he took a taxi, believe it or not. Though how he can afford a taxi, I'll never know."

"That'll take some explaining," Charles said. "I suppose you've contacted the firm?"

"I did," she said. "Long trip all the way out to Hagworthingham. That's a decent fare for the driver, better than the seven quid run to the supermarket."

"So he was there," Charles said and met Devon's stare.

"Alright, what else can we get on him? What did you get from the archives?"

"Clothing, guv. We've passed it on to Katy Southwell at the lab. She said she'd look at it immediately. We also dug the file out. It was digitised around a decade ago, but the images are just scanned copies of analogue images."

"Anything?"

"Well, it all points to Sutherland, that's for sure. The girl was found with a Hellebore in her hand, which, according to the girl's mother, was supposed to be in his lapel at their wedding. Plus, there were prints leading from the house where he was staying, across a field, and to the barn where the girl was found. These were proved to be Sutherland's prints."

"Anything else?"

"Yes. A hat and a pair of shoes matching those belonging to Sutherland were found out near the road about two miles away. It's thought he made for the road and flagged down a passing lorry to get him into town."

"That's exactly what he did," Charles said. "In a roundabout way, anyway."

"But what about Hugo Garfield's murder?" Devon asked. "We need to link him to the house. A taxi ride won't be enough."

"Southwell has tasked one of her team with that," Chalk said. "Someone called Pat. She said we'd hear news on that faster than the fifty-year-old clothing."

"Good," Charles said. "If we can put him at the house, then CPS will accept the prosecution."

"And if we can't?" Devon asked.

"Then we'll keep trying until we can," Charles told her, just as Forsythe walked in. "Ah, Forsythe, good of you to join us."

"Sorry, guv. I just had to speak to my wife."

"And how is life in paradise?" Charles asked. "Or shouldn't I ask?"

"I'd prefer not to speak of it if you don't mind," he replied. "In fact, I'd prefer not to even think of it. What's happening here?"

"Oh, it seems we're all redundant until we can prove that Sutherland is as guilty as his confession alludes."

"Sutherland?" Forsythe said. "What about Stow?"

"Oh, he's not even in the picture any more," Charles said with a laugh. "That was an hour ago. Things have moved on while you were..." He made the international hand gesture to mimic a phone. "You know?"

"Clearly."

"Sutherland has confessed," Devon told him. "He's been on the run since nineteen-seventy for the rape and murder of Polly Lavender. Now he's confessed to Hugo Garfield's murder, so we're waiting for CSI to back his statement up."

"So Stow is free?"

"For the time being," Charles said. "But I don't think it's the last we'll be seeing of him. He has a part to play in all of this, of that I am quite sure. In fact, if his statement is accurate then it was he who took the rope to the Garfield house."

"You what?" Forsythe said.

"I know," Charles replied, his hands held up in defence. "Apparently he went there with the sole purpose of ending his own life and framing Bobby Garfield in the process, and had it not been for the actual killer arriving and Hugo Garfield pottering about, he might very well have gone through with it."

"So John Stow went to the house on the Tuesday night and had an argument with Bobby and Hugo. He then returned on the Wednesday with the intention of–"

"Taking his own life," Charles finished for her, knowing she often found those words difficult to say.

"And Hugo's body was found on the Thursday," Devon continued, and she turned away in deep thought. "How would Sutherland have known that Stow was there if he hadn't been there himself? John Stow didn't even know about Sutherland until a couple of hours ago."

"It's not enough," Charles said.

"What about a fingerprint?" Chalk said, and she turned her laptop so they could all see a report from Katy Southwell. "Sutherland's fingerprints match those found on the door handles at the house. His DNA is still being tested but she's not hopeful."

"Which door?"

"Plural," Chalk replied. "The front door and the door to the study, along with John Stow's fingerprints."

"So his story stands up," Charles said. "We have the verbal confession of a man who has spent his life on the run and we have another man who claims to have tied the rope to the chandelier but left the house before he had a chance to do what he had intended. The question is, is that enough for the CPS?"

"It doesn't prove his confession is wrong, guv," Devon said. "If anything, it supports it."

"Aye, I know. But it's hardly signed and sealed, is it? It all seems a bit convenient, don't you think?"

"We still have the taxi, guv, and the CCTV. We can place him there and if his suggested motive is as he says it is, then that might be just enough to press charges."

"Aye, it might," Charles said. "I suppose it's all down to what Katy Southwell has to say then, eh? If what he says about Polly Lavender's murder is true, then I suppose that buys him a certain amount of credibility."

"We've done what we can, guv," Devon said. "We've got a confession."

"Aye, you're right," he replied heavily. "All right, let's call it a day, but I want to hear of any news the moment you get it, right?"

"Got it, guv," Forsythe said, dragging his jacket over his shoulders and closing his laptop. "See you tomorrow."

He was gone before any of them could respond and Chalk followed a few seconds after him.

"You walking down?" Devon asked as she buttoned her heavy coat.

"In a minute," he replied, then had a thought. "Actually, Devon, what are you doing tonight?"

"Tonight?" she said. "Nothing."

"No rhumba?"

"Zumba, guv," she said, clearly amused. "And no, not tonight."

"Fancy letting me treat you to a takeaway at my place?"

"Wow, I'm not sure if you're allowed to ask that, guv," she said with a laugh.

"Oh, I think I can," he replied. "It's all about context."

"Is that right? I'm not sure HR would agree."

"Let's not worry too much about HR, Devon. I'm a bit long in the tooth for any comments to be taken indecently."

She made a point of not disagreeing with him.

"Well, if I get a free takeaway, what's in it for you?"

"I just need some help with a wee project," he told her.

She gave it some thought and then perched on the desk behind her.

"You know I'm trying to lose weight, don't you?"

"So we'll get something healthy," he replied. "I hear Thai food is quite good."

"Thai food? Green curry? Maybe some Papaya rolls?"

"I have no idea what any of that is, but if that's what you want," he said. "Shall we say my place at six-thirty?"

"All right," she replied. "All right, you've got a deal."

"Excellent. I knew I could count on you," he told her. "Oh, and you might want to bring some old clothes. Something you don't mind getting ruined."

CHAPTER SIXTY-SEVEN

"Still think HR would have something to say?" he said, as he put a fresh cup of tea for Devon on the old tall boy.

She worked the excess paint from the roller and then placed the mucky end in the tray, leaning the long handle against a patch of drywall.

"Coercive, manipulative, and downright underhanded," she told him, reaching for the tea. "That's what this is."

"Aye, but you have to admit, there's no way anyone could suggest I meant anything untoward, eh?"

"No, guv," she said. "No, you've got me there."

"Anyway, this has got to be more fun than zoopla or whatever it is you do."

"*Zumba*," she said.

"Aye, that."

"Well, at Zumba, I'm not the biggest girl in the room."

"Ah," he said.

"And at Zumba, I don't get covered in paint."

"True," he replied. "There's that, I admit. But do they order you Thai food?"

She grinned.

"You've got me there," she replied, using the break to check her phone.

"Aye, I think this'll be nice when it's done," he told her, admiring her handiwork. "How long do you think?"

"Sorry?"

"Another hour?"

She stared at him, aghast.

"Less if we both get stuck in," she said.

"Aye," he replied. "An hour it is then."

"Dad," a voice called from downstairs.

"Here we go," he whispered to Devon. Then he called out, "We're up here, love."

"There's a bloke down here with Thai food. Surely he's got the wrong house?"

"No, that's for us," he replied. "It's all paid for."

They heard the mumbles of Vanessa thanking the man and sending him on his way, and then her footsteps on the stairs.

"What's going on?" she said when she came to the doorway and then nodded at Devon. "Hey, Anna."

"What does it look like?" Charles said.

"It looks like you're spotless and poor Anna is covered in paint, Dad. I think they call that abusing company resources or something, don't they?"

"Not quite," he replied. "It's just a good friend helping an old man out."

"But why are you painting it? This room hasn't been painted since I was a kid."

"Aye, I know," he said. "I thought it needed a good going over. Especially if we're to have a baby sleeping in here."

"In here?" she said, looking confused, and Charles smiled at her as he took her by the hand and led her along the landing.

"Aye, it's a nursery," he said and then pointed to the remaining rooms on the first floor. "That's your bedroom, that's your living room, and there's your bathroom. It's a flat."

"A flat? What about the house in Branston? I thought we agreed—"

"Oh, aye. I mean, the deposit is paid. The house is yours if you want it. Of course, you'd be alone for the most part with a screaming baby and you'd have barely enough money to feed yourselves or run that car of yours. If you want to go into town, you'll have to fight with a pushchair and a bus." He took a deep breath and caught her eye. "Or you could just live here. You can have the entire floor. I'll live upstairs on the second floor. You can live down here on the first, and we'll have the ground floor for a sort of communal space. You'd have money in your pocket, a live-in babysitter, and as for struggling with getting a pushchair on a bus, you could walk into town from here. There's food in the fridge, a garden for the wee bairn, and best of all, you won't have to be alone if you don't want to be."

"I see," she said, giving nothing away.

"Of course, if you'd prefer the house in Branston, I'd understand—"

"No," she said. "No, I love it, Dad. But this is *your* house. You don't want a screaming baby living here."

"Actually, I do," he told her. "Well, not so much the screaming but the baby. Aye, I do. Most of all, I want you, love."

"What's brought all this on? I thought you were keen on me moving out?"

"Ah, well, you know. Sometimes you just need a little time to reflect on things," he said. "A wee bit of separation to see the bigger picture, you know?"

"What he's trying to say, Vanessa," Devon cut in, "in your dad's long-winded way of avoiding emotional chit chat, is that there's nothing a father wouldn't do for his child. Screaming babies, stinky nappies—"

"And washing up and cleaning the kitchen?"

"Aye, well, we'd need to work something out there," he said.

"Maybe we can get a maid to come in a few times a week or something."

"You'd do all this for me?"

"Aye," he said. "Aye, I would."

"Sorry to be the one to ruin the moment," Devon said, and Charles turned to find her holding her phone up for him to see.

"What is it?"

"Katy Southwell," she said. "They managed to salvage some of the DNA from Polly Lavender's clothing."

"And?"

"And it's not Jimmy Sutherland's," she said. "Which, to paraphrase, gives his statement and his confession enough credibility to press charges on the Hugo Garfield murder."

"Sorry, love," Charles said to Vanessa, who shook her head dismissively. He turned his attention back to Devon. "So, let's get this straight. Stow went to the house with the purpose of—"

"Committing suicide," Devon said, foreseeing his hesitation.

"Aye, and Sutherland followed him inside. When Hugo spooked Stow and he left, Sutherland finished the job."

"We've got him on CCTV, we've got a statement from the taxi firm, we've got his and John Stow's fingerprints on the door handles, and if you're looking for a way to prove he isn't lying, his DNA *isn't* on Polly Lavender's clothing. It stands up, guv. We've got to charge him."

Charles dragged a stool from what was to be Vanessa's living room and then perched on it.

"So John Stow was telling the truth."

"He was telling the truth all along," Devon said.

"Aye, eventually," Charles said.

"Guv, the bloke was contemplating suicide. What do you expect him to do, just come out and say it? Do you know how hard it was for me to speak about it?"

"Aye, I do," he replied and smiled at her bravery for having done so. "By the look on your face, I get the feeling that's not all, is it?"

"No, guv," she said. "The database flagged a match for the DNA."

"Don't tease me, Devon," he said. "Whose is it?"

"Well, I could tell you, guv," she said. "But it all depends on how hungry you are."

"Devon," Charles said in a friendly warning tone.

"Garfield," she said. "Junior."

"Bobby Garfield?"

"He's got form," she added. "Joanne Childs' statement tells us he's more than capable of an assault."

"Of abuse, aye, but murder? He was what, thirteen or fourteen when it happened?"

"Maybe he had help?" Vanessa suggested, and they both turned to her. She raised her hands defensively. "Sorry, none of my business."

"No, you're right," Devon said, and then caught Charles' eye. "What did I just say? There's nothing a father wouldn't do for his child. I knew he wasn't clean. I could see it in his eyes."

"In his eyes, you say?" Charles said. "In his eyes..."

"Guv?"

"There's nothing a father wouldn't do for his child," Charles repeated, the phrase running over in his mind. "Nothing a father wouldn't do for his child."

"Guv?" Devon said.

"Get changed," he told her. "We're going out."

"What about the food?"

"Ah, I'll get you a burger or something. I know that's what you really want," he told her as he made his way down the stairs. "I'll be in the car and hurry up, will you? I want to swing by the station first. I've had an idea about something."

"Dad," Vanessa said, leaning over the bannister.

"Yes, love?"

She smiled at him and then reached down to kiss him on the cheek.

"Thank you," she said. "I'll take it."

He climbed back up the few steps and pulled her in for a hug.

"That makes me happy," he told her. "Now we just have to hope the wee bairn doesn't look like his father."

She pulled away and stared up at him with a confused expression.

"But I told you, I don't know who it is—"

"Aye, and you've spent more time at the station in the past week than you have in the twenty-odd years I've been there. Plus, a certain detective constable has been acting uncharacteristically coy lately – private phone calls, arguments with his wife, lunch dates. That sort of thing."

She said nothing but still held onto him.

"Just tell me if I'm wrong, love," he said, but she shook her head.

"You're not wrong," she replied. "Are you mad?"

"Mad? Me? Why would I be mad? I mean, my daughter has an affair with not just any old married man, but a man who works for me. He reports into me, for God's sake."

"It was a mistake, Dad," she said. "It was *my* mistake. I came to see you and he was outside, upset."

"What, so you consoled him by—"

"No, we just got talking. We had lunch a few times and things just went from there."

"Aye, it was a mistake, all right," he told her. "Happily for me, I'm in a position to make the bastard's life a misery."

"You're not going to fire him or have him transferred, are you?"

"Transferred? No," he said. "If he's the father of my first grandchild, then I want him where I can keep an eye on him. He's going to do the right thing."

"She's applied for a divorce, Dad. His wife, I mean. That's why he's been having the phone calls."

"And he wants to make a go of things with you, does he?"

"He does, but I've told him no. Not yet, anyway. I told him we should start slowly, and when his divorce is over, then we can see where we are. I don't want me or the baby dragged into his family affairs. That's not the way any child should start off in life."

He held her at arm's length, hoping that his warm expression gave her some comfort.

"I'm proud of you, love. That was a good decision."

"You're proud of me for getting knocked up by one of your junior officers?"

"Well, not so much. But I'm proud of the way you're handling it," he told her, as Devon emerged from the bathroom in clean clothes. She stopped in the doorway, clearly sensing that she'd interrupted something. He let Vanessa go and moved back onto the stairs. "One more thing, love," he said, and she peered down at him. "He's a good man. I'll say that about him."

"Thanks, Dad."

"And if things do work out between you, just know this," he said. "If he ever calls me Dad, I'll tear his bloody head off."

CHAPTER SIXTY-EIGHT

The sky was somewhere between darkness and light, but at that time tomorrow, the sun would only just be setting. The clocks would go forward, marking the onset of spring and bringing with it hope, new life, and warmth.

New life, Charles thought.

"How long have you known?" he asked, as they turned onto Beaumont Fee. She fingered the book he had collected from the station and then let it snap shut.

"About what?" Devon replied.

"Don't be coy. It doesn't suit you," he said, and she sighed.

"I didn't know for sure," she replied. "But I guessed when you told me about Vanessa's news. I'd seen them together a few times, in the cafe on the High Street and in the station car park. I didn't know about the divorce though."

"No?"

"Honest, guv. I had no idea. I just thought they were going through a rough patch."

He brought the car to a stop and killed the engine.

"What do I do, Devon? How do I play this?"

"Well, that all depends, guv. Do you want to drive her away

when it's taken you this long to build a relationship with her? Or do you think you can stomach having Forsythe as a son-in-law?"

"Oh Christ, when you say it like that."

"He's not all that bad," she said. "He's clean, he looks after himself, and he's actually quite intelligent."

"Ah, well at least my grandchild has a chance then, eh?" he said, as he shoved the door open. "Come on, let's get this over with." He met her at the front of the car and buttoned his coat. "Uniform?"

"En route," she replied.

"Good. And what about your schedule? I hope you're not planning any holidays in the coming weeks. You know, the older a crime is, the longer it takes to pull it together."

"It'll be worth it in the end, guv," she replied, as he reached up and gave three hard knocks on the door.

A few short moments passed before Charles reached up and gave another three knocks, harder this time. He turned to inspect the driveway. Bobby's car was there and parked beside it was the white BMW that belonged to his wife.

"Want to try the back?" Devon asked.

"You go," he said. "I'll wait here. Call out if you need me."

She disappeared around the side of the house and Charles stepped back to study the windows. Nothing moved. It was as still as the old house out in Hagworthingham.

He studied the cars, feeling the bonnets for warmth, but both were stone cold. The windows were tinted and the sky was dark enough that he had to use the torch function on his phone to peer inside. But both were empty.

The front door opened, startling him, and Devon filled the void.

"Guv," she said, and in that single syllable managed to convey a whole host of possibilities. She turned and led him into the dark corridor, and then stepped to one side when she reached Bobby Garfield's study. "We're too late."

He pushed the door open and slowly, inch by inch, Bobby's partner's desk came into view.

"Christ," he said aloud, for want of anything better to say.

Bobby Garfield was sitting in his leather chair with his head resting on his arms upon his desk. A half-empty bottle of whiskey accompanied a crystal tumbler and spread out before him were the contents of a pill bottle, and a framed photograph of himself with Rose Garfield, Dorothy and a teenage girl. "Ambulance," he told her, and he stepped forward searching for a pulse, examining the pill bottle and reading the label out. "Sertraline."

"Anti-depressants," she replied with her phone to her ear and then spoke to the operator, leaving Charles to deal with Garfield.

"I've got a pulse," he called out. "It's faint but it's there."

"Clear his airways," Devon said, as she reentered the room. "Lie him down on his side. Ambulance is on its way."

Charles manhandled Garfield to the floor and rolled him onto his side, where he left him there, stepping over him to Devon.

"Wait for the ambulance. Call me when you're on the way to the hospital."

"Where are you going?" she asked. "What if he dies before they get here?"

"Don't let him die," he told her. "Whatever happens, that man must not die."

"He's done a pretty good job of it, guv," Devon said. "He must have swallowed a dozen pills."

Charles stopped at the doorway and looked back at her.

"That is no suicide, Devon," he told her, pointing at Garfield on the floor. "That is attempted murder and I know exactly who's responsible."

"What? Who?" she said.

"The same person who killed Hugo," he called out as he marched along the corridor. "A father will do anything for his child, remember?"

"Right. So?" She came to the doorway and he turned in the hallway.

"So we've been looking at the wrong child, Devon," he said, and he held the book up, the book that he'd collected from the office. "And we've been looking at the wrong father."

CHAPTER SIXTY-NINE

The evening was cold and the effort of Charles' speed march through Lincoln had only served to dampen the back of his shirt, which the cold breeze seemed to take delight in. For many, the day was coming to an end. Shops were closing and staff were going home for the evening, whilst students and couples were only just getting started on the variety of reduced drinks on offer.

It was the same every year, Charles thought. He would complain that the winter seemed longer and colder than the last when in reality there was very little difference. The tail end of winter was always hard to bear, and it was only human nature to try and attribute the blame of that hardship onto an undeserving cause such as the climate.

He saw her from a hundred yards away– a rock in a stream of flowing bodies atop High Bridge. She checked her watch, glanced up and down the High Street, and then pulled her coat tightly around her. He thought for a moment that, even from afar, she might recognise him. But such was the state of her mind, she would only have eyes for one man.

And that man arrived in a flutter of coat-tails just as Charles settled into a nearby bench to observe. They embraced at first and then kissed. She buried her face in his chest and he held her.

It was time, Charles thought, as he pushed off the bench, and strode over to the bridge. He leaned on the handrail, peering down into the water, with the lovers a few feet behind him, oblivious to the world around them.

"It's a shame there's no busker today," he said aloud. "You could have had a wee dance."

He didn't turn but he knew the statement would have caught their attention.

"Inspector?" Stow said. "Inspector Cook, is that you?"

Charles turned, still leaning on the old balustrade, and smiled a greeting to them both.

"Mrs Garfield," he said. "Good evening."

She glanced around her and then back at Charles.

"There's no point running," he told her. "I've uniforms at either end of the High Street."

"What?" Stow said. "Why would she need to run?" He turned to her. "What's he talking about?"

"I'm talking about the death of Hugo Garfield, John," Charles said. "Her father-in-law."

"I don't understand. I thought Jimmy Sutherland confessed."

"Aye, he did. And a compelling confession it was too," he said. "Sadly, not compelling enough for me to be totally on board, despite the evidence. But what's evidence, eh?" He thumped his chest with his fist. "Sometimes everything you need is in here, eh? In the heart."

"You're not making any sense."

"Oh, really?" Charles said. "Well, I should apologise because this investigation has had me tied up in knots, I can tell you. I've got a man who, by all accounts, could have been killed by any number of people. I've got a list of suspects who were all in the area at the time and I've got more motives than I could shake a stick at. If I had my way, I'd have banged the lot of you up. You, for wasting police time, John, and you, lady, for a list of crimes as long as my arm."

"I assume you can prove I am guilty of each of those crimes," she said.

"Probably not," he said. "But there's only one crime I'm concerned with right now. Well, two if you count your husband, who is fighting for his life right now."

"What?" Stow said, and he pulled away from her.

"Wait, John. It's not what you think," she said, grasping for his arm, but he kept her at bay and stepped further away.

"A little lesson I learned when I joined the force," Charles told her. "When a man commits suicide with drink and pills, he doesn't put the lid back on the bottle, and he doesn't spread the pills out before him. There are always the outliers, but for the most part, they hang onto the bottle, and they tip the pills down their throat."

"That's not exactly evidence, is it?"

"Well, no, and I'm sure you will have been smart enough to remove your fingerprints from the bottle and the glass and the pill bottle."

She said nothing and made no show of denial or admission.

"Just as you wiped the surfaces of everything you touched in Hugo's house," Charles added. "Or was that Joanne?"

"Who?" Stow said.

"Joanne Childs, the cleaner," Charles said. "You met her in the local pub two weeks ago, didn't you, Rose?"

"I don't know what you're talking about," she replied.

"Oh, well, let me refresh your memory," he said. "Here's what I think happened. I think you and your beloved husband were going through your father-in-law's accounts, and you saw the payment made to Joanne's mother way back in the seventies. Odd that such a large sum of money should be paid to the housekeeper. Odd to most people, anyway. Except those who knew what the Garfields were like. Those who had experienced their cruelty first-hand."

"What are you saying, Inspector?" Stow said. "If you're going to make an arrest, I must insist that—"

"You can insist all you like, John," Charles told him. "I'm doing this here and now, and there's not a damn thing either one of you can do about it." He stared Stow down, until the time to continue was apparent, and he returned his focus to Rose Garfield. "If and when your husband wakes up, Rose, he will be charged with the rape and murder of your wee sister, Polly."

"What?" Stow said.

"But you knew that, didn't you? That's why you had to get him tonight. Because you knew the game was up. You knew that Sutherland would come clean and that Bobby's secret would be out. He would be carted off to spend the rest of his life in prison and any opportunity to get to him would be gone." She sneered at him like he was a piece of filth on her expensive shoe. "I just don't know how you stayed married to a man who did that to your little sister for so long."

"I didn't know," she snapped. "How could I have known? We all thought it was Jimmy."

"Ah, she speaks," he replied. "So let me guess, Joanne's little tale of woe gave you cause for doubt?"

"What he did to Joanne happened around the same time that Polly was murdered," she said. "It doesn't take a rocket scientist to work it out."

"No, just the wife of a successful lawyer," Charles replied. "So you planned their deaths. But you had to be smart about it. You would have known that John here had made a significant investment to buy land from the Garfields. How difficult it would have been to tempt Bobby into playing him one last time? How tempting it must have been for Bobby when you dangled John's demise before him like a carrot on a stick."

"You did what?" Stow said. "You put him up to it?"

"It wasn't like that—" she began.

"So you didn't contact Henry Gallant?" Charles asked. "If I look through your phone calls, would I find a call or two to him? An email maybe? Arranging a meeting between Bobby and him?"

"Well, of course, you'd find a call to him. He's a friend of Bobby's. Has been for years."

"So after your little chat with Joanne, you make the connection between your sister's death and Bobby, then you arranged for Bobby to ruin John here, giving him a motive. All you had to do was wait until he came to have it out with Bobby, which, of course, you knew he would."

"How could you?" Stow said. "You set me up—"

"John, no. It wasn't like that," she pleaded. "I just—"

"You just what?"

"She made a rash decision, John," Charles told him. "I don't think it was calculated. She panicked, and you were her only viable means of escape." He stared at Rose. "I'm right, aren't I?" She shook her head, and closed her eyes. "You're a destroyer of lives, Rose Garfield," Charles told her, and he held the book aloft for her to see.

"What's that?" she asked, peering at the cover. "Genetics?"

"I found it on Hugo's desk," he replied. "I never really paid it much attention until tonight. I even rushed back to the station to get it."

"It's a book," she said with a shrug.

"It was something somebody said about your husband. Something about them seeing the guilt in his eyes."

"So? He was guilty," she replied.

"It wasn't the meaning of the phrase that stirred something inside me," he said. "It was the statement itself. You have blue eyes, do you not?"

"I do," she replied, appearing confused, as did Stow.

"And Bobby, what colour are his eyes?"

"Blue also," she said.

"Aha," he said and slapped the book against his open palm. "What about Dorothy's?"

"My daughter?"

"What colour are her eyes, Rose?"

She gave it some thought and then shook her head.

"Brown, like my mother's."

"Brown, you say?"

"Yes, I'm sorry, but I can't see what any of this has to do with anything—"

"Page one-six-nine," he said, and tossed her the book, which she caught, but refused to open. "Shall I give you the abridged version?"

"I'm quite certain that you will," she replied.

"There is a zero per cent possibility of two blue-eyed parents having offspring with brown eyes."

"Excuse me?"

"It's a fact," he told her. "One of those little titbits of information you hear but have very little use for. Until times like this, of course. I must admit I had to reacquaint myself with the details, much as Hugo Garfield probably had to."

"I'm afraid you'll have to bring me up to speed," Stow said. "I don't see where any of this is going?"

"As much as I'd love to break the news to you, John, I prefer to maintain a level of decency, even to murderers like your friend Rose here."

She closed her eyes, but still, the tears streamed across her face. Beneath her coat, her chest heaved, and her lips pursed as she drew deep breaths.

"I'll start you off, shall I?" Charles said. "You learned the truth about your sister, and you wanted them both to pay. But why last week? Why the rush? A conniving woman with your resources, Rose, could have waited, would have waited, had you the time. You wouldn't have made such rash decisions, would you? But there *was* a time constraint, wasn't there?"

She made a show of stumbling across to the bench on the bridge and fell into it, clutching her chest.

"Rose, you need to start explaining," Stow said. "I'm sure this can all be cleared up. I just need to know the truth."

"It's Dorothy," she said weakly, and slowly she raised her head to look him in the eye. She's not Bobby's daughter."

"When was she born, Rose?" Charles asked, to which Rose looked away. "When is her birthday? Come on, you've got this one."

"September," she snapped.

"What year was she born?"

"Nineteen eighty-four..." Stow said, finally falling in with the conversation. "Are you saying that..." He paused and stumbled backwards, breathless.

"She's your daughter, John," she said and turned to sit upright, leaning forward with her elbows on her knees. "Hugo found out. I don't know how, but he did."

"Maybe it was this book?" Charles suggested.

"Maybe," Rose said and any sign of her denial was gone. "He told me he was going to remove us from the will, Dot and me. He promised not to tell Bobby—"

"But that didn't matter, did it?" Charles said. "You had to put your plan into action before the will was amended. You had to move fast and in doing so, you made mistakes. The biggest of which was Jimmy Sutherland."

"Oh Jimmy," she said quietly.

"You know he was prepared to take the blame for you, don't you?" said Charles. "Even though he'd never admit it, he'd rather spend his final years in prison than see you, the woman he once saw as his own daughter, go to prison."

"What will happen to him?" she asked, to which Charles simply shrugged.

"He'll be charged with perverting the course of justice and conspiracy to murder," Charles replied. "Unless, of course, you testify that he had nothing to do with it." He stepped over to her and looked down at the remains of a once confident and powerful woman. "I wonder if you have as much loyalty to him as he has for you."

Charles looked over his shoulder and nodded to the two uniformed officers who had closed in.

"Take her away and read her her rights," he told them.

"John," she cried out when they hauled her to her feet, but Stow simply shook his head and stepped back, his face a picture of loss and misery. "I did this for us," she said, as they led her away. "It was always you, John. I always wanted you."

"Stop," Stow called out, and the two uniformed officers sought guidance from Charles, who gave a quick nod. Stow approached Rose cautiously. He reached up and tucked her hair behind her ear, then slid his finger across her cheek, and she seemed to savour his touch.

"I would have given you the world, Rose," he said, and she closed her eyes as the tears began to stream. "You've destroyed me. Look at me. I'm an old man. I have nothing, and it's all because of you."

"Would it help if I told you I loved you?" she asked, and Stow took a step backwards. "I do, John. It's always been you."

But Stow said nothing. He glanced back Charles, who gave the officers the nod to continue removing her.

"It's always been you, John," she screamed at him. "Don't you see? It's you. You're all I ever wanted."

Stow stood with his eyes closed, reeling back and forth on his heels.

"I'm sorry you had to find out like that," Charles told him, as the two officers handcuffed her and led her away.

"What will happen to her?" Stow asked after a short pause.

"Can I be frank?"

"Please do."

"She won't see the light of day," Charles said. "She'll spend her last years in a prison cell." He shook his head. "Such a waste of life."

"And Bobby?"

"If he survives, he'll be tried for the rape and murder of Polly Lavender."

"What are his chances?"

"Slim," Charles said. "DNA is pretty irrefutable and when you consider the other allegations against him. Any jury would send him down in a heartbeat."

"So now nobody wins," Stow said quietly, and he turned to look Charles in the eye. "After all these years, nobody wins."

"Nobody wins," Charles agreed. "Least of all you."

"Least of all me," he replied with a little laugh that belied the gravity of the situation. "We all lose. Every last one of us."

"What will you do now?"

"I'll spend some time with my ma," he said, nodding. "Who knows, I might even enjoy my retirement."

"And Dorothy? She could probably use a dad right now," Charles suggested. "I think she even has kids of her own. That makes you a grandfather, John."

"I think I've had enough revelations for one night, Inspector," Stow replied, and he turned to walk away. "One more thing."

"Sutherland?" Charles asked, to which Stow nodded. "I'll do what I can, but I suppose it depends on if Rose wants to help him or not."

They both peered along the High Street to where she was being helped into the back seat of a liveried police car.

"Once more, his fate lies in the hands of another," John said, shaking his head. "It's funny, isn't it? Life, I mean. It's like that single event in nineteen-seventy mapped all our lives out for us and all we've been doing ever since is playing a predetermined role."

"Well, hopefully it's over now. You have a daughter, John. Grandkids too. Life could be very different for you."

Stow brushed the comment off with another laugh and a shake of his head.

"I wouldn't have the first idea about being a father," he said. "I mean, where do you start?"

Charles smiled at him.

"That's something I *am* able to help you with, John. You start as soon as you can. You hang on to them with both hands..." Charles began, and stepped over to Stow, holding his hand out for him to shake. Stow accepted, smiling gratefully, and Charles leaned in to offer his final piece of advice. "And you bloody well don't let them go, John."

CHAPTER SEVENTY
April 1, 2024

The world had indeed changed in the fifty-odd years since John had first ventured into the big, wide world. Horses did almost nothing for farmers now except occupy the minds of their daughters. Even the simple tractor was capable of far more than simply pulling machinery along. Every house had access to the internet, and even the bank of legal secretaries, of which Mrs Hyke was now in command, used computer-based software in place of the old, clunky typewriters they had used when John had first entered the offices of Swain and Swain.

Perhaps there was something more to the lyrics of that old song that John recalled. Perhaps there was more to the artist, as his name, it seemed, was mentioned almost every time the radio was turned on.

But some things never changed, and for that, John was glad. Daffodils still lined the fields, blackbirds still pecked at the moss on the roof tiles, and pools of rain still formed in the courtyard.

"Won't do you no good to stand there moping," Terry told him, as he dropped a heavy box onto the kitchen table.

"I know," John replied. He was standing at the kitchen door, letting the cool breeze into the house. "Do you remember that night you found me out there?"

"I do," Terry said. "Naked as the day you were born, you were. Aye, there's a lot I remember. Some memories are worth clinging to." He gestured at the box filled with his few personal possessions. "But most of them only weigh you down."

It was a curious thing to say, John thought, given that his solitary existence in the city had only been bearable with memories of home to cling to.

"Do you think you'll ever come back?" John asked.

"No. No, I doubt it. It's time for us to move on, John. Let it be," Terry said. "I'm old. Too old to be farming. No, we'll have to make do with what we've got."

"I can't," he said. "It just makes my blood boil."

"Then it'll boil you into an early grave. Mark my words. What's done is done."

"How can he get away with it?" John said and then kicked at the door frame. "It's all my bloody fault."

"Hey now, I won't hear that kind of language in here, thank you, and neither will your ma. And I'll thank you for not kicking the door. They'll be taking a bite out of me if there's damage to be fixed."

"I'm sorry, Terry. I just can't believe that this can be happening. How long have you been here?"

"Best part of my life," Terry replied, and he came to stand beside John briefly before nudging him outside. "Come on."

"Where are we going?"

"For a walk," Terry told him. "Your ma won't mind. Maybe we should say goodbye to the old place. Helps sometimes, you know?"

John followed him into the courtyard, and, avoiding the puddles and the mud, they crossed to the edge of the field where the daffodils grew in abundance.

"When the wildflowers bloom, the sun will come soon," he said, and John smiled.

"It's funny. I was thinking the same thing," John said. "If only for some sun."

"I were only twenty-five when my father died," Terry said. "Twenty-five and I took this on. They said I were mad, but I knew," he said, shaking his head and smiling at the idea of it all. "I knew I could do it."

"How old were you when you met Mum?"

Terry puffed his cheeks out and looked up into the sky in thought.

"Must have been thirty years old or thereabouts. Your ma was younger. Twenty-five, if memory serves. You were just a boy. I remember you back then. I always thought you'd wind up here, you know? I had these grand visions of enjoying my retirement, watching you out here working the land just as I'd shown you. Funny, eh? We'd have been in a right old pickle had you done that. We'd *all* be homeless."

"You're not homeless, Terry. I've secured us a cottage. It's not huge but it has a garden. Enough for an allotment."

"Ah, I don't worry about bills, John. What will be will be. Never worried about old Garfield's bills, did I? Now look at him. What good did it do him, eh?"

"Well, it's done now, isn't it?" John said. "And you don't need to worry about the cottage. I always said I'd take care of Ma and you, and I mean to."

Terry turned to look at him and he placed a huge, strong hand on his shoulder.

"They won't beat us, John," he said, shaking his head again. "No, this is a new start for us. That's all. We'll answer to no one. That's wealth, that is. That's true wealth. Happiness, a place to call home, and no reason not to smile."

John grinned at the words and at how Terry could have no idea of their significance.

"What are you two gossiping about?" a voice said from behind them, and they turned together to welcome his mother into the huddle.

"Just saying goodbye, love, that's all. We're just saying goodbye."

She stared out at the fields with them and John was reminded of happier times. Not many. But they were there, dotted amongst the bad. He remembered her helping them one harvest and how Terry had manhandled them both onto the hay bails, tossing them as if they weighed nothing at all. He remembered the year of the floods when they had all been out there gathering whatever they could before the rot set in.

"It's time," she said, in that way that only she could. "John, you load the rest of the boxes into the truck, will you? Terry, you give the place the once over."

"Do my rounds, you mean?" he said.

"One last time," she said. "Just to be sure."

She took John's arm and led him back towards the house. It was odd. He'd seen her age and he'd seen the effects that the farm life had had on her. But suddenly, now it was over, she seemed frail for the first time.

"Well, another chapter over," she said.

"Do you wonder what Father would have made of it all?"

She laughed the question off but squeezed his arm.

"You know Terry sees you as a son, don't you? There's nothing he wouldn't do."

"I know," he told her.

They walked for a moment in silence and then she pulled him to a stop in the middle of the courtyard.

"John, there's something you ought to know." She cast her eyes to the ground and then scanned the courtyard, as if every inch of the place held some memory or other. "He's a proud man is Terry. Prouder than most. And though he might not say it ever, he's grateful, you know? I don't know what we would have done without the money you sent. Old Garfield put the rent up so high that Terry could have been out here noon til night and we still wouldn't have managed it."

"Ma, you don't need to–"

"I do," she said. "Just listen, will you? You never were good at listening and I'm still your old ma."

He laughed a little and made a show of listening.

"You told me once, that day you went away, that you would take care of us. That you meant to, at any rate. Truth is, I thought you'd be home within a week. Never thought you'd stick it."

"Do you want to know something, Ma?" he said, and she peered across at him. "I very nearly didn't see it through."

"Well, I'm glad you did. I mean, you might have visited more, but I understand. You were busy. I see that now."

"I couldn't," he said. "I knew what I had to do, Ma. I had to knuckle down. I had to stop the distractions and focus on what I had to do."

"And you did it, didn't you?"

"I did, Ma."

"And I'm glad you did. Kept all your letters, I did. Still got them all in a box. And to think, when that Mr Fisher first came here and told us about your education, I could have sent him packing. Should have, if I'm honest."

"And then where would we be?"

"The point is, John, you ought to know how proud we are. Both of us. I mean, I don't think I'll ever get used to you speaking as you do. It ain't natural, is it?"

"It is," he said. "It's me now. But it's not how I speak or how I dress that matters. It's the whole package, Ma. Without my education, wrong or right, I would never have been accepted into Swain and Swain. Without Swain and Swain, I'd have been working on the farm with Terry. Don't you see, Ma? It all worked out. Everything happens for a reason, even if that reason isn't quite clear at the time."

"Well, we're proud and grateful and I'm not ashamed to admit it."

"Thanks, Ma," he told her, as the sound of a car tyres on loose gravel caught his ear.

"That'll be them," she said. "Come to get the keys and no doubt make sure we haven't taken that what we shouldn't have."

"Just let it be, Ma," he said. "To borrow Terry's words, what's done is done, and what will be will be."

"That's what your father would have said," she told him, as Terry emerged from the front of the house.

"You two better come and see this," he called, and the two of them wandered along the side of the house, arm in arm. They rounded the corner and saw, parked beside John's Jaguar, an old Mercedes, bearing a number plate that John recognised in a heartbeat.

"That's Mr Fisher's old car," he said, breaking free of his mother's grip to walk over to it just as the door opened.

Given the turn of events over the past few days, John wouldn't have been surprised if Mr Fisher, who had been dead for years, climbed out of the old Mercedes.

But it wasn't Mr Fisher who climbed out.

A long leg extended from the driver's side, bearing a smart, polished shoe and pressed black trousers. And the body that followed was tall and lean with a face that beamed down at John.

"Jimmy?" John said, marvelling at the man. Even without the scraggly, old beard, he was instantly recognisable with those gleaming eyes. "What the—"

"Hello, John," he said and then pulled him in for an embrace like a lifelong friend. "Good to see you, my old friend."

"But I thought you were—"

"Bailed, pending my hearing," he said. "In fact, I'm in the market for a criminal lawyer. I don't suppose you know of anybody, do you?"

"Oh, I'm retired, Jimmy. Didn't you know?" John said, and

then suddenly realised his poor manners. He pulled Jimmy forward and presented him to his mother and Terry. "Ma, Terry, this is Jimmy Sutherland."

"Well, I'll be," Terry said, a smile spreading across his face the opening of a spring flower. He stepped forward to shake Jimmy's hand. "As I live and breathe, I never thought I'd see the day."

"Mr Frobisher," Jimmy replied, nodding his head respectfully and then facing John's ma. "Mrs Frobisher."

"Well, John told us the story," she replied. "And a real pleasure it is to meet you, Mr Sutherland."

"Jimmy, please," he said, to which she nodded.

"Truth is that you've come at a bad time. We're to be off. New owners will be here soon to take the keys, and that's us done."

"Well, actually, that's the main reason for my visit," he said, and from his pocket, he withdrew an envelope, which he then handed to John.

"What's this?"

"Open it," Jimmy told him.

The envelope was instantly recognisable. It was quality stationery with the Swain and Swain logo stamped onto the rear.

John slid a finger inside and tore the paper open then extracted the single sheet of paper from inside.

"What does it say?" his ma asked.

"John?" Terry added. "Come on, don't leave us hanging."

John had to reread the three short paragraphs three times before he could make sense of it all. He stared up at Jimmy in disbelief.

"I don't understand," he said quietly. "The trust belongs to you?" He stared down at the letter again and saw the signatures at the bottom of the sheet. "Henry Gallant?"

"On behalf of the Garfield Estate," Jimmy said.

"He sold it to you? It was you who outbid me?" John said. "But why would you do that?"

"The same reason I've watched over you these past fifty years,

John," he replied. "Hugo Garfield destroyed any chance I had of a life. I've lived my life through you."

"But we could have owned the land. We would have been happy, Jimmy."

"And you will be," he said. "The trust has but one beneficiary, and his children, of course."

John shook his head and stepped back.

"No," he said, but Jimmy nodded.

"It's yours, John," he said. "The farm belongs to the trust, which effectively means it's yours."

"I could have bought it," he said. "You didn't have to do this."

"But I did," Jimmy said. "You'll get that money back from the Garfield Estate. It can't be held for long. And when you do, I think the three of you will be more than comfortable."

"I don't know what to say," John said.

"Well, God bless you, Mr Sutherland," Terry said, and he reached out to shake his hand again. "God bless you indeed."

"Work the farm," Jimmy said. "Or lease it out. Do as you wish. Be happy. By God, you've earned some happiness, the three of you."

"And when I die?" John asked. "What then?"

"Shame you've no children to speak of," his ma said. "If there's one thing missing from all this joy and merriment, it's a few little ones running around causing havoc."

"Actually, Ma," John said, dropping the letter to his side. He turned to face her and then took her hands in his. "There's something you should probably know."

CHAPTER SEVENTY-ONE

The persistent percussion was almost relaxing, and twice Charles felt his eyes close as his breathing fell in time with the various beeps given off by the machinery, the ventilator's hissing and sucking, and the dull hum of the light.

Nurses passed both left and right outside the room with the energy and stamina rarely seen in other professions. In fact, he thought, it was rarely seen in humans full stop, and was more akin to the natural behaviour seen in the animal kingdom. He could imagine the narration, performed by Attenborough, of course; nobody else came close to the man's talents.

'*Here we see a pride of nurses, each one with a multitude of tasks to complete. The juniors, denoted by their uniforms, listen intently to their elders, mimicking the behaviour of their senior counterparts so that one day, they might pass on that knowledge. And so the cycle goes. Rarely, do they stop for water, and when they do, their ears are ever pricked for the sound of a distant alarm. This particular pride, in Lincoln County Hospital, is coming to the end of a shift. Yet, not one of them will stop to rub their aching feet. Tirelessly they continue, until such a time when the new shift begins, and they can return to their families.*'

He smiled at the little scene in his head, and checked his

watch, just as a familiar voice rumbled somewhere outside near the little reception.

A few moments later, one of those junior nurses opened the door, and Charles nodded his approval to the nurse. The newcomer was familiar, yet Charles appraised the man as though meeting him for the first time. The man in the doorway shoved his hands in his trouser pockets, and shifted uneasily.

"All right, guv?" he said.

"Aye," Charles replied. "Aye, I'm just fine."

"What about him?" he said, and nodded sideways at Bobby Garfield. "Will he make it?"

"Oh, he'll make it," Charles told him. "He came round a few hours ago. One of the nurses gave him something to help him sleep."

"That's good," he replied, and then cleared his throat. "Devon said you wanted me to come."

"That's right."

"I was wondering why," he said. "You don't normally ask for me."

Charles listened, and then nodded his agreement.

"You're right," he said. "You're right, I don't normally ask for you." He took a deep breath, and clenched his fists, channelling any negativity into some far away place, for the time being at least. "I try to be a good boss, Forsythe. You know that, don't you?"

"I do," he said.

"And am I?" Charles asked. "A good boss, I mean. I'm not unfair, am I?"

"No, guv. Not to me, anyway."

"Because I would hate to think that those people under me were fearful, hesitant even. It doesn't make for a good team, you know?"

"I see," Forsythe replied.

"You see, I'd hate to think that the people in our wee team

spoke about me behind my back," Charles told him. "Or dare I say it, didn't respect me, for one reason or another."

"I don't think any of us do that, guv. We've all got a huge amount of respect for you."

"Aye, well that's good, eh?"

"I mean it, guv. As far as I know, we're all happy at work. No complaints from my end."

"And your personal life?" Charles said. "And I don't mean to pry, but it's not often I get to talk with you, man to man, I mean. Everything okay, is it?"

Forsythe hesitated, then drew his hands from his pockets and folded his arms, a defensive posture that gave him away in an instant.

"I think you know that it's not, guv," he said. "But respectfully, I've been doing everything I can not to let it affect my work."

"Aye, you have," Charles said, nodding his agreement.

"And I think you know something else," Forsythe added.

"Go on."

"Well, it's about Vanessa and me."

"Vanessa?"

"Your daughter, guv," he said, and there it was. No lies, no attempts to lead Charles down the garden path. He was impressed. "Things haven't been good for me at home for a long while. In fact, I can't remember the last time I actually stayed there."

"Your marriage, you mean?"

Forsythe nodded.

"We put on an act for the kids, but it's been over for some time." He stepped further into the room, until the light that hummed revealed every flaw in his face. "We're doing the whole divorce thing. We just have to tell the kids."

"When I asked you how your personal life was, Forsythe, I didn't mean to dig that deep."

"Well, you should know," he replied. "You should know that it's the last thing I would have wanted. A divorce, I mean."

"I'm sorry?"

"What I mean is that I haven't given up easily, guv. It's not like I'm walking away at the first sign of it getting hard," he said, and shrugged. "It's over."

"Right," Charles said. "So what now?"

"So now I move on," he said. "It's all I *can* do."

"I see," Charles replied. "And Vanessa?"

"With her," he said. "I want to be there, for the baby, I mean. I want to do the right thing. It'll take time, I know it will. But I'm not walking away. I've done that once, and I don't plan on doing it again."

"Serious talk," Charles said.

"I am serious," he replied, and Charles felt the balance of control shift in Forsythe's favour. "I know what we did wasn't exactly to the script, guv, but that doesn't mean it's bound for failure. I like her, and she likes me."

"Is that right?"

"It is," he said. "At least, that's what she tells me. She's going to have a baby, guv. My baby. It won't be easy, but we'll get through it."

"Is this your way of asking for my forgiveness, Forsythe?"

"No, guv," he said. "No, I don't need your forgiveness. I don't need your permission, either." Charles stared up at him in disbelief, but said nothing. "I'm just asking for some patience. I'm asking you to put some faith in me, believe in me, and most of all, trust me. I know it doesn't come easy. I've got a daughter, and if the tables were turned I'm not sure I could sit as you are now. I'm not sure how calm I would be."

"That comes with age, Forsythe. Nothing more."

A metallic rattle disturbed their little man-to-man chat, and they both looked over to Garfield, who raised his weary head looking definitively confused.

"What the bloody hell is this?" he said, pulling his hand against the handcuff that held him to the bed. "What's going on, and what are you doing here?"

Charles dropped his hands onto his thighs and shoved himself from his seat with a groan.

"You're under arrest, Bobby," he said. "For the rape and murder of Polly Lavender."

"Who? What are you talking about–"

Charles stepped over to him, and leaned down to whisper quietly.

"You know what they do to people like you, don't you, Bobby?"

"What, I don't know what you're talking about."

"You've had fifty years of fresh air and daylight," Charles told him. "I hope you made the most of it, because you won't be seeing any more of it."

"You can't prove anything."

"And remember, Bobby," he said. "Just remember this while you're lying in your wee cell, counting down the days until you meet your maker." Charles grinned. He couldn't help it, it just happened when he thought of what he was going to say. "John Stow is out there, a free man, a wealthy man, even. He'll die with a smile on his face, and he's earned that privilege," Charles told him. "What about you, Bobby? How will you die? Alone in a cell?" He shook his head. "No, I don't think you'll last that long. At least, I hope you don't." Charles straightened, and turned his back on Garfield. "Read him his rights, Forsythe, will you?" he said, as he made his way to the door. "I'll see you at the station."

"You can't do this," Garfield shouted. "Nurse! Nurse? Get me out of here."

Charles let the door swing closed behind him, and then took another deep breath, before walking slowly towards the exit.

"Guv?" A voice called out from behind him, and he turned to find Forsythe in the doorway.

"What is it, Forsythe?"

"If you want me to transfer, I'll understand," he said. "I get it. She's your daughter."

"Well, let's hope it doesn't come to that," Charles told him. "Anyway, there's your first murderer in there. Don't say I didn't give you a head start."

He started off towards the doors again, and was just about to hit the little button to exit, when Forsythe called out once more.

"Guv?" He said, and reluctantly Charles turned to face him. "Cheers. I really appreciate it."

Unsure if he was referring to Charles' daughter or the chance to arrest a rapist and murderer, Charles nodded once.

"Mess this up and you'll have me to answer to," he told him.

"Are we talking about Garfield, or..." Forsythe replied.

Charles left him with a grin, food for thought, and his next move to contemplate, as he turned and made his way down the long corridor.

"Guv? Guv?"

Forsythe's calls faded the further along the corridor Charles walked, but it was as he reached the bend that led to the main exit, that he stopped and looked back at the young man with his dark hair and hopeful expression.

"Do you know what a father would do for his daughter, Forsythe?" he asked, and Forsythe plunged his hands into his pockets again. "To keep her safe, to keep her happy, and to protect her from the world?"

"Go on," he replied, tentatively, and Charles grinned again.

"Anything," he said, feeling his grin subside as they two men locked distant stares. "Absolutely anything."

The End.

ALSO BY JACK CARTWRIGHT

The DCI Cook Murder Mysteries

A Winter of Blood

A Secret to Die For

The Wild Fens Murder Mysteries

Secrets In Blood

One For Sorrow

In Cold Blood

Suffer In Silence

Dying To Tell

Never To Return

Lie Beside Me

Dance With Death

In Dead Water

One Deadly Night

Her Dying Mind

Into Death's Arms

No More Blood

Join my VIP reader group to be among the first to hear about new release dates, discounts, and get a free Wild Fens novella.

Visit www.jackcartwrightbooks.com for details.

A NOTE FROM THE AUTHOR

Locations are as important to the story as the characters are; sometimes even more so. It's for this reason that I visit the settings and places used within my stories to see with open eyes, breathe in the air, and to listen to the sounds.

I have heard it said that each page should feature at least one sensory description, which in the age of the internet anybody can glean from somebody else's photos, maps, or even blog posts.

But, I disagree.

I believe that by visiting locations in person, a writer can experience a true sense of place which should then colour the language used in the story in a far more natural manner than by simply providing a banal description which can often stall the pace of the story.

However, there are times when I am compelled to create a fictional place within a real environment. For example, in the story you have just read, High Bridge, The Usher Gallery, and even Guildhall are all real places, whereas the Swain and Swain offices, The Garfield Estate, and the Grange are entirely fictitious. The George and Dragon in Hagworthingham is a fantastic pub, offering great food and good beer. So if you're in the area, stop by for lunch. You'll be warmly welcomed.

The reason I create fictional places is so that I can be sure not to cast any real location, setting, business, street, or feature in a negative light; nobody wants to see their beloved home town described as a scene for a murder, or any business portrayed as anything but excellent.

If any names of bonafide locations appear in my books, I ensure they bask in a positive light because I truly believe that Lincolnshire has so much to offer and that these locations should be celebrated with vehemence.

I hope you agree.

Jack Cartwright.

AFTERWORD

Because reviews are critical to an author's career, if you have enjoyed this novel, you could do me a huge favour by leaving a review on Amazon.

Reviews allow other readers to find my books. Your help in leaving one would make a big difference to this author.

Thank you for taking the time to read *A Secret To Die For*.

Best wishes,

Jack Cartwright.

COPYRIGHT

Copyright © 2024 by Jack Cartwright

All rights reserved.

The moral right of Jack Cartwright to be identified as the author of this work has been asserted by him in accordance with the Copyright, Designs and Patents act 1988.

All the characters in this book are fictitious, and any resemblance to actual persons living or dead is purely coincidental.

All rights reserved. No part of this publication may be reproduced, stored in a retrieval system or transmitted in any form or by any means, without the prior permission in writing of the publisher, nor to be otherwise circulated in any form of binding or cover other than that in which it is published without a similar condition, including this condition, being imposed on the subsequent purchaser.